Praise for Peter Spiegelman and **THICK AS THIEVES**

"Slick, sophisticated, and satisfying. . . . This is thriller fiction at its best." —Lee Child

"Spiegelman's ability to find glimmers of morality in a story populated by rogues, thieves and worse people . . . makes *Thick as Thieves* an enjoyable visit to a dark world." —*Pittsburgh Tribune-Review*

"A pure delight. . . . Heists, money-laundering, and smart plotting in a novel that's reminiscent of Elmore Leonard's best work." —Jeffery Deaver

"Spiegelman, who has written three thrillers since leaving Wall Street nine years ago, is being acclaimed for bringing some of the hands-on expertise and literary grace that John Le Carré brought to espionage novels to stories of capers, heists and double crosses." —*Weekend Edition*, NPR

"*Thick as Thieves* takes the suspense of a typical heist caper and ratchets it up several notches. . . . An elegant feat of fictional engineering." —*The Columbus Dispatch*

"*Thick as Thieves* is anything but 'thick'—it's sleek and subtle, with Spiegelman's rare eye for the telling detail. Thrilling in both tone and substance, these thieves will steal you away from whatever else you were doing, and leave you glad they did." —Don Winslow, author of *Savages*

"A thriller so nicely written you flip back a few pages to re-experience an especially well-turned bit of prose." —*Booklist*

"What really sets this apart is the quality of Spiegelman's writing. . . . It's not every day genre prose gets that kind of polish."   —*Kirkus Reviews* (starred review)

"*Thick as Thieves* is part magic, part alchemy and utterly entertaining. It is what all thrillers should aspire to be, and Spiegelman is that rare writer with both the heart and talent to pull off such an ambitious undertaking."

—Reed Farrel Coleman,
three-time Shamus Award–winning
author of *Innocent Monster*

"*Thick as Thieves* showcases the further development of Peter Spiegelman, one of our best writers of suspense and intrigue. His characters are forceful, smart, and his prose is supple, precise, and often poetic. Spiegelman gives us a deep inside look at scams and scammers of various sorts, and puts a big whirling plot into motion that ultimately delivers every satisfaction it promises at the start."

—Daniel Woodrell, author of *Winter's Bone*

PETER SPIEGELMAN

THICK AS THIEVES

Peter Spiegelman is the author of *Black Maps*, which won the 2004 Shamus Award for Best First P.I. Novel, *Death's Little Helpers*, and *Red Cat*. Prior to becoming a full-time writer, Mr. Spiegelman spent nearly twenty years in the financial services and software industries, and worked with leading banks and brokerages around the world. He lives in Connecticut.

www.peterspiegelman.com

ALSO BY PETER SPIEGELMAN

Red Cat

Death's Little Helpers

Black Maps

THICK AS THIEVES

PETER SPIEGELMAN

THICK AS THIEVES

A Novel

POCKET BLACK LIZARD

Vintage Books
A Division of Random House, Inc.
New York

FIRST POCKET BLACK LIZARD EDITION, JULY 2012

Copyright © 2011 by Peter Spiegelman

All rights reserved. Published in the United States by Vintage Books,
a division of Random House, Inc., New York, and in Canada by
Random House of Canada Limited, Toronto. Originally published in
hardcover in the United States by Alfred A. Knopf, a division of
Random House, Inc., New York, in 2011.

Vintage is a registered trademark and Pocket Black Lizard and colophon are
trademarks of Random House, Inc.

The Library of Congress has cataloged the Knopf edition as follows:
Spiegelman, Peter.
Thick as thieves / by Peter Spiegelman.
p. cm.
I. Title.
PS3619.P543T47 2011
813'.6—dc22 2011017855

Vintage ISBN: 978-1-4000-9705-0

www.weeklylizard.com

Printed in the United States of America
10 9 8 7 6 5 4 3 2 1

For my parents, Morton and Joyce,
and for my nephew Anthony, who we miss so much

"A plague upon it when thieves cannot be true one to another!"

—Falstaff to Prince Hal,
Henry IV, Part I, act II, scene 2

ACKNOWLEDGMENTS

Many thanks are due to many people for their help while I was writing this book: Reed Coleman, for his time and excellent ear; Nina Spiegelman, for her early reading; Denise Marcil and Abner Stein, for their encouragement and enthusiasm; Myron Glucksman, for any number of things; Sonny Mehta, for his support, advice, and supreme patience; and Alice Wang, for—really—more than I can say.

THICK AS THIEVES

1

INSIDE THE house now, the three of them stand still in the foyer, in the pale oblong of street light that falls through the transom, and Carr hears voices in the walls. A muted cough from the air ducts, a nervous murmur from the drapes, a creaking sigh from the paneling in the center hall—a muffled chorus, singing only to him. *Home early. Not the maid's night off. Tires in the driveway.* Carr's thighs are lead, and a clamp wraps around his chest. Adrenaline, he knows, but knowing doesn't help. He reminds himself to inhale, to exhale, not too fast. Above his chanting fear he can hear Declan's voice.

"Nothin' like a house in the dark, lad." The brogue that came and went, the rough laughter, the sharper edge of excitement, as if he were talking about a roller coaster. But Carr hates roller coasters, and always has. Inhale, exhale, not too fast.

The odors of the house come to him: lavender, cinnamon, lilac, vanilla, the chemical tang of a disinfectant—like a brothel above a bakery—but Piney Point Village is hardly that kind of Houston neighborhood. He takes another breath and catches a trace of cigars and of dog—an overweight, arthritic Lab that Carr knows is boarded at the vet's all week. Bobby flicks a penlight and follows its beam to a plastic box on the wall.

"No mess," Carr tells him.

"Yeah, yeah, I hear you," Bobby says, irritation and Brooklyn plain in his raspy whisper. He sticks the penlight in his mouth, pops the cover off the box with a thin screwdriver, and pries loose a circuit board from the bracket underneath. He pulls a coil of wire from the wall behind it and picks delicately at the board, teasing up the contacts. Bobby's moves are quick, and there's time to spare when he reaches into his pocket, pulls out something like a matchbook, and snaps it onto one edge of the board. A green LED blinks fast on the matchbook as it talks to the processor in the basement. *Don't worry, be happy.* The blinking is replaced by a steady glow, and Bobby lets the board hang by its wires down along the wall. He hooks the plastic cover on a corner of the bracket and takes the penlight from his mouth.

"Clean enough?" he asks.

Latin Mike answers. "Slick, *cabrón*, like always." Mike is forty, older than Carr, older than any of them, but his rounded San Diego accent makes him sound like a kid.

Carr nods. "Bobby goes downstairs; start by the door to the garage. Mike takes the master. Check your headsets first." Carr touches his own and swings down the mic on its wire arm. "You there, Vee?"

In the darkness Valerie's voice is close, as if her lips are at his ear. "Where else?" she says. Her tone is amber, smoky, a little weary. Carr can almost feel her breath. "All quiet out front. A guy walking a dog at the corner; a drunk in a beemer."

"And in back?" Carr asks.

Dennis answers. "Not even a drunk back here." His voice is young and reedy and tentative, like Dennis himself.

Carr looks at Bobby and Latin Mike. "You guys hear

everything?" Bobby barely nods; Mike won't muster even that. Carr looks down. "Clean shoes?"

Latin Mike snorts. "We virgins now, *jefe*?" he says, the *jefe* laden with sarcasm. "We never done this before?" He walks off, into the deeper darkness of the house, and Bobby follows.

Carr takes a long breath and lets it out slowly. He strains to hear them rummaging upstairs and down, but they're silent. No, not virgins. There's a half-moon table in the foyer, black lacquer with a vase of drooping gladiolas on top and a drawer beneath. Carr thumbs his own penlight and opens it.

CARR HAS progressed to the office, a mahogany annex to the living room, with many bookshelves but few books. There's a claw-footed desk squatting in the middle, and he's going through the center drawer when Latin Mike's voice crackles in his ear. "Got a box in the master, in the walk-in, behind the suits. Looks like a real piece of shit."

A surge of anger runs through Carr's gut. "Leave it," he says.

"Five minutes max and I'm in this thing."

"I said *leave it*."

"It's low-hanging fruit, *jefe*."

"We're not here for fruit. Now stay off the air unless you find it."

If Mike has an answer Carr doesn't hear it over Bobby's laugh. "You want low fruit, bro, you should see the liquor store goin' on down here. We lift a case of Dom, he'd never miss it."

Carr grits his teeth. There'd been none of this bullshit with Declan. With Deke, once they were inside, it was all business. There was no idle chatter, just that gravelly brogue calling out the numbers, and the clipped, whispered acknowledgments from each of them. Carr knows that Mike and Bobby are fucking with him, trying to get a rise, but he's not going to give them the pleasure. He takes a breath and is about to speak when Valerie cuts through Bobby's chuckles. "You girls want to shut the fuck up while this cruiser passes by?" she whispers.

Mike and Bobby go silent and there's a chunk of ice in Carr's gut. He kills his penlight. Valerie's voice is a low monotone. "Half a block down...two houses now...goddamn it, he's slowing down. Fuck—is there a backup you guys forgot about? 'Cause he's stopped right in front." Her voice gets softer and the sound of rustling fabric is loud in Carr's ear. He can picture her slouching low behind the wheel.

Bobby starts to talk but Carr cuts him off. "Quiet!" he whispers, and then to Valerie: "We burned or what, Vee?"

"I don't know," she whispers. "I don't...wait—he's rolling away. One house down...now two. He's at the corner, taking...a left."

Something releases in Carr's chest. "Dennis, anything?"

"He just went past. He's hanging a right on Smithdale."

Carr flicks on his light again. Bobby's voice leaps into his ear. "I didn't forget a fuckin' thing, Vee."

"You forgot how to keep quiet," Valerie says, the tension in her voice replaced by anger. "You forgot how to keep your head in the game—you and Mike both."

"Don't drag me into this, *chica*."

"Then shut the fuck up, the both of you, and get back to work."

It's ten minutes later when Bobby calls in. "I got it. On a table at the top of the basement stairs, in a bowl with loose change and gas receipts." Thirty seconds after that, the three of them are in the foyer again.

"Everything buttoned up?" Carr asks.

"Shipshape, *jefe*."

"Bobby?"

"Gotta clean this up," he says, pushing his chin at the box dangling down the wall. He hands Carr the card he's holding and digs in his vest for the screwdriver.

Carr runs his light over the ID card—hard gray plastic, with a picture of an office building on one side and a red nylon lanyard clipped to one end. He turns the card over and looks at the bar codes and mag strip and photo of the bland, balding man in the center. It's a better picture of Jerry Molloy, he thinks, than the portrait above the living room mantel.

2

THERE ARE candles burning in green glass spheres, and green paper lanterns hanging, and the air above the patio is tinted the color of an aquarium gone bad. It smells of citronella, and cigarettes, and a hundred clashing colognes. Valerie walks from the bar, a pitcher of Shiner Bock in each hand. She wears a short, flowered dress that clings to her as if it's wet, and her bare arms and legs are gleaming. Her dark blond hair is pinned in a haphazard pile, and her long, limber body is like a burning fuse as she twists through the crowd.

Every eye in the place—male and female—follows her back to the table, though Carr tries to avoid watching. Looking is what she wants, he thinks, and it feels too much like strings being pulled. Still, over the top of his glass, he looks—and so do Bobby, Latin Mike, and Dennis. Because, despite how long they've known her, how many times they've seen her work a room, there is always with Valerie the promise of something they haven't seen before.

Their table is in a far corner, and the four men sit with their backs to the low cinder-block wall that separates the patio from the surrounding hardpan lot. Carr watches the crowd, which is watching them, and he doesn't care for the attention.

Valerie slides the pitchers into the center of the table and sits next to Carr. "What's your problem?" she asks.

"You riled up the natives, *chica*," Mike answers, before Carr can speak.

"Place needs something," Valerie says. "The music sucks." She's smiling and her cheeks are flushed.

"He don't want them noticing us, right, *jefe*?"

Carr leans back and looks up through the rafters and the open roof—at the hovering mosquitoes, the flickering bats, the washed-out stars above. A warm breeze works its fingers beneath his shirt. He's had three beers, and there's a pleasant foaminess somewhere around his forebrain. He knows where Mike is going and he's too tired to follow. He keeps quiet but it doesn't help.

"Like they took us for locals before she crossed the floor?" Bobby says.

Mike gives Bobby a low five. "We blend in, *cabrón*; we natives." Latin Mike looks at Carr and frowns. "They get a bad vibe from us, *jefe*."

Carr drains his beer glass. "Vibes are one thing; Vee makes us memorable."

"Memorable for sure," Bobby says, and winks at Valerie, who winks back.

Mike snorts. "Face it, *pendejo*, we fit better in Caracas or Recife than we do up here."

Dennis wipes sweat from his face and joins in. "Down there we're just *norteamericanos*—oil workers, contractors, whatever—nobody gives a damn. Just a few more Yankees passing through."

"Speak for yourself, *yanqui*," Mike says. "But the point is, what the fuck we doing up here? Too much homeland security horseshit—what we need the headaches for? It's not like we have problems finding work."

Carr sighs. "Not this kind of work."

Mike downs half his beer and points a finger at Carr. He's smiling, but with him that's a tactic. "This kind of work is too fucking complicated—too many moving parts."

"You used to worry about the same shit five years ago, if I remember right, but things turned out okay."

"Damn straight I was worried. We had a good thing going, fishing where the fish were stupid—why mess with what works? But Deke was a man with a plan, and there was no arguing with him. Plus, I had faith in the guy."

"And you don't in me."

"No offense, *cabrón*, but you're not Deke."

Carr leans forward. "Sure, Mike, no offense."

"For chrissakes!" Valerie says, and slams her own glass on the tabletop. "Why don't you two get a room if you're going at this bullshit again. This was supposed to be a party." Bobby smirks and Dennis giggles with relief. Under the table Valerie's hand finds Carr's thigh. He doesn't jump, but it's a near thing. Her palm is hot through the fabric of his jeans. Carr nods slowly and reaches for a pitcher. He proffers it across the table.

"Let me top that off," he says, and Mike holds out his glass.

Valerie is right, Carr knows: they've gone around like this a dozen times or more, and there'll be time enough to go around again. But not now. Now, the night before they work again, it's time to drink. It's a lesson he had from Declan, who was ever alert to the peril of idle hands.

"Busy is best for these nippers," he'd told Carr. "Otherwise it's all worry and gossip and chewin' the arses off one another. Keep 'em busy, and when they've done their chores, get 'em pissed." More than tradition, these outings are an antidote to the jitters and jumps and sheer stir-craziness that come to a boil on the eve of every job. But like so much else he's learned from Declan, Carr knows he doesn't do it quite as well. Pirate king, father confessor, jolly Jack Falstaff—Carr is none of these, though he has developed other talents: watchfulness, patience, an attention to detail—the talents of a planner, a technician. Not exactly inspirational, he knows. Not like Declan. Still, one does what one can.

Carr works a smile onto his face and fills glasses until the pitcher is empty. Valerie's hand is gone now, and the music is louder, if unimproved. Valerie is dancing with Mike to something twangy, and Dennis watches them, tapping the tabletop in time to nothing Carr can hear. Bobby is eyeing the local talent. The peaceable kingdom. Carr finishes his beer. He leans back and looks at the wrung-out sky and thinks of limes.

Declan was cutting them the first time they met—a bet with a barman at a marble and frosted glass palace in Las Lomas. Teddy Voigt, Carr's immediate boss at Integral Risk Associates, and the closest thing he'd had to a friend there, had arranged the get-together, not forty-eight hours after Carr had been fired and just forty-eight hours before Carr had to vacate his company-owned apartment—the graceful exit being one of the things Carr had relinquished when he'd hit his most profitable client in the face.

Hunched over the granite bar, Declan was a rhino at a tea party: red-faced, craggy, and ancient next to the silken youth that crowded the club—more like one of the bodyguards loitering on the sidewalk outside. The paring knife was nearly lost in his fist, but the edge of the blade was a blur and the slices he cut were translucent green petals. Whatever the bet was, Declan won going away, and whatever the prize, Declan declined payment and instead bought the barman a shot of Patrón. Which, Carr came to realize, was essential Declan: good with bartenders, good with knives, good with tactical mercy.

Good at other things too, Carr learned as they bar-hopped

across the leafy night, from Las Lomas to an English pub in Polanco to a hipster saloon in Condesa. Good at Gallic bonhomie and fatalistic, self-deprecating humor. Good at oblique but relentless interrogation. Good at large volumes of pricey tequila, chased by even larger volumes of beer. Good, despite how much he'd had to drink, at negotiating the unforgiving chaos of traffic in Mexico City.

Good too at throwing an elbow into a man's windpipe, then breaking his wrist, for slapping a woman to the pavement. That took place in the doorway of their last stop: a workingman's tavern in Santa María la Ribera that was little more than a dim hallway drenched in nicotine and sentimental guitars. The patrons seemed to take the violence in stride, if they noticed it at all, and the smile never left Declan's face. He'd made his pitch to Carr at a table near the kitchen.

Carr comes back to the sound of breaking glass. Dennis and Valerie are on the dance floor but they're not dancing. There's a stunned look on Dennis's face, and a local boy, a wide receiver gone to seed, is laughing and grabbing Valerie around the waist. Latin Mike and Bobby are on their feet, smiling eagerly as three doughy cowboys shoulder through the skittish crowd to help the wide receiver. Valerie looks angry, and looks at Carr, who has visions of broken bottles, flashing lights, the cowboys hauled off in ambulances, his crew simply hauled off.

"Shit," he mutters, and hoists himself off his chair.

IN THE Ford, on the way back to the hotel, adrenaline has burned off the alcohol and left them with a different kind of buzz. Carr is at the wheel, always three miles over the limit, nice and steady, while Valerie works the radio. Dennis has his face in the rush of humid air from the open window in back, and Bobby and Mike are smoking and joking.

"Fucking Vee," Bobby says, "that guy's gonna be picking his balls outta his nose for a week." He puts a fist forward and Valerie knocks it with her own.

"The way he mauled me, I should've kicked him again."

Mike catches Carr's eye in the mirror. "Three times was enough, *chica*," he says. "Four would make you *memorable*." He and Bobby laugh and Carr shakes his head and pulls into the hotel lot.

Dennis is pale and wobbly getting out of the car; he crosses the parking lot at a jog and disappears into the hotel. Valerie, Bobby, and Mike take their time. Mike lights another cigarette, props his elbows on the Ford's roof, and looks across at Carr.

"Eight o'clock tomorrow," Carr says. Mike and Valerie say nothing. Bobby looks at the low hotel, the rows of windows, mostly black, and the vestigial balconies. He nods absently and heads for the lobby. Carr follows, rubbing the bruises on his forearms and knuckles, not listening to Mike and Valerie, who stand by the car and speak softly.

Carr leaves his room dark and lets his eyes adjust to the yellow haze that seeps through the curtains from the sodium lamps outside. From the window he can see the parking lot and, if he cranes his neck, the car. He can make out Latin Mike's shape, tall, with a plume of cigarette smoke above, and Valerie's silhouette, very close by. Just how close? Carr can't tell from his vantage, and in a while he tells himself he doesn't care. A while after that he stops looking.

The air in his room is like an airplane's: metallic, exhausted, and too cold. Carr switches off the AC, and a ticking silence descends. And then dissolves in the babble of a television from next door. Carr switches on the AC.

His work clothes hang in the closet, and his bag is packed but for his shaving kit and what he's wearing. He strips off his jeans and polo shirt, folds them, packs them away, and looks around the room, rehearsing in his mind the routine for wiping it down: front to back, left to right, floor to head height. Then he brushes his teeth and gets into the shower.

When he comes out, Valerie's key is on the desk. Her shoes are by the nightstand, her dress on the chair, and Valerie herself is in bed, under a sheet, with a hand behind her head and her blond hair fanned across the pillows. Carr can smell her perfume and her sweat, and the cigarette smoke that clings to her like cobwebs. *Just how close?*

"Is he going to behave himself?" Carr asks.

"He'll behave tomorrow."

"And after that?"

Valerie shrugs. "You think you can get to sleep?" she asks.

"No," Carr says, and fastens the chain on the door.

3

THE PRAIRIE Galleria, a ten-story structure on Prairie Street, not far from Minute Maid Park, once housed, among other tenants, the Houston offices of a national bank, the Houston outpost of an international consulting firm, and half a dozen energy trading houses. Those businesses are gone now, bought out, broken up, or plain dead, but their bad luck is still etched on the building's blue glass skin, which is stained and cracked in some spots, and missing altogether in others—patched with plywood sheets like rippled, gray scabs.

The current occupants are making the best of the current economy. They're an eclectic bunch, including accountants, lawyers of various stripes—bankruptcy, tax, and divorce the best-represented specialties—a bail bondsman, two dealers in used office equipment, and several real estate liquidators. With the exception of the bail bondsman, none of these firms conduct regular business on Saturdays, so the lobby is quiet when Carr approaches the reception counter at 8:37 a.m.— just two uniformed guards who, Carr knows, work only weekend shifts. The cooling system is cycling low, and the air is thick and smells of someone's breakfast. Carr keeps close to the right-hand wall, out of view of the single security camera. His deck shoes squeak on the marble floor and a line of sweat worms down his ribs. *Inhale, exhale, not too fast.*

Carr hitches up the strap on the nylon briefcase slung over his shoulder and pushes the horn-rimmed sunglasses up on his nose. He makes a show of searching the pockets of his sagging blue blazer. The guards have never seen him before, but whatever curiosity they experience is overmatched by heat and apathy, and they barely raise their heads. Carr shifts the Styrofoam coffee cup to his left hand and searches more pockets. The performance settles him down and he nods at the guards and puts a eureka look on his face. He fishes the ID card from his pocket and slides it through the reader on the turnstile that stands between him and the elevator bank. The light on the reader blinks from amber to green and the barrier swings away and Carr walks through. He stops on the other side.

"My guys haven't been in yet, have they?" he asks.

The guards look at each other and back at Carr. "What guys?" the bald one asks.

"IT guys, coming with new computers."

"Nobody's been in."

Carr looks at his watch. "Should be soon. You'll send 'em up?"

The bald guard nods, taps a finger on a keyboard, and squints at the text on the screen. "Yep. That's Molloy, on six?"

"That's me," Carr says, and steps into a waiting elevator. He keeps his head down, away from the camera in the corner, and presses the button for six.

The sixth floor is warmer than the lobby, and quieter, and all Carr can hear after the doors close behind him is the elevator sliding down and the faint push of air from a ceiling vent. Once upon a time, Carr knows, the whole floor belonged to a law firm. It was where they kept their library and conference rooms and archived records, until the markets went south and everything else followed. Then the law firm shut down, the building changed hands, and the new landlords invested in new doors, new wiring, and lots of wallboard, and turned all that teak paneling and Berber carpet into five separate office suites.

Carr looks at the nameplates. To his right, two lawyers and a forensic accountant; straight ahead, behind heavy glass doors and a roll-down metal gate, in the largest suite on the floor, a company called Portrait Capital; and to his left, in the smallest office, Jerry Molloy, tax attorney in semiretirement, currently concluding a one-week visit to his Hill Country home. Carr removes his sunglasses, pulls latex gloves from his briefcase, and turns left.

Molloy's lock is a joke—old and tired—and it surrenders after a few bumps with the power rake. The alarm is even worse—no motion detector, and just a single magnetic contact on the door frame. But Carr doesn't have to fiddle it; he has the code, copied from the slip of paper Valerie discovered taped beneath Molloy's desk blotter two weeks before. Molloy had gone out to lunch—without setting his alarm—and Valerie was ostensibly visiting a divorce lawyer one floor up. It had taken her all of six minutes to find it. A dispirited chirping comes from the smudged plastic box on the wall. Carr taps the keypad and the box goes silent. He locks the office door, wipes a sleeve across his forehead, and looks around.

There isn't much to see. The space is partitioned into two rooms: the one Carr is standing in, with a small window, a small filing cabinet, a small desk for Molloy's part-time secretary, and carpeting the color of car exhaust; and Molloy's office, which is a larger version of the same. Both smell vaguely of old cigar smoke, and neither holds anything of interest to Carr. He takes off his blazer, folds it on Molloy's desk, and rolls up his sleeves. Then he crosses to the far wall and opens a door.

Behind it is a small utility closet, where electrical and telecom lines branch out from the conduits that carry them between floors to provide local service. There are junction boxes on the wall: gray for telecom, beige for electrical, flimsy white plastic for the security system. They're mounted next to the vertical PVC conduits, and bundles of cable snake into and out of them. Carr pulls a penlight and a much handled sheaf of papers from his briefcase and flips pages to the plan of Molloy's office.

The plans tell him that this closet is a recent addition, built when the original office space was subdivided. It shares a wall with another, larger utility closet in the suite next door—a hastily erected wall of gypsum board hung on metal studs. Carr raps on the board and it makes a hollow sound. He pulls a tape measure and a pencil from his bag, checks the plan, and marks a rectangle, two feet wide by three feet high, on the closet wall. Then he takes a headset out.

"You there, Vee?" he says.

"Where else?" she answers. "Everything okay?"

"Fine. Send them in."

Carr looks out the window and watches Bobby and Latin Mike emerge from a rusting blue van parked nose out in the lot across the street. Each has a nylon bag slung on his shoulder, and each is carrying a Dell computer box. Even from six floors up Carr can see the tension in their strides. They wear jeans, dark T-shirts, and sunglasses, but neither really looks the part of IT geek. Bobby comes close—scruffy, freckled, pale, and slightly bloated, as if he lives on fast food—but Mike is a far cry. His heavy shoulders and battered, angry good looks transcend wardrobe and typecast him as a hardcase, a badass, a thief. Still, Carr knows they'll pass muster with the listless guards in the lobby. They disappear into the Prairie Galleria, and Carr looks again at the van. He tries to make out Valerie behind the wheel but can't.

"Anybody else come in?" he asks.

"The painters and the carpet guys," she answers, "about five minutes ago."

"How many today?"

"Five—same as last week."

The ever-hopeful owners of the Galleria have been painting walls and replacing the carpets in the building's common areas, two floors every Saturday. Carr knows the schedule, and knows they're working downstairs today, on four and five.

"Nobody else?"

"Not yet."

There's a knock on the door and Carr opens it for Bobby and Mike. Bobby pulls on gloves, looks around, and shakes his head. "What a dump. I had to sit here all day, I'd shoot myself."

"That's why it's good you're not an accountant," Mike says.

"Molloy's a lawyer," Carr says. He points at the closet.

Bobby crouches at the wall, looking at Carr's marks and rechecking the plan. He taps on the wall and shakes his head some more. "Sounds like quarter-inch. Cheap bastards."

Bobby takes a drop cloth from his bag and spreads it beneath Carr's rectangle. Then he removes plastic goggles, a battery-powered reciprocating saw, a set of blades in a plastic box, and a rectangular strip of heavy felt. He's humming softly as he selects a blade, locks it in place, and wraps felt around the saw's motor. Carr doesn't know the tune, but knows that Bobby is nervous. Carr himself is fighting the desire to pace. Bobby squeezes the trigger on the saw and smiles at the dull whirring sound.

"Like a whisper," he says. He wipes sweat off his forehead, sets the blade along a penciled line, and cuts. He's quick and quiet and neat, and in less than a minute he hands Carr a two-by-three-foot panel of wallboard.

"See—quarter-inch. I could've used my Swiss Army knife."

He takes a penlight from his bag and shines it in the hole he's cut. He looks at the metal studs and the back of the wall in the utility closet next door. He taps the wall several times, then takes a Phillips-head screwdriver from his bag and punches a hole in the board. He turns to Latin Mike, who takes the screwdriver from Bobby and hands him the device he's been assembling.

It's an under-door camera, a hand-held video unit with a tiny lens mounted on the end of a thin metal snake. This model has its own light source and an infrared attachment. Bobby powers it up, feeds the snake through the hole, and starts working the controls. Mike leans over his shoulder and peers into the monitor. Carr gives them room and goes to the window.

The sky is yellow and greasy, and though it's hours till noon, the sidewalk already shimmers with heat. Carr's shirt is wet, stuck to his back and ribs, though only some of that is from the temperature. He takes a handkerchief from his pocket and wipes the back of his neck. He looks at the van and thinks of Valerie.

Last night, afterward, they'd been welded together by sweat. The droning of the air conditioner swallowed every other sound, and Valerie's weight on him, and the heat that seeped from her to cover him, and the scent of her skin and of her hair that fell in a honey cascade across his shoulder, swallowed every thought of movement. They were perfectly still and perfectly quiet until she spoke, softly, in his ear.

As he had many times since the first day he'd met her, Carr wondered about Valerie's accent. Like so much else about her it was malleable, indeterminate, like smoke. There were hints of Canada in it sometimes, around the edges of her *r*'s, and at other times a suggestion of farther corners of the Commonwealth—South Africa, or maybe Australia. Other times her speech was flat and neutral, like a newscaster's— straight out of Kansas. It was as supple as the rest of her—

stretching, bending, shaping itself like putty to suit the job at hand. Last night, her accent was diluted British, a Surrey childhood not quite undone by decades in the States. He'd heard that one before. He'd heard the sentiment too, though not as often. Twice before, to be exact, twice in the four months they'd been sleeping together.

"We could sleep in. Get room service. Spend the day in bed."

Speaking was an effort for Carr, his words rising up from deep water. "There's no room service here, and we have plans for tomorrow."

"I'm not talking about tomorrow, or about this dump. I'm talking about afterward, someplace with a real bed. Someplace we could take time."

"Time for what?"

"Time out. Time to see what's what—what this is all about."

"Are you asking me to go steady?"

Valerie hadn't laughed or snapped, but simply kissed his ear and gone quiet for a while. "You told me this was it for you," she said eventually. "You said so more than once. So you need to plan for afterward. I'm saying that maybe our plans can line up."

Twice before, and last night was lucky number three. Carr still didn't know what to make of it.

Bobby calls him back. He has the saw in hand again, and Latin Mike is stowing the camera. "It's clean in there—no motion detectors, no infrared, just four walls and a door—your basic utility closet."

Four walls, a door, more junction boxes, and the processing unit of Portrait Capital's security system, which is to Jerry Molloy's alarm as a Porsche is to a vegetable peeler. And that's fitting, as Molloy's office holds only yellowing tax files, while Portrait Capital's safeguards more substantial assets.

4

THERE ARE no golden bezants over the door, no neon signs in the window, and no furtive customers lurking out front, but Portrait Capital—Marius Lucovic, founder—is nonetheless a pawn shop, albeit an upmarket one. It doesn't trade in forlorn wedding rings, Grandma's sad china, or handguns of dubious provenance, but the basic deal offered at Portrait—valuables handed over as collateral against a loan—is the same as what's on the table down by the bus station, and the customers are similarly desperate. There are differences, of course: the pawnbrokers at Portrait Capital may be seen by appointment only; they deal exclusively in works of art, authenticated antiques, and pieces of serious jewelry; and the smallest loan that Portrait will consider is for a quarter of a million dollars. Lucovic started the company just after the crash, and business has always been brisk.

Which would, at first glance, seem to explain the motion detectors, pressure sensors, and video cameras, but not quite. While it's true that Portrait Capital often has valuable items on its premises, they're never there for longer than a few hours at a time, and never overnight. Any collateral brought to the office is sent out again by armored courier at the end of the day, to a high-security, climate-controlled warehouse near Ellington Airport. So all the hardware Lucovic installed at the Prairie Galleria is not to defend his high-priced pawn. No, it's to protect the inventory of an entirely different Lucovic enterprise—fencing diamonds.

Diamonds have always been Lucovic's specialty, from his first jewelry store smash-and-grab as a teenager in Zagreb, to his days running conflict stones into Western Europe. Diamond money bought him his ticket to the States, his house in River Oaks, his condos in Vegas and L.A., and the nut to start Portrait Capital. Diamond money is what he launders, month in and month out, through Portrait's several bank accounts, and diamonds are what Carr and Bobby and Latin Mike have come to carry off.

Bobby cuts through the wallboard into Portrait Capital's utility closet—another neat two-by-three-foot section—gets down on all fours, and crawls through. Mike is next, pushing the computer boxes and tool bags, and Carr is last.

This closet is three times the size of Jerry Molloy's, a small room really, and the beams of Bobby's and Mike's utility lanterns cast heavy shadows in the corners. Carr brushes off his pants and joins Mike and Bobby in gazing at the security unit—a large black box, forbiddingly blank but for the name, Ten Argus, in yellow.

Bobby wipes his face on his sleeve and kneels beside the processor. He runs his hand along the bottom edge of the black box, finds a latch, and opens the cover. Inside is an array of densely packed circuit boards, banks of status lights, and three cooling fans. Cables from the sensors installed throughout the office suite feed in through a conduit at the back of the box, along with two dedicated telephone lines and the power supply. Two gray bricks sit at the bottom of the box—backup batteries. Bobby trains his light on it all and stares, as if searching a crowd for a familiar face. He shakes his head.

"It looks different," Bobby says softly. He reaches into a bag and pulls out several sheets of circuit diagrams and starts to hum. He studies the diagrams, while Mike unpacks one of the Dell boxes—Styrofoam, a laptop, a bulky antistatic bag, and cables. Carr gives in to the engine racing in his chest, and paces the little room—four paces by three. He walks to the door, puts his hand on the knob, and imagines what would happen if he opened it and walked across a pressure sensor or stepped into a crossfire of infrared beams. No Klaxons or cruisers, Carr knows—Lucovic doesn't welcome attention, and especially not from the police—but a fast, armed response, the security company guards first, followed closely by Lucovic's own men.

"Okay," Bobby says to no one. He's found what he's looking for in the thicket of chips, and he folds his diagrams away. Mike powers up the laptop. Bobby opens the antistatic bag and pulls out a large circuit board. He sets the board beside the security system and cables it to the laptop. Carr can see, in the dense mosaic of chips on the board, two large chips with the TEN ARGUS label. Bobby kneels over the laptop and starts typing.

Bobby calls it the Ten Zombie, and he and Dennis built it with specs and components they pinched from a dealer in Sugar Land, whose own offices were scandalously insecure. *Zombie* because, once connected, it will look to the monitoring units on the other end of the dedicated phone line just like the Ten Argus unit installed in the humid little room at Portrait Capital, though in fact it is a hollowed out version of that system, receiving input from no sensors, and reporting only what Bobby instructs it to report. And Bobby has directed it to murmur incessantly that everything is perfectly fine.

Connecting it—swapping the Zombie for the real thing—is the tricky part: the monitor software makes allowances for power surges and line glitches, and that's what Bobby wants the swap to look like, but his window is only seven seconds wide. Latin Mike and Bobby stand by the black box, Mike's hands poised over the phone jacks, Bobby's over the power lines. Carr holds the laptop and the Zombie board, and keeps his eye on his watch. They've practiced this a hundred times or more.

"On three," Bobby says.

They finish with two seconds to spare, not their best time but close. Bobby checks and rechecks the laptop screen, watching the back-and-forth over the phone lines. He gives a thumbs-up and closes the laptop, and Carr gives up an ancient breath. Mike shakes the tension from his arms and shoulders. Their shirts are dark with sweat.

Bobby and Mike pick up the tools and the boxes, and Carr opens the door. The air in the corridor is ten degrees cooler. He blinks in the light, wipes his eyes, and touches his headset.

"We're in," he says.

"Making good time," Valerie answers.

"Things okay down there?"

"It's a fucking swamp," she says.

The office suite is done up in leather and dark wood, someone's notion of staid and bankerly, as gleaned from watching old TV shows. It reminds Carr of a funeral home. Carr leads the way to Lucovic's office, skirting the reception area where the video cameras stand watch. They pass a floor safe, a glossy, black monster with a handle like a ship's wheel, and the name of a long-defunct bank in gold leaf across the front. It's empty, they know, but Mike gives it an affectionate pat.

Lucovic's office is locked, but not seriously, and once Carr opens it, Mike and Bobby make space. Lucovic's leather chair goes to one side of the room, and his mahogany desk goes to the other, which leaves a wide patch of gray carpet in front of the mahogany credenza that stretches across the back wall. There are bookshelves on top of it and file drawers beneath, and behind one set of drawers—the false ones—is the safe.

It's a Guard-Rite T2100, with steel skin, six thick bolts that anchor it firmly to the floor, and room enough inside to accommodate four bowling balls. Mike spins the combination dial. It's an Ames and Landrieu R720 lock package, and he's drilled ten of them in the past two weeks. Today will make eleven. He opens the other Dell box and unpacks his tools.

Carr watches Mike assemble the drill rig, and Bobby lay out the bits and the borescope. He's pacing again, and Mike doesn't like it.

"You're fucking up my rhythm, *cabrón*. How 'bout you do that someplace else?"

Carr walks his fear and boredom into the hall. He studies the door to Lucovic's office, and the door frame, and the floor, looking for an unseen contact switch, a pressure plate, some other hidden, independent alarm—something Valerie might've missed during her two-week stint emptying trash cans with the cleaning crew. He strains to hear heavy footsteps approaching, even as he tells himself that Valerie doesn't miss those kinds of things.

And then it's Declan's voice he's hearing again, back in Mexico City, making his pitch at a table by the kitchen. Declan had not hemmed or hawed, but jumped right in.

"I'm a robber, Mr. Carr, a robber plain and simple—cash and highly liquid items only. No art, no stocks, no bonds unless they're the bearer variety, no finished jewels, no cars or boats or fancy stamp collections. Just cash and its closest cousins."

Carr squinted, convinced that Declan was drunk and that this was a joke whose reeling logic eluded him. "A bank robber?" he asked eventually. "Teddy said you were a consultant."

"Not a consultant." Declan laughed. "And I don't touch banks. I don't touch payrolls or cambios either, nor armored cars nor safe deposit boxes—no official money for me. Too much official firepower looking after that stuff, and anyway, who wants to crawl into bed at night with images of sobbing widows in his head, and big-eyed orphans turned out in the cold? Takes the joy from living, don't it? So it's black money only I go for. There's plenty of that lying about, and it leaves you with a nice clean conscience afterward."

Carr peered at Declan through smoke and his own drunken haze, still waiting for the punch line. "So, you rob from the rich and give to...?"

"Myself, Mr. Carr. And it's rich shites I rob from—drug runners, gunrunners, whore runners, human smugglers, kidnappers—the very worst swine. I've lightened the till on all of them."

Carr pulled on his beer, but it didn't help to anchor him. "I can't imagine they're very happy about it," he said finally. "And they've got plenty of firepower of their own, and no hesitation using it."

"That they do." Declan laughed. "But the upside is they don't go whining to the *polizei* either, except maybe to the ones they've got on payroll. And when it comes to security, they tend to go for quantity, not quality, if you know what I mean. Heavy stuff, lots of tech sometimes, but not subtle, and typically with some very large blind spots. And, of course, the boys and me are stealthy bastards—they don't know we exist until we're over the threshold, and then it's in fast, out fast, and clear out of town. We don't leave footprints, and we never—but never—fish the same stream twice."

"Security in obscurity," Carr recited—an old lesson that he knew was only sometimes true. "So what's the downside of your business?"

"What you'd expect: people get cross, they brood over

things, they have long memories, and if they catch you they'll kill you all kinds of dead—by which time death will seem like a mercy. But like I said, we're dead sneaky: never been pinched; never come·close. We're phantoms, Mr. Carr— black cats tippy-toeing in the black night."

The smoke that swirled around the room seemed to fill Carr's head. "I've got to have a talk with Teddy Voigt. I don't know what he's been telling you about me, but I—"

Declan laughed again. "Teddy said you might be just the ticket."

"The ticket to what?"

"To bigger and better, Mr. Carr—a step up in the league tables."

"I'm not following."

"I'm running a nice enough carnival now. I've got a strongman, a fire-eater, a boy who bites the heads off chickens, and I'm the barker that keeps it all going. Our show does fine, Mr. Carr, a reliable money-spinner, but it's still just a carnival, and I've got bigger plans. I want me a full-blown circus, with three feckin' rings and a fat box office every show. But for that I need a ringmaster: someone to sort out the elephants and monkeys, and stuff the clowns in their wee cars. Someone to make sure the trapeze girl doesn't land in the lion's cage, you see? You understand, Mr. Carr, I need a planner, an organizer. Teddy says that's you."

Carr's mind was stuttering, and organization was the last thing on it. He could muster no more than an adolescent shrug, but Declan had momentum enough for both of them.

"Teddy says you've got an engineer's eye for operations— a talent for breaking big problems into bite-size ones, for finding the shortest paths and the points of failure, and coming up with contingencies and fallbacks. He says—"

"Teddy's talking out of school. He should know better."

The smile widened on Declan's chipped red face, and he

ran a hand over his thinning hair. His eyes were cold and probing through the smoke. "He says that you're careful too—that you always pack the belt *and* the suspenders. Caution is a virtuous thing in a planner."

Carr could never put his finger on just when he'd begun to take Declan seriously, to believe that his talk of robbers and ringmasters was more than just drunken digression, or the overture to some elaborate scam. Maybe it was in the long silence that followed Declan's speech, as the smoke and sorrowful music pressed closer, or while Carr sipped at the coffee he'd ordered to replace his unfinished beer. Or maybe, on the heels of another failure, another firing, adrift once again, Carr had been a buyer from the start.

"Maybe you could do with a bit more caution yourself. How do you know I won't go home and call the police?"

"And tell them what? My name? My phone number? You know as well as anyone how disposable those are. And besides, I do my sums, Mr. Carr—I think I know you better than that."

Carr shook his head. "Fucking Teddy."

"Don't go blaming Teddy, either—not too much anyway. Yes, he tells me some things—I expect it for the fee I pay him—but I do my own legwork besides. So I know about your unfortunate disagreement with your client, and the nice right cross that put an end to your career with Integral Risk. I know about your housing problem, as well. And I know about your brief period of service to your country— very noble that—and how they tossed you out on your arse after all that training. Decided you're not the kind of glad-handing wanker Langley likes for their agent-runners. Imaginative bunch up there, eh?

"And I know how Teddy recruited you to IR after that, and bounced you around the region a bit, before setting you down in Mexico. And I know that you send a check once a month to your old dad up in Massachusetts. Stockbridge, is it? It's not everything about you, I'm sure, but it's enough to give me some comfort you won't be running to the Garda. You're too smart for that, Mr. Carr."

The smile was there, and the furry, conspiratorial chuckle, and there was only the briefest gust of icy air—like walking past an open freezer—when he met Declan's blue gaze. Carr found the implicit threat comforting somehow—a kind of corroboration.

"Many people get killed in your business?" Carr asked finally.

"I won't say no eggs get broken, but we try to avoid it. And truth be told, these aren't altar boys we're dealing with. They're dead-enders—hard boys, or so they fancy themselves—bad insurance risks on the best of days."

"I was wondering more about your own guys."

"When it comes to me and mine, *safety first* is my motto. I'm pleased to say I haven't lost a man yet."

"*Yet.*"

Declan shook his head. "If it's risk you're worried about, I can't change that—it is what it is—but if it's crime that gives you pause, then I'd ask you to think about who it is I'm robbing. They're pricks, every one of 'em—none worse in the world. I'm no Robin Hood, but the fact is I hurt 'em where they live—square in the wallet—which might be more justice than they get from anyone else." Declan smiled again, more broadly this time, impossibly charming, and then he drained his beer. "So what d'ya say, Mr. Carr, you want to run off with the circus?"

Safety first . . . haven't lost a man yet. Carr shakes his head, banishing the echoes of Declan's voice. No, Carr thinks, you hadn't lost a man until four months ago, when you lost two—shot full of holes and burned to a crisp on the side of the Trans-Andean Highway. And too bad one of those rigid cinders was you.

Then Bobby is shaking him, whispering urgently. "The fuck's the matter with you? You don't hear that?" Bobby points toward the reception area, where the voices are coming from. Carr wipes a hand across his face and listens. They're muffled and indistinct, but he can make out two men, talking and laughing.

"*Chingada!*" Mike's voice is low and harsh. He's standing, clenched, in the door of Lucovic's office, and he's holding a Glock.

"What are you doing with that?" Carr whispers.

"Scratching my ass, *cabrón*—what the fuck you think I'm doing?"

Carr shakes his head. "Stay here, both of you, and put that thing away."

"Time to pack up?" Bobby asks.

"Just stay," Carr says, and he crosses the office suite to a teak-paneled partition that reaches nearly to the ceiling and that on the other side forms the long curving back wall of Portrait Capital's reception area.

The voices are louder here but still muffled, and Carr can tell they're coming from outside the glass doors. Carr lies on the floor and peers through a gap between the corner of the partition and a potted tree. The reception area is still dark, the metal gate is still down, and the glass doors are still closed, but beyond them, in the dimly lit corridor near the elevators, there are two men sitting on the floor. Their T-shirts and baggy white pants are spattered with paint, and they are smoking a joint. The dope smell is cloying and powerful, and it reaches Carr quickly even across the still air. He rolls back around the corner and nearly collides with Bobby, who is holding a little Beretta.

Carr looks at the gun. "For chrissakes—you too?" he whispers.

"Is it the rent-a-cops from the lobby?"

"It's the painters from downstairs, getting high. You want to shoot them?"

Bobby tucks the gun into his back pocket. "So are we fucked or not?"

"I don't know yet," Carr says. He stretches out on the floor again, peeks around the corner for another moment, and then sits up. "Give it a minute. They're down to the roach—let's see if they go back to work when they're done."

"Don't know if Mike's got a minute—he's twitchy as hell."

"He's not alone," Carr says, and he gets low and takes another look. "They're done," he whispers. "The one guy's getting up. He's pocketing the roach. Now the other guy's up. They're...fuck these assholes!" Carr turns the corner and stands quickly.

"What's going on?" Bobby asks, but Carr is crossing the office suite at a jog, headed back to the utility closet. Bobby follows. "What's going on?" he asks again.

"They're rattling doorknobs."

"Shit! Did we lock Molloy's door?"

"I don't know," Carr says, and he drops down to crawl through the hole in the closet wall.

"Fucking thieves," Bobby mutters, and he drops too.

They almost make it. Carr is halfway across Molloy's office, headed for his secretary's, and Bobby is just emerging from the utility closet, when there are whispers in the hallway, and the handle on the office door begins to turn. Carr pulls his headset off, jams it in his pocket, and turns his back to the office door. He stands by Molloy's desk and picks up Molloy's telephone. His tone is conversational when he speaks, but his voice is loud—as if the connection is bad.

"Got it, honey—two cases of Lone Star, a case of tonic water, the steaks, the macaroni salad. Anything else?" Bobby freezes in mid-stride, then walks slowly backward until he's up against the wall. His gun is out again and he's sighting along the wall, toward the office door. Carr glares at him and shakes his head minutely.

There's more murmuring in the hall, a suppressed laugh, and the office door begins to open. Bobby works the slide on the Beretta, and Carr slices the air with his fingertips— a gambler refusing a card. Bobby scowls.

"I'll be a while longer," Carr says loudly. "Couple of hours, at least. No, I won't forget the tonic."

The door opens wider and the smell of weed reaches Carr. He's certain he can feel eyes on his back, but his own eyes are locked on Bobby against the wall. And then there's movement in the closet, and Latin Mike is there, lying prone, looking down the barrel of his Glock.

Carr swallows hard. "And the macaroni salad—I won't forget." His voice is shaking and he's trying to catch Mike's eye, but Mike won't see him, won't see anything but the door that's opening wider still. Carr's lungs lock up, his body tenses, and he takes a half-step to his right, right into Mike's sight line. Bobby draws an audible breath; Mike's Glock doesn't waver.

And then there's laughter in the hallway, a giggled "*Fuck it*," running footsteps, and the office door falling shut with a decisive click.

The silence afterward is ringing. Carr is conscious only of the pulse in his ears and the sweat running over his ribs. Latin Mike crawls back through the closet wall, and Bobby follows. Carr locks the office door and goes through too, then stands in Lucovic's office while Mike drills the safe.

Two hundred twenty-seven thousand dollars in neatly bundled cash; three million, give or take, in loose polished stones.

5

WHEN THE adrenaline washes out, Carr thinks, it's like another country—another planet altogether. On this planet, on this evening, they look like film stars by the swimming pool: Valerie in a slate-blue shift, dark glasses, and a loose French braid; Dennis, Bobby, Mike, and Carr himself all freshly showered, shaved, in crisp shirts and shades of their own. The late-day sun throws sheets of orange light across the pool, the fieldstone deck, the wrought-iron chairs and tables, the sinuous olive trees, and a wide swath of Napa Valley hillside below. The waitress delivers another bottle of Chardonnay, another plate of cheese, and another basket of warm bread to their table. She leaves, and they have the terrace to themselves again.

Latin Mike sips and sighs and stretches in the cooling air. "Nice," he says. "Whose choice?" Carr nods toward Valerie, and Mike smiles. "You can book all my hotels, *chica*." She lifts her wineglass and smiles back.

"Lucky to be here, no, *jefe*?" Mike continues. "Those two stoners could've screwed us up but good."

Carr shakes his head. "The luck was that you didn't start banging away. Otherwise we'd be picking brains off our lapels around now, instead of drinking wine."

"That'd work too," Mike says. "My tastes are simple."

"So instead of nobody knowing anything, we'd have had maybe ten minutes to haul ass before the cops got there. And that works for you?"

Mike shrugs. "Not everybody's so squeamish, *cabrón.*"

Carr takes off his sunglasses. "Not everybody's so stupid, either."

"You saying Deke was stupid, bro? 'Cause he didn't mind a little juice."

"He didn't mind when there wasn't another option."

"Traffic moves fast. There's not always time to figure the options."

"Which is why you're not supposed to figure anything— you're supposed to listen to me. For chrissakes, Mike, we've put months into this gig, and you nearly ended it in the first act."

Valerie mutters something, and Dennis shifts nervously in his chair. Bobby clears his throat. "Which is something we've been wondering about," Bobby says, "ending it in the first act, I mean."

It was hard travel from Houston—dusty, hot, and bumpy—and though he's washed off the grit, Carr can still feel the ride in his shoulders. He looks at Bobby and then at Latin Mike. "We made a deal," he says, "a commitment. We've got big sunk costs in this thing, and so does Boyce. He's not going to like it if we walk away."

Mike clasps his hands behind his head. "*Señor Boyce—el padrino.*"

"Fucking ghost, more like," Bobby says.

Carr rises from the table and walks to the terrace railing. He looks at the darkening vineyards and sighs. He's been down this road before with Mike and Bobby, more than once—do the job, don't do the job; one last run, or not—but with three and a quarter million in swag in a room upstairs, the potholes and blind curves are less theoretical now.

"You've worked for him longer than I have, Mike," Carr says. "You were working for him when I signed on."

"True that, *cabrón*, but I've never met the guy. None of us have had the honor—only Deke and you."

"I didn't ask for it—it's the way Deke set it up. It's the way Boyce wants it."

"But you see how it makes a guy nervous."

"You never had a problem before—no worries about the intel he feeds us, or the logistics; no complaint about the splits or the banking service; no gripes at all that I heard about."

Latin Mike nods slowly, but concedes nothing. "Still, a guy gets older, he starts to like the bird in the hand, right, Bobby?"

Bobby smiles. "Three bucks and a quarter—we used to call that a nice payday."

There's wood smoke in the air, something fragrant, mesquite maybe, mixing with the scents of warm earth, bay laurel, and sage that rise from the hillside. Carr breathes in deeply.

"Back when Declan brought me on, you guys thought half a buck was Christmas morning. Times change; prices rise. Three and a quarter isn't what it used to be, especially after expenses. It's not beach money anymore."

Mike empties his wineglass. "And you're all about retirement, right, *jefe*?"

"I thought we all were. I thought that's what we said the last five times we had this conversation. But if you're saying something different, let's not dick around. Tell me now and I'll tell Boyce when I see him day after tomorrow."

Bobby pops up, as if he's sat on a tack, but he's smiling. "Nobody's saying anything. We're just thinking out loud."

Valerie's laugh is like ice in a glass. "Is that how you split the labor, Bobby—Mike thinks, and you do the out loud part?"

Bobby flips her the bird, but he's laughing too, and so is Dennis, and so—finally—is Mike. Carr is still watching purple shadows spread over the valley when the waitress reappears and says that their table is ready.

It's set with heavy linen, battered silver, and votive candles in thick blue glass. Valerie is at the head, between Bobby and Latin Mike, and Carr sits at the other end, between Dennis and the vacant chair. Valerie's playing hostess tonight, smiling, laughing, keeping glasses filled and conversation weightless. It's a part she plays well: conspiratorial and flattering with Mike; flirtatious and profane with Bobby; and with Dennis simply present to be gazed upon. Carr can relate; he can't look away either.

Candlelight flickers on her arms and throat and softens her elfin features. Her green eyes glow and, as the night wears on, her braid loosens and two honey-colored strands slip down to frame her face. Always in motion, the face, the hands, the voice—lifting, lilting, insinuating. It must be exhausting, Carr thinks—it exhausts him just watching her, but he watches just the same. The room darkens, the crowd thins, wine bottles march steadily past, good soldiers all, and by the time the entrees are cleared Carr is drunk and drifting backward again, to Costa Alegre.

IT WAS off-season in Chamela—white mornings, the narrow pastel streets empty until noon—and Carr was on R & R between jobs, nursing a row of bruised ribs. He was sticking close to his rented casita, swimming, reading, sleeping, and he'd never have seen her if not for Fernando.

Fernando did alarms for Declan when Carr first joined up, and his brother Ernesto did surveillance, but their skills didn't line up with Declan's ambitions and they'd slipped into retirement about a year later—Neto to a sport fishing business on the Riviera Maya, and Nando to invest in Jalisco real estate. Carr had always liked the brothers, their unfussy competence and soft-edged cynicism, and he'd been happy to hear from Nando and accept his invitation to drive up the coast for lunch by a hotel pool.

Nando was thicker, darker, and more jocular than he'd been the last time he and Carr had shared a meal. He was working steadily through a platter of chicken tacos and a long story about some condos he was building in Manzanilla when he paused and pointed with his beer to the far side of the pool. "*Oye, cabrón*—you like a little mystery?"

She wore a green two-piece, and her skin was the color of toast. Her hair wasn't blond then, it was a sun-streaked copper, cut blunt to her shoulders, and there was a tattoo on her lower back, a tangle of blue Sanskrit, that looked as if it had been there a while, but which proved to be window dressing. The freckles were real though, and so were the quick green eyes. And the catch at the back of his throat. And the ache he felt through his arms and fingers.

"*Muy bien, no?*" Nando continued. "At first I think she's a tourist, but then I'm not sure. All week I see guys make their play, and all week she's ice. She shuts them down before they get a word out—even me, if you can believe it. Then these skinny guys check in a couple days ago, from up north, and suddenly she's Miss Congeniality. She lets them buy her drinks, lunch, dinner, whatever, and they're practically slitting each other's throats to get next to her."

"You think she's a working girl?"

"She's working something, *cabrón*. I just can't figure out what."

Nando was flying up to Monterrey that afternoon for his niece's *quinceañera*, and he picked up the check before he left and promised to let Carr buy dinner when he returned. "You keep your eye on her, bro. Maybe you can tell me what the mystery is all about." It took him three days to work it out.

Carr spent a few more hours poolside that afternoon, watching her talk to the skinny men. The next day, he took a room at the hotel and followed her: to the beach with the tall skinny man, into town with the balding one, on the cliff-side hiking trail with the blond one who wore a strand of Buddhist prayer beads around his wrist. Poolside, in the cottony twilight, the men bought her drinks, fidgeted, laughed too long, and looked away from one another and scowled.

The day after that, Carr spent some dollars with the hotel staff to learn that her name was Carrie Lyle and that she was from L.A. The three men were from Milpitas, California, and they'd each given the same address on McCarthy Boulevard when they'd registered. Online, in the hotel's business center, he found that the Milpitas address was the headquarters of Null Space Integrated, a manufacturer of specialized graphics chips, and that the men were NSI's three most senior design engineers. Of Carrie Lyle he could find no trace at all.

A pro then, trolling for technical intel, or maybe for talent. It didn't surprise Carr, but the knowledge left him feeling somehow disappointed, as if such mundane loot wasn't deserving of her performance. Because it really was an exceptional performance—maybe the best he'd seen—subtle, unhurried, and finely calibrated to each member of her small audience. He saw it in her body language—the way she arranged herself at their sides—and he heard it in the snippets of conversation he'd managed to steal. She was tentative, almost shy, with the tall man; coltish, nearly awkward, with the bald one; and with the blond Buddhist she was ethereal and dreamy. Three women, beckoning.

It didn't seem much work for her to reconcile her various

selves when she entertained the three men at once. It was a matter of small adjustments as far as Carr could tell from his corner of the patio—something in her laugh, her posture, the way she touched her hair. A matter of little intimacies bestowed like candies: a fingertip on the back of a hand, a tanned thigh pressed for a moment against a pale one, a tanned foot sliding on a pale ankle, a hand on a nervous hip. The skinny men were like cats under a full moon, and at his shaded table Carr himself felt a lunar itch and an urge to howl.

So, mystery solved. Carr sighed heavily at the squandering of talent and hoisted himself from his seat. He headed toward his room and wondered what he and Declan might not get up to with someone like her on their crew. They'd been talking about recruiting someone with that kind of knack—a roper, a honeypot—but neither of them could come up with a likely prospect. Carr slid his key into his door and wondered if Carrie Lyle, or whatever the hell her real name was, might do. And then a gun was in his back and a hand was on his neck, pushing him inside.

The man didn't wait until the door had closed. "The fuck you want, motherfucker?" His voice was American and nervous.

Carr turned slowly and took a slow, deep breath. The man was maybe thirty, and wore jeans and a polo shirt. He had short, black hair and a narrow frame, and something about his tapered head, and the way it swayed on his neck, reminded Carr of an otter. The man was sweating and breathing hard, and a vein throbbed at his temple faster than Carr's pulse was racing.

"The fuck you want with her?" the otter said, and Carr sighed with relief that this was about Carrie Lyle and not some older piece of business. He studied the damp face. He didn't think he'd seen the otter around the hotel, but he knew he wasn't perfect when it came to those things.

"Want with who?"

"Don't screw with me, asshole. You're fucking bird-dogging her, and I want to know why."

The gun was a little S&W, and Carr didn't like the way it jumped around in the otter's hand. "You mean the redhead? Take a look at her, brother—what do you think I'm interested in?"

The otter almost spit. "Right—that's why you duke the desk guy a hundred bucks to see all those registration cards."

Carr nodded slowly. She'd set up trip wires. She'd had someone watching her back. Carr was impressed, even if her guard dog was a lightweight. She'd known someone was trailing her and still she hadn't broken stride. Carr took a half-step closer. The otter didn't notice. "I wondered what she saw in those geeks," he said. "A girl like that—I couldn't figure it. I still can't."

The otter swallowed hard. "Bullshit. What are you—NSI security? Something private?"

Carr took another step forward and put a quaver in his voice and a frightened look on his face. "Seriously, I'm not anybody," he said, and he raised his hands in the air. "I'm just here on vacation from—"

Carr jabbed his thumb into the otter's throat, then into his eye, and then he took the otter's gun. The man gagged and put his hands to his face. Carr pushed him backward into a chair. He tried to get up and Carr pushed him down harder and flipped him over. The otter had a wallet in his hip pocket and Carr took it, and slapped the back of his head when he tried to resist.

According to his driver's license, his name was Kenneth Kern, from Van Nuys, California, and according to his business card, he was a partner and senior investigator with Victory Security Services, Inc. Carr tossed the wallet at Kern's feet.

"I don't work for NSI," Carr said. "And I could give a shit what you guys are up to. I just want five minutes of her time—a quick chat, and nothing else." He emptied the S&W while he spoke, and put the bullets in his pocket. Then he popped the cylinder out of the gun and tossed what was left into Kern's lap. He held up the cylinder. "She comes to see me, I'll give this back."

She showed up around midnight, wearing a gray linen shift and an expression of impatience and disdain. She looked years older than she had poolside, and even ignoring the little automatic in her hand, she was about as seductive as the taxman.

Valerie's voice was flat and without accent. "Your five minutes started fifteen seconds ago, so if you've got a pitch, make it now."

Carr handed her the S&W cylinder. "I promised your boss I'd give this back."

She snorted. "Kenny's barely the boss of his shoelaces," she said, and dropped the cylinder into her purse. She looked at her watch again.

Carr nodded and said his piece. Two days later, after she'd e-mailed the specs for NSI's next mobile phone chip to her client in Shanghai and shorted a thousand shares of NSI stock, Valerie arrived for lunch in Chamela. Her expression was wary when Carr greeted her at the door of his casita, and warmed only slightly when Declan offered her a drink.

HIS PHONE is jittering on the bedside table, and Valerie is shaking his arm. Carr wipes a hand across his face and gropes for the light. Seven people have his number: the three men he was at dinner with hours earlier; the woman he's in bed with now; Mr. Boyce, who rarely calls; Declan, who's dead; and Eleanor Calvin. The caller ID shows a 413 area code, and Carr calculates the time in Stockbridge—five twenty in the morning. He takes the phone into the bathroom, turns on the light, and shuts the door on Valerie's curious gaze. He runs water in the sink, and when he speaks his voice is thick and distant.

"Mrs. Calvin, what's the matter?"

She's seventy, about the shape and size of a hockey stick, but despite the early hour her voice is blue jay bright. "It's not a good night for him, dear. He's been walking the floor for hours, and now he's calling for you."

"Calling me for what, Mrs. Calvin?"

"You know how hard he can be to follow. He's talking about your summer break, and a job—an internship, I think—at the State Department. I'm missing part of it, I'm sure, but I think he's angry because you're supposed to call someone about it, but you haven't."

The light in the bathroom is harsh and broken, the surfaces too shiny, and it all feels like sand in his eyes. In the mirror, his features are pale and smudged—a lost boy look, Valerie would say. Emphasis on the lost, Carr thinks, and for an instant Declan's voice flashes in his head: *Neither sober nor quite drunk enough*.

"That was a dozen years ago, Mrs. Calvin."

"It's not a good night for him."

"Would it help if I spoke to him?"

"It would help if you came for a visit."

"Soon, Mrs. Calvin. Did you tell him I'll be back there soon?"

"I did, dear, but honestly I'm not sure the ambassador knows who I am right now."

Carr lets out a long breath. "He wasn't an ambassador, Mrs. Calvin."

"Of course not, dear. Now wait just a minute and I'll get your father."

6

IT IS raining in the Berkshires, a warm patter from a low sky. The waxy leaves shudder, branches bow under the gray weight of water and humid air, and the odors of damp wood, moldering paper, and rodent piss rise from the clapboards and curling shingles of his father's house. Carr stands on the front porch and feels the old lassitude creep over him like a fog. It's been years since he's spent more than a night or two in the sagging Victorian pile, but its musty gravity is insistent.

The reek of long neglect and decay is the perfume of Carr's adolescence—of the year he spent here with his father and mother following their abrupt, chaotic decampment from Mexico City, and of the boarding school holidays he endured in the years after his mother's death. The creeping torpor—the feeling of lead in his bones, cotton wool in his skull, and breath coagulating in his lungs, of life coagulating around him, even as it surges ahead in the world beyond the slumping stone wall—is what has kept him away, except for days here and there, since the morning he left for college. Part of what has kept him away.

Eleanor Calvin is at his side, her wiry, freckled hand on his arm. She wears paddock boots, pressed jeans, and a rain slicker—a bright yellow flame against the overcast. Carr eyes the knee-high stacks of newspapers and magazines that run the length of the porch. Calvin follows his gaze.

"It's hard to keep up," she says. "He has so many subscriptions, they accumulate faster than I can get to recycling."

The piles of *The New York Times*, *The Wall Street Journal*, the *Financial Times*, *The Washington Post*, *Foreign Affairs*, and *Foreign Policy* are yellowed and dissolving. To Carr they look no different from the ones he saw the last time he was here.

"I told him he can get them all online," Carr says.

Eleanor Calvin nods sadly. "It's difficult for him sometimes, remembering the passwords. And then he gets angry."

"Nothing new there—angry is his usual state."

Calvin frowns and shakes her head. "It's because he's scared of what's happening to him." She pats Carr's arm. "It's what the doctor said, dear—there'll be good days and bad, and over time more of the bad ones. But today he's good, and you should enjoy it. I told the ambassador you were coming, and he's looking forward to it."

Carr sighs, but doesn't correct her.

Inside the light is gray, as it always is, regardless of weather, time of day, or season of the year. Arthur Carr is in the dining room, at the head of a long table that is layered in newspapers, folded laundry, and heaps of unopened mail. He looks up from his *FT*, blinks his gray eyes, and pushes half-glasses into a still dark hairline. His face is long, angular, and academic-looking, the skin of his cheeks pink from shaving, the fine nose veined from drink. It isn't Carr's nose, which is twice broken but otherwise unmarred, and the eyes are different too: Carr's are hazel, like his mother's, but still the resemblance is pronounced. Which always startles Carr and makes him uneasy.

"You're sunburned," Arthur Carr says. "How do you manage that from behind a desk? Or do they have you in the field now?" Still the Ivy League drawl, but higher-pitched now—an old man's voice.

Carr isn't sure which *they* his father means. He's left his employment status vague since being fired from Integral Risk, adopting Declan's usefully elastic *consultant* when pressed. It's been months since his father has pressed. "I had some vacation time," he answers.

"Well, don't waste it here," his father says. He points a long finger at the dining room window and the neon yellow form of Eleanor Calvin standing on the porch. "I told her not to bother you, but she gets so damned dramatic."

"It was no trouble—I'd planned to come next week. I just moved things up a little."

Arthur Carr turns back to his newspaper, rattling the page. "At any rate, you must be glad to get out of that sewer."

Carr has been vague about his living arrangements too. His father believes that he's still in Mexico City. "It's not so bad," Carr says.

His father snorts. "Long as you don't need to breathe the air, or drink the water, or drive ten blocks in under an hour. I don't know how you stand it."

"It's not so bad," Carr says again.

"*Not so bad?* You don't know what you're talking about. Twenty years down there, I could never stand it."

Noxious shitholes was the phrase his father favored, and he used it often—more often with a few drinks in him. Carr remembers him red and fuming, a glass in one hand, the other gesturing at a broad window, and the low, smudged skyline—of what city Carr can't recall—that lay beyond, hunched under a shelf of smog. He remembers his mother too: pale and still and quiet before his father's wave of complaint, always in a dress and heels, always with a cigarette. He doesn't remember the details of his father's rants, but the broad strokes were all the same: the wrong political connections, the wrong family ties, the wrong school ring; the inept boss, the paranoid boss, the vengeful boss; favors and grudges; being passed over, and passed over again. Thwarted. And so it went in Lima, São Paulo, Buenos Aires, Asunción, Quito, San Salvador, Managua, Ciudad Juárez, and Mexico City.

Carr remembers his father's rising voice, his mother's massive silence, and his own clenched dread. It was a swooping, taloned thing that seized his chest, seized his voice, and chased him through the houses that blended one into the next.

They were different, it seemed, only in their addresses. Always walled and gated, with leafy courtyards and burbling fountains, their rooms were cool and quiet, their furnishings heavy, dark, and carefully arranged—like store displays, and just as lifeless. Carr can still recall the sour odor of spilt wine that lurked in the sofa cushions, and the smell of singed fabric—the remnants of one of his parents' parties, or maybe of a prior resident's. Not their sofas, of course, and not really their houses: they were just the latest in a long line of temporary lodgers—in and out in two years, maybe three. The attendant cooks and gardeners and maids, always dark and wary, had greater claims on those places.

He made friends from time to time, other Foreign Service brats, and he remembers his quiet envy of the houses that they lived in. Not very different from his own in shape or size, they'd been transformed by an alchemy unknown to his family from anonymous showrooms into homes, with photos on the mantel, bicycles in the drive, and a carved pumpkin at Halloween. They made wherever he was living seem like a rented van.

Arthur Carr wasn't an ambassador; he wasn't even close. The highest he'd climbed in nineteen years was to the number three spot in the Economic Section of the embassy in

Mexico City. That was his final posting, and he'd lasted barely ten months.

His father is up now, leaning at a sideboard that is littered with white plastic grocery bags. A flock of ghosts, Carr thinks, and they make a noise like dry leaves as his father brushes them aside to find a rocks glass. Carr checks his watch as his father pours an inch of scotch and swirls it around.

"You look like your mother when you look like that," Arthur Carr says.

"A little early, isn't it?"

"Is it?" his father asks, and lets his reading glasses fall to his nose. "And just what the hell do I have to wait for?"

The rain has lightened to a mist when Carr returns to the porch, and the air is warmer and more cloying. Eleanor Calvin is staring at the treetops and the leaden sky.

"There's a salad for lunch," she says. "There should be enough for both of you. And there's roast chicken for dinner, and some new potatoes."

"I booked a room at the Red Lion," Carr says. "I can eat there." Eleanor Calvin sighs, still looking up. She's waiting for something. "Do you need a lift home?" Carr asks.

She shakes her head. "It's just a mile, and hardly raining."

"It's no trouble, Mrs. Cal—"

"Do you remember my daughter, dear?"

Carr recalls a rangy blond girl, a few years younger than he. A rider, he remembers. "Annabeth, right? She went to law school down south."

"She's still there, in Atlanta. She had a baby six weeks ago, her second little girl."

Something frozen drops into Carr's gut. "Another granddaughter—I had no idea. Congratulations."

Eleanor Calvin takes a deep breath. She looks at Carr, who is looking at the floorboards. "She wants to go back to work, dear, and she needs help with the children. She's got plenty of room, and she's asked me to move in."

Carr is focused on his breathing, fighting the light-headed feeling. He flexes his fingers, which are suddenly cold. "I had no idea," he says again, softly. "Look, I know he's difficult. If it's the money, I could—"

Eleanor Calvin frowns. "It has nothing to do with money," she says sadly. "You've been more than generous, dear. And you know how fond I was of your mother. But Annabeth and her girls need me now, and truth be told these winters get longer every year."

Carr is still staring down, shaking his head slowly. "When?" he asks.

"Two or three months, I think. I've listed the house. I've got some cleaning up to do before they can start showing it, but I can go before it's sold."

"I need time."

"Of course you do, dear. It's a big change. It'll be a big adjustment for your father."

"That woman who filled in for you—the one who came when you went to Florida—could she come on full-time?"

A pained look crosses Eleanor Calvin's weathered face. "But, dear, I thought you understood—your father needs more than home care now. Atlanta aside, I don't know that I could do for him much longer. It's getting more… complicated."

"Complicated how?"

A blush spreads across her lined cheeks. "He's…he's starting to have bathroom problems, and last week the police picked him up at ten at night, a half mile down the road from here. He didn't have shoes on and his feet were bleeding. I wish I could do more, dear, but really the ambassador needs a different sort of care."

"He wasn't an ambassador," Carr says, but only to himself.

. . .

ELEANOR CALVIN gives him three months, and leaves Carr on the porch, figuring furiously. Some of his figuring is about timing: three months is bad. He has scheduled thirteen more weeks for the job, including a one-week contingency. Three months would fall at the endgame—the close of the third act. It couldn't be worse, and he'll have to beg or bribe her for an extra two weeks.

But most of his figuring is about money. His father has next to none, and Carr has been paying for his care for several years: every month an envelope stuffed with used hundreds to Eleanor Calvin. The arrangement works well for both of them: a tax-free income for her, and the anonymity of cash for him. But cash won't fly with a nursing home. They will have forms to fill out, contracts to sign, and bank accounts, employment, and income to verify—and all in his actual name. Which is, of course, impossible.

And which assumes he can even find a place that will take his father. Eleanor Calvin had done research and pressed some papers on him—a list of websites with information on facilities for the elderly, and on Medicare, Medicaid, and Social Security, is folded in his pocket, along with a list of nursing homes in the Berkshires. He scanned them once, twice, but they turned to Greek.

Arthur Carr calls from the front hallway: he wants his lunch. Carr goes inside and finds Eleanor Calvin's salad, and watches his father eat it and drink more scotch. Clouds thicken in his head as he listens to his father's monologue, which skips like a stone from war to stock markets, to the decline of the West, to Eleanor Calvin's cooking, to her designs on the family silver.

Eleanor Calvin thought Carr should tell his father sooner rather than later about her move, but Carr has no stomach for the conversation. His father's talk grows angrier and more tangential with each refill, and as the day fades Carr wonders if his father will sleep soon, or if he should start drinking too. Instead he walks across the hall into the living room.

It's dimmer than the dining room, and more chaotic, with newspapers and magazines and precarious stacks of books on nearly every surface. There's an upright piano against one wall, a block of ebony and dust, and on top, in tarnished silver frames, lying facedown, are photographs. Carr stands them up.

They're desiccated and yellowed behind their smudged panes—ancient-looking, like bugs in a collection. His grand-parents—his father's parents—starched, pale, and unsmiling beside a long, dark sedan. His father, young and smirking amid a group of distant cousins. They are gathered by a pine-edged lake, all in dark shorts and white shirts, like camp-ers or a Bible study group. His father again—older, taller, in cap and gown and an already bitter smile, the Battell Chapel and a bit of New Haven street behind him. And then, in the most tarnished frame, the photo he is looking for, of his mother, her black hair loose, her eyes shining, her white teeth and a curl of smoke visible between her parted lips.

He called the picture by different names as a child, because he didn't know where it was taken or what she was doing in it, and so he made up different stories about it. *En el jardín. En la fiesta. En el baile. In the garden*, because his mother stands before well-tended hedges, with a bed of blue flowers visible over her shoulder, and a vine with red blossoms wind-ing up a trellis. *At the party*, because she wears pearls and a floral dress, and holds a champagne flute, and because she might be laughing. *At the dance*, because her hair is sweeping past her shoulder, her neck is long and curved like a dancer's, and she might be looking at someone—a partner—outside the frame. He still doesn't know which of those stories was the right one. Maybe all of them.

His father says something from the dining room, but Carr can't make out what. He waits for more, but nothing comes. After a while he sweeps a pile of magazines from the sofa and lies down.

The phone, burring in his pocket, wakes him from a clammy sleep. It's dark now and he turns on the porch light as he steps outside to answer. The air is like a cool cloth on his face. Mr. Boyce, who almost never calls, is calling.

"You're not in California," he says. His voice is heavy and smooth, an amber syrup. "You're supposed to be in California today, and you're supposed to be out here tomorrow."

"I'll be there. I'm flying out of Boston first thing."

"Is there a problem?"

"No. No problem."

1

BACKLIT ON the fourteenth tee, Mr. Boyce is a slab of granite escaped from the quarry, or spare parts from Stonehenge. Carr walks up the cart path, and from fifty yards features emerge in the monolith: massive arms and shoulders, a corded neck, a shaved head, black and gleaming against the blue sky. *Rockefeller Center*, Carr thinks, *the statue of Atlas*. He thinks it every time he sees Boyce. Carr stops walking as Mr. Boyce sets up over the ball. The driver is like a blade of grass in his hands, and though Carr has seen him play many times before, he is always amazed that the heavily plated torso can coil and release with such ease. There is a slashing noise, a gunshot, and Mr. Boyce looks down the fairway and nods. Then he beckons to Carr.

This is the twenty-second time they have met, and their twenty-second meeting on a golf course, though never on the same course twice. Today they are in Wisconsin, just outside Madison, at a private club set beside a lake, amid hills drenched in green. As he was the first time Carr saw him, in Atlanta, under a punishing August sun, Mr. Boyce is wearing tailored black. And, as always, he is golfing alone, walking the course, and carrying his own bag.

Which isn't to say he is without retainers. There are two

of them today, trailing behind in a golf cart: a large man in khakis and sunglasses, with short red hair, whose name Carr has never learned but who drives Mr. Boyce's cars, and next to him Tina, who is slim and white-blond, whose oval face is as smooth and empty as a mannequin's, and who, Declan once told him, kills people for Mr. Boyce. Tina looks up from a glossy magazine through dark, rectangular glasses and smiles.

A frisson of tension ripples through Carr's gut as he walks down the fairway and cuts through the dull throbbing in his head. Ahead, Mr. Boyce seems too large for the landscape. It's an illusion, Carr knows, though not of the light off the lake, nor even of Boyce's considerable mass. Rather, it's the aura he casts—of power barely controlled, of destructive potential contained, but just for now.

"Like a chainsaw," Declan said that first time in Atlanta, "or a crate of blasting caps. You want to walk careful around him, young Carr. You want to keep a little distance."

The menace is palpable, but always implicit. In all their meetings, Mr. Boyce has never been other than exact, economical, and watchful. Still, he's the only man Carr knows of who made Declan nervous.

It was a long drive, three hundred yards at least, and the ball sits on the right side of the fairway, at the bend of a dogleg left, not far from the rough. The green is uphill, 150 yards away, and ringed by bunkers. Mr. Boyce walks slowly around his ball. In person his voice is even deeper— the rumbling of an earthquake.

"I expected you earlier," he says, "by the ninth hole."

"My flight was delayed."

Boyce nods. "Thunderstorms over New York, I know." The wind is gusting off the lake and Boyce studies the tree-tops and the distant flag. He scatters bits of grass from his fingertips and watches them fly.

"What do you think—blowing left to right, about twenty miles an hour, a little less on the green with that stand of trees. You make it a seven iron from here?"

"You know I don't play," Carr answers.

Mr. Boyce shakes his head. "Too bad. There's a lot you'd like about it. The precision, the planning—everything just so."

"Maybe in my retirement."

Boyce chuckles, which sounds like an air horn. "I admire your optimism." He pulls a seven iron from his bag and takes an easy practice swing. "Everything fine with your father?"

"Sure," Carr says quietly.

"Sure," Boyce repeats, and then all his attention is on the ball. Again there is the slash, the gunshot, an arc of cut grass in the air, and the ball bounces on the green—once, twice, now rolling toward the pin. Boyce turns back to Carr. "So tell me how you're spending my money."

And for the next two holes Carr does exactly that, pausing only for Boyce to strike the ball. On the seventeenth tee he finishes, and Boyce asks questions.

"Where are the stones now?"

"Here."

"On you?"

"They're in the trunk of your Benz, in the first-aid kit, underneath the cold packs."

A rueful smile crosses Mr. Boyce's face. "You broke into my car?"

"I'll need them in the Caymans. I need you to hold them for me till then."

"And what about the cash?"

"I'm using it for expenses."

"I want receipts," Boyce says.

"You'll get them."

Boyce looks down the fairway. It's a short par four, 330

yards, and he takes the driver from his bag. "You think three's enough to buy you in?" he asks.

"More would be better, but the right references and the right introduction should convince him there's a steady supply."

"And Bessemer is the guy to introduce you?"

"He's the best bet."

"You're sure of that?"

"Of course not. But he's known Prager for years, he's been referring clients to him, one way or another, for a while, and he's approachable. He's the best bet."

"It's your call," Boyce says, and tees up his ball at the tips. "And what about the woman—Chun?"

"Valerie has a good feeling about her."

"*Good feeling?* I like to base my investments on a little more than that."

"If we want to add six months to the timetable, then we can look elsewhere. If not, then Chun's our girl."

Boyce shakes his head. "Let's hope it's a *great* feeling," he says, and another gunshot echoes across the lake. The ball hits the fringe and bounces onto the green. Boyce nods slowly as it rolls, then he turns to Carr and leans his hip against his driver, as if it were a cane.

"So Valerie's doing all right?" he asks.

"She's doing fine."

"And Mike and Bobby, and the kid?"

"Dennis. They're fine too."

"Must be an adjustment for them, not having Deke there. A different rhythm for them—a different style."

"This isn't the first time we've been around the block together."

"But you're not part of the crew anymore. You're the boss now. Management."

Carr pinches the bridge of his nose and looks at Mr. Boyce, whose eyes are like black stones. "It's all good."

Boyce taps the toe of his golf shoe with his driver. "Deke ran a tight ship—very firm, very hands-on. He wasn't worried about being liked—"

"He didn't have to worry—everybody liked him."

"Regardless, that wasn't his focus. His focus was on having his orders followed. He was a good soldier that way— a good platoon leader. It's not an easy job, and not everyone's built for it. Some people need to be liked; some people get lazy or stupid."

"Which one of those do you think is my problem?" Carr says.

The wind subsides for a moment, and the smells of grass and loam and trapped heat rise up, as if the ground has opened. Mr. Boyce straightens, and Carr takes a step back. "You'll know when I think you have a problem," he says, and Carr can feel the bass rumble in his chest. Boyce looks at him for a while, sighs, and drops his club into his golf bag.

"You have anything for me?" Carr asks.

Boyce points at Tina, who is already headed for the tee with something tucked under her arm. "She'll fix you up," Boyce says, and he turns toward the green.

CARR AND Tina sit on a bench off the cart path, in the heavy shade of an oak. The air is cool here, and Tina's legs shine white in the shadows.

"The new stuff's at the last tab," she says, and she opens the latest British *Vogue* while Carr opens the latest edition of Curtis Prager's dossier.

Carr remembers the first time he read it, six months back, in a hotel bar in Panama City, and remembers Declan's whiskey-furred voice as he slid it across the table. *Last job of work we'll need to do, boyo. It's the feckin' sweepstakes.* The lined red face split in a grin. Carr has read and reread it countless times since then—all but memorized it—but still he looks at every page.

A picture comes first, Curtis Prager years ago, emerging from the back of a black car. He is lithe, tanned, and shiny, his features finely sculpted, his hair like blond lacquer on his neat head, his shoulders square. An Apollo of finance, Carr thinks—a gilded man for a gilded age. All that's missing is a laurel wreath.

After the photo are the puff pieces about him that appeared in financial trade rags in the United States and Europe with great regularity before the crash. In tone they run a narrow gamut from fawning to sycophantic, and they all tell the same tale: of the tow-headed prodigy, home-schooled in Cincinnati until age sixteen, then off to Princeton, Harvard B-school, and Wall Street after that. By age twenty-five, he was the youngest managing director in the history of Melton-Peck; by twenty-eight he was the head of all trading there; and by thirty he was out the door—off to seek his fortune as a hedge fund manager, with a very large fortune in bonus money already in hand, and a flock of investors following behind him, all eager to pay for the privilege of having the wunderkind manage their money.

And so the birth of Tirol Capital, which from the first charged staggering fees, made a mania of secrecy, and cultivated an air of exclusivity to rival any Upper East Side co-op or private school. The formula worked well for Prager and, along with the outsize returns he reported year after year, helped make Tirol one of the fastest growing funds of the new century.

Besides the money, and the truckloads by which it arrived at Tirol's Greenwich, Connecticut, doorstep, the articles discuss Prager's many good works. There are lists of scholarship funds, endowed chairs, research laboratories, and hospital pavilions that bear his name, and pictures of Prager and the missus—tall, blond, disdainful—at an endless series of charity events. Black ties, white ties, polo shirts and sunglasses—the dress code varies, but never the smiles, which are tight and entitled. Smiles of any sort are in short supply in the next set of clippings—the ones from the trials.

There were two of them, the first just before the markets collapsed, the second just afterward, and despite the torch-and-pitchfork temper of those times, both ended in hung juries. The press attributed this to the complexity of the government's case against Prager—the difficulty of making money-laundering and conspiracy charges stick, the arcane financial instruments involved—though some in the U.S. Attorney's office grumbled darkly, and not for attribution, about jury tampering.

The feds were about to have a third go when their only witness, a former Tirol compliance officer named Munce, drove his Lexus off a dark road in Litchfield County, and through the frozen skin of the Housatonic River. His blood alcohol level was twice the legal limit, and there was ice on the roadway, but still the feds had both Munce and his car stripped down to their frames. The autopsies found nothing, though, and the most they could do to Prager were a dozen stiff fines for a dozen obscure record-keeping violations.

But the mere fact of his indictment, along with the implosion of the markets, had already dealt much worse punishment to Prager and his firm. Tirol was losing investors at a slow bleed before the first trial began, and like a broken hydrant afterward, and by the time the feds imposed their fines, the firm was down to a measly billion or so in assets under management, and a handful of clients in Florida, Latin America, and the Caribbean.

News coverage of Curtis Prager dropped off sharply four years back, after the fines—a mention in the *Greenwich Time* of the sale of his North Street estate, another in the *New York Post* of his divorce and exodus to the Cayman Islands. After which the press had bigger, more blatant frauds to cover, and the entries in the dossier switch from press clippings to what Carr recognized on first reading as intelligence reports.

"Where does Boyce get this stuff?" he'd asked Declan at the time.

Declan had shrugged and, typically, answered a different question. "He likes to keep an eye on the competition." Carr stopped asking about what other lines of business Mr. Boyce was in, though he's never stopped wondering.

About Curtis Prager's business, the reports leave little doubt. With a labored dispassion typical to the genre, and with no mention of sources or methods, they describe how Prager, having relocated to the Caymans, closed down what was left of Tirol Capital and established Isla Privada Holdings, a firm whose ostensible business is the acquisition, consolidation, and management of small banks and trust companies in the United States, but whose actual purpose is to deliver financial services to organized criminals.

A comprehensive list of services too, according to the reports, especially for a relative newcomer to the field: bulk cash processing, foreign exchange, electronic funds transfer, access to a network of overseas correspondent banks, provision of fully documented shell corporations, asset management, even tax consultation—everything a crime syndicate might require to launder large sums of money, move them around the world, invest them, and bring them home clean.

The reports say that Prager is still building his business, and that his client base is still small—a Mexican drug cartel, a Colombian cocaine syndicate, a smuggling ring out of Panama, and a Salvadoran private army that expanded from death-squad work into regional arms supply. But he has grander things in mind, and his marketing efforts have recently spread beyond the Caribbean and Latin America to Central Europe and Asia. The list of Prager's clients stopped Carr in his tracks the first time he read it. He peered across the table through the smoke from Declan's Cohiba.

"We know some of these guys," Carr said. "We hit them twice, they're going to take it personally."

"It's not them we're hitting, boyo, it's their banker. Deposit insurance is his problem."

"You're thinking about a cash shipment?"

Declan shook his head. "Keep reading."

The lightbulb went on two paragraphs down, in the midst of a dry discussion of the common back office used by the banks that Isla Privada owns. The centralized processing system gives Curtis Prager ready access to all of the accounts in all of the banks in Isla Privada's portfolio, and—with the help of an obedient, well-paid, and meticulously incurious operations and accounting staff—makes it a simple matter to commingle licit and illicit cash and hide dubious funds transfers in a forest of legitimate ones.

Carr had looked up at Declan, who was grinning like a shot fox. "That back-office system of his is a fecking magic lamp," Declan said. "The great Prager rubs away, wishing for some clean money, it spews a bit of smoke, and *poof*—out pops a wire transfer! Any given time, he can move a hundred million at least with that lamp, boyo. I say we do a bit of wishin' of our own."

"You say something?" Tina asks him. She's lifted her glasses off her nose, and her gray eyes are motionless. Carr shakes his head. "You sure you're okay?" she asks. " 'Cause you look like a fucking ghost."

"I'm fine," Carr says. He flips past the profiles of Prager's staff—his security chief, his tame accountants and auditors—and leafs through the technical section. Floor plans of Isla

Privada's offices on Grand Cayman and of Prager's beach-front compound, the makes and models of alarm systems, registry listings for Prager's sloop and his motor yacht, the tail number of his G650—Boyce's people are good at this sort of thing, and it goes on for pages.

Carr squints at a column of figures and rubs his head. He turns to the last tab and scans the latest updates.

There are pictures of a party by a long swimming pool, at night—men in linen trousers, women in gauzy shifts, waiters in starched jackets, and in the background a line of luminous surf. Carr recognizes it as Prager's Grand Cayman beachfront.

"These are from his party last week?" he asks. Tina doesn't look up from her magazine, but nods. "You bought yourself one of the caterer's people?"

"Rented," she says.

"Another fund-raiser?"

Tina nods again. "For a local grade school."

"Prager schedule the next one?"

"Just before Labor Day—right before he leaves on his prospecting trip."

"Still off to Europe?"

"And Asia now. Lot of money to be washed out there. He'll be gone about five weeks."

"So, Labor Day—that's about eleven weeks."

"Ten," Tina says, and turns another page of her magazine. Carr keeps studying the party photos.

"I don't see Eddie Silva here."

"Next picture," Tina says.

It's a photo of a fifty-something man, thick, with a salt-and-pepper buzz cut. It's a daytime shot, and he's coming out of a bar. His eyes are smeared and his face is like pitted pavement. "He's off the wagon?" Carr asks.

Tina nods. "Again."

"That's what—the third time in five months?"

"That's what I make it."

"Hell of a thing for the head of security."

"Nice for you though."

There are more photos at the back of the folder, and the very last one stops Carr. It's another shot of Curtis Prager, and like the first picture in the file it shows Prager climbing from a car, though this car is a Bentley, and the street, sunny and white, isn't in New York, but in George Town, on Grand Cayman. Prager is wearing jeans and a guayabera. His hair is long, curling, bleached from the sun, and his mouth is open, as if he's about to speak.

Carr flips to the front of the file and then to the back again. There can't be five years between this photo and the first one, but in the interim Prager's face has aged fifteen years at least. His skin is hide brown, seamed, and pulled too tight over the fine bones. The cords of his neck are like rigging, and his eyes are adrift in a sea of lines and shadows. His mouth looks wider and hungrier—weathered, but avid too, Carr thinks. Prager's thrown off the collar and found himself some appetites to indulge—found that indulgence agrees with him. So, more a pirate than ever; more Bacchus than Apollo now. Carr shakes his head. They hated this kind of thinking at the Farm, and his trainers dinged him for it more times than he could remember. Projection, they called it. *Don't impose a narrative, for chrissakes—let them tell their own stories. An agent gets an idea there's something particular you want to hear, all he'll do is sing it to you. He'll have you chasing your tail right up your backside.* Still, he looked like a pirate.

Tina is holding a flash drive and looking at him. "File's on here," she says.

Carr closes the dossier and pockets the drive. "You have anything else for me?"

"Anything like...?"

"It's been four months, for chrissakes."

"I told you, it's slow going. We don't have a lot of friends down there."

"So four months of digging and nothing to show?"

Tina closes her magazine and places it on her lap. "Not exactly nothing," she says.

Carr draws a hand down his face. He is awake now, fully, for the first time today. "Exactly *what*, then?"

"Not a hundred percent sure. A guy one of our few friends knows met another guy who pilots for a vineyard down there. He flies in and out of an airfield near Mendoza. His brother works part-time at the same field, doing maintenance on the prop planes. The rest of the time, the brother works at a private field northwest of town, a dirt strip on an *estancia*."

"Bertolli's place."

Tina nods. "Works there on Tuesdays and Fridays. And word is he told his big brother that one Friday morning, four months back, before he could even get his truck parked, the foreman waved him off. Told him *hasta la vista*—go home, no work today. No explanation besides there was a party going on at the ranch that night, which seemed weird to the mechanic because he knew that Bertolli was away in Europe for two weeks. But the foreman gave him a day's pay anyway, for doing nothing, so he didn't ask questions. He did notice something as he was driving out the gate that morning, though: a truckload of men driving in."

"What men?"

"He'd seen some of them around the ranch before, but they scared him and he always kept his distance. Bertolli's hard boys. The mechanic tells his brother they looked like they were there to work."

Carr stands slowly and puts a hand on the back of the bench. "Which Friday morning was this?"

"Four months back, the second Friday of the month. That makes it the morning of the twelfth."

After a while, Carr clears his throat. "That's the morning of the day before," he says.

"Mr. Boyce says not to read too much into it."

Carr looks down at Tina, and at his own face, black in her black lenses. "It doesn't take any reading," he says quietly. "They knew he was coming. They were waiting for him."

8

AT 9:35 a.m. Howard Bessemer will leave his blue, Bermuda-style cottage, turn right on Monterey Road, turn right again on North Ocean Boulevard, and drive south, past the Palm Beach Country Club, to the Barton Golf and Racquet Club, there to meet Daniel Brunt for a ten o'clock court. He will play no more than two sets of tennis with Brunt, and afterward drink no more than two iced teas, and then he will shower, dress, get in his car, and drive across the Royal Park Bridge for lunch in West Palm Beach. This is Howard Bessemer's routine on Tuesdays and Thursdays, and this being 9:33 on a Tuesday, Carr knows that Bessemer will soon appear. Because if Carr, Latin Mike, Bobby, and Dennis have learned anything in the weeks they've been watching him, it is that Bessemer is a man of routines.

Tuesdays and Thursdays: tennis and lunch. Mondays and Wednesdays: golf and cocktails. Friday mornings: sailing. Friday afternoons: more cocktails. And Friday nights straight through Sunday afternoons: high-stakes poker, cocaine, and whores—two, sometimes three, at a clip—all in a basement below a Brazilian restaurant, not far from the medical center. They can set their watches by Bessemer, and they love him for it.

The garage door opens, and the blue BMW pulls out. Bessemer has the top down, and his thinning blond hair is a tattered pennant in the breeze. Right and right again, and Bobby waits another fifteen seconds before he pulls the gray painter's van away from the curb. Carr calls Latin Mike.

"We're gone," he says into his cell.

"We're in," Mike replies, and in the side mirror Carr sees Bessemer's front door swing shut.

This stretch of Ocean Boulevard is flat and straight— a corridor of stucco walls, hedges, and gated drives, whose usual quiet is deepened by a sense of off-season abandonment. Traffic is sparse, and Carr can see Bessemer's BMW blocks ahead, shimmering in the heat. The Atlantic appears to their left in flashes, in the alleys between properties— white, heaving, covered in sunlight.

Bobby tugs his painter's cap lower. "Got another doughnut?" he asks. Carr hands him a powdered sugar, rolls down his window, and lets in the salt breeze and the smell of ripening seaweed.

Bessemer is nimble for a thickset man. He tosses his keys in a neat arc to a valet in a pink polo shirt, hitches his tennis bag on his shoulder, trots up the steps of the Barton, and disappears into its Spanish colonial facade. The valet slides into the BMW and wheels the car around the crushed shell drive. On another Tuesday he would head due west, fifty yards down a service road to the club's parking lot—but not today. Today, half of that lot is being resurfaced, and only the cars of Barton members are being parked in the other half. The cars of staff, and of guests like Howard Bessemer, go around the corner, to the unattended lot of an Episcopal church. Carr and Bobby are parked across the street when the BMW arrives.

The valet drops it into a slot next to a Porsche and sprints off toward the club. Carr takes a black box smaller than a deck of cards from the backpack at his feet.

"Two minutes," he says, but he doesn't take that long. When he returns he has another small box in his hand, like the first but caked in mud and dust.

"Korean crap," Bobby says, disgustedly. "Second one that's died on me this year. The fucking Kia of GPS trackers."

Bobby drives around another corner and down an alley. They park beside a dumpster and Carr takes a camera from the backpack. He sights through the viewfinder, and through a gap in the green court windscreen, and finds Bessemer and Brunt on their usual court. He has plenty of pictures of Bessemer—the benign, round face, the watery, perpetually astonished blue eyes, the ingratiating smile—and of the tanned and simian Brunt, but just now Bessemer is talking to someone Carr hasn't seen before, a tall, knobby man, awkward and embarrassed-looking in tennis whites. Carr takes half a dozen photos and checks the results on the camera's little screen.

Bobby picks through the doughnut box. "Used to be, a guy like Howie did a little time, laid low awhile, then hooked up with a charity board," he says. "Raised money for cancer or something. Now he can't even get membership in a fucking tennis club—has to be like a permanent guest. Fraud and embezzlement—you'd think he was skinning live cats. I guess that fucking Madoff really queered it for guys like him."

Carr smiles and passes the camera to Bobby. "Do we know this guy?" he asks.

Bobby looks at the screen and speaks through a mouthful of Boston cream. "Howie had a lunch and a dinner with him last week. I call him Ichabod. Don't know his real name."

"Time to find out," Carr says.

Time, in fact, to pick Howard Bessemer's pockets and rifle through his sock drawer, down to the lint and the last stray pennies. The dossier from Boyce has given Carr and his crew a head start: the basics of Bessemer's story. The early chapters are straightforward enough: a young man of mediocre intellect and even less ambition—not to mention a DWI arrest on his eighteenth birthday—finds a spot at the university that generations of his family have attended, and where his grandfather has recently built a gymnasium. Not much new there.

The middle passages are similarly predictable: a degree after five and a half years, a record distinguished only by his term as social director of his fraternity and three more DWI arrests—though no convictions—and yet Howard still wangles a place in the training program at Melton-Peck, where his great-uncle was once a board member. A job as an account manager in the private bank follows, as does a marriage, a promotion or two, a co-op on the Upper East Side, a baby, and finally a rancorous, pricey divorce. Again, nothing novel, except that it is during this period that Bessemer met Curtis Prager. They overlapped at Melton-Peck by two years, and when Prager started up his first hedge fund, Bessemer referred clients to him—and eventually became one himself.

It's in the later chapters that things get more interesting, and that the Bessemer story plays out in the New York newspapers, and in the records of the U.S. District Court, Southern District of New York. It becomes the tale of an affable private banker who for years poached funds from the accounts of certain customers to bolster the investment returns of certain others. A banker who, when caught knee-deep in the cookie jar, sang long and loud to the feds about the inner workings of an elaborate tax evasion scheme that involved several of his well-heeled clients and a pair of Swiss bankers, and featured hundreds of large wire transfers that somehow managed not to appear on anybody's suspicious activity reports.

Cooperation and a guilty plea bought Bessemer a reduced sentence—eighteen months in Otisville—but he could've gotten off with even less. The feds had dangled another offer before him, just before his trip upstate: a suspended sentence in exchange for testimony against Curtis Prager and Tirol Capital. But Bessemer declined. Mr. Boyce's dossier dryly lists two possible reasons, neither of which involves Howard's unwavering loyalty.

One hypothesis is that, despite his friendship with Prager, Howard was never a Tirol insider, so he simply didn't know enough to be useful to the feds. Another—a favorite of the prosecutors, and encouraged by the conspiracy theories of the ex–Mrs. Bessemer and her frustrated lawyers—is that Howard knew plenty, but kept quiet because Prager had helped him hide assets during his divorce. Eighteen months of medium-security time, their reasoning went, was more appealing to Howard than writing off five million or so in hidden funds.

Bessemer did his time without incident, and when he was released, two years back, he settled himself in Palm Beach, in the Bermuda-style cottage he'd inherited from his grandmother, and with a modest income from a trust she'd left.

A good start, but not enough for Carr's purposes. Nor is his own research—not yet. Seventeen days of arm's-length observations have given Carr the routines—the tennis, the lunches, the poker, and the whores—and the comfort that Bessemer does almost nothing to safeguard his home or his person, but Carr needs more than that, and for more he needs to get close.

So Dennis and Latin Mike are even now in Bessemer's cottage, with an hour to work before the maid arrives for the weekly cleaning—time enough to plant the microphones and cameras, tap the landline, skim the mail and the garbage, and for Dennis to work his dark magic on Bessemer's laptop:

sniffers, keyloggers, screen scrapers—enough spyware to turn Bessemer's computer into a digital confessional every time he switches it on. Carr checks his watch. Time enough.

Bobby wipes his chin and opens the van door. "Give me the Nikon," he says, as he unzips his painter's coveralls. He brushes stray crumbs from the AT&T logo on the polo shirt he's wearing underneath, tosses the coveralls in back, and straps a phone man's tool rig around his waist. Carr hands him a palm-size camera from the backpack, and Bobby drops it in the pocket of his cargo shorts.

"The last jelly's mine," he says, and Carr watches him shamble down the alley to the Barton's small loading dock.

For the job of following Howard Bessemer around Palm Beach, Bobby is Carr's first choice. Valerie is distracting, and besides, she is otherwise occupied in Boca Raton, and Dennis is too jumpy. He sweats and fidgets whenever he has to playact, and his anxiety glows like neon. Latin Mike is poised and utterly capable but, with Carr at least, sour and taciturn. His shuttered face and silent disapproval wear on Carr and remind him of his father.

Bobby is easier to take, especially without Mike around. Without Mike to impress, he's more relaxed and accommodating—funnier, and less inclined to carp or balk. More likable. Carr knows that Bobby isn't as comfortable with him as he is with Latin Mike—Carr lacks Mike's working-class credentials—but one-on-one, Bobby gives him the benefit of the doubt. And, most important, Bobby likes to talk.

A steady stream of it has issued from him as he and Carr have tailed Bessemer—a miscellany of profanity-laced observations on Bessemer's choice of car and clothing, the latest heartbreak served up by Bobby's beloved, despised Mets, the crappy house he, Mike, and Dennis are staying in, the ass of any woman who crosses his line of sight, his Brooklyn boyhood, his truncated air force career—McGuire Air Force Base, Ramstein, Aviano, and back to McGuire for the court-martial—his shrew of an ex-wife. A grab bag, but short on the topic that interests Carr most—the topic that has circled his thoughts like a scavenging bird ever since his last conversation with Tina.

Carr tries to keep in mind his long-ago training, incomplete though it was, on agents and their early cultivation. *Walk softly. Come at it obliquely. Keep your shopping list to yourself. Let them broach the topic first, but change the subject the first time they do. Change it the second time too.* But he was impatient at the Farm—one of his many failings—and he's been impatient in Palm Beach too, and in neither place did it help his cause. His instructors scowled and shook their heads, and so did Bobby.

Another truck, another alleyway, three days before.

"For fuck's sake," Bobby said, "you ask about this I don't know how many times. What else is there to say about it?"

Carr put on a pensive look. "I've got no one else to ask, Bobby. Valerie wasn't there, and Mike won't say shit about it."

"Well, you know it all already. Deke thought it was a layup, but it wasn't. Bales of cash sitting in a barn on Bertolli's ranch. No real security besides a little local talent, and the ranch being at the ass end of nowhere, and all we have to do is drive in, deal with the locals, load up, and drive away—straight through to Santiago. Deke had a flight lined up out of Los Cerrillos. The driving-in part was fine; after that it was a shit storm."

"You had two trucks."

Bobby sighed. "Two vans—Fords—four-wheel drive conversions. Ray-Ray lined 'em up in B.A., and we drove 'em north. Me and Mike in one, Deke and Ray-Ray in the other. You know all this."

"Deke decided who rode where?"

"Deke decided everything. Ray-Ray was the best driver, then me—so he split us up."

"And he rode with Ray."

"He always got a kick out of the kid."

"Everybody did; he was a good kid. So you drove in the main gate?"

Bobby squinted at him. "You not listening the first ten times I told it? We came up a service road—three miles of washboard in the pitch-fucking-black—and clipped the chain on a cattle gate. It was another two miles from there to the airstrip and the barn."

"And then you hit trouble."

"Soon as we got out of the vans. They came around back of a tin hangar on the other side of the strip—four big four-by-fours—and fucking fast."

"You didn't get into the barn?"

"Didn't get closer than twenty meters. We got out of the vans and they lit us up like fucking Vegas."

"They seem like regular security, or something laid on especially for you guys?"

"The fuck should I know? All I know is they could shoot."

"Deke said there wouldn't be much opposition."

"That was the intel."

"Where'd he get it from?"

"Might as well been from a cereal box, for what it was worth. He'd been looking at Bertolli a long time, I know that, but he always played his sources close to the vest. He was big on that *need to know* crap."

"You guys put up a fight?"

"It was like pissing in the wind. We had MP9s; they had like a dozen guys with AKs. Mostly we ran like hell."

"But not in the same direction."

"It was Deke's call—split up and regroup in Mendoza. We

had a fallback off the Avenue Zapata, near the bus station. He and Ray-Ray went out the main gate, me and Mike went out the way we came."

"And only you and Mike made it."

"Only by the hairs on our asses, lemme tell you—those motherfuckers were serious. Two-plus hours hard running down Highway Forty, and those bastards were bouncing in my mirrors the whole time. We could barely put a mile between us and them. Half busted an axle, and my rear panels were like Swiss cheese. Wasn't till we got to town that I could shake 'em."

"Just the one truck after you guys, though—just one of those four-by-fours."

"One was enough."

"So the other three were on Deke and Ray-Ray?"

"The fuck should I know? All Deke said was that they were on his ass. He didn't say if that meant three trucks or one."

"He called just once?"

"And I could barely hear him then. The service isn't great out there."

"He didn't say that he wasn't going to Mendoza? That he was making for Santiago instead?"

"He said they were on his ass, and that was it. If he'd said anything about Santiago, or not showing up at the fallback, we wouldn't have spent two days waiting in that fucking hole, peeping through those moldy curtains, and jumping every time a toilet flushed."

"So no idea how Deke and Ray-Ray ended up westbound on Highway Seven?"

Bobby ran a thick hand down his face. "Come on, Carr—enough already with this."

"You were there, Bobby—you must have an idea."

"Like what—they were cut off, couldn't get back on Forty,

took one of those horse trails to Seven, and got tagged in the mountains? You don't like that story, make up one of your own. You know as much as I do about what happened."

"You were there."

"And you weren't, and you don't know how to give it a rest. Look, everybody gets that you never liked the deal—you and Val both. Not enough planning, too rushed, whatever. You guys made it clear, and it turns out you were right. Nobody thinks it's your fault, Carr. Nobody holds it against you, except maybe you."

"I'm not holding anything. I just want to know why it went bad."

"There're a million reasons. Crappy planning, crappy intel, crappy roads, crappy luck—take your pick. Who knows why, and who the hell cares? Deke is gone, and so is Ray, and picking at the roadkill won't bring 'em back. You feel guilty, find yourself a priest. Talking to you about this is like talking to my Irish grandma, for chrissakes, or talking to a cop."

Carr had smiled at that. He hadn't been talking like a cop, but he'd been listening like one. That was the sixth time he'd gotten Bobby to tell the story, the third time since his talk with Tina, and every time Bobby had told it just the same way, down to the pitch-fucking-black, the bastards bouncing in his mirrors, the half-busted axle, and the moldy curtains. Always the same details—never more, never less, never different. Every time. The same.

Bobby comes up the alley, wiping the corner of his mouth, and Carr comes back.

Bobby unhitches his tool belt and tosses it into the van. "Ichabod's name is Willis Stearn," he says. "I got more pictures. I got a number and an address too. And I knocked over the kitchen for a tuna on white with the crusts cut off. Fucking master criminal, huh?"

Carr nods. "Nobody better, Bobby."

9

IN THE maze of machines and shining bodies, it is her shoulders that he finally recognizes. They're angular and broad for a woman, with well-defined deltoid muscles and a faded scar—a ragged-edged dime of unknown origin—over her left scapula. It appears and disappears beneath the edge of her sweat-darkened tank top as she works the fly machine. Carr forces himself not to stare, but to keep drifting around the perimeter of the vast gym.

It has taken him ten minutes of drifting to find Valerie, and no wonder. Her hair is shorter now, and expensively tinted—a champagne and honey cap with bangs swept to the side—and her skin is biscuit brown. But the hair and tan are just window dressing, sleight of hand. The real transformation runs deeper, and Carr is no closer to working out the trick now than he was in Costa Alegre.

So she is older today—thirty-five, maybe forty—and very fit. But also tired, though not from the exercise. It's a longer-term fatigue, a kind of erosion—the product of a beating tide of disappointment, wrong choices, bad luck. Its etchings appear at the corners of her mouth and around her eyes, in her dye job, and in the concentration she puts into her workout. They tell a story of assets carefully managed but dwindling nonetheless—an inexorable spending of the principal. Carr has stopped and is staring again, and now she knows he's here.

This is another bit of magic he can't work out—some radar she possesses. Her look is fleeting—less than that— the barest flick of her eyes on the way to glancing at the wall clock, but Carr reads the anger there. He drifts back to the lobby, out the doors, and across Mizner Park to his Saturn.

In twenty minutes Carr is at the Embassy Suites, in a pale blue room with a view of some dumpsters and of planes departing the Boca Raton airport. Forty minutes after that Valerie is at the door, in flats and a sleeveless orange dress. She smells of honeysuckle, and her hair is still damp from the shower. She walks past Carr and sits at the end of the bed.

"What the hell were you doing there?" she says. Her voice is tight with anger, and Carr hears something else in it—the hint of a twang, a whisper of Texas or Oklahoma.

"I told them I was interested in a membership," he says. "They let me walk around."

"I don't give a damn what you told them. What the hell were you doing? We were supposed to meet here. You want to fuck this up while we're still at the gate?"

"Was Amy at the club?"

"She had a yoga class this afternoon; she left half an hour before you showed up. But that's not the point. The point is I don't want you there. I don't want to be seen with anybody there. Jill's supposed to be on her own."

"You take the yoga class with Amy?"

Valerie's lips purse. "Monday. I join the class Monday."

"You talk to her yet?"

"In the locker room, to say hello," Valerie says, and slips off her flats. Her bare feet are tanned; her toenails, like her fingernails, are pale pink.

"She knows who you are?"

"She knows I'm Jill. She's heard me talk about being new in town."

"That's not much."

"It's enough for now. Get this for me," she says, rising and turning her back to Carr. He slides her zipper down.

"You have a better read on her?"

"I know she takes care of herself. Yoga, spinning, weights, laps in the pool—she's at the club every day. She spends money on her hair and nails, and serious money on her wardrobe. St. John, Carlisle, Akris—nice stuff. Low-key, but classy. And that handbag of hers is no knockoff. Twenty grand, easy. She's a loner, though. Never says more than a word or two to the staff, or to another member. Never has guests."

"But she says hello to you."

Valerie nods, and lets her dress fall in an orange pool at her feet. She wears no bra, and her panties are sheer orange silk. "I'm sociable," she says.

She throws the spread off the bed and pulls down the blanket and top sheet. Carr leans against the desk. His heart is pounding and his words catch in his throat. "You see the video Dennis and Bobby shot of her house?" he asks. Valerie nods. "What did you think?"

"It's modern—lots of glass."

"I meant about the security."

"No surprise: she's president of a bank, and it's a pain in the ass. She's in a gated community, so there's the gatehouse, the authorized visitor lists, the prowl cars, and lots of rent-a-cops—who, by the way, are all strapped. Bobby said the house itself is wired pretty good too—not that it slowed him much.

"On top of that, there's the bank's security people. She's got a retired sheriff's deputy that drives her everywhere in that nice black Benz, and her office, her car, and her house all get swept weekly for electronics."

"On a set schedule?"

She shakes her head. "That'd make life too easy. And as far as her work laptop goes, Bobby says it rides to the office with her in the Benz and comes home the same way, and when she stops at the gym, it waits in the car with her driver."

Carr nods. "Dennis send you anything from her personal computer?"

"He spiked it, and he's supposed to send me her e-mail and her browser history. He confirmed it doesn't have the Isla Privada software on it, and none of the security hardware to access their network." Valerie sits cross-legged on the bed and pulls a pillow onto her lap. "You think I'm not doing my homework?"

"Maybe you saw something I didn't."

Valerie shakes her head. "It's what we thought: we want access to Isla Privada's network, we need their hardware; we want access to that—to Amy Chun's equipment, anyway—we need somebody who can hang out in her house. And that would be Jill."

Carr nods slowly and sits up on the desk. "How's your apartment working out?"

She shrugs. "Mid-nineties generic. Lot of corporate types in the building, on long-term business trips, plus some divorced dads with cars they can't afford. I can see a slice of the Intracoastal from the balcony. It's right for Jill."

"We could've met there."

Valerie narrows her eyes. "No we couldn't," she says, scowling. "I told you: Jill's on her own."

"Yeah, I got that. You color in any other parts of Jill's life?"

"I'm waiting for the take from Amy's computer," she says. Valerie looks Carr up and down. "You're perched on that desk like it's a lifeboat. We sinking or something?"

"I'm trying to figure out if you're going to keep snapping at my ass. I'm thinking maybe I can hide behind this thing."

Valerie is still for a beat, and then she sighs. "Yeah. Sorry. It takes me a while to let her go. I can't switch her off just like that." She snaps her fingers, like a branch breaking. "Jill's pretty much had it with men. She's a little angry."

"I get that."

Valerie sighs again, longer and more heavily. "Not me, though. I'm not angry." She pats the mattress beside her, and Carr crosses to the bed.

AFTERWARD, COVERED in gooseflesh and the sour breath of the air conditioner, Valerie pulls him back from the edge of sleep. Her head is on his chest, and her fingers comb gently through his pubic hair. Her voice is husky.

"Let's play geography," she says.

Carr sighs. He can't remember who started it, or when they started playing, but it's become a fixture of the long stretches the crew spends together in cars, in vans, in darkened rooms—a way to relieve the monotony of sitting for hours with earpieces jammed in their heads, watching, listening, waiting. Dennis called it retirement geography, and it was simple to play: tell a story about what you're going to do once you've made your nut, and where you're going to do it—your dream of life afterward. Which, Carr thought, told you a lot about a person.

Bobby's ideal retirement changed venues now and then—shifting from Nassau, to Vegas, to Macao, to Monte Carlo, and back to Nassau again—but regardless of the particular locale, it was always the same: a high-roller suite at a high-end gambling resort.

"These new villas, they have private elevators right down to the casino floor, and private hostesses who spoon-feed you caviar and wipe your ass with silk. I'll make sure they all have pictures of my ex, with orders to shoot on sight." A simple man, Bobby, with a simple plan.

Latin Mike's vision of his golden years was also straight-forward, if less gilded: he wanted off the grid. "A thousand acres in the high desert. I put up a wind turbine, solar cells, and a tall motherfucking fence. I have a few horses, maybe a goat, and nobody needs to send me a Christmas card."

Ray-Ray had a second career in mind—a ski school in British Columbia, with a bar attached. "I'll run the tourist babes up and down the mountain all day, and at night I'll ply their sore little bods with alcohol."

And Dennis dreamed of setting up a venture capital shop on Sand Hill Road and financing the next Google. Bobby always laughed at that. "You're a fucking pure breed, Denny; you're geek to the bone."

Carr didn't play the game, and neither did Valerie. He would simply shake his head when his turn came around; she chose deflection.

"I'm falling off the map, boys," she said, the last time Bobby tried to goad her into it. "Over the edge, like those ships when the world was flat."

Bobby laughed. "C'mon, Vee—that's not how you play."

"Fuck you—you think I want you guys showing up on my doorstep, looking to borrow money?"

Of all of them, Declan liked the game best, and he was best at it. It called to some Celtic storytelling gene in him, and he would spin elaborate yarns about his retirement by the sea. Over the years he'd had several shores in mind: Hoi An, in Vietnam, and Hua Hin, in Thailand, La Barra, in Uruguay, was a favorite for a long while. He would talk about them at length and in detail—the weather, the waters, the cuisines, and local real estate markets. Carr remembers him hunched over binoculars, waxing poetic about asado and fish empanadas, while the smell of his cigar filled the van.

"Yer young now, but you'll see, when yer all wizened bas-tards like me, you won't want to be working or whoring or—

forgive me, Mike—roasting in the feckin' desert. You'll want a cottage by the sea, I'm telling ya, and a boat, and maybe a garden with a fruit tree. And who knows, but maybe you'll want to do some breeding yerselves. Me, I'm hoping the local publican has a daughter of marrying age, or maybe the baker—a homely but grateful girl. That's the ticket, lads." The gravel whisper went on and on about the meals he'd cook, the wine he'd drink, the darts he'd play, and the dog he would buy.

Carr rubs his eyes and sits up in bed. "I thought you didn't like that game," he says.

"I didn't," Valerie says, "when it was just a game. Now it's less abstract. Come on—you show me yours…"

Carr shakes his head. "I have nothing to show. I haven't given much thought to afterward."

Valerie sighs and settles herself again, her cheek on his thigh. "Bobby said you were talking to him about Mendoza. Asking about what happened again."

"And?"

"And it worries him."

"Worries him how?"

"He thinks you're picking at something, and he doesn't know what. He's worried you're taking your eye off the ball."

"Screw him. He should keep his mind on his own goddamn job, and let me take care of mine."

"He says you feel guilty."

"Bobby's a psychiatrist now? That's a sure sign of the apocalypse."

"I don't like what happened down there either. It was a waste, and I was as broken up about it as anybody—but I don't feel guilty."

Carr shakes his head. "No offense, Vee, but I'm not sure you're the best yardstick."

Valerie sits up and pulls a sheet over her breasts. "If I wasn't such a cold-hearted bitch, I might take offense at that," she says with a bitter laugh. "Maybe I didn't know those guys as long as you, but I trusted them with my life more times than I can count. I trusted them to back me up, and they didn't disappoint. Not ever. Ray was like a kid brother, for chrissakes, and Deke…"

She looks at the ceiling and breathes deeply—once, twice—to steady her voice. "We told Deke what we thought about that job—you and me both. We said everything there was to say about the planning, the intel, the risks—everything and then some. Maybe you remember, he was pretty pissed at us when he left. I thought the two of you were going to come to blows. You tell me, what else were we supposed to do?"

Carr shrugs. "We should've been more convincing."

"Right—'cause Deke was always so open to suggestions."

"He listened to me."

"He listened when he felt like it, but he didn't listen then. And really, how many ways can you say *bad idea* and *stupid fucking plan*? I think we tried them all."

Carr runs a hand through his hair. "Maybe it wasn't just the plan that was bad. Maybe something else was going on."

Valerie sits up and looks at him. "What the *fuck* are you talking about?" Carr shrugs again, and Valerie's hand is on his biceps. "*Something else* like what?"

"I don't know. Bertolli might've gotten wind of something."

Valerie shakes her head. "Are you for real with this? What was Bertolli going to get wind of? The only guy as insane about operational security as you are was Declan. You really think he got sloppy with that?"

"Maybe somebody got sloppy for him."

"You're not serious with this paranoid shit, are you? You think Bobby or Mike dimed him out? Or maybe you think it was me?" She slides her palm up his arm, over his shoulder, to his neck. The smell of honeysuckle is strong. Her voice softens. "Guilt does that, you know—it makes you paranoid. You feel bad, you feel responsible, so you feel like there's a bill coming due. Then you're looking over your shoulder every other minute, waiting for it to arrive. Paranoid."

Carr rolls away from her, out of bed, and goes into the bathroom. He turns the water tap, drinks from a cupped hand, and looks in the mirror. The angular face, the cropped black hair, disheveled now, his mother's hazel eyes, smudged with fatigue, the wiry frame, the white sketch marks of scars here and there, are somehow unfamiliar to him—pieces he can't assemble into a working whole. He stands in the bathroom doorway. Valerie is sitting cross-legged, the sheet down around her waist.

"Our being down there wouldn't have changed anything," she says, "except maybe we'd be dead on the side of a road too. So we were someplace else—so what?"

"I know where we were," Carr says, his voice rising suddenly above the drone of the air conditioner. "I know what we were doing."

Valerie laughs, and there's a note of satisfaction in it— a long-held theory finally confirmed. Jill's twang reappears in her voice. "So you feel bad about that too—that we were in St. Barts, fucking, while it was going on. You sure you weren't raised Catholic, or maybe Jewish? 'Cause, baby boy, you got the guilt down cold."

"You and Bobby can talk it out in your next session. Compare notes."

"That might be deep water for Bobby," Valerie says, and throws off her sheet. She pushes past Carr into the bathroom and runs the shower.

Carr watches as she steps in—the muscles in her back, her brown ass, her skin flawless but for the ragged-edged dime on her scapula. "Why the hell are you talking to Bobby about this anyway?" he says.

Valerie works her fingers through her water-darkened hair. "I thought you wanted me to—that you wanted my help with these guys. To take their temperature—make sure their heads were on right. I thought we both wanted this job over and done with, and done right. Then, if you want, we can work out that guilt and whatever other little bugs are crawling around your head. We could have ourselves some fun afterward."

Valerie builds a creamy lather on her arms and breasts and belly. She beckons to Carr, and through the scrim of water and curling steam her smile is bright.

THE SKY above the hotel parking lot is gray, and it's heavy with car exhaust and the metal heat of the fading day. An erratic breeze sends a paper cup back and forth across a patch of cracked cement. Sitting in the Saturn, Carr is similarly restless. He doesn't know why he started talking to Valerie about what happened in Mendoza, or why he stopped. Maybe he was fishing for something—for her to tell him to forget his suspicions, call them paranoid shit, and remind him to keep his mind on the job. He thinks about the game she tried to play—retirement geography, and all those stories of *afterward*. He hears his own voice—*I haven't given much thought to afterward*—and wonders if maybe he should.

Certainly, *afterward* is easier for him to think about. Easier than thinking about how Bertolli's men came to be waiting for Deke in the dead of night. Or why Bobby always tells the story just the same way. Easier than dealing with Mike's snide comments and hostile silences. Or finding a useful handle on Howard Bessemer. Or thinking about Valerie and Amy Chun. Easier by far than thinking about his father, and the tar pit of brochures, applications, and FAQ pages Carr has drowned in every night for nearly three weeks. Assisted living facilities, nursing homes, dementia units—the nomenclature sticks to his arms and legs, and fills his ears with static. Eleanor Calvin has left messages—six, eight, Carr has lost count—but he hasn't returned a one.

So *afterward*. The problem is, Carr doesn't know much about *afterward*—with Valerie, or with anyone else.

His relationships with women haven't lasted long—a few weeks, a month or two—no longer than the gaps between his jobs with Declan. But there was a sameness to them all, a sense of melancholy that suffused them from the start—the feel of a beach in midwinter.

The women themselves were not much alike, not at first glance anyway. Hannah was from Seattle, a filmmaker shooting a documentary on the Costa Rican rainforests and staying in the same hotel as Carr, in Puerto Viejo. Ann was from Zurich, a geologist with ABB, analyzing core samples taken off the Belize coast and drinking at night in a bar in San Pedro that Carr also favored. Brooke was a UNICEF pediatrician from Toronto, on vacation in Antigua between a stint in Haiti and a posting in Phnom Penh, and she and Carr dove the same reefs.

The list went on—different ages, different nationalities, different professions and appearances, but still, a sameness. They were all nominally married, but they were solitaries by nature—self-sufficient, emotionally reticent, even prickly. They were all obsessive about their jobs, and chronically exhausted by them. And they all possessed a certain brand of low-key intellectual charisma—a smart-girl glamour—that pulled at Carr like the moon pulled the seas.

The other thing they had in common, of course, was Carr himself. He understood something of his own appeal. Yes, he was attractive enough, enthusiastic and inventive enough, articulate and reasonably amusing when he had something to say, and smart enough to keep quiet otherwise. But his main draws, he knew, lay elsewhere. He was convenient. He was unburdened by backstory. And he was, without question, impermanent. It made him the perfect time-out from the rest of their lives—ephemeral, essentially anonymous, as disposable as the aliases they knew him by. And it left Carr entirely ignorant of *afterward*.

His thoughts find no forward traction with Valerie, and inevitably they slide back, to St. Barts. The vast, glassy plain of Flamands Bay, the crescent of bone-white sand, the white umbrellas, like a line of portly nuns, and their rooms over-looking it all. Their rooms that they never left. All that time working together, and St. Barts was their first time. And there, amid the ravaged bedding and the ruins of room service trays, was the first time it occurred to Carr that perhaps things didn't have to be quite so temporary.

Then the calls came in. The first was at five a.m., local time. Bobby's voice was low and flat and affectless, difficult for Carr to understand. It wasn't until after he'd hung up that Carr realized Bobby was in shock. The next calls, hours later, were from Mike, and they were confused and angry and scared. By then Carr had packed his bag and arranged his transit to B.A.

The heat has put him nearly to sleep, but there's movement across the lot, a flash of orange and short blond hair, and Carr wakes himself. He sees Valerie get into her Audi and drive off. He counts off thirty seconds and starts up the Saturn.

She takes Military Trail south and Palmetto Park east, to a stretch of stores and low apartment buildings. Valerie's building is glass and concrete, and as generic as she described. She pulls into the residents' lot, and Carr parks across the street. He doesn't see her enter, but in a while he sees a row of lights in some third-floor windows, and a slender orange figure crossing a room. In another minute he sees Valerie on a balcony, a glass in her hand, her face turned east, looking perhaps at a slice of the Intracoastal.

It is full dark when she goes inside again and draws the curtains. Carr watches her blank windows for an hour after-ward, and then gets on 95 and drives back to Palm Beach.

10

NO PALMS on this street—barely any green at all besides a runty saw palmetto, and its fronds are mostly gray. Bobby was right about the house; it's crap: a low concrete bunker the color of dishwater, with barred windows, a tin-roofed carport, and a sagging school yard fence. In a neighborhood where chipped breeze block and auto parts on the lawn make up an architectural school, it's still the worst house on the street. But the locals don't worry much about how the hedge next door is clipped, or if they do, they know better than to say. Which makes the house crap but also ideal. A jet passes low, directly overhead. It casts a broad shadow and shakes Carr's stomach, and leaves behind the tang of spent kerosene.

Carr has been here only twice before, but still it's more than familiar to him, a cousin to every workhouse they've ever used, in more bleak neighborhoods, by more airports, harbors, and rail yards than he can count. He knocks twice and waits. His head aches, the midday glare makes his eyes water, and, though he had nothing stronger than soda water the night before, he feels hungover. The kerosene smell settles in his hair and clothing. He can feel it on his skin. Dennis opens the door.

The lights are on in the living room, and all the shades

are drawn. There's music playing, propulsive Colombian hip-hop, but it's fighting a losing battle with the air conditioner rattling in the wall. The living room furniture— a spavined sofa, a lumpy recliner, some battered kitchen chairs, a side table pitted with burn marks—is pushed up against the walls, and the center of the space is dominated by two long tables with plastic tops and folding legs. Bobby and Latin Mike sit at one, peering into the same laptop screen. Dennis folds himself at the other, behind an uneven berm of equipment—laptops, printers, routers, modems, a laminating machine, and a tangle of cabling. Like every other workhouse.

Carr winces at the music and the odor—of cigarettes and burned coffee—and locks the door behind him. He places the white paper bag he's carrying on Bobby's table and tears it open. The smells of tomato sauce and grease waft up to mix with the entrenched aromas.

"Two meatball and two sausage and pepper," Carr says.

"Just in time," Bobby says. "Denny was starting to look like a plate of wings to me." Bobby reaches across, takes two of the foil-wrapped torpedoes, and passes one to Dennis. Latin Mike sighs and takes a long pull on his cigarette.

Bobby tears the wrapping off his sandwich and takes a bite. He makes small grunts as he chews, and red sauce runs down his chin. Latin Mike shakes his head. "You never heard of a napkin?" He reaches across Carr for a sandwich and carefully peels the foil away.

Bobby looks at Carr. "You not eating?"

Mike laughs. "*Jefe* don't need to eat with us. He's got that nice café by his condo. All those white tables, and the waitresses in their aprons, right, *jefe*? Not a place for workingmen like us, Bobby."

Carr looks at Mike, who smiles and eats his sandwich. There's nothing in the grin beyond his usual bullshit—the theater of labor versus management that he's compelled to perform every time he has to report progress. He did it when Declan was alive, and Carr has learned to bear it.

Carr smiles. "Yeah, they wax your Bentley with every meal. How about telling me what's up with Bessemer."

Dennis giggles behind his monitors. Mike wipes his mouth and hands carefully. "Well, it looks like Howie's got himself a job since gettin' out. And he's been busy at it. Eight days take from the wires we planted, and we got what we need. Howie's making valuable contributions to his community."

Dennis giggles again. "Real valuable," he says.

"A public servant," Bobby adds, laughing.

Carr sighs, and the throbbing in his head is more insistent. "Dennis, you want to turn down the music? And how about we skip the banter?"

Dennis kills the hip-hop. Latin Mike smiles and turns his laptop toward Carr. "Look for yourself. This is off one of the cameras we put in his house—the one behind his desk."

A window opens on the laptop and fills with a murky image: the back of a leather chair, the surface of a desk— scuffed wood, a blotter, a green shaded lamp, a computer keyboard and monitor. Beyond the desk, beside a darkened window, is a pair of green leather club chairs. Howard Bessemer is in one, and Daniel Brunt, his frequent tennis partner, is in the other. Their voices are muffled but entirely intelligible, and they both sound slightly drunk.

"Is her name actually Natasha?" Brunt says. "They can't all be named that, can they? And is she even Russian, or is she from Latvia or one of those other places?"

"I have no clue where she's from, Danny. Really, I don't ask."

"But you know she's eighteen, right?"

"I know what they tell me."

"Because the last thing I need, Bess, is underage issues."

"You don't need any issues, Danny. Nobody does."

Carr taps the mousepad and the video pauses. He looks at Mike, who is smiling. "Whores? They're talking about whores?"

"Russian whores, *jefe*."

"Howie takes Brunt to his poker parties?"

"Not that we've seen," Bobby says around a mouthful of meatball.

"So...?"

"Howie is a *player, jefe*. This little Pillsbury *pendejo* is a *pimp*."

Dennis clears his throat. "I think he's more of a pander, technically, or a procurer. I mean, the girls don't work for him."

"Whatever," Latin Mike says. "The point is, he's lining 'em up for Brunt. And not just whores."

"And not just for Brunt," Bobby adds.

Carr looks at the image of Howard Bessemer, frozen on the laptop screen—the round, unlined face, the high forehead catching the dim light. Carr shakes his head. "What else besides whores?"

"Danny here likes his Vicodin," Bobby says.

Latin Mike turns the laptop around again, and works the keyboard. "We got the best stuff from the cameras in his house, and the mics in his car and his tennis bag," Mike says. "They all know better than to put this shit in e-mails. This one's from the car." He turns the laptop around again. There's no picture, but a voice comes on. It's lazy, low, entitled. Carr doesn't recognize it.

"*...more of that stuff you got last week? That was very nice— very mellow.*"

Carr stops the playback. "This is who?"

"Nick Scoville," Dennis answers. "Howie sails with him. He's got a smack habit."

Bobby laughs. "And his golfing buddy Tandy—he likes

coke with his whores. He likes really fat whores, by the way. The other golfer, Moyer, is into ice, and lots of it."

"Nice friends," Carr says, and hits PLAY again. Bessemer's voice comes on.

"I'll talk to my guys and see what they can do."

"See what they can do with price, Bess. I mean, it's pretty shit but it's not cheap."

Carr hits STOP. "Who are these *guys* he's talking about?"

Mike takes the laptop again and brings up a photo. He turns the screen back to Carr. "They're brothers," Mike says.

There are two men in the photo, both stocky and dark, one muscular, the other just fat. The muscular one wears a gray suit and a white shirt, open at the collar. The fat one wears jeans, a black T-shirt, a rumpled blue blazer, dark glasses, and a three-day beard. Carr recognizes the backdrop: the frosted glass front of the Brazilian restaurant beneath which Bessemer spends his weekends.

"Mister *GQ* is Misha Grigoriev," Bobby says. "The dough boy is his baby brother, Sasha. Russkies, in case you couldn't guess. Came over when they were teenagers, by way of Jersey. Now they're local bad boys, with a little bit of everything going on. They own the Brazilian place and two others like it in Jupiter and Vero Beach. They got a string of high-end call girls here in town, and a couple of small-time dope guys on staff. They got a gambling joint down in Boynton Beach. Like everybody else around here, they got a construction business to pump the money through, though these days I can't see how that flies so well."

Carr looks sharply from Bobby to Mike and back. "Where'd you get all that?"

Latin Mike scowls and mutters something in Spanish. Bobby puts up his hands. "Don't worry—we didn't leave tracks. I bought drinks for a stumblebum vice cop who couldn't find his own dick to piss with, and doesn't know me from Adam. And Denny did some crazy shit with a fed computer."

"A DOJ server," Dennis says, and smiles sheepishly. "And I made it look like all the traffic went in and out of Moscow."

Carr nods and looks at the Grigorievs on the screen. "Are they connected?"

Bobby shakes his head. "According to the feds they're independents."

"And Bessemer works for them?"

"He's a middleman," Bobby says. "A freelancer. He's buying the dope from the Grigorievs' people, marking up the price, and selling to his buddies."

"He's fronting the money?" Carr asks, and Dennis nods. "For the whores too?"

Another nod. "Yeah—with a markup. He relays the where, when, and how many to the Grigorievs' man, and the whores show up."

"He making much money?"

Bobby shrugs. "His margins look pretty thin. The Russkies aren't giving him any breaks on price. Play the one with Sasha, Denny—from Howie's car."

Dennis fiddles at the keyboard until another voice comes on. This one is deep and impatient, with a trace of an accent.

"You have a problem, you talk to Willy, not me, right?"

"But this stuff isn't for me, Sash—you know that. It's for my friends, and the price—"

"I don't know about any stuff, and I don't want to know, Howard. You don't talk to me about this crap, you understand? What Willy says is what goes, okay? He don't know who this is for, and he don't care, right? All he knows is you, and shit costs what he says it costs, and that's it, right? What you do after that is your thing."

Bobby hits STOP. "He's whining about the price of coke. They charge Howie one-ten a gram, which is full retail and then some for around here."

Carr draws a hand along his jaw. "This is a lot of risk he's taking," he says, "especially for a guy with a record. What the hell's he doing it for?"

Latin Mike blows out smoke in a disgusted blast. "*Cabrón*, who gives a shit why he's doing it? It's enough we know what he's doing. Like you said, it's a big risk for a guy like him, and that makes it a good handle. A handle like this, we pick him up and carry him anywhere we want."

Another jet passes, shaking the glass in the windows. Carr rubs a palm over his chin. "It's not enough. We get only one shot at Bessemer, and we need to make it stick. We need to know all the strings there are to pull. I want to know why he's doing it. Is it just money? Is it something else?"

"*Hijo de puta!*" Mike flicks his cigarette across the room and jumps to his feet. There's a burst of red against the cinder block, and a smoldering ember on the carpet, and Mike's chair tips back. He points at Carr. "The *fuck* is up with you? This thing is lined up like dominoes. What's wrong with knocking it over?"

When he finally answers, Carr's voice is quiet. "I said we don't know enough yet."

"I tell you what's not enough," Mike says, and he cups a hand around his crotch.

Bobby has stopped chewing, and Dennis is frozen at his keyboard. The room is silent but for the chugging of the air conditioner and the receding rumble of a jet. Blood rushes in Carr's ears as he stands. "I don't recall you ever making quite that argument to Declan, Mike."

Mike smiles and steps forward. "That's 'cause Deke had a pair."

Carr nods. "And most of the time he managed not to confuse them with his brains."

Mike steps forward until his chest is nearly touching Carr's. He looks down at Carr and smiles wider. "That's right, *pendejo*, I'm just a dumbass chicano. What the fuck do I know? What kinda dumbass thing will I do next?"

Carr forces his breathing down—*inhale, exhale, not too fast.* He can smell the cigarettes on Mike, and the coffee, and the cologne. He studies Mike's throat—the pulse in his carotid artery, the soft spot below his Adam's apple—and tenses his fingers. He nearly jumps at Dennis's nervous cough.

"I…I know what Valerie would say if she were here." Dennis's voice is cracking. "Something like *put 'em back in your pants.* Don't you think, Bobby?"

Bobby's laugh is too loud. "Yeah, or maybe *sit the fuck down.* Right, Mike?"

Mike shrugs, but his gaze never leaves Carr. "She's not here now. And what the fuck does she care how long this takes? She's not living in this shithole. She's like Carr—got herself a nice apartment with a view of the water and everything."

"But that's what she'd say, Mike, and she'd be right." Bobby tries to catch Carr's eye and fails. "She'd be right, Carr," Bobby says. "We got to keep our heads in the work."

"She's not here now," Carr says quietly.

Dennis stands, still holding his sub. "For chrissakes, I didn't sign up for this kind of thing," he says, and backs away until he hits the wall. When he does a large meatball is ejected from the end of his sandwich. It lands with a wet thud on the carpet between his feet. All three men turn to look first at Dennis, and then the meatball.

Bobby's voice is low and grave. "Look at that—you made the kid shit himself."

And then, suddenly, air returns to the room and the four men are laughing. Carr's shoulders relax, and Latin Mike rights his overturned chair. "You better clean that up, Denny," Mike says. "I don't want to be steppin' in it."

"I don't know," Dennis says, "I think it goes with the carpet."

The men laugh again, and Latin Mike lights a cigarette. Carr moves to the door and turns the lock.

"I don't want this to take longer than it has to," he says, "but we need to know more. Give it a week—if we don't turn up anything else, we'll go with what we've got."

Carr closes the door behind him and hears someone lock it. He walks down the cracked path, through the rusting gate, and it is only when he's around the corner that he takes a breath.

11

HIS APARTMENT is in North Palm Beach, on Ocean Drive, and even the parking lot has a water view. Carr locks the Saturn and stops to watch the flashes of lightning on the horizon. The sky is purple, going to pitch-black at the eastern edge. It's the verge of something that might ripen to a hurricane, or amount to nothing more than rain. The forecast is muddled with conditionals—colliding zones of warm and cold seawater, churning air masses, equivocal fronts from Canada, butterfly wings over Africa—too many variables. Carr can empathize with the weathermen.

Too many variables. Why is Bessemer doing what he's doing? Will his Russian friends care when he gets burned? Why is Mike such an unremitting asshole, and how does he know about the view from Valerie's apartment? Carr pockets his keys and pushes through the briny air to the lobby.

Here he is Gregory Frye, investor in distressed real estate, down from Boston for an indefinite stay. The doorman greets him by name and makes a joke about the Red Sox, and Carr smiles and nods and gets on the elevator.

He leaves the lights off in the apartment, pulls six beers from the refrigerator, and settles on the sofa, before the tall windows. He opens a bottle and drinks half in one pull, and he's watching the distant lightning when his cell phone burrs. Eleanor Calvin's number appears on the display, and he tosses the phone to the other end of the sofa, where it glows like a ghost light in a theater.

"Shit." He sighs.

He's been trying, since he left Stockbridge, to dredge up some warmth for Arthur Carr—to find a happy memory of his father or, barring that, any memory that isn't tainted by anger, disapproval, or disappointment. Maybe he's been looking for that for most of his life. The best he's done lately is La Plata, southeast of Buenos Aires, out in the Río de la Plata.

They were sailing then, just the two of them, in an eighteen-footer his father had rented for the day. The wind was from the east, the estuary was brown and choppy, and the sun was waning but still bright. Carr was twelve.

He remembers his father in a faded blue polo shirt, shorts, and bare feet, his arms ropy and brown, and his face shaded by a long-billed cap. They'd been running through man overboard drills for most of the afternoon, steering figure eights again and again to rescue an orange life vest that his father kept flinging over the side.

"There goes Oscar," Arthur Carr would say, and toss the vest again.

His father did the spotting and fished out the vest when they came alongside; Carr was in the cockpit, one hand on the tiller, the other on the lines.

"Bring her around—*quickly* now—the man *is* drowning, after all. Now come to his windward side—*his* windward— that's good. Now ease up on the sheets. Let them luff, for chrissakes—you don't want to run by him!" Carr had gone through it too many times to count that afternoon.

For the last drill of the day, his father wanted Carr to do it all—spot, sail, and haul in the victim. "Pretend for a moment that you actually had a friend, and it was just the two of you out here. Now what would happen if your friend went in? What would you do—watch him drown? You can't just sit there and watch." And over the side the vest went once more.

"You're on your own now," Arthur Carr said.

Carr's heart was pounding, but he kept his head on a swivel, kept his eyes on the bobbing patch of orange, and kept them off his father, who crouched in the companion-way and stared at him like a baleful bird. He guided the boat away from the vest and, when he had enough room, tacked smartly. He panicked for an instant as the bow swept around and he lost the vest in the loping brown swells, but he found it again, and lined up on its windward side. He came in on a close reach, and let his sails luff. As the boat slowed, he scrambled under the boom. He kept low, gripped a stanchion with one hand, and ducked under the lifeline. He leaned out, but the vest was just beyond his straining fingers. Carr slid his hand up the stanchion to the lifeline and leaned out far-ther. And then a big swell hit.

There was a forward pitch, a sickening drop, scrabbling fingers, rushing, flooding cold, and a blow to the head that ran through Carr's whole body. There was bubbling and roaring, and no time to call out, and no breath to call with. The shadow of the boat rose above him and began to fall again, and then Arthur Carr had a fist through the front of his life vest—was dragging him up through the brown water, up into the air, and dropping him on the cockpit bench.

Carr coughed and sputtered, and his father wrapped a blanket around him and studied his face. He peered into one eye and then the other, and put alcohol and a bandage over the gash on his cheek, where he'd slammed into the hull. Then he took the tiller, turned the boat back toward the marina, and shook his head in disgust.

"Now you're both dead," his father said flatly, "you and your nonexistent friend."

That's the best he can do: an afternoon more than two decades back when his father hadn't actually flown into a rage, had instead been only casually cruel, but had cared enough to pluck him from the river. Though he wasn't sure about the caring part—saving him might simply have been easier than explaining his absence to Carr's mother.

Carr takes another pull on his beer and empties the bottle—his third somehow. Blue light is rippling through the sky, and a red light is blinking on his phone in the corner of his sofa. Mrs. Calvin has left another message. He opens a fourth beer, takes a long swallow, and hears his father's voice again: *You can't just sit there and watch.*

But watching is what he's best at—what he's always been best at, from when he was very small: the comings and goings of neighbors; the shopkeepers in their storefronts, sweeping, chatting with customers, hectoring clerks; the deliverymen; the embassy drivers; the maids and cooks and gardeners; and his parents most closely of all. His father didn't like it—it made him edgy, he said—but his mother didn't mind. In fact, she encouraged it, nurtured it, made a virtue of it, and a game.

He remembers sitting on her lap, in the tall windows of one of their houses, looking out on a tree-lined avenue. Was he even five years old? She would place a pale finger on the glass and point, and he would follow her gaze. Then she would put her hand over his eyes. *¿Qué ves, mijo? What do you see?*

And he would tell her. A man with a dog. A lady in a hat. A blue truck. A green taxi. A grandpa at a café table. He remembers the softness of her palm across his brow, the smell of her hand—gardenias and tobacco. *And what is the old man doing?* Reading a newspaper. Smoking. Drinking from a cup. *What kind of cup? What color hat? How large a dog?* They would go on and on, in English, in Spanish, as afternoon went down to dusk. He would lean against her, sleepy, her voice warm and husky in his ear. *¿Qué color es el coche, mijo? And how many men are in it?*

When his father returned from work—always furrowed and simmering, his tie askew—the game would stop, and it was as if his mother had left the room. As if she'd left the house altogether. She took him from her lap, and her arms were stiff and cool. Her hazel eyes were narrow. She spoke quietly, and only in English, and she said very little. Mostly she listened to Arthur Carr's litany of irritations and slights, nodding without ever conveying agreement.

Carr remembers his father's voice—droning at first, and growing louder as the cocktails took hold. He remembers his father's rumpled shirts, damp spots under the arms, and his father's broad, sloppy gestures. He remembers his mother's rigid shoulders, a vein thrumming in her neck, her stillness otherwise. He would try to catch her eye sometimes—offer up a grimace or a conspiratorial smirk—but it was as if he wasn't there. Or she wasn't. Other times, he would perch in the window and continue their game on his own, but inevitably his father grew irritated.

"It's like living with a goddamn cat," Arthur Carr would mutter, pulling him from the sill. "Nobody likes a cat."

More lightning, another beer, and Carr thinks about his father's anger and his mother's distance, and he remembers the maps.

His mother was a great one for them. Maps and guidebooks and histories and almanacs—but especially maps. When word of a new posting would come, despite Arthur Carr's grumblings—or perhaps because of them—she would smile, haul out the maps, and study them.

"Should we just stumble around like tourists?" she would say to Carr. "Get lost on our way to buy ice cream? No—we must know something about this place. We can't have people think you are *un hombre inculto*."

Carr remembers her at the dining table, half-glasses balanced on her nose, a cigarette burning in an ashtray, a cord of smoke twisting to the ceiling. The books were open in an arc in front of her, and the maps were unfurled. Her hair was pulled back and tied with a black ribbon.

"Here's where we will live, *mijo*," she said, pointing with a sharp red pencil. "And here is Daddy's office, and the new school." She made neat red check marks as she spoke. "Here is the museum, and the *fútbol* stadium, and the port, right here, and three train stations, and the main post office. Here is the airport, and the television studio, and the radio station, and the power plant. And see—here is the park, *mijo*, and the carousel."

And he remembers wandering the cities with her, remembers the narrow streets and the squares—cobbled, noisy, sometimes with a fountain, a dark arcade, or a looming church. His mother would hold his hand through the crowds, and buy him a lemon ice, a slice of melon, or a skewer off the grill. Then she would find a bench or little table and smoke and watch the people while Carr ate. They would sit for what seemed like hours to Carr, but he didn't mind. She would run her fingers through his hair, and sometimes, after he'd eaten, he would lean against her and doze.

Often, he recalls, she would meet someone she knew. Or they would meet her. And why not: the whole world seemed to stroll through those squares. Carr recognized some of the men and women, from embassy parties he thought, but most of them were strangers to him. They spoke mainly in Spanish to his mother, though some spoke in English and some in Portuguese. They would stop long enough to say hello, to talk about the weather, to shake hands and offer a cigarette or a book of matches. They all stared at him.

He remembers the heat of the stones, the smells of rotting fruit and grilling meat, the cool damp of the arcades, the drone of many footsteps on the cobbles, the feel of her dress as he leaned against her. Gardenias and tobacco.

And then there is a voice behind him, and a cool hand on the back of his neck.

"I thought you'd know better than to sit with your back to the door."

12

HE JUMPS, and his beer goes flying, and Tina smiles.

"At ease, soldier," she says.

It's the first time he's seen her away from a golf course, the first time he's seen her without Mr. Boyce, and the change in context is disorienting. For an instant Carr wonders if she's come to kill him, but decides probably not. If she had, he would probably be dead by now. Probably, too, she would've worn something else.

She's dressed in black shorts—very short—a black tank top, and black flip-flops. Her black sunglasses are pushed into her white-blond hair. Her arms and legs are ghostly, and her hands, long-fingered and elegant, are raised. Her gray eyes are steady.

"The door was locked," Carr says.

"Guy like you should get better locks," Tina says, lowering her hands. "Sorry for the surprise."

"You could've called first."

"Don't like phones," she says. "Besides, I like to keep in practice."

Carr wipes his hands on his pants. "It doesn't seem like you need much. And somehow I don't think that's the only reason you're here."

She smiles thinly. "Mr. Boyce didn't want to pull you away, but he does want to know how things are going."

"And he doesn't like the phone either?" Tina nods. "So you're here to check up?"

"More like checking in."

"I don't remember a lot of checking in with Declan."

She shrugs. "Does it need explaining?"

"I'm not Declan—I get it."

Tina sits on the sofa, slips off her shoes, and folds her legs beneath her. "No need to pout," she says. "So how about we open a couple more beers, and you tell me what's what, and I do the same?"

Carr looks at her more closely, and his disorientation becomes bewilderment. Tina out of school is less guarded—relaxed, almost funny. Her voice is soft and liquid—intimate in the confines of a room. And her pale, oval face, always smooth and empty at those golf course meetings, has an appealing touch of irony at the corners of her eyes and mouth.

"You want yours in a glass?" he asks. Tina shakes her head.

TINA'S HAD three bottles by the time Carr's made his report, and Carr has had two more. His head is cottony, and Bessemer's work as a procurer, though no less mystifying to him, is more amusing as he tells it to Tina.

"Maybe it's not all that different from private banking," Carr says, smiling. "It's all about keeping the clients happy."

Tina shakes her head. "Guy's a few cards short of a deck, for sure. It's a big gamble just to pick up some extra income. Can't blame you for wanting to find out why."

Carr shrugs. "And what about you? Anything new with our pal Prager?"

"Not much. His security guy, Silva, has fallen off the wagon again."

"Christ," Carr says, drinking the last of his beer. "It's a wonder he has a liver left."

"I'm not sure he does. And this time he's fallen off the radar too. He was on a tear in Homestead last week and we lost him."

"Probably staggered into the Everglades."

"We'll let you know if he staggers out again," Tina says. "You need any help with Bessemer, or maybe with his Russian friends?"

"If I do, what's it going to cost me?"

Her smile is chilly. "The deal doesn't change: we front your expense money, and we get paid back—plus finance charges—off the top. Services rendered are at cost plus."

Carr counts off on his fingers. "Expenses, finance charges, cost plus, finder's fee, management fee. You guys are fucking crooks."

Tina laughs, and it's surprisingly girlish. "We don't do pro bono." She drains her beer bottle and thrusts the empty at Carr. "But you want to do for yourself, fund your own expenses, save a little money, it's okay with us."

A frown darkens Carr's face. "That didn't work out so well for Declan." He takes Tina's empties and his own to the kitchen, and returns with two fresh beers. Tina is standing at the window, watching the distant storm.

"Speaking of which," she says. Carr takes a deep breath, trying to chase the wool from his head. He stands next to Tina. Their reflections are like ghosts in the glass. "We had a talk with somebody down there," she continues. "Somebody who used to work for Bertolli."

"*Somebody* who?"

Tina shakes her head. "Somebody who worked security for him, up until a few months ago—security in Mendoza."

Carr leans forward. "Did he say anything about how they knew Deke was coming? Who they got the word from?"

"He didn't know anything about that. He was strictly an order taker; he didn't ask questions, didn't even think about having questions."

"So what use is he?"

"Everything we heard about that night—everything we heard from you—says that your guys got tagged almost as soon as they pulled up to that little airstrip."

"That's the way it was told to me, every time—that they'd barely gotten out of the vans."

"And they never got inside the barn? Never laid eyes on the cash?"

"That's the way I heard it. I assume that you've heard something different."

She nods again. "This guy says that your people didn't get hit coming out of the vans; they got hit coming out of the *barn*. He says when it was all over that night, Bertolli was short almost two million euro."

In the glass, Carr sees Tina watching him. "And this guy is who?"

"I told you, he worked security for Bertolli."

"So he's what—some brain-dead kid with a gun? And your friends down there just tripped over him? Or did he volunteer his services?"

"He's no genius, but he's no walk-in either. Our friends worked hard to turn him up, and they spent some money too. He was hiding out in B.A. Seems he'd had a falling-out with his crew chief up in Mendoza. Something about the chief's sister."

"And your friends believed him?"

"I did too."

"You spoke to him?"

Tina nods. "Went down there last week."

A jagged white line lights the horizon, and the afterimage flares behind Carr's eyes. He takes a long pull on his beer. "Two million euro," he says. "Maybe it burned with Declan's van."

"I asked about that. This guy said Bertolli had them sifting through the wreckage, looking for some trace. They didn't find one."

"There wasn't much left of that van," Carr says.

"If you say so."

Carr turns to look at her. "What's that supposed to mean?"

Tina keeps her gaze on the horizon. "You're the one had eyes-on. You were at the salvage yard; you were at the morgue. I wasn't."

"Eyes-on," he mutters, and the traces of lightning vanish from beneath his lids, replaced by twisted metal, blistered paint, melted upholstery, charred, fire-stiffened limbs, blackened flesh, and naked, shattered bone. And the smell, even days after, even in the air-conditioned bays of the city morgue. . . . It comes over him in a wave, and the beer in his gut threatens to erupt.

"You okay?" Tina asks.

"That van was like a fucking shell crater. I'm not surprised they didn't find anything. They blew the hell—"

"Yeah, that's another thing," Tina says, cutting him off. "According to this guy they didn't run Declan off the road. According to him, they were hauling ass on Highway Seven, but Declan got way out in front. They lost sight of his van for like twenty minutes. They were thinking about turning around when they saw a flash up ahead of them, and a column of smoke. The van was wrecked and burning on the roadside when they got there, but they didn't see it happen."

"I saw the bullet holes—in the rear bumper, in the side panels. As twisted up and black as everything was, you could still see those."

"He didn't say they weren't firing at it—in fact, he said

they chewed its tail up pretty good—he just said they didn't force it off the road."

Carr shakes his head, steps away from the window. "Am I supposed to make something of that? He said they shot up the van. Maybe it blew a tire. Maybe the gas tank was leaking and there was a spark. So Bertolli's men weren't around to see it go up—so what?"

Tina perches on an arm of the sofa and draws a knee up under her chin. She examines her toenails, which are perfectly manicured and glazed white. When she looks back at Carr, her gray eyes are as steady as ever. Her voice is vaguely amused. "A girl can't win with you. You bitch when we don't turn up anything, and you bitch when we do. You make what you want out of it, I'm just telling you what I've found.

"We're looking at this only because you said you wouldn't go on with the Prager gig otherwise—and it's the only reason Boyce agreed to split the costs with you. You don't like how we're going about things, you don't want to hear what we learn—that's cool. He's got other ways to spend his money, and I've got other ways to spend my time."

Carr looks at her for a long minute, and then smiles. "And here we were getting along so well."

She shrugs. "Honeymoons never last."

Carr sits at the other end of the sofa and puts his beer on the floor. "Two million euro. If it didn't burn in the van, and Bertolli's boys didn't pocket it themselves—"

"I seriously doubt that. Bertolli's got them terrified."

"Then where did it go?"

"I figured you'd have a theory."

"Your guy didn't see anyone else out there? No cars, no trucks?"

"I asked a few different ways; he said no. But it's remote as hell up there, with lots of twists and turns, and fucking dark. Somebody running without lights...who knows?"

Carr reaches for his beer, and looks through the brown glass at the dregs that remain. "Two million euro—it's not pocket change."

"Nope," Tina says. "Maybe you want to ask your boys if they've seen it lying around."

Carr drains the bottle. The beer is warm and mostly froth, and he nearly gags getting it down. He shakes his head at Tina. "I don't want to," Carr says, "but I will."

13

BOBBY CALLS in the morning, to say that Bessemer has broken his routine.

"He's playing tennis with Stearn today—just the two of them, no Brunt. And they're having lunch afterward. That's new and different for a Thursday."

Carr's head is like bad fruit, but he drags himself to a sitting position and tells Bobby he'll meet him in an hour. He raises the shades and squints into the milky sky. Then he stumbles to the shower, where the blast of water hurts, and then helps.

Carr finds street parking and meets Bobby in the alley behind the Barton Golf and Racquet Club. Bobby has traded the painter's van for a gray sedan. He has the AC on and the cold air is like a second shower. Bobby is drinking a blue slushie from a plastic cup the size of a sap bucket.

"Howie's jumpy today. He got that way when Brunt called, and told him it was just going to be Howie and Stearn on the tennis court. Got more that way when Stearn called to invite him for lunch after."

"Stearn makes him nervous?"

"Haven't seen them alone together much, but I think so.

He lets him win at tennis. Double-faults if he's about to beat the guy."

"He does the same with Brunt, and he lets those other guys beat him at golf. That's Howie's thing. We know what Stearn does for a living?"

"Rich and retired, like most of Howie's friends. Denny tells me he was over in London for twenty-plus years, with an American bank—a portfolio manager or something. Got fired in a merger, and came here after that. On a couple of boards around town—the hospital, the art museum. On the board of a prep school, up north."

"He married?"

"Wife spends the summer in Maine. Kids are grown."

"Nothing obvious that would make Howie nervous."

"Come on, the guy looks like some kind of zombie scarecrow. He makes me a little tense."

Stearn wins the second set when Bessemer double-faults, and the men sling their racquet bags and walk to the clubhouse. Bobby pulls the car around and they follow Bessemer's BMW as it follows Stearn's Mercedes from the Barton.

Lunch isn't far. They travel south from the Barton, then east, then south again, on South Ocean Boulevard. Carr and Bobby are a hundred yards back when the Mercedes and then the BMW pull through the black iron gates of Willis Stearn's estate. Driving past the entrance, Carr catches a glimpse of lawns like carpet and, in the distance, a mustard-colored villa. He swears softly.

"We've got a mic in Howie's racquet bag," Bobby says, as they round the corner, "but I'm betting he leaves it in the car."

"Which means we're deaf and blind."

The properties here are large, and private, and the security patrols are not lazy. The closest parking spot Bobby finds is nearly half a mile away, a dirt patch at a construction site. It's beyond the range of the mic in Bessemer's bag, and just at the limit of the one in his car, but in any event there's nothing to hear besides distant traffic and the occasional growl of thunder. Bobby switches off the engine.

"The GPS will tell us when he moves," Bobby says. He reaches for a laptop on the backseat and balances it on the console between them. Then he settles himself lower behind the wheel and runs his straw around the bottom of his empty cup.

Carr takes a deep breath. "Dennis come up with anything else on Bessemer's friends?"

"He's looking. Mike's on it too, or will be when he gets back from Boca."

Carr turns in his seat. "What the hell's he doing down there?"

"Val needed a replacement for one of the cameras she's gonna use in Chun's house. Mike brought it down."

"Why the hell didn't she call me?"

Bobby puts up a hand and arranges his meaty face into as close as it comes to a conciliatory look. "She calls me direct sometimes. She's done it before. It's not a problem."

"It's a problem for me, Bobby. I want to know who's doing what, and where. And if she called you, how come you didn't go down there?"

Bobby clears his throat and suppresses a smile. " 'Cause I'm here with you, looking at Howie."

Carr sighs and peels his shirt from the upholstery. "Run the AC."

Bobby does, and the two of them sit without speaking, watching some stonemasons build a long wall. They are shaping and fitting the rocks, and their hammers sound like gunshots to Carr. The air conditioner dries the sweat on his skin but does nothing for the throbbing in his temples. Tina's words reverberate there: *Bertolli was short almost two million euro.* Two million euro—Declan thought there'd be more.

THEY WERE in Port of Spain, in the bar at the Hyatt Regency. Wind was shaking the windows, and the city lights were lost behind low clouds. The place was empty, and they were all a little drunk. Declan was like a red-faced witch over a cauldron.

"The bastard doesn't trust banks or bankers," he said. "Oh, he uses them—he's got to with the feckin' money he makes on all that crap he smuggles in—but he likes to keep some cash on hand. Nothing big, mind you, we're talking three to five mil in euros—he prefers them to dollars. Keeps enough around for incidentals and traveling funds, in case he has to move in a hurry, which he's done a few times—out of São Paulo, out of Ciudad del Este, out of Argentina and back again. He's quite the jackrabbit, Señor Bertolli is.

"I had this job lined up years ago—had it all worked out—but the fat fuck skipped on me. Hightailed it out of Argentina when a new government came in, with his wife, mistresses, and various bastards in tow. Got away about a minute before the PFA knocked down his door. Took all his cash with him too. But that party's gone now, and so Bertolli and his money have come home."

Carr was slow on the uptake. He'd been working on the Prager job all day—peering at floor plans and wiring diagrams. His eyes were gritty and his head full of numbers, and he didn't get the point right away. Declan was annoyed.

"Wake up, Carr—it's the feckin' expenses. The up-front costs on the Prager job are running twice what we expected, and they'll run higher still. I don't know about you, but I don't want to be paying such a big chunk of my take in finance fees to the grand Mr. Boyce. It's usury what he's chargin'! This deal is lovely—a quick in and out, three bucks easy, and then we don't need his feckin' financing."

That was all he'd had to say to convince Mike and Bobby and Ray-Ray, who were already antsy from too much planning, and who were never happy paying anyone for anything. Some part of Carr had known right there that it was a losing battle, but still he spent the next week in increasingly heated, increasingly pointless argument with Declan. He and Valerie both—though that night, in the Hyatt bar, she'd just stared into her drink and said nothing at all.

CARR'S HEAD drops, and he realizes he's been dozing. Bobby is watching him. "Up late?" he asks.

Carr wipes his chin. "Anything from Bessemer?"

"His car hasn't moved, and there's nothing on the mic but seagulls."

Bobby has a cooler in the back, and Carr pulls a bottle of water from it. He takes a long pull and looks at Bobby. He doesn't want to ask about it—doesn't have the energy today—and besides, he knows what the answer will be. But still...*Bertolli was short almost two million euro*. He clears his throat.

"At Bertolli's place that night," Carr begins, and at the mention of the name Bobby's face colors with surprise and anger.

"You're *fucking* kidding me with this!" he says, and then the laptop pings twice, loudly.

Bobby sits up fast. "Bessemer's moving," he says, and he throws the car into gear and guns it through the dirt lot. There's a curtain of dust around them; the laptop slides from the console and Carr catches it mid-flight. Bobby pushes through the side streets and they hit South Ocean

Boulevard in time to see Bessemer's convertible pull out of Stearn's place. His top is still down and his thin hair is flying as they pass him going north.

"Fast lunch," Bobby says, and he slides the car through an easy U-turn and into the northbound lane.

"I'm not surprised," Carr says. "Did you see Bessemer's face? He looked like he was about to throw up."

Two miles up South Ocean Boulevard they watch him do just that, in a garbage can by the side of the road.

14

"**A LOT** of phone time for Howie tonight," Dennis says, "and he didn't sound good."

They're at the workhouse—Carr, Bobby, Dennis, and Latin Mike—and the pent-up heat of the day is suffocating. Mike is tilted back in a kitchen chair, clean-shaven, hair slick from a shower. The half-smile on his face sets Carr's teeth on edge.

"He called the Caymans a few times," Dennis continues, "his pal Prager's number, but he never got past the help. Then he called his pimp. Took him four tries to go through with it. First three times, he hung up before anyone answered."

"Prager didn't take his call?" Carr asks.

Dennis shrugs. "The secretary said he wasn't in, but she had to go away and check before she said it. The second time, she told him Prager would get back to him."

"Has he?"

"Not yet."

Mike grins nastily. "I thought Prager was his friend," he says. "That's not so friendly, *jefe*."

"And the pimp?" Carr asks. "What was going on with the three hang-ups?"

"He didn't want to pull the trigger," Bobby says.

Carr squints at him. "Pull the trigger on what?"

Dennis shakes his head. "He didn't say on the phone."

"Who's the pimp?" Carr asks.

"Calls himself Lamp. Works for the Russian brothers."

Mike dangles a cigarette from his lip, but doesn't light it. "Howie's gotten whores for his friends before. How come he's nervous now?"

Bobby shakes his head. "The guy is freaked about something. The way he blew his lunch this afternoon—I thought his socks were gonna come up."

Carr looks at Dennis. "You find out more about Bessemer's friends?"

Dennis taps at one of his keyboards. "Plenty," he says, "though I'm not sure it amounts to anything. Brunt and Moyer are retired money guys, like Stearn. Moyer was a bond trader; Brunt was an investment manager."

"They all work at the same place?"

"Different companies, different places. Stearn was in London, Moyer in New York, and Brunt was in Chicago."

"And the other two guys?"

"Tandy is also retired. He was a partner in a law firm up in New York. He got downsized a few years back—him and half the firm. As far as I can tell, Scoville has never worked. Lives in the guesthouse on his mother's property, a few miles down the road from Stearn. Besides sailing and heroin, lying around the pool seems to be the only job he's ever had."

"Married?"

"Not Scoville, but the rest of them are."

"Any of them have records?"

"Scoville took a couple of possession busts in New York, one with intent to sell. He got probation and rehab."

"Any of them friends with Bessemer before he came down here?"

"Not that I can tell."

"So Howie is what to them—the only guy they know who knows the rough trade?"

Mike lights his cigarette and chuckles derisively. "We trying to get inside their heads now too? Who gives a fuck?"

Carr ignores him. "And we think Howie's doing this... why?"

Bobby sighs. "Same reason people do most things," he says, "for the money." He looks at Dennis.

"The guy's chronically short," Dennis says. "The divorce cleaned him out pretty good. His house is paid for, but his grandmother's trust throws off barely enough income to cover the taxes and his liquor bills, and she set it up so he can't get at the principal."

"My *abuela* was a bitch too," Mike mutters.

"I thought Prager was hiding money for him," Carr says. "What happened to that?"

Dennis shrugs. "It's not in any of the accounts I can see, though I can't see into Isla Privada."

Carr shakes his head. "When's Howie meeting the pimp?" he asks.

"Monday," Bobby says, "outside the Brazilian place. I'll be there."

Carr looks at Latin Mike. "We'll all be there."

"Sure, *jefe*," Mike says, smiling. "All of us."

THE NIGHT is close and the airport throws sheets of flashing light against the low clouds. The smell of the jet fuel, of the house, of Mike's cigarettes, and of his own sweat are caught in Carr's clothing, and he walks the long way around the block to get to his car. He's halfway there when he hears footsteps behind him and whirls.

Latin Mike chuckles from behind the glowing end of a cigarette. "That's slow, man. I want to hurt you, you be all the way hurt by now."

He steps from the shadows and Carr takes a slow, deep breath to quiet his pulse. "You going out again?" Carr says.

"Just for some air. Not enough in that dump tonight. And you?"

"To bed. You want something?"

"Me? No, I got what I need—but you're still looking for something."

Carr sighs. "We've been over this. I want to know more before we go at Bessemer. I want to know why—"

A barking laugh, and Mike blows smoke into the blinking sky. "I'm not talking about Bessemer. Bobby says you're still asking him about Mendoza. Says you did it again today."

Carr takes another deep breath. "And?"

"And I want to know what that's about."

"It's *about* what it seems to be about: I want to know what happened, what went wrong. Bobby didn't tell you?"

"Bobby tells me everything, *jefe*. But why you keep asking him about this? You think he's gonna tell you something new? You think he doesn't get what you're doing when you ask the same questions over and over? That you're calling him a liar."

"I didn't know it was upsetting him so much."

"Sure you did. So why don't you cut it out? You still got questions about what happened down there, ask me."

"Why, are you going to tell me something new?"

Mike barks again. "I'm gonna tell you to fuck off."

"So nothing new."

Another laugh. "You want new, maybe you need to get different questions."

"Maybe I have one."

Mike smiles and rolls out a line of smoke rings that break on Carr's shoulder. "Give it a try, *cabrón*."

"Okay. Did you get into that barn before Bertolli's guys turned up?"

In the long silence that follows, a car passes, a jet passes, someone shouts from somewhere in Brazilian Portuguese. Mike flicks his cigarette into the street. He shakes his head and laughs to himself. "Deke was always so hot on you— always talked about how smart you were, how good at planning, how you saw angles other people didn't, how you thought big. It was like you were his kid or something.

"Me, I never got it—and I told him so. More smoke than fire, I said. Too much complication. Too much bullshit. After a while, he didn't want to hear it: told me to shut up or move on. I thought about that a long time, and decided to stay. I liked Deke; I was used to him, and I liked the paydays, so... I didn't change my mind about you, but I kept my mouth shut. But when the old bastard bought it, I tell you I was ready to book. I would have too if this gig had been any smaller, and if Bobby and Val hadn't asked me—shit, they *begged* me—to stick it out."

Carr kicks at a piece of broken pavement. It skips and skids and ends up in a storm drain. He laughs softly. "I don't hear anything new, Mike, and I don't hear an answer to my question."

Mike's fists clench and his arms swell. "Here's my answer, *pendejo*—if you're running this thing, then *run it*, and if you're not, then shove off. 'Cause this is the last *fucking* job I'm doing, and if it turns to shit, it's *you* I come looking for. No one else—just you. So get your mind off Mendoza and Declan and Bertolli's *fucking* barn, *cabrón*, and get it on Bessemer and Prager."

Mike turns and walks back into the dark, and Carr sees his lighter flare as he fires up another smoke. "Was that a *yes* or a *no* about the barn?" Carr calls, but Mike doesn't answer.

15

THEY LEAN together like schoolgirls, flushed and whispering as they stroll the pink arcades around Mizner Park. They're not quite holding hands, but it takes a second look to be certain. Valerie—Jill—is in a summer dress: spaghetti straps and long, tanned limbs. On her day off, Amy Chun, president of the Spanish River Bank and Trust Company, wears a tan wrap skirt, a white T-shirt short enough to expose a narrow band of midsection, and low sandals. She's in her mid-forties, slender, shorter than Jill by two inches, and more darkly tanned. Her straight black hair is done in a loose braid, and her sunglasses are sleek and smoky.

They pause at the window of a jewelry store. Jill points, Amy takes off her glasses, nods, and they both laugh. Jill walks on and Amy watches her.

Carr's chest aches and he realizes he's been holding his breath. He sighs and runs down the car window. A damp breeze wanders in. Not even two weeks since Jill joined Amy Chun's yoga class, he thinks, and already she's set the hook deep.

Valerie's voice was tired and raspy on the phone the night before, and she was reluctant at first to talk about Chun—like a magician asked to explain her very best trick—but Carr had insisted.

"She's better than I'd hoped," Valerie said. "Basically, she's got no life. She goes from work to her workout to her house, and then it's more work, into the night."

"No friends or family?"

"I haven't seen any friends, and the only family she's got are her parents, in Vancouver. No, it's all work for Amy. But the little time she's not grinding away, she spends online— and not just shopping, either."

"What's she doing—looking at pornography?"

"A little, but that's not what I'm talking about. Amy is a stalker—a cyber-stalker, anyway. I went through the take from Dennis's spyware—her e-mail, her browser history— and it's plain as day. She's keeping tabs on someone named Janice Lessig."

"Who the hell is she?"

"She runs a little company out in the Bay Area—makes organic bread and shit like that. She lives in Berkeley, plays the cello in a couple of amateur groups, has two daughters, and a domestic partner named Elaine."

"I repeat—who the hell is she?"

"She and Amy went to B-school together, twenty years ago, and they were pretty tight. I think maybe she's Amy's *road not taken*."

"They were lovers?"

"I can't say for sure, but they wrote some articles for their B-school review together, and their last year there, they were its coeditors."

"That doesn't mean—"

"Dennis dug up a copy of the school's student directory for their last year. The two of them lived at the same address off-campus. The same apartment number."

"And you think Chun still has a thing for her?"

"She visits Lessig's Facebook page every night, and the Radclyffe Hall Bread Company's website too—the pages with Lessig's pictures on them. Ditto the websites of the Piedmont Amateur Strings and the Shattuck Quartet. And it's not like these pages change very much. She even cruises the website of the private school Lessig's kids go to. It's got a picture of Lessig on it, from when she came in for career day. On top of which, Amy Googles Lessig a couple of times a week. I don't know how else to read all that."

"Is Chun in touch with her?"

"Not that I can tell. No e-mail to or from Lessig—and Amy saves her e-mail since like the beginning of time. She never posts anything on Lessig's Facebook page. Dennis found her Christmas card list on the laptop, and Lessig wasn't on it."

"Okay, Chun is still carrying a torch for Lessig. What do you do with that?"

"Use it to fine-tune Jill. So now she has red highlights in her hair, and her clothes are a little more crunchy-granola. Now she cooks, and wants to start a catering business. And she sings, and someday she wants to have kids."

"You cook and sing?"

"I do a lot of things."

Sitting in his darkened living room, looking at a distant light on the black ocean, Carr had swallowed hard. "What about Jill's backstory?" he asked eventually.

"The same," Valerie said. "She's still been through the wringer; she's still looking to change her life."

Carr shifts in the front seat and watches them. Her walk is new, he thinks—a bit less assertive, a bit more coltish—and her accessories are different too: dangly earrings, a looped necklace of colored glass beads, a row of thin gold bracelets. And there are tattoos now: a complicated henna braid around her right biceps and a narrower one around her left ankle. Carr slouches lower as they pass.

There are other people in the park: other couples, off-season tourist families, people walking dogs, but it is Jill and Amy who draw the eye. It's more than beauty, Carr thinks. Something about their attraction to each other, the simmering anticipation, the wisps of steam before a full boil. It's in the air between them, like a magnetic field—invisible, but palpable nonetheless.

Carr hears faint, intermittent music—a bossa nova spilling from one of the stores when its automatic doors slide open. It's a familiar tune but the door slides shut before he can place it. He watches the women and struggles to recall the tune, and he's taken suddenly by an aching loneliness—like the last student left at school at the start of a long holiday. The door opens, closes, opens again. The music seeps out, and Carr has it: Jobim playing "Lamento," and he hears another version of that song.

An infinitely worse version, the one he remembers—the scraping of a quintet that didn't know half the notes, and didn't care much for the rest. They were playing in a beachfront bar, and he and Declan were there with several bottles between them. They were two days gone from Bogotá, and the crew was $5.7 million richer for it—the take from the first job that Carr had planned end to end. Carr felt like he'd just graduated from something, and Declan—creased and unshaven—was beaming. The sky was six shades of violet and the first stars were lit, and all was right with the world.

Declan lifted a glass. "Brilliant, lad—feckin' brilliant. They never saw us—never even dreamed of us." He'd said it before, but Carr didn't mind the repetition. He lifted his glass in return.

Declan laughed. "Those spreadsheets at Langley didn't know what they had, did they? Couldn't recognize a natural right there in their midst."

Carr never liked this subject, and he shrugged and looked away. "A natural what?"

"A natural spy, lad—a fella bred for the secret life."

"They would've disagreed with you."

Declan shook his head disgustedly. "What the hell did they know? I've run across my share of company men, and they're about as subtle as a dog humpin' yer leg. They think it's all about sales, fer chrissakes—that if you can charm Granny into buying an estate car, you can nick war plans from the North Koreans. Was that it, lad—you weren't enough of a salesman for 'em?"

Carr shrugged again. "They don't explain much."

"They must've said something."

"They didn't think I had the temperament for it. They said I had a problem with authority."

Declan smiled broadly. "And who doesn't that's worth a goddamn?" he said, and raised his glass in a toast. "And that was all? That was enough to shitcan you?"

Carr took a long pull on his drink. "They didn't think I'd be good with agents."

Declan squinted—indignant on his behalf—and refilled his glass. "What the hell does that mean?"

"They didn't think I'd be good at running them. They thought I had a tendency to see what I wanted to see and hear what I wanted to hear, and that when time came to squeeze them hard, or burn them, I wouldn't have the stomach for it. *Overly invested* they called it."

"Sounds like feckin' psychobabble to me."

"They were big on that," Carr said.

"Well, fuck 'em, I say! Big outfits like that, they don't appreciate the solitary man. Don't understand him. A fellow like yerself makes 'em nervous. You don't fit their molds—so they don't know what moves you, what levers to pull."

Carr filled his own glass, and Declan's too. "But you've got that figured out, have you?"

Declan drank and nodded. "To lead men, you must know what they love."

Carr laughed. "And that would be what?"

"For you, solitary Carr, I'd say it's being a ghost. You love drifting through the drab workaday mess—all the tinkers and tailors and doctors and bankers; you love watching their monkeyshines without actually being a part of 'em. You're in it, but you're not—not really. You're like a feckin' specter."

Carr hid his surprise behind another drink, and slid the bottle to his side of the table. "Now who's into the fucking psychobabble? You're hammered."

"It doesn't mean I'm wrong. You love flying above it all, looking down like yer on an airplane, or yer floating over a reef, watching the wee fishes. That was the appeal of Integral Risk, wasn't it—your clients, their lives, the things they got up to—it was like an aquarium, and you on the other side of the glass."

Carr looked at him for a while and nodded slowly. "Tell me you don't like that aspect of it—being apart from things."

"How else could I recognize it in you? 'Course I like it— I'm a solitary too, at heart, so I know the appeal. You feel invulnerable, somehow—you've no connections, no dependents, no hostages to be taken. Nobody can lay a finger on you, 'cause yer just not there. It's better than bulletproof. But some advice from an aged bastard: you want to watch you don't get overly fond of it. You step out of the flesh and blood world long enough, it's hard to step back in."

Carr held the bottle up, saw the moon turn amber in it. "That assumes you ever lived there in the first place."

Declan laughed. "Ah, Carr, save yer tragic tale for the ladies, and pass me that feckin' bottle."

Sweat rolls down Carr's ribs, and his head is bobbing in the heat. He shakes off sleep and memory, and gets out of his car. Jill and Amy are a block and a half away now, and he follows them down the arcade. They're window-shopping—clothing, handbags, shoes, more jewelry—pointing, laughing. They pause outside a furniture store, and again at a real estate office.

Carr trails them to an outdoor café. They take a table near a tiled fountain and order iced teas. The air is thick and the palms and bougainvillea hang in limp surrender, but Jill and Amy don't seem to mind. Even in the shade, their arms and legs are shining. Jill reaches for the sugar, nearly tips her glass, just catches it, and laughs nervously. Carr shakes his head at the performance.

It's the seamlessness that impresses him most, the integration of elements small and large into her fabricated persona. The endearing clumsiness, the slightly funky clothing and accoutrements, the accent and the diction, the attitude, the wear and tear: all Jill, all of a piece. He wonders how she's done up her apartment, what's in the glove box of her car, and what's on her iPod. Not a false note, he's sure.

The heat is a weight on his shoulders, and he finds a bench beneath a palm. He thinks back to Costa Alegre, to Valerie's easy shifts between the three engineers. He recalls the other men and women he's watched her seduce over the years, and the characters she's inhabited to do it—doctors, lawyers, Indian chiefs. . . . He watches her sip tea, and something about the dappled light on her legs reminds him of Port of Spain, the perpetual overcast of the two months they spent there, laying the groundwork for the Prager job.

Declan installed them in one of the new glass towers on the waterfront, in seven apartments—Declan, Bobby, Ray-Ray, Dennis, and Mike on the seventh floor, Valerie and Carr on the ninth. After which Declan, Bobby, Ray-Ray, Dennis, and Mike developed a sudden fondness for cricket, and decamped most afternoons to Queen's Park, leaving Carr and Valerie squinting into their laptops. *Fucking Cinderella* was Valerie's grumbled gloss on the circumstances.

At first they worked separately—digesting Boyce's dossiers, ferreting out additional information, collecting technical data—and met in the evenings to compare notes and drink beer. Later they worked in Valerie's apartment, assembling and disassembling the framework of a plan, again and again, until they had something that might float.

He stared out her living room window a lot, at the highway and the rush of cars, at the shipping containers stacked along the wharves, like the ruins of an ancient city, at the ocean like beaten lead. A pearly light filled her place, along with a perfume—something with lime and orange blossom and vanilla.

Valerie went to buy lunch one afternoon, leaving him there alone. Carr walked through every room and thought about looking inside her medicine chest and her closets, but didn't. He stared for a long time at the pile of books by her bedside. They were paperbacks, slim volumes by Borges, Fante, Akhmatova, Didion. He leafed through them, and when he heard her key in the lock he piled the books up again. He was standing at the living room window when the door opened.

Was it then that things began to simmer, or had it started long before? Either way, she leaned in closer after that, touched him on the hand or the arm often, didn't look away. Her apartment felt smaller, and Carr felt a surge of anger and disappointment whenever the cricket fans returned.

The phone shudders in his pocket and it brings him back to his bench. He looks down the arcade and sees Amy Chun, alone at her table. He reaches for his phone, and Valerie is on the other end, whispering angrily.

"I don't know what you think you're doing here," she says, "but you've seen enough for one day. Now clear the fuck out before you queer my play."

16

MONDAY NOON is too early for Lamp. He grimaces at the sky, adjusts his sunglasses on his peeling nose, and fiddles with the visor on his open-top Jeep. Then he hoists up his iced coffee and takes another needy pull. He does it all very slowly, as if he's half asleep, and the other half is in some pain.

Carr watches from a wine bar across the street and decides that Lamp looks like his job. Not the pimp job, but the other one, which, according to Dennis, is owner and manager of Lampanelli's Surf n' Sport, in Riviera Beach. He's forty-ish and tall, with sandy hair, a tan, and a gut edging toward sloppy. He's wearing a pink T-shirt and khaki shorts, and has a tattoo of a parrot on his left calf and a look of annoyance on his unshaved face.

Lamp glances around the parking lot. The Grigoriev brothers' Brazilian restaurant is closed today, and the lot is empty but for his Jeep. He checks his watch. Carr hopes that Lamp finds some patience, or is tired enough to stay put for a while. Bobby and Latin Mike have called to tell him that Howard Bessemer is en route, but moving slowly due to traffic and what seems to be a lethal hangover.

"Looks like he's been living on bad fish and toilet water,"

Bobby said, laughing. "We're about half a block back of him, and twenty-five seems to be his top speed today."

"Hungover or reluctant?" Carr asked.

"Both," Bobby said.

Definitely reluctant, Carr thinks, and for several days now also reclusive. Bessemer didn't leave his house for his usual weekend poker and whore festival, or for anything else. Lunch and dinner were delivered three days running, along with parcels from the local liquor store. And televisions were on around the clock in the kitchen, the living room, and the bedroom, though Bessemer watched none of them, but wandered from room to room drinking gin and smoking joints. When he did pause, it was to collapse wherever he was standing, and to sleep for a few hours. Then up again and back to work. The only other breaks in the action—besides his occasional puking—were when Bessemer tried calling Prager. None of his attempts was successful.

The waitress brings Carr another soda water. He watches Lamp drain his iced coffee cup. On the street beyond the far side of the parking lot, Carr sees the van where he parked it, long before Lamp pulled in. Dennis is in back, with a couple of laptops and wireless broadband cards. He looks for Bobby and Mike, but doesn't really expect to spot them. They're good enough that he won't see them climb into the van. There's movement in the foreground and Bessemer's BMW rolls into the lot.

Despite the clear skies, Howie's got the top up, and from Carr's vantage he's no more than a ghost at the wheel. He leaves a parking space between his car and the Jeep and kills the engine. And then he sits. And sits. Unmoving, with his white hands on the wheel, as if at any moment he might drive off again. Lamp is as puzzled as Carr, and after a while he holds his wristwatch out toward Howie's car and taps the face with his finger. Howie gets the point.

He opens the door slowly and cringes like a vampire in the midday sun. Lamp looks Howie up and down and shakes his head. Howie leans against the Jeep and starts talking, and Carr curses another conversation he isn't going to hear.

Whatever Howie's saying, he's saying it fast, and Lamp holds up a hand and looks irritated. Howie pauses, rubs a hand over his face, and starts again, more slowly this time. Lamp listens and begins to shake his head, and the look of irritation is replaced by one of vague disgust. Carr's phone vibrates.

"Me and Mike are in the van," Bobby says. "You see this?"

"I see it," Carr answers, "but I have no idea what he's saying."

"Whatever it is, Lamp's not crazy for it. You'd figure a guy like him has heard it all before."

Lamp is still shaking his head, and Bessemer is still talking, leaning more heavily now against the Jeep. Finally Lamp holds up a hand and points at Howie's car. Howie begins to speak again, but Lamp points once more and pulls a cell phone from the pocket of his shorts. He waits until Howie is back in his car, and then he makes his call.

"Who do you think he's calling?" Bobby asks.

"Wish I knew," Carr says.

Lamp talks for a while, glancing now and then at Bessemer. Then he nods his head and punches off. He rubs a hand across the back of his neck, rolls his shoulders, and punches in another number.

This conversation is longer, and Lamp walks around while he has it. He circles his Jeep slowly, inspecting bumpers and kicking tires. Finally Lamp pockets his phone and walks over to Bessemer's car. He raps on the window and Bessemer runs it down. Lamp leans over, props his forearms on the sill, and starts talking.

"Put this on speaker," Carr says into his phone.

And Bobby does. Lamp's voice comes on, hollow, choppy, but the New Orleans accent clear.

"You on for Friday night," Lamp says, "but don't let's make this a regular thing. This kinda product's not for me—too many problems. Too much fucking risk. Your pal want something like this again, you gotta go elsewhere, you get me, bro?"

Howie nods.

"And the folks that bring her, you pay them up front—in cash—or she don't get out of the car."

Howie nods again.

"And best not to fuck with these folks, Howie, you know? Or even talk to them too much."

Lamp doesn't wait for another nod, but climbs into his Jeep and drives away. A cloud of dust hangs over the asphalt, and Bessemer rests his forehead on his steering wheel. He sits this way for five minutes, and then he too leaves.

17

BOBBY AND Mike follow Bessemer from the Brazilian restaurant, and when it's clear he's headed home, they call Carr, who drives with Dennis to the workhouse. They open one of Dennis's laptops and bring up the mics and cameras in Bessemer's cottage. They watch Bessemer fumble ice into a glass, hold a bottle above the tumbler, and pour for a long time. Then they watch him wander to his office and drop heavily into a chair.

They both start when Bessemer's landline rings. Howie doesn't move, but lets the machine answer. It's Willis Stearn, nervous but excited.

"Just calling to see if you'd worked things out—if we're on for Friday, and if she's...if everything is per our discussion. Call me back."

Howie mutters to himself after Stearn hangs up, and finally he speaks out loud. "*Fuck!*"

Then he hauls himself from his chair, digs in a desk drawer, and comes out with a cell phone. He finds a number in its memory, presses a key, and sets the phone on the desk. A woman answers, her voice thin through the phone speaker, and Bessemer asks for Curtis Prager. And gets him.

It is the first time Carr has heard Prager's voice, and it's deeper than he expects, and calmer. It's an oddly denatured voice too, lacking any regional accent or twang—an anchorman's voice, but without the practiced affability. His pleasantries are mechanical and distracted, lacking any actual warmth—a sociable shell over an icy core.

"What can I do you for, Bess? I understand you've been burning up the phone lines."

Bessemer hems and haws for a while, and Carr hears him swallow hard. Finally, he comes out with it. "It's my money, Curt—I need my money back."

There is a long pause from Prager. "Where are you calling from?" he asks.

"Don't worry, I follow the rules—I'm on a prepaid cell, just like you said. It's been a very long time, Curt—years, for chrissakes—and I really need my money."

Prager chuckles patronizingly. "I heard you the first time. We've talked about this before, Bess. Often. You know it's not a simple matter."

Bessemer's voice is nervous but determined. "I know you always make it sound complicated, but I'm still not clear why that should be."

Again, the chuckle. "We've been over it again and again."

"A simple wire transfer—I'm not sure why it's more involved than that."

Another sigh, longer, more impatient. "How many ways can I say it?" Prager asks. "Transferring the money is the easy part. Provenance is the problem."

"But that's . . . isn't that *my* problem?"

"The hell it is," Prager says brusquely. "Who do you think will be the second person the feds want to talk to, as soon as they've eaten you for lunch?"

"We could break it into several transfers, in smaller amounts. I know you know how to—"

Prager's voice turns colder. "That's called *structuring*,

Bess, or maybe you've forgotten. And the feds are always thrilled to find it. It tells them they're on the right track. I know they'd especially love to see it in your bank account."

"They're not still watching me," Bessemer says, with more hope than conviction.

"Really? Is that what all *your* security people tell you? Because *my* security people tell me something different. They say that the feds are still fascinated by what flows through your accounts, and that Tracy and her fucking lawyers do their best to keep them interested."

Dennis looks at Carr, puzzled. Carr shakes his head. When Bessemer speaks again, his voice is a white flag. "I need money, Curt," he says softly.

"I know," Prager says. "And believe me, I'm working on getting it to you. In the meantime, if you need something to tide you over, I'm sure we can work it out. We can do what we've done before: package it as a consulting fee, for client referrals. As long as we give it documentation, and keep it to small amounts, it should be fine."

Prager's reassurances are met with silence. A skeptical silence, Carr thinks, and maybe Prager thinks so too, because his next words are lower and somehow more threatening. "What's the matter, Bess—after everything we've been through, you suddenly decide you don't trust me? All these years, and I still haven't proven I can keep my word?"

Bessemer coughs and sputters, but his declarations of trust come too late: Prager has already hung up.

"What was all that about the feds?" Dennis asks. "We're the only ones following Howie around. And who the hell is Tracy?"

"She's Bessemer's ex," Carr says. "I don't know what the rest of that shit was about." Carr is still rubbing his chin when Bessemer makes a second call—this one to Willis Stearn.

"Friday night, at nine," Howie says when Stearn picks up. His voice is clipped, almost angry.

"At your house?"

"That's what you asked for."

"And she's—"

"It's what you asked for, Willis."

"How old is—"

"For chrissakes, Willis, she's what you fucking ordered!"

Bessemer hangs up, and Dennis stares at Carr, his Adam's apple twitching. They watch on the laptop screen for a while, while Howie drinks in silence

"Tell Bobby and Mike to come back," Carr says finally. "He's not going anywhere."

BOBBY AND Mike bring a lot of beer with them. They all sit around the folding tables in the workhouse, in the glow of the laptop screens. An oily, late-day rain beats at the windows.

"How much gin you think Howie's gonna put away tonight?" Bobby asks between swallows of beer. "I bet he makes it through the bottle, but doesn't hold it down. How about it—anybody want to start a pool?"

Mike drags on a cigarette. "Howie's delivering the goods to Stearn on Friday," he says. "We get video of that, we can put whatever kind of leash we want on him. What do you say, *jefe*—we ready to roll on this?"

Dennis slams his bottle down and some beer sloshes out the top. His face is red, and his reedy voice is trembling. "Video? Are you saying we're just going to sit there and watch while this shit happens?"

They all look at him, surprised. In the time they've known him, they've never heard Dennis raise his voice beyond a goofy laugh. Latin Mike shakes his head, and Carr leans back in his chair.

Bobby looks into his beer. His voice is quiet. "C'mon,

Denny—we've seen bad shit before. Most of what we do is watch scumbags, and if they're not doing boring shit, they're doing bad shit. We've seen people get knifed, get shot, get the crap kicked out of 'em. Get killed. We've done a little of that ourselves."

"This is different. Those people were scumbags too, and they were all adults. Bessemer is talking about a *kid* here."

Mike laughs bitterly. "Jesus," he says, and looks at Carr. "Why don't you talk to him? Tell him to grow up or something." Carr doesn't answer, and Mike shakes his head. He turns back to Dennis. "We don't even know for sure what Stearn ordered, bro."

"Bullshit," Dennis says. "You *know* this girl they're talking about is a kid. Why else would Howie's pimp be so nervous—not to mention Howie shitting his pants?"

"And what do you want to do about it—call the *policía*? Or maybe you're gonna ride to the rescue yourself—go snatch her from Bessemer's place and leave her on the church steps, wrapped in a blanket."

Dennis stares at nothing. "I...I don't know what to do about it," he says softly. "I just don't want to sit there watching—*recording*—while shit like that goes down."

Mike snorts. "You want somebody else to work the video, so you don't have to see?"

"That's not the point."

"You sure about that, junior? Maybe your conscience just needs a little wiggle room."

"Fuck you," Dennis says to Latin Mike, and then he turns to Carr. "If we're going to roll Howie up," he asks, "what are we waiting for? Let's do it now—tonight."

"Which does what, *cabrón*—besides save you from seeing something you don't want to see? The kid they're pimping out would be in the same shit regardless, on top of which we give up some leverage on Bessemer."

Bobby runs a hand through his hair and sighs. "We're not cops, Denny."

Dennis pushes his chair back from the table. "I'm not saying we are. I'm just saying.... Fuck—I don't know what I'm saying."

Mike blows a plume of smoke at the ceiling. "So what are we doing, *jefe*?"

Carr studies his beer, thinking about Prager, recalling the threat heavy in the anchorman voice. *What's the matter, Bess—after everything we've been through, you suddenly decide you don't trust me? All these years, and I still haven't proven I can keep my word?* It had left Bessemer scared, but scared of what?

"There's something we're still not seeing," Carr says softly.

"*Hijo de puta!*" Mike shouts. "What else is there to know? And why the *fuck* do we need to know it?"

Bobby puts a hand on Mike's shoulder, but Mike shakes it off. Bobby looks at Carr. "He has a point: we've got video and sound of the guy buying and selling drugs, arranging hookers for his buddies, and come Friday we'll have him in the middle of who knows what kind of sick shit. What else do we need?"

Carr shakes his head. His voice is low and raspy. "The feds offered to let him walk away from eighteen months in prison if he rolled on Prager, and Bessemer turned them down. Prager's got a grip on him, and I want to know what it is. We get only one shot with Bessemer, and I want to go in holding all the cards."

"I thought he kept his mouth shut because Prager helped him hide money from his wife," Bobby says. "What else—"

Mike cuts him off. "We got the fucking cards already. We got Bessemer with his dick hanging out, and this time he won't be looking at some bullshit Wall Street summer-camp jail. He'll be looking at real prison for the shit we've got on him. There's no way he has the balls for that."

"There's something we're not seeing," Carr says again.

"You're saying you want to wait?" Bobby asks.

He shakes his head slowly. "I'm saying between now and Friday, I want to know what's going on."

"And how the hell we gonna find out?" Mike asks, disgusted.

"That's not your problem," Carr says.

ON HIS apartment's balcony, Carr switches to rum. He puts his bare feet on the railing and tilts back in his chair, and his thoughts skid like bad tires. He thinks about the rain and the heat, and sees Bessemer, slumped over the wheel of his BMW, and wonders again what hold Prager has on him. He sees a light on the water, bobbing and blinking in the dark, and he wonders who might be out there—so far out—on a night like this. He leans forward and squints, but loses sight of it.

The wind shifts, and the smells of wet earth and decaying vegetation come in. He thinks about his father's house, the gray light, his father's eyes, the list of nursing homes Eleanor Calvin has given him, and the messages from her that he's continued to ignore. The light reappears on the water and vanishes again when he tries to fix on it—like a dust mote, he thinks, almost imaginary.

The wind shifts again and a sweet smell—some night-blooming flower—washes across the balcony. He thinks about Valerie—Jill—and Amy Chun leaning close, and wonders how they're spending this rainy evening. He thinks about Tina, curled like a cat on his sofa, about Bobby and Mike, and Bertolli's missing money. He thinks about the wreckage of the van, and Ray-Ray and Declan, and the morgue smell that still rises sometimes from his clothes.

And he thinks again and again about Dennis—his red face, his reedy voice, his disgust. *Are you saying we're just going to sit there and watch while this shit happens?* It seems to Carr he's been doing that for a while now, one way or another. With Declan, and before that with Integral Risk.

It was raining in Mexico City, a halfhearted drizzle on a warm spring day, when Carlos Morilla summoned him to his office tower out in Santa Fe. He was chairman and CEO of Morilla Farmacias, and Integral Risk's largest client in Mexico. Carr was the account manager.

Morilla's face was dark and shuttered as he told Carr to have a seat. His voice was rumbling, and his English without accent. There was not the usual offer of coffee. Morilla slid a blue Integral Risk folder across the desk.

"You are telling me that my Patricia is homosexual?" he said. "My only daughter—a lesbian? This is your finding?"

Carr took a deep breath. "The report draws no conclusions, sir. You requested that we observe Patricia and her friend for a period of time and document their activities. That's what we've done."

Morilla frowned. "Is there another conclusion one could reach?" Carr said nothing and Morilla's face had grown even darker. Morilla sighed. "She is very young, Patricia, and she has led a sheltered life. She is very impressionable—susceptible to the influence of... of the wrong sort of person. So there is something else I would like you to take care of."

Carr thought he'd never gotten proper credit for the patience he'd shown. He hadn't interrupted Morilla's commands, even when the executive's voice had shaken, his face had reddened in a way that reminded Carr of his father's, and he'd snapped his Montblanc pen in two. Carr remained quiet and composed throughout, and when Morilla was done, Carr had taken a deep breath and explained things slowly and carefully.

"Integral Risk is a corporate security firm, sir, and while we deeply value the business we have done together, this is simply not the sort of job we can undertake. It is neither in your best interests, nor in ours. I think, with time to reflect, you might also see that this is not the wisest course for your family."

It was this last suggestion—that someone else, the hired help no less, might know what was best for the Morilla family—that Carr realized too late he should have kept to himself. Morilla had colored deeply, but said nothing for a long time. Then he picked up the phone and called the general manager of Integral Risk Latin America—Carr's boss's boss.

Carr hadn't minded the weeklong enforced vacation. He went to the seashore. He swam every day, and read and drank at night. What he'd minded was learning, when he returned, that Luisa Rios, an art student at UNAM, had had her face slashed from her left earlobe to the corner of her mouth and her right arm broken in three places.

The wind rises, and the sounds of the rain and ocean and thrashing palms merge into a great wave, and Carr's chair is slipping out from under him, falling backward, and Carr with it. The jolt knocks the breath out of him, and his glass breaks on the balcony deck. He carries the pieces inside and dries his face. Then he picks up his cell phone.

"You up for a road trip?" he asks when Valerie answers.

18

THE CHEERLEADER figure is sloppy now, and the etched features are blurred. Her skin is lined and lax, like her paint-stained jeans, and her brown eyes are wary. The avid smile—so much on display in the wedding announcements Carr found online—is nowhere in sight, and her hair, lacquered chestnut in those photos, is curled by the ocean air, sweat-dampened, and streaked with gray. The cheerleader's older sister, Carr thinks: wiser certainly, but angrier too, with little left in the way of expectations. He is certain that more than just time has worked these changes on Tracy Holland—six years of marriage to Howard Bessemer doubtless played a part.

Holland lays her roller in the metal tray, and wipes her hands on her T-shirt. She sweeps hair off her forehead and gazes at Carr suspiciously.

"We rang the bell," he says, smiling. "But no one answered."

Holland frowns and looks at Valerie. "You're the one who called yesterday, about the film? Megan…?" Her voice is scratchy.

Valerie walks through the French doors. She steps around the ladder and the paint cans and extends a hand. "Hecht,

Megan Hecht. Looks like we caught you in the middle of something."

"A place this age, there's always something," Holland says.

Carr nods. The white shingle pile, all porches and dormers, must be 150 years old at least. It sprawls against a hillside, above a rocky stretch of Maine coast and a choppy sea—Townsend Gut emptying into Boothbay Harbor.

Valerie pushes her plaid sleeves above her elbows and looks around the dining room. She smiles appreciatively at the meticulous paint job—dove gray with intricate eggshell trim. "This looks like a pretty big project."

"Scraping and sanding were the hard parts; this is just boring," Holland says. She looks at Carr. "Who is he?"

"Brian," Carr says, putting out a hand.

"Brian helps me with research," Valerie says, "and scouting locations."

"And getting coffee," Carr adds, but still there is no smile from Tracy Holland. She wipes a forearm across her brow, drinks from a sweating bottle of Sam Adams, and moves through the French doors to the porch. Carr and Valerie follow.

"A documentary about Wall Street wives," Holland says, doubtfully. "Not the most sympathetic subjects in the world, are they? Probably do better with a reality TV show—some crap about a bunch of women you love to hate. That's more like it."

"You may have a point," Valerie says. "But as I mentioned on the phone, our director thinks women like you have some interesting stories to tell. A perspective on the crash that we haven't seen before."

"*Women like me,*" she says. "I'm not sure what that means." Holland leads them to a pair of wicker armchairs. She and Valerie sit, and Carr leans on the porch rail.

"Do you mind if we tape?" Carr asks, and reaches for the camera case slung over his shoulder.

Holland frowns. "Yes, I mind. I'm still not sure if I want to be involved in this."

"Sure," Valerie says soothingly. "Talking is great."

"But why talk to me? It's not like Howard and I were boldfaced names in New York. The most coverage he got was when he got arrested."

"The kind of storytelling we do—it's about taking the particular experiences of individuals and finding the broader themes. You and your husband led a certain kind of life in New York: his job, the Upper East Side co-op, private schools, charity boards. Now that's all over—the market, his career, that whole life. And you seem to be a kind of refugee. There are other Wall Street wives in that spot. More than a few."

Tracy Holland sips some beer and looks out at the water. She chuckles again, more bitterly this time. "By which you mean what—women who made deals with the devil, only to find the devil couldn't hold up his end?"

Valerie's smile turns confiding. "Is that what happened," she asks, "a breach of contract on Satan's part?"

Holland smiles back. "Isn't that how those deals always end?" she says. "But you should probably talk to those other wives. It was a long time ago, and I don't think I'm typical of anything."

"No?"

"I'm pretty sure none of my old friends do their own painting, diminished circumstances or not."

"You keep in touch with many of them?" Carr asks.

She squints at him, surprised he has spoken. "No."

"What about your ex-husband? Do you think he was—"

The squint turns into a scowl. "My lawyers deal with him. I don't."

"I was just going to ask if he was typical of men who worked on Wall Street then."

"You think there was only one type—a bunch of Gordon Gekko wannabes in suspenders and slick hair? Kind of out-dated, isn't it?"

Carr makes a conciliatory nod. "I'm sure they're all unique, but maybe they had motivations in common."

"You mean greed."

"It's what makes the markets go, and what inflates bubbles—according to popular wisdom, anyway."

Holland takes an angry swig. "You seem to know it all. I don't see why you need me."

Valerie looks at Carr and coughs discreetly. "I'm sure we know hardly anything," she says, "but I'm hoping you can educate us. What made Howard tick? What led him to Wall Street?"

Holland holds the beer bottle against the side of her neck and sighs. "He wasn't typical. Not one of those people who always had their sights set on a Wall Street career. Basically, most of Howard's trust fund was gone by the time he left college. He needed to work, and he didn't think he could get a job anywhere else."

"It's not like bagging groceries at the supermarket," Valerie says. "There was a lot of competition for those jobs."

"There still is. But Howard didn't have to worry about that—he had family connections at Melton-Peck."

"So it was the only firm that would hire him?"

"So Howard thought. He also thought it was the only thing he was cut out for."

"Banking?"

"He said he wasn't enough of a quant to be a trader, and that he didn't have enough energy to be in sales. He said that catering to the whims of people richer than he was was the closest thing to planning parties for his fraternity, and that was all he was ever good at. Hence private banking."

Valerie nods slowly. "Sounds like he gave it a lot of thought."

Tracy Holland sighs again, more deeply this time. "Another way Howard wasn't typical. Wall Street people aren't much given to self-reflection, not the ones I knew anyway. Howard was different that way."

"Introspective?"

"Enough to know his own failings, though not enough to do anything about them. Does that make him better or worse than the guys who never give it a thought?"

"Doing something is always the hard part," Valerie says. "What were they—his failings?"

"Jesus—where to begin? Always taking the path of least resistance? No impulse control? Chronic self-pity? How about his sense of entitlement? Or his whining about the burdens of growing up with the appearance and expectations of wealth, but without the actual money to back them up?" She takes another sip of Sam Adams and sighs. "You don't have the time, and I don't have the energy."

"Doesn't sound particularly appealing," Valerie says. "Or easy to live with."

"He wasn't."

"So why did you?"

"I found Howard kind of cute, at first—like a blond, blue-eyed teddy bear. He was funny and self-deprecating—more the class cutup than the quarterback types I usually went with, and I liked that. He was sweet, and easy to be with, and if I'm being honest, there was the economic factor too. Fading trust fund or not, Howard seemed to be at the start of a good career when I met him. And where was I then—a pre-K teacher at a private school, and filling in part-time at Sotheby's. That's what a fine arts degree got me—that, and my house painting skills."

Valerie nods. "So cute and funny didn't do it in the long haul?"

"They never had a chance: the longer he worked at the

bank—the more time he spent with those people—the more drinking and whining there was, and the less there was of cute and funny. And having a baby just made it worse. He was useless as a father—well-meaning, I guess, but useless." Holland pauses and laughs bitterly. "Of course, the gambling, the drugs, and the hookers didn't help much."

"Are you serious?" Valerie asks, and Tracy Holland nods.

"Who do you mean by *those people*?" Carr asks. "Who was he spending time with?"

Another frown from Holland. "His clients, his colleagues—all those people."

"Was Curtis Prager in that group?"

The frown deepens, and an icy silence settles on the porch. When Holland speaks again, her voice is tight and low. "I'm the wrong person to talk to about him. Maybe I'm the wrong person to talk to altogether."

The silence expands until Valerie clears her throat and points at Holland's beer bottle. "You have another of those around?"

Holland is surprised, but after a moment she stands. Valerie raises a hand. "Brian can get it, if you tell him where."

Holland pauses and nods uncertainly. "In the kitchen, in the fridge."

Carr takes his time, going back through the dining room and down a hall. The kitchen, when he finds it, is another work-in-progress: new cabinets and countertops, raw wallboard where tiles will go, the smells of sawdust and paint still strong in the air. The old refrigerator is forlorn in a slot that's sized for a larger model. There are layers of paper stuck to it with magnets, and Carr flicks through them. Bills from a dentist, an electrician, a plumber, an invoice from a fuel oil company. There's a calendar too, with drawings of lobster traps and fishing buoys on it, and a dense scrawl of appointments in red ink. Beneath all these there are photographs of a boy.

They are badly rippled by the salt air, but still his resemblance to Howard Bessemer is plain. The same blond hair, though considerably more of it, the same round face and benign, guileless smile. The photos cover a range of ages: at six or seven he is dressed as a colonial soldier, trick-or-treating with a tricorn hat and plastic musket; at eight he's at the helm of a sky-blue sunfish; and at nine and ten and eleven, he's playing soccer—blond hair flying amid clouds of dust and turf. His face is a mask of concentration and resolve. And then a door slams, and there are knobby footsteps behind Carr, and the boy himself is there.

He's twelve now, small and solid and still a soccer player. His cleats and knees are muddy, and his jersey is stained with grass and sweat. His cheeks are red and his thick blond hair is matted. His head is canted as he stares at Carr, and his face and eyes are without expression.

The eyes are dark and wide-spaced, like his mother's, and Carr thinks the camera missed what's important in them: the wells of suspicion, the watchfulness, the deliberation, and the stillness—the sense that the boy is always preparing for the ground to shift beneath him, or to fall away altogether, always waiting for another shoe to drop.

Carr smiles. "You must be Simon," he says. "I'm Brian."

The boy nods slowly, weighing Carr's words and his own reply. "Where's my mom?" Simon Bessemer asks eventually.

"On the porch, with my boss. I'm supposed to bring beer. What position do you play?"

The boy pauses again, considering. "Defense."

"Fullback?"

"Defensive mid."

"You must be fast," Carr says. The boy nods, and Carr

points at his soccer jersey. It's blue, with a broad gold band across the chest. "Boca Juniors?"

Simon Bessemer raises an eyebrow and nearly smiles. "The home jersey."

Carr nods. "I've been to some of their matches."

The near smile turns skeptical, and the boy looks suddenly like his mother. "In Argentina?" Carr nods again, but the disbelief doesn't fade. "I watch them on satellite," the boy says, "on the soccer channel. You're a friend of my mom?"

"We're doing research, my boss and I, for a documentary about Wall Street. About banking."

The boy's forehead clouds with questions, but he doesn't ask any. "My dad worked in banking," he says finally, "when we lived in New York."

Carr nods again. "You must've been pretty young then. You remember much about it?"

Simon Bessemer studies Carr for another moment and shakes his head. "I don't really know him," he says. "I haven't seen him in a while." And he turns and leaves the kitchen.

His footsteps recede down the hall and up a flight of stairs. Carr looks again at the pictures on the fridge. Something in the boy's eyes is familiar, though he cannot say what at first. Something about the watchfulness, and the suspicion. Something about the deliberation. Later, after he has delivered a beer to Valerie and brought another one for Tracy Holland and excused himself again, it comes to him. He is in a hallway powder room, sluicing water on his face, and he looks up, into the mirror, and there it is.

19

"**PORTLAND TO** JFK at eight," Carr says as he comes down the wharf. "Then we pick up a rental and drive to East Hampton."

Valerie grimaces. "Eight *a.m.*? Do we have to be such fucking early birds?"

Carr smiles at her. She takes his hand, and they walk farther out. "There's a worm waiting for us," he says. "At least, I hope there is."

Valerie nods. "Tracy was pretty clear about it," she says. "The date it went from merely intolerable with Bessemer to call-in-the-lawyers bad. She knew when it was, and where he'd been, and she knew that whatever he was doing, he'd been doing it with Prager. Of course, the fact that it was the weekend of their fifth anniversary, and Howard was supposed to have been at home with her, probably helped it stick in her mind.

"Before that weekend—according to her—he was just a middling-to-bad husband and dad, out drinking with clients too often, paying no attention to her or the kid when he was at home, whining all the time. After that weekend was when it went south in a big way: the gambling and drugs and whores—usually with Prager as his wingman. Or vice versa."

"Sounds like a worm to me," Carr says.

What's left of daylight is sputtering out in the low brick skyline of Portland. The sodium lights along the wharf cast an amber glow on Valerie's face. Her hand is warm in his. She leads Carr to the railing, and they look out at the swaying boats.

"She didn't like you," Valerie says after a while.

"Yeah, I got that."

"You shouldn't take it personally—she doesn't like men. She's permanently angry."

"I got that, too. Is it all thanks to Howard?"

"He just finished the job. Her dad started it, and there were others in between."

"You got all that from a beer?"

"It was six beers, each, and it helped that you made yourself scarce." Valerie unwinds her hand and slips it around his waist. "Besides," she says, "I'm a good listener. People open up to me."

"So I've seen."

"Most people, anyway." She looks at the harbor again and starts to whistle something Carr almost recognizes.

He is fairly certain she isn't drunk—he's seen her drink much more than the beers she had with Holland and the bottle of wine he and she shared in the hotel lounge, and with no discernible effect. No, this evening she's something different—something open and unguarded, and seemingly without calculation. A Valerie he hasn't seen before? A performance he hasn't seen, anyway. She leans against him at the rail, and her scent mixes with the smells of diesel and low tide.

"You like the water, don't you?" she asks. "Diving, sailing—all of that."

"I do."

"You grew up around it?"

"I learned to sail when I was a kid."

"Who from?"

"My father."

"You were close to him?"

Carr looks at the bobbing lights and the water, nearly black now. He shakes his head. "I liked it in spite of him."

"An asshole?"

"Like Tracy Holland—permanently pissed off."

"At you?"

"At life; at the world; at my mother. I was a convenient proxy."

The wind picks up, colder now, and Valerie shivers beside him. Carr takes off his blazer and hangs it around her shoulders. Valerie rubs her hand up and down his forearm. "Poor baby boy," she says, chuckling.

"Are you making light of my troubled childhood?"

"Did they smack you around? Or each other?"

"No."

"Then we have different definitions of *troubled*."

"You have that kind of trouble?"

She looks up. Her face is flushed from the wine, and Carr can feel the heat rising from her. "I was too cute to get mad at."

"Even then?"

She nods. "Still, it sucks having an asshole for a dad. Probably sucks worse for a guy. Role models, and all that."

"You're watching too much daytime television down in Boca."

Valerie wraps his jacket around her and laughs. "It explains so much, though—Deke's appeal to you, his big, bluff paternal thing, why you're still picking at what happened in Mendoza like it's a scab."

Carr steps back from the rail. "Definitely too much television."

"Oprah can't tell me shit, babe. You think I can do what I do without knowing what makes people tick? Now tell me Declan wasn't a father figure to you."

"I can't say I've given it much thought."

Valerie laughs. "Of course not."

Carr takes another step back, and puts his hands in the air. "Deke had big plans, he ran a good crew, and he was a good soldier—disciplined, focused, a good motivator. He kept his head in the game, and he made us all rich. That's what I know."

"You're remembering a different guy," she says. "Yes, he thought big, and he ran a good crew—but disciplined? Focused? C'mon, Carr—that's what he had you for. And half the time, he didn't want to listen. Deke liked any excuse to light it up, and you know it. He got bored too easy, and deep down he was a fucking cowboy. Toward the end, it wasn't even down that deep. Personally, I think it was some sort of midlife crisis."

"That's bullshit. Besides Mendoza—"

"I'm not just talking about Mendoza, and you know it. There was César, and before that the Russians in Nicaragua. Before that, there was—"

"That's enough, Vee," Carr says, and his voice is icy.

"Don't go all Eastwood on me now—we were almost having a conversation."

"You were doing the talking."

She smiles at him, and there's a little pity in it. "Okay," she says softly. "But you're remembering a different guy."

She takes his hand again and leads him down the wharf, past a yellow cigarette boat, a chrome-heavy sport fisher, and a big white catamaran. She's whistling again, softly, and Carr sighs.

"What about you?" he asks. "No lingering mommy and daddy issues?"

She laughs. "You don't know anybody more mentally healthy than me."

"Most of the people I know are borderline sociopaths. Your parents stay together?"

Her laugh is sharp, and it echoes like a shot on the water. "They were both military, so they knew how to fight. It was like a nonstop cage match."

"But you have no issues."

She shakes her head and slips her arm around him. "It doesn't always have to be like that, you know—like my parents, and yours. Like the battling Bessemers."

"I haven't seen many examples to the contrary."

Valerie moves in front of him, and slides her hands under his shirt. They're cold and smooth against his ribs, and a shudder runs through him. "Maybe that's what we'll do afterward," she whispers. "You and me. We'll conduct a little research to find some happy couples. We'll be like archaeologists."

"You think we'll have to dig them up?"

Valerie laughs, and her mouth is hungry on his. "Early morning tomorrow," she whispers. "We should call it a night."

20

CARR ARRIVES at the workhouse at three p.m. on Friday. He has swum, showered, shaved, and dressed in a blazer, jeans, and dark glasses. No one inside the house looks as good.

Bobby is bristled and fragile, and he's working slowly though a liter of Coke and an egg sandwich. Latin Mike is also unshaven, vaguely jaundiced, and unconcerned with anything beyond the cup of coffee on the table before him, the cigarette burning in his ashtray, and the bottle of Advil in his hand. Dennis is green, shaking death. Carr lets the door slam behind him and smiles when they wince.

"I see you've been busy while I was away," he says loudly. Mike ignores him, and Bobby flips him the bird over his sandwich. Carr chuckles. "How's our man Bessemer doing?" he asks.

Dennis wipes sweat from his forehead. "Pickled. He was at the gin again last night, and didn't get up until noon. Hasn't been out of the house yet today. Stearn called him an hour ago, to check that his party was still on for tonight."

"And?"

"Howie told him nine o'clock."

"Has he spoken to Prager again?"

"He's tried twice—yesterday and the day before—and got nowhere."

Carr nods. "And Amy Chun? How's she coming along?"

Dennis taps on his keyboard. "Good. I pulled some stuff from her laptop—her personal one, not the Isla Privada equipment."

"And?"

Dennis manages a smile. "She's been e-mailing Val—Jill, I mean. She talks about how she misses her, how much she enjoys hanging out with her."

"Fuckin' Vee," Bobby says through a mouthful of egg.

"Chun's also been searching for anything and everything about Jill Creary on the Web," Dennis says.

"No more stalking Janice Lessig?"

"Not for a while now."

"What's she finding on Jill?"

"Everything we put out there, everything Val asked for. Footprints in New York and in Boston. Modeling, PR, cooking school."

"Chun does all the looking herself? No professional help?"

"All by herself," Dennis says, and scrolls through some e-mail. "Her last note to Jill, she talks about the two of them going on vacation together."

Carr shakes his head. "That's fast."

Mike rouses himself from his coffee to smile bitterly. "A real heartbreaker, that Vee."

Bobby laughs, takes a bite of his sandwich, and wipes his mouth with the back of his hand. He looks at Carr. "You gonna say how your trip went?"

"It went fine, Bobby."

"Fine as in you had a nice little vacation, or fine as in you found something out about Bessemer?"

Carr smiles, but says nothing.

"Asshole," Bobby says, and he takes a long swallow of Coke. "What time do we set up at Howie's tonight?"

Carr's smile widens. "I'm thinking six."

Latin Mike scowls. "Why the hell we need to get there so early? Stearn won't show till nine, and the pimp's people won't be any sooner."

"We don't need to wait for them," Carr says. "We don't need them."

Dennis looks up. "What?"

"We don't need them. We're set for tonight, without them."

Confusion and relief play across Dennis's pale face. "What about Stearn, and Lamp? They're expecting—"

"Howie will sort them out for us."

Latin Mike shakes his head. "Guess *jefe*'s trip worked out okay."

Bobby looks at Carr. "How do you want to work it tonight?"

"We give Bessemer no time to think," Carr says. "I want fear, confusion, and compliance."

Bobby nods, and burps loudly. "You sound just like my ex," he says.

21

WATER GURGLES in the shower drain as Howard Bessemer presses a towel to his face, and then he hears his front door open. He leaves damp footprints on the tiles as he steps cautiously out of his bedroom, and a puddle forms where he stands frozen and stares openmouthed at the men in his entrance foyer.

Carr hands the laptop to Latin Mike. "Set it up in the living room," he says, and Mike nods and walks off. Carr looks at Bessemer. "You want to get your pants on, Howie, or are you good like that?"

Bessemer wraps his towel more tightly about his waist. His mouth closes and opens again and a sound comes out, but it's not a word.

"Pants, Howie."

Bessemer squints, and takes a step backward. "Wha . . . What?"

Carr points to the bedroom. "Pants."

"Who. . . . Who the hell are—"

"Get your fucking pants on, Howie," Carr says, smiling, and he unbuttons his blazer and lets Bessemer see the Glock in his belt. Bessemer backs slowly into the bedroom, and Carr counts to twenty. When he walks to the bedroom door, he finds Bessemer holding the telephone handset, staring at it.

"Just out of curiosity, Howie, if the phone was working, just who do you think you'd call?"

Bessemer drops the phone and stumbles on the edge of his towel. Carr waits in the doorway while Bessemer dresses in Madras shorts and a polo shirt that's too tight across the gut. Then he walks him into the living room.

It's a long, bright space, with Persian rugs on the floor, equestrian sketches on the walls, and teak and rattan furniture that is old but still solid. Latin Mike is standing at a black lacquer cabinet whose doors are open to reveal barware and bottles. He pours two fingers of Glenlivet into a tumbler and offers the bottle to Carr.

"Not just now," Carr says. "You have the disk?" Latin Mike produces a DVD case and scales it across the room. Carr plucks it from the air. "Collect his cell phones. They should be in the office." Mike downs the scotch and nods, and Carr carries the DVD to the laptop that is open on a low teak table by the sofa.

"Have a seat, Howie," Carr says.

Bessemer draws himself up and takes a deep breath. "Just who the *hell* are you, and what do you think you're doing in my house?" The teddy bear face is damp and pink, and the voice is shaky.

Carr puts a hand on Bessemer's shoulder, spreads his fingers across Bessemer's collarbone, and digs. Bessemer cries out and collapses to one knee. "What the fuck!" His face is red and there are tears in his eyes.

Carr yanks Bessemer to his feet again. "On the sofa, Howie. Shut up, and watch the movie."

Bessemer perches unsteadily on the edge of the sofa and Carr slips a disk into the laptop. It whirrs and hums and a video starts to play. And Howard Bessemer goes pale.

Carr stands silent for several minutes, watching the video and watching the teddy bear split at the seams. When he sees Bessemer's hands tremble and his chin quiver, Carr clears his throat. "Guess it's true what they say about the camera, Howie—it adds ten pounds, at least. But still, it's easy to tell it's you. Easy to identify your friends too: Brunt and Scoville, Tandy and Moyer, and if you wait just a minute you'll see Lamp and the Grigoriev brothers as well. See—you can even make out their license plates. And the audio is good quality—nice and clean—you all sound like yourselves."

Bessemer moans, and Carr puts a hand on his shoulder, gently this time. "This is just the highlight reel, Howie. We've got hours more of you guys—phone conversations, payments being made, dope being delivered, girls…lots of stuff."

Bessemer waves his hands, as if he's shooing away gnats. His voice is a frightened whisper. "You…you're cops," he says.

"Oh no, Howie." Carr laughs. "We're much worse than that."

22

CARR IS sitting in an armchair, drinking soda water from a highball glass and leafing through a month-old copy of *The New Yorker*, when the teddy bear groans and lifts his head from the waste can. Carr places his glass on an end table and watches as Bessemer's gumdrop eyes dart about the room—ceiling to floor, wall to wall, lingering over the laptop, and coming to rest finally on the highball glass on its coaster and the Glock beside it.

Carr smiles benevolently. "All done throwing up? You want some water now?"

Bessemer shakes his head and sits back on the sofa. He runs a hand through his thin hair and across his mouth. His eyes dart some more, and then light on a brass clock atop the liquor cabinet.

"Yes, it is getting late," Carr says. "Time to call Stearn, and Lamp. Tell each of them that the other one has canceled on you. Tell them that you don't know why, and that you'll have to get back to them to reschedule. Best to be brief and vague." Bessemer looks at him and squints, as if straining to remember something. "Are you sure you wouldn't like some water?" Carr asks again.

"Who *are* you?" he asks.

Carr shakes his head and calls out: "Can we get Howie a phone?" Latin Mike emerges from the kitchen with one of Bessemer's cell phones. He tosses it to Bessemer, who jumps as if it's a hand grenade. Mike laughs.

"Stearn," Carr says, "and then Lamp. Then we'll talk."

"Who…?"

"Make the calls, Howie."

And Bessemer does. He's both brief and vague, and all the time he talks, he never takes his eyes off the gun on the end table. When he's done, he hands the phone back to Carr and lies back on the sofa. He closes his eyes, presses his fingers to them, and opens them again. He looks surprised to find Carr still there.

"I'll have that water now," he says.

Carr goes into the kitchen and brings out a glass, with ice. Bessemer sits up and drinks it all. "Who are you?" he asks Carr.

"Gregory Frye," Carr answers, and puts out his hand. Bessemer's grip is soft and damp. "And I'm not a cop."

"Then what the hell are you doing in my house, acting like it's your goddamn house? Who *are* you, and what the hell do you want from me?"

Carr chuckles and finishes his drink. "I'm the guy who doesn't care what you're doing with Willis Stearn or Daniel Brunt or Nick Scoville, or Tandy or Moyer, or Lamp, or the Grigoriev brothers." Carr points at Bessemer's glass. "Refill?"

Bessemer blanches, and Carr wonders if he's going to vomit again. But Bessemer rights himself, smooths his hair, and sits up straight. "I don't know what you're talking about."

Carr shakes his head. "Let's not do *that*, Howie."

Bessemer wipes his forehead. "I'm going to call the police."

Carr sighs and hands him the telephone. "Really, Howie,

the dramatics are a big waste. You pretend, I threaten, and round and round we go. Why put yourself through it? You must be tired after the past few days. All that worrying. All that running around. It's a long way from the Upper East Side, isn't it? From Otisville too—though maybe not quite as long."

"I don't know what you're—"

"It's hard to argue with video, Howie."

Bessemer sits frozen with the phone in his hand. His polo shirt is mottled with sweat, and his face is a crumbling mask of fear and confusion. His eyes race around the room again and come to rest on his Persian rug. He doesn't resist when Carr takes the phone from him.

"What do you want?" Bessemer asks softly.

"I want to meet a friend of yours."

Bessemer squints again. "Who—Willis? Nicky? Danny Brunt?"

"None of those guys."

"Well, I don't have any other friends. Not anymore."

"You've got at least one, Howie—an old friend."

He shakes his head. "I don't know who—"

"Curtis Prager. I want you to introduce me to Curtis Prager."

Bessemer straightens his shoulders, and lines of defiance appear around his eyes. "Who is—"

Carr sighs. "You steered investors to him when he was starting Tirol Capital. You put your own money in. He helped you hide some of it when your wife was divorcing you."

"He didn't—"

"Your wife's lawyers thought he did, even if they couldn't prove it."

Bessemer's mouth stiffens. "I don't know him."

Carr shakes his head regretfully, and his voice falls to a

whisper. "I'll put up with a certain amount of drama, Howie. I suppose it's unavoidable. But I won't tolerate lying. And especially not this kind of thing—it's insulting. You might as well call me an idiot. My clothes, my grammar, my reading this magazine and bringing you water, may have given you the wrong idea about me. You may think I'm very different from Lamp and the Grigorievs and the other trash you've been hanging with, but in the ways most relevant to your health, I promise you I'm not."

Bessemer's body softens and slumps. Carr claps him lightly on the shoulder and carries his highball glass to the kitchen. He returns with it refilled and Bessemer looks at him.

"What do you want with Curtis?" he says.

"To meet him. To do business."

"I'll give you his number. You can call his secretary and make an appointment."

Carr laughs. "I had a more personal intro in mind."

Bessemer drinks some water and spills more down his shirtfront. He wipes his mouth with his fingertips, gathers his breath, and sits up straighter. "Listen, Mr. Frye, you might've done me a favor tonight—keeping me from doing something I wasn't looking forward to—so I'll give you some valuable advice, for absolutely no charge: I don't know what business you think you want to do with Curtis Prager, but whatever it is, you don't want to do it. Whatever it is—and I'm not asking what—I tell you, it won't work out. It won't end well, for you or anyone else involved. Anyone besides Curtis."

"And who knows better than you?"

Bessemer slumps again. "What's that mean?"

"It means your own business with Prager hasn't panned out so well. It means he has your money and doesn't want to give it back, so now you earn your gambling, coke, and hooker money by dealing dope to your friends and procuring prostitutes for them. And call me Greg, Howie."

Bessemer blanches and swallows hard, and Carr smiles to himself. "Who are you?" Bessemer whispers.

"Wrong question. You should be asking, *What's in it for me? What can Greg Frye do for me?*"

"And what would that be?"

"I can get you out from under, Howie—out of the low-margin fetching and carrying you do for your pals, out of your grandma's bungalow, out of scratching at the doors of clubs that won't have you for a member. I can get you out of this life altogether. I can get your money back—your money and then some."

Howard Bessemer stands and shakes his head. "I...I want no part of that."

"No part of what, Howie?"

"If you're thinking about...I don't know what you're thinking about—all I know is I want no part of it."

Carr sits back in his chair. He nods slowly and drums his fingers on the armrest. "Not surprising, I guess. You heard that offer before, or something like it, just before they put you on the bus for Otisville. *Talk to us about Curtis Prager and get out of jail free.* But you didn't bite then."

Bessemer's eyes are wide now, and he's pointing. "You *are* a cop!"

"I'm not, Howie, and don't yell."

"Then who the fuck are you?"

"Again, wrong question."

"No—I don't *care* what you can do! Whatever you're thinking, forget it. You can't—"

Carr holds up a hand, cuts Bessemer off, and lets quiet descend on the room. He takes a deep breath. Time to climb the ladder, he thinks, and his own heart begins to pound. "If you don't care what I can do *for* you," Carr says, "then worry about what I can do *to* you."

"I don't—"

Carr cuts Bessemer off again. He works a hard look onto his face and an angry edge into his voice. "I'm not just talking about video of you and those country club shitheads doing lines, Howie. Drugs and whores are not even frosting on this cake."

"What—"

"And I'm not one of your ex-wife's asshole lawyers, either. I'm not stupid enough to think you kept quiet just because Prager sheltered funds for you. And I certainly don't think it's because you're a stand-up guy."

"I don't know what you're talking about," Bessemer says, so softly Carr can barely make it out.

Carr stares at him. Time to step onto the platform. "I'm talking about the hold Curtis Prager has on you, Howard— the reason you kept your mouth shut and did your time, and the reason you're still taking his shit today. I'm saying that *I know*, Howard. I know, and I have no problem using it."

"Really, Mr. Frye—Greg—I don't know—"

Carr takes a deep breath. Time to dive. "Sarah Cotter," he says evenly. "Sarah Cotter."

In the silent seconds that follow, the dive becomes a spinning, sickening free fall. Puzzlement supplants fear on Bessemer's face, and Carr is suddenly sure that he's gotten it all wrong—that he and Valerie somehow read too much into what Tracy Holland said, heard what they'd wanted to hear, and connected dots in East Hampton that formed no hidden picture at all, but were nothing more than . . . dots. Bessemer squints at him, and Carr feels his temples pound and a line of sweat slide down his spine. His mind races through unlikely alternate plans—a desperate landscape of threats and blandishments—as the silence expands. And then Howard Bessemer sways before him, his knees buckle, and he sits abruptly on the sofa, as if his spine has turned to water.

Carr breathes a long sigh and lets his voice soften.

"After all these years, it's still an open case, but I guess that's no surprise. A young woman like Sarah Cotter—just twenty-three—hit and run so early in the morning, and not a witness to be found. No forensic evidence either—no paint transfer or tire tracks, nothing. The police out there don't get too many cases like that."

Bessemer is staring now, at nothing in the room. He's paper-white, and his hands are shaking. "You're a cop," he whispers, and to Carr it sounds like a plea. He sits on the sofa and puts a hand on Bessemer's shoulder.

"I'm really not," he says quietly.

Bessemer looks at him—disappointed, Carr thinks. "It was so early," Bessemer says after a long while. His voice is low and exhausted. "The middle of the night really—no light in the sky at all—and there was fog too, like goddamn soup. I still wonder what the hell she was doing out there in the dark. Who rides a bike in the dark like that?"

"She was training for a triathlon."

"I read that in the papers. But still—what the hell was she doing there?"

"That time of night, the fog—it must've been hard to see."

Bessemer squints at him and shakes his head. "That's what Curtis said, when I drove back to his place—*even sober, you'd never have seen her, Bess*. Then he woke up his security guy and told me he'd take care of everything. And fuck me if I didn't believe him."

Bessemer hangs his head, and a shudder runs through him. Carr claps him on the arm. "You can't change the past, Howie, but you don't have to be a prisoner of it."

Bessemer shrinks from his hand. "What bullshit," he says. "What total bullshit. What you really mean is that I can trade one jailer for another—Prager for you."

Carr sighs, crosses the room again, and picks up his gun. He blows a speck of something off the barrel and slips it into his belt. "You're looking at it the wrong way. I've put a carrot *and* a stick on the table: you help me out and you get your money back and get out of this life; you don't help, and... well, we both know how that goes. With Prager, you get only the stick—and you've been getting it for years. I figure you've got to be a little tired of it by now."

Bessemer makes a sound halfway between a groan and a bitter laugh and pushes his hands through his thin hair. "I need something more than water," he says, and points to the liquor cabinet. Carr nods. Bessemer walks unsteadily to it, and finds a bottle of Bombay Sapphire inside. He pours some into a glass, drinks half, and coughs. He shakes his head slowly.

"You're planning on...on stealing from him?" Bessemer struggles with the word *stealing*, as if just speaking it is enough to bring down thunder. Carr looks at him and says nothing, and Bessemer takes that as an answer. "If I got involved in this—if I helped you—and Curtis found out, prison wouldn't be the problem, if you know what I mean. Curtis and the people who work for him—the people he knows—they're capable of—"

"I know who they are, Howie, and what they're capable of. You get your money back, you can afford to go somewhere else. To be somebody else."

"What—an alias? A new identity?"

"You're really happy with the old one?"

"But I...I wouldn't know how—"

"It's not hard, Howie. I can show you."

Bessemer drinks the rest of his gin and massages his temples with his thumbs. He rummages again in the liquor cabinet. He comes out with a mirror, a razor blade, a silver straw, and a small white envelope. He taps a pile of white powder onto the mirror and draws it into six thin lines. He bends over the mirror and four of the lines disappear. He looks up at Carr.

"First Curtis, then Misha and Sasha, then Stearn, and now you," Bessemer says, sniffling. "I don't know why this keeps happening. Sometimes I feel like I have a sign around my neck—*kick me*, or something."

"The Grigorievs are squeezing you?" Carr asks, and Bessemer nods. "Stearn too?" Another nod.

"The brokering that I do—with the drugs and the girls—Misha and Sasha got me into it. I ran up a big tab with them—bigger than my cash flow could handle—and they suggested a way I could pay it off. *Suggested* isn't quite the right word actually."

"Insisted?"

"That's closer. Anyway, that's how it got started, but this thing tonight, with Willis…I've never been involved in anything like that before. When I found out what he wanted, I tried to beg off. I told him I didn't have those kinds of contacts, but he wouldn't hear it. He said I was getting a reputation around town, and that I needed to be careful. He said things could get awkward for me if rumors got back to the police." Bessemer offers Carr the straw.

Carr smiles. "Not just now."

Bessemer snorts another line. "You see, I haven't been lucky recently. So how do I know, if I get involved with this, it won't turn out the same? What assurance do I have?"

Carr nods and smiles sympathetically. "Other than my word as the guy holding the gun, you have none. But you also have no choice. Not to put too fine a point on it."

Bessemer looks at Carr and then looks down at the mirror atop the liquor cabinet, at the last line of cocaine, at his own reflection. He bends, snorts the final line, and wipes his nose with the back of his hand.

"Who are you supposed to be?" he asks, sniffling. "When I talk to Curtis, what am I supposed to say?"

"I'm a guy you met in Otisville, a good guy, someone who

helped you when you were inside. Say that we've stayed in touch, and now I'm in the market for a banker. We'll do the details later."

"And when you meet with him, then what happens?"

"I do a little business with him."

"You know it won't be that simple, right? Curtis checks. He checks on everything, very carefully, and then he double-checks."

Carr nods and finishes his soda water. "Don't worry, Howie. I'm double-checkable."

23

"**HE SOUNDS** like a whiner, and more than a little screwy," Tina says to Carr, as the tide runs over their bare feet.

Carr looks at her over the top of his sunglasses. "He's both of those, and a lush to boot. And a cokehead."

"Well, I feel much better." Tina laughs. "And I can't wait to tell the boss. He'll love it that your whole plan hangs on a guy like this." They turn and walk north through the creaming surf. The hem of her gauzy black skirt and Carr's rolled cuffs are damp with foam.

"I can't say I'm thrilled myself," Carr says, "but it's not like there were a lot of options, or a lot of time."

Tina shrugs and watches the ocean, glassy and orange in the late daylight. "How's Bessemer adapting to his new circumstances?"

"He's self-medicating on gin and blow, but he's behaving. I've got a babysitter with him all the time, and I think he likes the company."

"When push comes to shove is he going to cooperate? Is he going to stick to the script with Prager? Will he be convincing?"

"He'll get there. Right now he's mostly scared."

"Of who?"

"Of Prager; of me."

"Who's got the edge?"

"We're holding the same threat over his head, but I'm the guy in his living room with a gun. Plus, I've got the carrots."

"And he believes in them?"

"He wants to, but he's not sure."

"So maybe he's not completely stupid," Tina says, tracking a gull as it swoops above some flotsam. "That was a nice piece of research up north, by the way, with the Cotter thing. A big roll of the dice, for sure, but it worked out. You could be a cop."

Carr shrugs. "Bessemer's ex was the key. She gave us the where and the when. That made it a whole lot easier to figure out the what—especially since it happened in the off-season. It was a big deal for the papers out there—the only real news they had to report at the time. And the place they found her—that stretch of road—it was one of the routes you'd take if you were driving from Prager's place to the highway."

"Still, a risky play," Tina says. "It hasn't occurred to Bessemer that Prager can't rat him out without implicating himself in the cover-up?"

"He said he tried that line of reasoning once, and never again. Prager told him he could get a dozen people to swear that it never happened—that Bessemer drove off in the middle of the night and didn't return, and that Prager wasn't even in East Hampton at the time."

Tina nods, still following the gull as if she's taking aim. They come to a hotel beach, and a hotel bar with shaded tables. Tina points. "I need to get out of the sun."

Carr orders an iced tea, Tina a lime soda. She takes a sip and shakes out her hair. It shimmers like white tinsel. "When are you going to have him make the call?" she asks.

"In a few days. I want him to settle down a while longer, and I want to go over the story with him some more."

"Dennis fix up your past?"

Carr nods. "Bumped some servers at Justice and the Bureau of Prisons. Frye did federal time for receiving stolen property. Overlapped eight months with Howie in Otisville. Before that, a money laundering beef, with charges eventually dropped. Nowadays, he's based in Boston. Has a nice little online business selling jeweler supplies to the trade."

"Too bad it's bullshit—I bet he could get me a deal on some earrings. How are things going in Boca?"

Carr takes a long swallow of iced tea and looks into his glass. "Val says it's going well."

"Love is in the air?"

"She's got Chun locked in. She'll be all but moved in there soon, and then she can plant whatever we want, and clean it up again before the security sweeps."

"She was a big help with Bessemer's ex, I guess. A regular Watson to your Holmes."

Carr nods. Tina rests her heel on the edge of her seat. Her skirt falls away and her bare leg is like ivory. She brushes sand from her bare foot. "You don't like talking about her," she says.

Carr's voice is carefully neutral. "Are there questions I haven't answered? Something you want to know that I haven't told you?"

"You and she have a thing going, once upon a time? Or maybe going on now?"

Carr's face is taut. "Who's asking—Boyce or you?"

Tina lowers one foot, raises another, brushes away sand. A tiny smile flickers on her lips. "You're a big boy, and nobody's playing chaperone. It's just not typically the best management technique. *Don't shit where you eat*, et cetera. Fucks up unit cohesion. Doesn't help command judgment much either."

The sun has dropped behind the hotel tower and the sky

is washed in violet. Carr drops some bills on the table. "Let's walk," he says.

Carr heads for the shoreline. The sand is cooler, and he turns north again, for a jetty a quarter mile away. Tina is silent at his side.

"How are things in the Prager compound?" Carr asks eventually.

"Same same," Tina says. "He's getting ready for his prospecting trip to Europe and Asia. Silva still hasn't surfaced from whatever glass he's climbed into."

"Good," Carr says. He stops and digs a flat stone the size of a silver dollar from the sand. He launches it in low, spinning flight over the smooth water, and it bounces and jinks more times than he can count before vanishing into a gray swell. "And down south?" he asks. "Are we making any progress there?"

"Maybe. Our guys were in Santiago, trying to locate the pilot Declan made his exit arrangements with. They went trolling at the bars near Los Cerrillos—the pilot bars—and got a hit. Found a charter operator named Guerrero. He's got a light jet, a Hawker, and he's apparently used to working for cash, and with no questions asked. You know the name?"

Carr shakes his head. "Is he the guy Declan hired?"

"He told my guys he took a deposit from someone that sounds a lot like Declan."

"Declan's plan was to go to São Paulo. From there, there were a lot of options to get back to Port of Spain. Where was this Guerrero supposed to go?"

"He wouldn't say. He wouldn't say anything else without money."

"Your guys didn't want to pay?"

"My guys check with me first. I told them I'd come down and see for myself. I'm flying out of Miami tomorrow."

Carr stops and looks at Tina. The tide rushes up over

their ankles and he sees a shiver run through her. "This is a lot of personal attention," he says.

Tina takes off her sunglasses and nods. "You got me interested."

CARR'S PHONE burrs as he opens the door to his apartment. He answers without looking and Eleanor Calvin's voice takes him by surprise. She is just as surprised by his.

"I didn't think I'd actually reach you," she says. "I've tried so many times."

"I've gotten your messages, Mrs. Calvin, but things have been crazy at work."

"I'm sure, dear."

"How's your move coming? Are you showing the house yet?"

"I've got an offer on it—two, actually. The real estate agent thinks there might even be a third one coming. They all want to close soon."

Carr stands in the darkened living room and takes a deep breath. "Oh," he says.

"Have you settled the arrangements for your father, dear?"

"I'm working on it, Mrs. Calvin."

"I know it's difficult for you, but there isn't much time."

Carr walks to the window and leans his head against the glass. "I'm aware, Mrs. Calvin."

"I know you are, dear, and I didn't call to talk about this. The ambassador is a little agitated this evening, and he wants to speak with you."

"Agitated about what, Mrs. Calvin? I really don't have—"

"I'm not sure what's upset him, but he's insistent. He's been...difficult all day, and I'm afraid he's been drinking."

Carr sighs. "Put him on," he says.

His father's voice is scratchy and attenuated across the ether, and he sounds to Carr like an old recording of FDR. Nothing to fear but fear itself. He seems at first more angry than drunk.

"She lies to me, you know. Tells me she's done things when she hasn't. Tells me she hasn't done things when I know she has. And she takes things. That's why I can never find a goddamn thing in this house."

"Mrs. Calvin doesn't take things, and she doesn't lie. She's not your maid either."

"You're taking her side."

"There's no side to this."

"You're just like her, you know."

"Like Mrs. Calvin?"

"Don't be thick. You're just like her—always watching—like a goddamn cat. Quiet like a cat, and arrogant—no one can tell you anything, oh no. And stubborn—goddamn stubborn— just like her. Everything on your terms, and you won't let go until you're goddamn good and ready."

"I don't know what you're talking about, Dad," Carr says, and he sighs heavily. "What is it you're upset over?"

"I can't find it. I spent all day looking. Looked in her room, in your room, even got up in the goddamn attic, and I can't find it."

"Can't find what?"

"The *plata*. I can't find her *plata*."

Carr puts his hand out in the darkness and finds the back of a chair. It fails to anchor him in the present.

Plata. Carr gave it that name, the family story went, when he was three or so, and speaking his first words of Spanish. They were in Lima, and the *plata* was an S. T. Dupont cigarette lighter, a tiny, weighty slab of silver that the young Carr liked to play with. It was a gift to his mother from her sometimes tennis partner, the courtly, ever-smiling Sr.

Farías—commemorating not only their success in the Club Regatas mixed doubles tournament, but also his appreciation of Andrea Carr's help in landing the Spanish journalist an interview with the new American ambassador.

Hector Farías turned up all over Latin America, bouncing from country to country at least as often as the Carrs. And whenever they found themselves living in the same cities, Farías and Andrea Carr resumed their tennis. Carr's recollections of him are mostly blurred and, he knows, mostly composites. Farías in tennis whites, drink in hand, his hair wavy and damp, his teeth like white tiles. Farías at a consular reception, his shirt like a cloud, his shoes like glass, smoke curling from his smiling mouth. Farías on the living room sofa, straightening his tie, tugging at his cuffs, grinning at Carr, while his mother, cheeks burning, stepped quickly to the window and smoothed her skirts. Which living room was that?

His clearest memory of Farías, though, is from a photograph in a Buenos Aires newspaper. It was already three months old when he saw it on his father's desk, and they'd been in Stockbridge for almost that long, sorting through boxes others had packed for them so hurriedly in Mexico City. The unannounced visits from the dark-suited, block-shouldered men, their long discussions with his parents—together and separately—behind closed doors, the trips his parents made to Boston and Washington, had all grown less frequent. It was a good photo—not grainy at all—Farías with a trench coat over his broad shoulders, flanked by a pair of uniformed policemen, his hands thrust awkwardly before him, the handcuffs snug around his wrists. *Un Espía Cubano* was the caption.

"I can't find it," Arthur Carr says again.

"Why do you want it?" Carr asks.

"It's none of your goddamn business why I want it. Maybe I want to light a cigar. Maybe I want to burn down the house. Why the hell do you care? I just want it."

Carr drops into the chair and looks out at the empty night. He sighs again. "You're not going to find it."

"Because she took it. I told you, she takes things."

"Mrs. Calvin didn't take it."

"Then where the hell is it?"

"It's in the. . . . It's with her—with Mom. You buried it with her, Dad."

24

"**A FULL** boat," Howard Bessemer says to Bobby. "Jacks over eights." He sweeps the chips from the center of the dining table into the large pile already in front of him. "It's just not your night."

It is nine a.m., and sunlight is streaming through the windows of Bessemer's dining room, reflecting from the white plaster walls, refracting through the crystal ashtray, the highball glasses, the bottle of gin on the table, and the curtain of smoke above.

He turns to Carr and smiles. "Top of the mornin', Gregory," he says. Bessemer is a dissipated teddy bear today, in seersucker pajama bottoms, a New York Athletic Club T-shirt, and a three-day beard that is a dirty-blond shadow on his pudgy cheeks. His blond hair is bent at odd angles, his gumdrop eyes are red and shiny, and so is the new cut at the corner of his mouth. He picks a joint from the ashtray, lights it, and takes a long hit. "Deal you in?" he asks.

"Not just now, Howie," Carr says, and he hands Bobby one of the grocery bags he's carrying. "Let's make coffee."

Bobby follows Carr to the kitchen and empties the bag onto the counter. Egg sandwiches, bagels, fruit salad in a plastic tub. There's a TV on the counter and Carr switches it on and turns up the volume. He tosses Bobby a pound of ground coffee. "Late night?" Carr asks, his voice low.

"Howie couldn't sleep. He wanted to play cards, so we played."

"You get high too?"

Bobby yawns and flips him the bird. "Yeah, baby, I'm trippin' on Coca-Cola and potato chips."

"You hit him?" Carr asks. Bobby spoons coffee into the machine. "Bobby?" Carr says again. Bobby fills the coffee-maker with water and presses the button. He looks at Carr but stays silent. "Bobby?"

"It was nothing. Mike was a little torqued up, and Howie was whining about something and Mike told him to shut up. Howie got mouthy and Mike got pissed."

"And hit him."

"Barely."

"For chrissakes, Bobby, we need him in one piece."

"Hey, I broke it up right away. And it's not like we're keeping the guy around long-term."

Carr frowns. "While we've got him, we need him happy."

"I'm down like two hundred bucks to the guy. That's not happy enough?"

Carr shakes his head. "What's got Mike twisted up?"

"Who the fuck knows?" Bobby says, unwrapping a sandwich. "It's gettin' so he's almost as moody a bastard as you."

Bessemer has finished his joint when Carr carries a sandwich and a cup of coffee into the dining room, and he's stacking his chips into neat columns before him.

"I make it two hundred fifteen dollars I've taken off him," he says.

"He's good for it. Sorry about the bruise."

Bessemer shrugs. "Your other friend is kind of an asshole, Greg. No fun to hang with at all."

"He'll take it easy as long as you do, Howie. Everybody's

a little stir-crazy, and the sooner we move things along, the better."

"Amen to that," Bessemer says, and takes a slug of gin. Carr takes the glass from him and slides the sandwich and coffee in front of him.

"Let's do breakfast now, Howie. Then we'll do the story."

It takes Bessemer two sandwiches, three cups of coffee, and a long shower before he's ready, and then he and Carr settle in Bessemer's office. Sunlight seeps around the edges of the shades, but Carr leaves them drawn. He sits at the desk and turns on a brass lamp. Bessemer sprawls in a studded leather chair.

"Take it from the top, Howie," Carr says.

And Bessemer does. He's got the facts down cold: how he met Greg Frye in Otisville, where Frye was serving out the last months of a federal sentence for trafficking in stolen diamonds; how Frye had helped him learn the ropes there, and avoid the predations of the rougher trade; how they've kept in touch over the years; and how Frye has come down to Palm Beach in search of a banker, and—possibly—a business partner. And his delivery is solid: offhand, uncomplicated, adorned with enough detail to be convincing, but not enough to be dangerous. Bessemer is an apt pupil—at home with deception—but Carr knows that drills are one thing and live fire something else entirely.

Bessemer yawns and rubs his eyes. "I might crash right here, Greg," he says.

"Not yet," Carr says. "You think Prager's going to be interested?"

Bessemer smiles. "You're asking me now? I thought you knew it all."

There's a drinks tray on the credenza behind the desk, and Carr pours a gin and hands it to Bessemer. "You actually know the guy."

Bessemer sits up, and curiosity sparks in his bloodshot

eyes. He sips at the gin. "Curt will be interested enough to talk. Why wouldn't he be? I've referred clients to Isla Privada before, and even if he doesn't take them on, he always talks. Talking's free, he says. Besides, he'll like the synergy."

"Meaning?"

"Meaning a client who can broaden his business model is better than a plain old client to him. Curt will like the idea of taking your money—assuming there's enough of it— but he'll like the diamonds even more. Someone who can take cash in exchange for diamonds, and who can do it in quantity—that's going to appeal to him. Diamonds are a lot easier to move than cash. And if you tell him you've got a network of people around the world who can do the transaction in reverse—take in diamonds and pay out cash—well, that's a new model." Bessemer takes another drink and smiles at Carr. "Assuming your story is solid."

"It is."

"Because if it isn't—if it's not granite—"

"It is, Howard."

"You're confident," Bessemer says, finishing his drink. "That's good."

"You should be confident too. You should be thinking about what you want to do afterward, when you get your money back."

Bessemer sighs and looks at his empty glass. "I have been thinking about it."

"And?"

Bessemer furrows his broad brow. "I don't know. I'm skittish about making plans. Seems whenever I do, things never work out. Sometimes I think the best way for me to make sure that I *don't* do something is for me to make a plan to do it."

Carr shakes his head. "Kind of self-defeating, isn't it?"

"Self-defeat's my best thing."

"Maybe this is an opportunity to turn over a new leaf."

"That kind of plan is always the most disappointing."

"Then start small."

Bessemer nods slowly. "I could get myself cleaned up—lose some weight, ease up on this." He holds up his glass. "Maybe try to get fit."

"All good ideas."

"Then maybe I could spend some time with my kid. He's twelve now, and I haven't seen him in…a long time."

"Baby steps, Howie. Baby steps."

BESSEMER STRETCHES out on the office sofa and dozes. He shifts around occasionally and murmurs words that Carr can't make out. Asleep he looks younger, Carr thinks, and much like his son. Carr empties ashtrays and fills the dishwasher and makes himself another cup of coffee. He looks out the window, at a jet crossing the sky, and thinks about Tina, flying down to Santiago, and Guerrero, who may have been Declan's pilot. He thinks about Declan, and his hastily sketched exit plan from Mendoza, and he remembers Valerie's words on the wharf in Portland.

You're remembering a different guy, she said, and Carr knows she's right. Sometimes it seems that he's remembering several different guys. It's like a hall of mirrors, and everywhere there's a version of Declan—short, tall, skinny, fat…

There's the grinning red pirate who recruited him in Mexico; the wise mentor who taught him the ropes; and the tough, charismatic soldier who executed plans with precision and economy, improvised like Coltrane whenever things went sideways, and always led from the front.

Then there's the melancholy, whiskey-voiced raconteur, sitting in a darkened bar, spinning out tales of his days in the service—in Ireland, the Middle East, and at unnamed stops along the Silk Road—of the hell he raised with other crews, and the swag he hauled away. And there is the weary campaigner, aging, aching, and contemplating retirement with a mix of anticipation and dread. Those incarnations didn't turn up often, and when they did it was always just before a job, or just after one.

And then there's the Declan Valerie had in mind—the erratic, reckless Declan, the willful, capricious one. It's hard—impossible, really—for Carr to reconcile her version with those others, but he can't say he hasn't seen them before. He has, in bits and pieces, several times over the years. And especially toward the end.

He hears Valerie's voice again: *There was César, and before that the Russians.* They were the last jobs they worked, before Mendoza, and she was right about them—Declan hadn't been at his best.

César was a transporter, and he'd ship pretty much anything to anyplace, according to Mr. Boyce and Tina. He'd started out, like so many in the region, with drug shipments, and found natural synergies in the movement of small arms and cash. Then, in the early years of the new century, he diversified into transporting heavier weapons, hijacked electronics, pirated software and DVDs, and human traffic headed north. Despite his success, or perhaps because he kept so busy spending its fruits on hookers, Ferraris, and thoroughbred horses, César had, over the years, underinvested badly in his own security infrastructure.

"I've seen 7-Elevens with tighter perimeters," Tina had said.

The perimeter she was talking about was in Puerto Barrios, Guatemala, around a waterfront compound where César kept an office, some odds and ends of his shipments—a pallet or two of flat-screen TVs, a crate of RPGs—a climate-controlled garage for some of his Testarossas, and $6.8 million in shrink-wrapped packs of hundred-dollar

bills. The money was in a cinder-block annex to the Ferrari garage, and it should've been a simple job—three sleepy
guards, a fence to scale, a video feed to interrupt, an alarm
system barely worth the name, and a safe room that wasn't.
In and out, unseen and unheard, in seventeen minutes flat. It
should've been simple, but it wasn't, because Declan developed something of a mania for César.

Not that that was difficult to do. César was unlikable in
the extreme—a thug, a beater of women and children, a liar,
a casual killer, and an all-around swine. Though he was, in
truth, no worse than any of the other people they stole from,
Declan had for some reason decided that he was.

"I think it's his girth, boys," he confessed over beer one
night in a Puerto Barrios bar. "He's such a fat fuck, and he
dresses like. . . . What's he dress like, Bobby?"

"Like an L.A. pimp, Deke, circa 1977."

"Not even that well, lad. And he's an insult to those cars
of his. I just don't know how he jams his guts behind the
wheel." It was a running joke through all their planning, and
then, on the night of the job, in an instant it wasn't.

Carr was on the fence, and Declan, Bobby, and Ray-Ray
had the safe room. Carr watched through the nightscope
as Bobby and Ray-Ray came out, bags over shoulders, and
headed toward him.

"Where's Deke?" Carr said into his headset.

There was a pause, a whispered chuckle, and then Declan's
raspy voice. "Leavin' a little something for that feckin' sack,"
he said, and Carr saw him in the doorway of the Ferrari
garage—saw him pitch something in underhanded, and then
come running.

"Might want to add some quick, lads," he said, and then
the night lit up with an orange flash, a muffled blast, a symphony of breaking glass, and a shock wave that Carr felt even
fifty yards away. He tore the nightscope from his head.

"What the fuck?" Bobby and Ray-Ray shouted, nearly in unison.

Declan was laughing when he reached them, and laughing later that night, when they passed a bottle around in the cabin of a sport fisher, halfway to Belize.

"He didn't deserve those cars, the fat shite. All I did was restore order to the universe. And what the fuck was he gonna do with that box of pineapples anyway? Nothing so productive, I'll guarantee you." He looked at Carr. "Why're you being a feckin' old woman about it, anyway? It's fireworks is all—nothing to fret over. It's like a tonic."

Bobby and Mike and Dennis and Ray-Ray had laughed with him; Carr and Valerie had not.

Nobody was laughing after Nicaragua, though. The Russians were called Dudek, and they were actually from Ukraine—two cousins who cashed out of the army and headed west when the Evil Empire dissolved. And weapons were their specialty. They bought them, sold them, shipped them, serviced them, and trained clients in their use. And unlike César, they did not leave piles of money about in cinder-block sheds. They did, however, keep some petty cash on hand—$5.1 million, more or less—in a safe in the back office of Dudek Air Charter, not far from the Managua airport. The safe was a serious one, as was the security around it, which relied less on technology than it did on the presence of many guys with guns.

Carr hadn't liked the job at first, hadn't seen a way of doing it that didn't devolve into a full-on firefight, but Declan had pushed, and eventually he'd come up with a plan. It relied on distraction, misdirection, and some painfully tight timings, but if it played as written, it would get them in and out without a shot fired. Carr was pleased with it; Declan less so. It was late, and they were sitting in the shitty kitchen of a shitty house, in a city—Managua—full of shitty houses.

"The way in is okay, I guess, but the exit is too clever by half. We'll have the swag in hand, fer chrissakes, we don't need yer feckin' floor show. We just head for the door."

"And do what," Carr had said, "shoot your way out? Those aren't rent-a-cops at Dudek, those are mercs—mostly kid mercs. They're not big on judgment or hesitation or worries about mortality—theirs or anyone else's. You light it up with them, it's not a halfway thing."

"I know who they are, boyo, and the last thing I need is a lecture on firefights. Not from you. I'm saying yer plan is riskier than it has to be because yer shy when it comes to heavy lifting—you always have been. You're delicate, so to avoid the shootin' you have us wastin' time in that stairwell, while you sing and dance. Well, I say that's a higher risk. I'd rather do the shootin' than wait around fer someone to do it to me."

"I'm talking about a series of flash-bangs on the other side of the building, to draw them off. I'm talking about a wait of a minute, ninety seconds tops. We make some noise, and then you leave, and if you do meet people on the way out, you'll meet fewer of them."

"So you say. But what're you so worried about, boyo— you'll be on the outside, out of harm's way."

"There are risks we can minimize, and risks we can't. The exit plan falls in the first category. If I'm worried about anything, it's that you don't see that. I'm talking about a minute, Deke, a minute and a half tops."

"You shy because they're kids? Is that it?"

They went back and forth like that, until the sky grew pale and everyone but Latin Mike agreed with Carr, and Mike stayed silent. Finally—peevishly—Declan folded. And then, three nights later, as he and Bobby and Mike were on their way out of the Dudek Air Charter building, he changed his mind.

No one laughed after that. Not Bobby or Mike, who had taken a round through his right arm and who Carr had never seen so pale, and not Declan, who'd taken a round in his left thigh and killed three child soldiers along the way. The wound didn't seem to bother Declan much on the drive west, from Managua to the Pacific coast, nor did it stop Carr.

"We had a plan," Carr said.

Declan's smile was thin and cold. "You know what they say about those, boyo: they don't survive the first shot."

"We all agreed on it."

"And since when was this a feckin' democracy?"

Carr stared for a long while, and then shook his head. "What the fuck is the matter with you?" he whispered. Declan stopped smiling, but had no other answer.

It's nearly nightfall when Mike arrives, and there are clouds in the darkening sky, and approaching thunder. Mike has a six of Corona under one arm, and a bucket of fried chicken under the other.

"Howie's still sleeping," Carr says, as he passes Mike in the doorway. "Don't hit him again." Mike starts to say something, but Carr keeps walking.

DENNIS IS eating dinner when Carr arrives, a Cuban sandwich and a beer. He's bent over a laptop, wearing headphones, and he doesn't look up when Carr opens the door. Carr raps on the table, and Dennis starts and pulls the phones off.

"I'm looking at the latest from Chun's place—the wires Vee laid down."

Carr pulls a chair alongside Dennis's. "And?" he asks.

Dennis colors. "It's good," he says. "Actually, it's great."

The image is clear, despite the low light: Amy Chun in her home office. The tiny camera is planted in a bookshelf behind her desk, and the view is over and above her right shoulder. She's wearing a sleeveless white shirt, and there's a mug of tea steaming in a corner of her desk, next to her cell phone. She is pushing aside the keyboard of her home computer and opening up the laptop she carries every day to and from her office suite at the Spanish River Bank and Trust Company.

"Laptop keyboard is nice and clear," Dennis says. "Vee did a good job with placement."

Chun takes a fingerprint scanner from the desk drawer and plugs it into the laptop. From her purse she takes something like a keychain fob, with a tiny LCD strip down the center—an automatic password generator. A log-on window opens on the laptop, and she types in a password, one part of it from memory, and the rest from the screen of the password generator. Another window comes up, and Chun presses her thumb onto the fingerprint scanner. The laptop screen flickers and then her cell phone chimes. Chun picks it up, listens, picks up the password generator again, and keys a code from its screen into her cell phone. The laptop screen flickers again and she's into the network shared by the Spanish River Bank and Trust, and the rest of the banks owned by Isla Privada.

Carr shakes his head. "We knew how all that worked, we could save ourselves a lot of trouble."

Dennis stiffens beside him. His tone is frosty. "It's a virtual private network with multifactor authorization, including an out-of-band security feature, and I know exactly *how* it all works. What I'm missing is the checksum for Chun's thumbprint, the algorithm her key fob is using to generate those one-time passwords, and the authentication chip inside her laptop. If I had all that, *and* Chun's private password, *and* a phone on the network's call-back list, then we wouldn't need Vee in there at all, and I could log on to the Isla Privada network whenever I wanted. Give me Curtis Prager's private password on top of that, and we could all go home right now. Now *that* would save us trouble."

Carr suppresses a laugh. "I stand corrected," he says quietly. "We got Chun's part, though, didn't we?"

"We got it," Dennis says. "We got her password and we got account numbers."

"Nice job," Carr says, and claps him on the shoulder. "What else is on the tape?"

"Vee comes on," Dennis says, blushing. He fast-forwards several minutes, and a shadow crosses Amy Chun's desk. A moment later, Valerie's—Jill's—hip leans against Chun's arm. She's wearing a short white T-shirt and panties with lace trim, and she's carrying a rocks glass. Carr can't tell what's in it, but he can hear the ice. Jill rests her arm on Chun's back.

"I'll miss you," Jill says.

"It's just a day," Chun says, looking up at her. "New York and back. I'll be home before eleven."

"You'll call me?"

"Why don't you meet me here?" Chun says, and she slides her hand beneath Jill's shirt.

Jill inhales sharply and her hips shift. Her voice is choked. "Hurry and finish," she says, and she exits the frame to the tinkle of ice.

"Christ," Dennis whispers.

Carr lets out a deep breath. "Is that it?"

Dennis blushes again. "There's more...in the bedroom. The light is low, so the picture's not great, and the AC is blowing, so the sound is—"

"Play it."

Dennis clicks on another video file, and a dim, sepia-shadowed image appears: a heap of pillows, a tangle of dark blankets, two pale blurs on a paler, rectangular field. There is the faint shifting of sheets, the sound of someone drinking, someone sighing.

Amy Chun's voice is a tentative whisper. "Have you been...*out* for a long time?"

Valerie—Jill—laughs. Her voice is sleepy and soft. "I never thought about it that way; I never was really *in*. I've known how I felt since grade school, and I've never pretended anything different."

"Your parents?"

"They were too busy fighting with each other to pay much attention to me. I was in college before they noticed."

"They didn't care?"

"If they did, I didn't notice, and pretty soon I was out of there."

"My parents would notice," Amy Chun whispers, "even from Vancouver. And they would care. So would my board of directors."

"It's your life, Amy, not theirs. Your one-and-only life, and your happiness."

"Coming out is no guarantee of happiness."

"Nope—I know plenty of unhappy couples—of all persuasions. But *not* coming out—that *is* a guarantee."

Sheets rustle and someone exhales slowly. There's a sound of ice in a glass. "I'm happy now," Amy Chun says quietly. "Happier than I've been. Definitely happier than my parents are."

"They don't get along?"

"Never."

"It doesn't always have to be like that, you know—like my parents, and yours."

There's more shifting, and a giggle. "No?" Amy Chun asks.

"Maybe that's what we should do, you and me," she whispers. "Go away together and conduct a little research, to find some happy couples. We'll be like archaeologists."

There's more sighing and rustling, and the clip ends. Dennis lets out a long breath and pushes back from the table. "She is good," he says. "Sincere. Believable. Like scary good."

Carr looks at the image frozen on the screen—two women, bare, clinging to each other in the wreckage of the bed. He nods but doesn't speak.

25

ALL SUBTROPICAL financial districts look alike, Carr thinks. The broad, divided boulevards; the lush foliage at street level; the towers soaring above; the German cars at curbside, each with tinted glass and a large, watchful driver; the overcaffeinated, expensively suited young men who stride along, mesmerized by their BlackBerrys and chattering maniacally into the ether; the young women—stylish, tanned, with impossible heels, impossible legs, impossible self-possession. It could be Avenida Paulista, Avenida Balboa, or a stretch of Reforma, but it's not. It's Brickell Avenue in Miami, and Carr is walking north, following Valerie.

He's kept his distance all the way down 95, but now she's out of her car and he's out of his, and he needs to be careful. The lunchtime rush helps and hurts: Carr hides in the crowd, but so does Valerie, and he's nearly lost her twice since she gave her car to the valet at the Four Seasons and set out on foot. It's clear today, and cooler than it has been, but that just means it feels like ninety-something. Carr's shirt is stuck to his back, but Valerie, when he catches a glimpse, looks cool and crisp in a pale gray skirt and sleeveless white blouse. She crosses Brickell and heads west on Tenth Street.

Bessemer's call to Curtis Prager that morning was

anticlimactic. Sitting in his dim office, Carr at his side, Bessemer had phoned Prager's private number, only to learn that Prager is away until tomorrow, and please try again. And so an unexpected day off for Carr. He'd consigned Bessemer to Bobby's care, driven down to Boca Raton, and phoned Valerie from a spot fifty yards from her apartment building. Where she'd lied to him.

"I could drive down," he'd said, "and take a room. We could have lunch at the beach."

Valerie had yawned loudly. "That sounds nice, baby— really nice—but I've got to get some rest. I've been up late every night this week, and I'm supposed to meet Amy again tonight. I've got the drapes closed, and I'm going back to sleep."

Carr wasn't sure why he hadn't believed her, why he'd waited in his parked car after she'd hung up, why he'd followed her little Audi, half an hour later, when it pulled out of the building lot and made its way to 95. Maybe it was because her yawn had been too elaborate, or because he could see from his parking space that her drapes were wide open. Maybe it was the memory of her conversation with Amy Chun, the night before, and what she'd said to him back in Portland. *Maybe that's what we should do, you and me— go away together and conduct a little research, to find some happy couples. We'll be like archaeologists.*

SHE TURNS north again at First Avenue and passes beneath the elevated tracks of the light-rail. She crosses the street, to a compact shopping plaza in the shadow of the Metromover, and goes into a coffee bar. Carr keeps walking on Tenth Street, enters the plaza from Miami Avenue, and stands in the shade of a stunted, bushy palm tree. The coffee bar is busy, but through the wide front window Carr can see

Valerie slipping through the crowd toward the back of the room. He edges closer and sees her settle on a bar stool at a narrow counter along the side wall, in front of a keyboard, a mouse, and a monitor.

Carr can't make out the screen from where he is, but Valerie reads for a while and then types. She's at the computer for about three minutes, and then she pushes away from the counter and leaves through the back door.

Carr jogs into the coffee bar, shouldering past customers and ignoring the angry looks. A twenty-something man in linen pants, a Daddy Yankee T-shirt, and lots of body ink has a hand on Valerie's bar-stool when Carr steps in front of him.

"Hey, I'm sitting here, man," he says, and he puts his coffee cup on the counter.

"You definitely are," Carr says softly, "in about thirty seconds." Carr finds the browser icon on the desktop and clicks on it.

"I'm sitting here *now*, man," the twenty-something says, "so get the hell out of my way."

"Yep, absolutely," Carr says, watching the browser open, "I'm out of here."

"You talk, but you don't move your ass." The twenty-something puts a hand on Carr's arm and pulls, and his face seizes up in a grimace. Carr has his hand around the man's wrist and fingers and has bent them back at impossible angles. The twenty-something's face is pale and his knees begin to buckle, and Carr eases up on the finger lock.

"Another second," Carr whispers, and he opens the browser history. The screen is empty and Carr stares at it a moment and says: "Fuck." Then he hits the back door at a run, leaving the twenty-something rubbing his wrist and gasping and the few patrons who've noticed anything shaking their heads.

She's a block and a half down First Avenue, walking in

the shade of the Metromover tracks, and Carr is just in time to see her turn east on Eighth Street, back toward Brickell Avenue. He sprints to close the gap.

She walks briskly down Eighth Street and crosses Brickell as the light changes. Carr waits on the other side of the street and watches Valerie disappear into a tower of white stone and green glass.

When Carr steps into the building, Valerie is nowhere in sight, and security is already eyeing him. And why not—no one else in the lobby is as rumpled as he is, or as damp with sweat. He walks over to the building directory and scans the list of tenants. Software companies, law firms, management consultants, but more than anything else banks and broker-ages. And, Carr notices, mostly foreign firms.

"Can I help you, sir?" the guard asks. He's big and uni-formed, and so is his hovering partner.

"Think I got the wrong address," Carr says, and he exits into the midday heat.

There's a Starbucks next door to the building, and a wine bar on the opposite corner. Carr likes the sight lines from the wine bar better, though neither are perfect: there are too many ways out of the green tower. Still, he takes a window seat and orders a bottle of soda water and a ham sandwich on a baguette.

The traffic churns past on Brickell while Carr eats and watches and wonders. What was Valerie doing in the coffee bar, where she had no time to drink coffee, but time enough to delete her browsing history? Surfing? Sending? And if sending, then sending to whom? And why do it there, when she has Internet access back in Boca Raton?

Privacy and anonymity are the obvious answers, and both worry Carr. He and his crew are the only people in a position to eavesdrop on Valerie's laptop. What might she be doing online that she'd want to hide from them? And who might she be doing it with?

After an hour, the lunch crowd has thinned on the street and in the wine bar, and the air-conditioning has dried him off, but Carr has seen no sign of Valerie. He worries that he's missed her in the wash of people, or that she's left another way, and he pays the check and steps outside. The humidity is like a wet hammer, and Carr is sweating before the light changes. There's a shaded plaza beside the green tower, with white pergolas, razor-straight rows of palm trees, tables with umbrellas, and a view through the lobby glass of the elevator banks. Carr heads for one of the tables, and when he stops in his tracks he's not sure at first what it is that's stopped him.

Something in the corner of his eye. Something he knows. Broad shoulders held just so, a thrusting gut, an aggressive, pumping gait—a familiar bulk. In the lobby, in the shuffling clutch of people at the elevator doors. When Carr picks him out, there's a rush of noise in his head—gears grinding on one another—and he's frozen, flat-footed, in the plaza. He might as well be waving a flag. It's sheer luck that Nando doesn't look over.

"What the fuck?" Carr says to no one, and he steps behind one of the manicured palms.

Nando crosses the lobby and pushes through the doors. He's wearing a tan suit and an open-collared French blue shirt, and he's carrying a tan briefcase. He's thicker and darker than when Carr last saw him, years ago in Costa Alegre, and more prosperous-looking than ever. He's on his cell as he crosses Brickell and heads south. He's still talking when he enters another office tower, this one clad in brushed metal and gray glass. He's alone in the elevator when the doors slide shut, and Carr watches the numbers climb to eight.

Security in the gray building is lazy, and no guards brace Carr as he scans the lobby directory. The assortment of firms is only slightly different here—more lawyers, fewer consultants—but there are still plenty of foreign banks. The eighth floor, in fact, is nothing but banks.

Nando is inside for about an hour, after which Carr follows him down Brickell to another building—gold glass this time. Carr can't tell which floor he's headed to—there are too many people on the elevator with him—but there is no shortage of banks here either. Nando reappears fifty minutes later. Carr is buying gum at a lobby kiosk and readying himself for another walk in the heat when Nando turns not to the Brickell Avenue doors, but toward the back of the lobby and the enclosed passage that leads to the building's parking structure.

Carr comes down the passage in time to see Nando board an elevator. It stops on the third parking level and Carr jogs up the stairs. He comes out of the stairwell and hears footsteps echoing, a car door closing, and an engine turning over.

"Shit," he whispers, and he waits at the stairs as Nando drives by in a white rental.

Back on the sidewalk, Carr looks up and down Brickell Avenue, but sees no sign of Nando's car, or of Valerie. He walks up the street to the gray tower with the lax security. Around the corner he finds the tower's four-level parking structure and, on its lowest level, the loading dock. There's security there—two guys in rumpled uniform shirts and sneakers—but they seem only semiconscious. Carr checks the block and climbs a low wall into the parking structure. He bounces hard on the fenders of three parked cars—Lexus, BMW, Rover—and their lights flash and their horns blare. He steps behind a wide pillar, and when the security slackers wander over to investigate the alarms, Carr slips into the loading dock and into the service elevator and rides to eight.

Three banks—all foreign—have offices on the eighth floor, but only one has a reception desk. The blonde behind it looks barely out of middle school, and she has a fizzy voice and a manic smile.

"How can I help you today?" she says.

Carr puts on a beaten look. "I'm hoping you can help me out with my boss," he says. "He's was in here a while ago, and he thinks he left his BlackBerry. Now he is rip-roarin' pissed—like it's my fault he can't keep track of his stuff."

The girl nods in solidarity and sympathetic understanding of irrational bosses. "I haven't seen anything lying around."

"He was in about two hours ago. Black-haired guy, big, dark, in a tan suit and a blue shirt."

The blonde nods. "New accounts," she says, and she picks up the phone. "Britty, you find a BlackBerry over there? That new client, Mr. Reyes—he thinks he might've left his here." She listens and nods and smiles at Carr. "She's checking," she tells him. Then she listens again and frowns. "Thanks anyway, babe," she says into the phone, and she shakes her head.

He is barely aware of the walk back to the Four Seasons, and surprised to find himself there. More surprised to find that Valerie's car is still in the lot. He gets into his own car and finds a spot with a view of the hotel entrance and waits.

The afternoon rush washes about him, and so do the questions. Mr. Reyes? New accounts? What is Nando doing in Miami? And what the *fuck* is he doing with Valerie? The questions spin around like water in a drain, and there's orange in the sky when he realizes he hasn't been watching the hotel, or anyway that he hasn't been seeing it.

A dinner crowd is arriving, and the valets cast long shadows as they dart among the idling cars. Carr watches them run, and watches the pretty crowd disappear inside, through the revolving doors. And then he sees a couple step out.

The woman is first, and Carr recognizes Valerie right away, though her blouse is untucked now, and her hair is damp, as if from a bath. It takes him a moment longer to recognize the man, who pauses in the doorway and then walks forward, slips a thick arm around Valerie's waist, and rests a large hand on her hip. Mike.

26

"**YOU'RE NOT** yourself this morning, Greg," Bessemer says to Carr. "Need some more coffee?" He reaches across the kitchen counter and fills his mug.

Latin Mike looks at Carr with no expression, and Carr looks back. "I'm going now," Mike says, and Carr nods.

Bessemer squints at him, curiosity plain on his round face. "Rough night?"

And it hasn't ended yet, Carr thinks. The rum brought him no sleep, and even now there's a blur around the borders of things, and a hollow echo to every sound. His thoughts want to wander, to drift sideways, to skid. They steer the wrong way and then hit the gas until the skid becomes a dizzying spin.

They left the hotel separately—Mike first, then Valerie. Carr followed Valerie back to Boca, back to her apartment, then out again to Amy Chun's place. After an hour of watching dark windows, he left her there. Then he drove back to North Palm Beach and started to pace. Sometime past midnight the drinking began.

Drinking, pacing, replaying how many moments, again and again, in his head. Poolside at Chamela. Her apartment in Port of Spain. More workhouses and hotel rooms than he could count. And more questions. When did his suspicions begin? What set them off? When did she meet Nando, and how? Why, along with the sensation of having missed a stair, does he feel something equally jarring—something a lot like relief?

Round and round he went, unable or unwilling to get to the middle of it, to get a purchase on the central problem: the dimensions of her betrayal. What has she done? What is she in the midst of doing? Who is she doing it with? Who can he trust, and what the hell should he do?

Howard Bessemer is still holding the coffeepot, still squinting at him. "Are we going to make that call today, Greg?"

Carr looks at him but says nothing.

Drinking, pacing, staring at the ocean. *What the hell should he do?* His options are limited to exactly two: finish the Prager job, or cut and run—and the second choice is more or less a nonstarter. Mr. Boyce has fronted a lot of cash on this job, and if Carr decides to fold, he's going to want it back—and with a nice return. Yes, Boyce is currently holding the diamonds the crew picked up in Houston, and they'll go some way to paying off the debt, but Carr has no intention of being stuck with the balance. Neither does he want to spend the rest of his life looking over his shoulder, waiting for Tina to appear.

Sometime before dawn, he decided he couldn't stand his apartment any longer, and he walked across the road to the beach, leaving his shoes at the edge of the sand but bringing the rum. The sand was cold, and in the moonlight the breakers looked like white smoke rolling toward him.

He thought of Tina and looked over his shoulder and laughed out loud at the notion of telling Boyce what was going on. Or rather telling him that *something* was going on, but that Carr didn't know exactly what it was. Not much of a thought, really—not much of an option. At best, Boyce would pull the plug on the job himself, and still want his money back. More likely, he'd decide the whole shit storm was an unacceptable breach of operational security—a terminal breach. And there, over Carr's shoulder, would be Tina again.

Walking down the beach, he stepped on something slippery and colder than the sand. A jellyfish. He braced for the sting, but felt nothing and kept walking.

The bottom line is, he needs Prager's money, needs what it can buy. A few months back he'd calculated that he had enough put away to do what he wanted for as long as he wanted, but that calculation is out of date. His father's situation and Mrs. Calvin's impending departure have thrown his cash flow assumptions to the wind. He needs the money.

Bessemer clears his throat once...twice. "I'm thinking that maybe you're not into this today, Greg—that your mind is elsewhere. Greg?"

So, finish the job. Easy enough to say, but it begs the question of who he can trust while he's doing it. He's been asking himself that since Declan's death, or maybe even before, but now it's acquired a particular urgency.

Working the paranoid calculus—that's what his instructor at the Farm had called it, an atypically neat turn of phrase from an otherwise lumpish fellow. Tracing the lattice of connections, mapping the shifting landscape of who-owes-who and who-owns-who, of loyalty, grudge, and pressure. Who's in bed with whom? Who's working what angle? Who benefits? Nando and Valerie. Valerie and Mike. If Mike, then Bobby as well? They were both in Mendoza, after all. And what about Dennis?

The answer—the short answer—is to trust none of them, not for a second, not as far as he can throw them, not even half that far. But nothing is ever so straightforward. The practical truth is, if he's going to finish the Prager job, then he needs them—all of them. And they need him. They have to trust one another to carry out their assigned work—to watch one another's backs. Like birds of a feather and bugs in a rug, arms linked in a chorus of "Kumbaya." Thick as fucking thieves—right up until the moment they transfer the money out of Isla Privada's accounts. Then the question becomes how to survive their success.

Dawn found him standing frozen at the shoreline, surrounded—as if in a minefield—by acres of clumped seaweed and the glistening bodies of jellyfish. His ankles ached with cold, and his head was filled with shuffling images of burned and broken metal, Declan's skewed grin and blackened limbs, and Valerie in the dark. He could almost summon her smell and the feel of her skin, but the rising light and the ocean breeze swept his conjuring away. Surprise? Sadness? Anger? Relief? Like the seaweed, they're tangled too thoroughly for Carr to pick apart.

Bessemer is standing now, a look of alarm replacing the curiosity on his face. "Are we calling or not?"

Carr looks at him. "Pour me another cup of coffee," he says, "and get the telephone."

27

THEY'RE FOLLOWED from the airport on Grand Cayman—two men in a muddy blue Nissan, as inconspicuous as it's possible for a single-car tail to be. Carr spots them as he turns the Toyota onto Dorcy Drive.

"They were at the rental counter," he says, "but that's not a rental car." Bessemer starts to turn in his seat, but Carr puts a hand on his arm. "Use the mirrors," he says. Bessemer does, and his brows crease in confusion.

"The driver was outside passport control," Carr says, "but he wasn't on our flight."

"You think they're following us?"

"I know they are. You ever see them before?"

"I don't think so," Bessemer says, and there's worry in his voice.

"This a usual thing for Prager?"

Bessemer shakes his head. "If it is, I never noticed."

They're quiet after that. Bessemer watches the Nissan in the rearview. Carr watches traffic and looks at the landscape of the northern edge of George Town, which is flat, cluttered, and homely under a pale sky. Carr lowers his window and the smell of ocean rushes in, mixed with odors of asphalt and exhaust and brackish salt marsh. He glances at Bessemer, who is still looking in the mirrors, and whose face has tightened with fear.

"Strip malls and SUVs," Carr says. "Just like Florida."

Bessemer nods stiffly. "The north side's nicer. This your first time down here?" Carr smiles but doesn't answer, and Bessemer's eyes dart back to the mirror.

"They're just watching, Howie. They're not going to do anything."

Bessemer's nerves have been fraying since the call to Curtis Prager, which, when it finally happened three days before, had gone as well as Carr could've hoped. Bessemer had stayed on script and had managed to sound convincing about it. And, because Prager doesn't like phones, he hadn't had to talk for long. Bessemer told Prager that a good friend, Greg Frye, was in town, looking for a money manager. *And when I heard about the business opportunity Greg's got, I thought of you right away, Curt.*

Prager asked how good a friend this was and how Bessemer knew him. When Bessemer explained that he was an Otisville friend, Prager went silent for a long while—so long that Carr wondered if they'd been cut off. When Prager finally responded, he was brief.

"You know I'm always happy to meet prospective investors, Bess. So if you've got the time, you and your friend should come down here. We'll hit some balls, we'll put some lines in the water, and we'll see what bites."

Bessemer started fretting as soon as he hung up. "I thought all you wanted was an introduction, Greg. I think I've held up my part of the bargain."

"So far, so good," Carr said.

"You never talked about a trip."

"It's a short trip, Howie."

"But you never said—"

"Prager invited both of us down. It would be a little awkward if I showed up by myself."

Bessemer paced and worried his lower lip. "It'll be awkward for me if Curtis thinks I've lied to him. Awkward as in dead."

"Don't be dramatic."

"*Dramatic?* I'm not the one holding somebody hostage in his own house, or blackmailing him into being part of some kind of scam. I'm not the dramatic one."

Carr had almost smiled. "Don't be so negative, Howie. This doesn't have to be complicated: we go down there, we hang out, and then we're done. Stay focused on what you get out of this: your money, your life back, a fresh start."

"I don't know," Bessemer said, shaking his head and walking to his liquor cabinet.

"The upside, Howie—focus on the upside."

They're on Tibbetts Highway now, the Nissan still with them, a quarter-mile back. They come up a gentle rise and on his left, beyond the big hotels, Carr sees the beaches, the ocean, and the cruise ships at anchor, each one as graceless as a Soviet apartment block. Away to his right, North Sound is like a pale blue plate, and the feathered wake of a powerboat like a fracture line across it. Closer on the right is the broad dome of a landfill, with a thousand white gulls wheeling above. Carr glances at Bessemer, who is drumming his fingers on the armrest and still staring at the mirrors. Carr understands nerves—his own are like confetti.

He saw Valerie the day before he left Palm Beach. She drove up while Amy was at work, and he took a room at the Marriott. She said not a word about Miami or Nando or Mike, and Carr managed not to ask. Managed not to speak much at all that afternoon, unless spoken to—and there wasn't much of that at first. Later, when the sheets and pillows were on the floor and they were sideways on the bed, Valerie had questions of her own.

"They're set up down there?" she asked.

"Dennis went yesterday. Bobby and Mike go tonight."

"They must be happy to get out of that dump."

"They were getting stir-crazy. Forward motion calms everybody down."

"Everybody, including you?"

"I want to get it done as much as anyone."

"And afterward?" she asked softly, and slid a bare foot up his calf. "You ever been to New Zealand? It's really something down there—Middle Earth, just like in the movies. I know a place where we could have a cottage to ourselves, just us, a few thousand acres, and some sheep. Nothing to see out the windows but cliffs and sky and ocean. What do you say—you take care of the airfare, and I'll pick up the tab at the Wharekauhau?"

"New Zealand's a long way."

"You can afford it. And besides, isn't that what you want—something far away?"

He had no answer for that, so he nodded vaguely and went into the bathroom. When he came out, Valerie was standing by the balcony doors. She'd opened the drapes to the width of her shoulders, and she wore nothing but the long bar of light that came through the glass. Carr stared at her for some time, looking for he didn't know what. A mark? A sign? Some sort of clue? But there was nothing except that body, slender, wanton, tinted pale saffron by the streetlight. She turned to look at him, and her face, half in shadow, was suddenly exhausted.

"We moved a lot when I was a kid," she said quietly. "Base to base—never anyplace longer than a year or two. My mother was useless around the house, but my father could do things, and he'd always try to fix up whatever crappy billet we'd been assigned. He'd paint, hang pictures, plant a window box, that kind of thing. But those places weren't ours, and all the petunias in the world couldn't change it—

couldn't make us belong somewhere. I get the feeling you know what that's like."

"I know."

"I'll be glad when this is done. I'm tired of hotels and furnished apartments and putting on these lives like somebody else's clothes. I want someplace I can sit still. Someplace that's mine." The air conditioner came on and she shivered in the breeze. She wrapped her arms around herself. "I want my skin back."

Carr swallowed hard, and Valerie stepped away from the window and began to collect her scattered clothes. "Something's on your mind," she whispered.

Did they show, he wondered—the questions that still spun through his head? He shrugged. "Prager, Bessemer, a bunch of things."

"You need help," she said. "Let me help you."

THE RESORT grounds are vast: a golf course, clubhouse and marina on the sound, and, across West Bay Road, a curving, coral-pink hotel complex on Seven Mile Beach. The Nissan doesn't follow when Carr turns through the main gates, but any relief he feels is short-lived. There are two more men in the lobby, watching them from behind day-old newspapers.

28

THEY'RE IN a fourth-floor corner suite—two bedrooms separated by a living room, a kitchenette, a wet bar, a terrace, and glary views of pool and ocean. While Bessemer explores the bar, Carr carries his bag to a bedroom and drops it on a luggage rack. He steps into the bathroom and runs water in both sinks. Then he opens his cell and calls Bobby.

"Not bad here," Bobby says. "You can practically smell the offshore cash."

"It's very fragrant," Carr says. "You guys clean when you came in from the airport?"

"Sure. Clean last night, clean today. Why?"

"Two guys were with us on the drive here, and another pair picked us up in the lobby. I see one of them down by the pool. I don't know where his partner is."

"You think they're Prager's?"

"I hope like hell they are," Carr says. "We don't need new players at the table."

"His security guy was supposed to be a joke."

"Maybe he's on the wagon again."

"Fucking drunks," Bobby says, "you can never count on 'em. I got your stuff; you want me to bring it over?"

"And you can check out the babysitters while you're at it.

Howie and I will take a walk around the grounds, starting with the bar by the pool. We'll meet you back here. You need a key to the suite?"

Bobby laughs. "Now you're just being a prick," he says, and hangs up.

THE CAIMAN Lounge is a broad expanse of terra-cotta tile, bleached wood, and sliding glass doors that let the bar merge with the patio around the pool. Carr and Bessemer pause at the entrance. Carr doesn't see Bobby—doesn't see anyone besides a few off-season honeymooners sitting close. He and Bessemer take a table near a large aquarium. Carr orders an iced tea, and Bessemer a gin and tonic. Bessemer is transfixed by a green and blue triggerfish swimming lazily behind the glass.

"Ridiculous fish," he says. "Goofy-looking. It reminds me of my ex-mother-in-law."

"Triggers are aggressive," Carr says. "They'll take a chunk out of you if you get between them and the next meal."

"Definitely my ex-mother-in-law."

Carr nods, and then he spots the lobby men. One takes a seat at the bar and orders something. The other walks in from the pool patio, sits at a table in back, and studies a menu. Bessemer is rambling on about his former in-laws, and Carr tunes out to regard the minders from the corners of his eyes.

Polo shirts, thick necks, bristly haircuts, heavy, confounded brows, and a general air of unfocused anger. Corporate security types, he thinks—ex–law enforcement, ex-military—the kind of foot soldiers he used to hire and fire at Integral Risk. The waitress delivers their drinks, and Bessemer interrupts his ramble to clink glasses. Carr sits for another ten minutes, not listening to Bessemer, not looking for Bobby, and then he gets up.

"Let's walk, Howie."

And so they do, for half an hour or so: around the pool, down to the beach, back to the lobby, in and out of the pricey shops, and through the barbered gardens. And the two minders stroll with them—never obviously, not to Bessemer at any rate, never too close, but never really out of sight. Carr leads them on a final turn around the marina, then back across West Bay Road and through the lobby again. He and Bessemer are alone on the elevator to the fourth floor. When they return to their suite, Bobby is there, drinking beer. He's got the blinds drawn, and a Marlins game on the big plasma screen.

Bessemer is in the doorway, about to speak, when Carr raises a hand to stop him. Carr looks at Bobby and lifts an eyebrow.

Bobby holds up what looks like an old-fashioned beeper with a stubby antenna on top. "It's okay," he says. "I swept it. It's clean."

A tentative smile falls from Bessemer's face. "What's clean?"

"The room, Howie," Bobby says. "And a pretty nice room too. First-class all the way with Greg, huh?" Bessemer nods vaguely, still confused.

"What did you see?" Carr asks.

"Just the two buzz cuts. They looked like a couple of water buffaloes, waddling around after you."

"What are you talking about?" Bessemer asks. "Who's a water buffalo? Are we still being followed?"

"It's all good, Howie," Carr says, shaking his head. He sits in a chair across from Bobby and opens the brown plastic grocery bag that Bobby has left on the coffee table. Inside, wrapped in a hand towel, is a holstered Glock, and beneath that a small box, about the size of a deck of cards. Carr opens it and empties the contents into the palm of his hand: three black, one-gigabyte flash drives.

"Gave you two extra, for backup," Bobby says. "Prager plugs it in and we're good to go."

"He doesn't have to open a file or read the directory?"

"Nope. All he has to do is plug it in and the worm loads."

"You make it sound easy," Carr says.

Bobby shrugs. "You're the guy who's got to get him to do it."

Bessemer's eyes lurch from the gun to Carr. "Do what? Plug what in?" His voice is brittle and shaky.

"Not to worry, Howie," Carr says, and then he nods at Bobby. "I'm going out, but he'll keep you company while I'm gone."

"Gone where?"

"No place far," Carr says. "We'll call Prager when I get back." And then he goes into his bedroom, rummages in his bag for a bathing suit, and opens his phone.

Tina's hotel is down the beach from Carr's—practically next door, she said, but it turns out to be a mile-and-a-half swim. The water is warm and clear, but there's rough surf around the reefs, and a powerful undertow at a break in a sand bar, and it takes Carr almost forty minutes to make the trip. He's breathing hard when he pulls off his fins and mask and walks out of the ocean. His shoulders and thighs are burning.

Tina is waiting for him in a white canvas beach cabana, the last tent in a curving white line. She's lying on a lounge chair, wearing a black two-piece swimsuit and big black sunglasses. Her skin is pale and petal smooth, and Carr can feel her eyes on him as he crosses the sand.

She hands him a heavy white towel. "I'm impressed," she says, "but wouldn't driving have been easier?"

"Sure," Carr says, drying his hair. "Except I didn't think you'd want me bringing my minders along."

Tina sits up and pulls her glasses off. Her eyes are narrow. "What are you talking about?" she says softly.

"Minders. Two of them—big biceps, high and tight hair, milling around the lobby. Not to be confused with the pair who tailed me from the airport."

"Where did you leave them?"

"On the hotel beach, trying to pick me out of a few dozen people snorkeling offshore."

"At some point they're going to realize you're not coming in."

Carr shrugs. "They can tell the lifeguard."

Tina looks into the middle distance. "No idea of who sent them?"

"They've got that corporate look, but otherwise no clue."

"Prager's?"

"That's the optimistic interpretation."

"It seems awfully diligent for Eddie Silva."

Carr nods. "Surprises were inevitable down here: security immediately around Prager is what I know least about."

"Bessemer was supposed to be your ticket around all that."

"And Silva was supposed to be a useless lush."

Tina makes a sour face and raps her sunglasses idly against her lounge chair. "So much for theories," she says. "What did you do with Bessemer?"

"Bobby's with him, at the hotel."

"He and Mike and the kid settled in?"

Carr nods. "In a place on the sound, with a yard and a dock and a straight shot to the airport. They like it better than West Palm."

Tina gives him a speculative look. "You want the stones?"

Carr sits. "That's why I'm here."

"And I thought it was just to see me," Tina says. There's a canvas beach bag at her side, and she reaches in and pulls out a large nylon shaving kit, blue with a zippered top. She tosses it to Carr, who catches it and opens the zip. The diamonds are in three plastic bags inside. Carr takes them out and weighs each one in his palm. "Everything here?"

"Except what I used for belt buckles and toe rings," Tina says.

Carr smiles and makes a show of weighing the bags again. "As long as you left me enough to get Prager's attention."

"From the minders, I'd say you already have it."

Carr puts the stones back in the zippered case. He looks at Tina and gets another questioning look in return. "You worried?" she asks. "About these guys following you around?"

His first impulse is to laugh, and he almost does. Not because he isn't worried about being followed—he is. Out from behind the listening end of a microphone, outside of anonymous cars and vans, Carr feels naked. The minders have simply added a spotlight and pointing finger. No, the almost laughter isn't because the buzz cuts don't scare him, it's because they're at the end of a long line. In the crowded landscape of Carr's fear, they are mere foothills beside Valerie, Mike, and Nando, beside his galloping suspicions about what really happened on that bleak highway to Santiago, beside his dark fantasies of what might happen here afterward, if his crew is successful in stealing Prager's money.

His second impulse—and it surprises him—is to tell her. The idea of giving voice to his fears, saying them aloud, confessing them to Tina, makes him dizzy for an instant. Words well up in his chest. They bubble and rush and nearly spring forth, and then he remembers who he's talking to. The half-smiling woman on the lounge chair vanishes, replaced by a slender figure—a riding crop in a black dress—standing in the deep shade at the edge of a golf course. So Carr swallows the words with his laughter and shrugs.

"I'm not crazy about working the front of the house," he says, "being the face Prager sees, the one he'll remember."

"First time for everything."

"First and last time for this."

"You never know—you might develop a taste for it."

"Not going to happen," Carr says, shaking his head. "Last

time I saw you, you were headed down to Santiago, to have a look at Guerrero. How did that go?"

Tina sighs. "I wish I could say it was a breakthrough, but it wasn't."

"Guerrero wasn't Declan's guy?"

"He was the guy all right, but that was it. He had nothing to tell us."

"Nothing at all?"

"Declan—or somebody very much like him—put down a cash deposit to fly that Saturday night. He paid cash, and booked for four passengers, plus baggage."

"Going where?"

"São Paulo."

"Declan."

"Sounds like. Unfortunately, that's all this Guerrero had to say. The date came and went, the guy didn't show and didn't call, and Guerrero happily kept the cash. End of story."

Carr's jaw clenches. "Which leaves us where?"

"No place great," Tina says. "It takes us back to our two original questions: Who gave Bertolli's men the heads-up, and what became of Bertolli's missing money?"

"How about Bertolli's former security guy down there— the one your people turned up?"

"How about him?"

"We could go back to him—push a little harder, or sweeten the pot—get him to do some digging into who warned Bertolli."

Tina is doubtful. "The guy was pretty scared..."

"So that's it then? I've spent my money on dead ends?"

"You want to keep spending, I'll keep my guys working— knocking on Bertolli's man again, trying to turn up another source, whatever. But if we're going to do that, then we've got to work it from the other end as well."

"Meaning what?"

"Who knew Declan's plans, and who was in a position to leak them? And who might've benefited from doing it? Those are the questions—and I think you know who you need to ask."

A gust of wind blows through the canvas walls of the cabana. Carr hunches like an old man and pulls the towel around his shoulders.

TINA BUYS him a T-shirt and flip-flops from her hotel's gift shop, along with a beach bag for his fins, mask, and diamonds, and she drives him back to his hotel. They say little in the car, and she drops him at the roadside just past the resort's flower-draped gate.

Bobby is watching television when Carr returns, a Dodgers game now. Bessemer is snoring in his room, diagonal across the bed, one arm flung out in a desperate reach for something. Carr closes the bedroom door.

"He went down about an hour ago," Bobby says. "The guy is not looking forward to seeing Prager."

Bobby is gone when Bessemer teeters into the living room, wiping crust from his eyes and spittle from his chin—a bedraggled teddy bear. He squints at the television, and then at the evening sky.

"Jesus," he says. "What time is it?"

"Time to make a phone call, Howie," Carr says.

Bessemer's hair is a weed patch, and he pushes clumsy fingers through it. "Call to who?"

"Come on, Howie, wake yourself up."

"You want to call Curt now?" he asks. His voice is a rusty hinge. "I don't think that's a good idea, Greg. Really, I'm not my best."

Carr shakes his head. "Room service will fix you. Coffee and a club sandwich."

Bessemer waves his hands and drops onto the sofa. "No, really, Greg, now isn't a good time. How about I give you Curt's number? Just say that I told you to call."

Carr goes to the bar and fills a glass with crushed ice and Coke. He places it on the coffee table in front of Bessemer, takes a seat next to him, and drapes an arm across Bessemer's hunched shoulders. Carr's voice is low and intimate, almost a whisper.

"And how about I put your face through those glass doors, Howie, and drop you four floors off the terrace? Because unless you pull yourself together and remember who you're talking to, that's exactly what I'm going to do. And I'll be long gone while they're still figuring out which pieces of you go where. So drink your soda and have a think, Howie, but don't take too long. I'll get the room service menu."

Carr gives Bessemer's shoulder a friendly squeeze as he finishes, and he sets a cell phone down next to the sweating glass.

29

ISLA PRIVADA Holdings is headquartered in a six-story slab of concrete and tinted glass that would be anonymous in an actual city, but that in George Town is a soaring office tower. It's off Elgin Avenue, not far from a police building that looks like it's made of orange sherbet. Carr parks next to a Land Rover with a large man leaning on the bumper. He's wearing a dark suit and fiddling uncomfortably with his shoulder holster, and he gives Carr a hard look as he and Bessemer pass, but Carr knows it's just for practice.

It's not yet noon, but the asphalt is already soft underfoot as they cross the parking lot. Bessemer is shaved and combed and barely bloodshot, but his steps are hesitant.

"We take it nice and easy, Howie," Carr says softly as they approach the glass doors. "And we keep things simple."

Carr has said it before—spent much of last night saying it. "You introduce me, and you let me talk. He asks about Otisville, you stammer, look embarrassed, and you let me talk. Just do what you said you always do when you arrange these get-togethers—make the introductions and fade into the woodwork."

"Why are we doing it at his office?" Bessemer asked a dozen times or more. "He always has me over to the house.

I've never even been to the office before. Curtis hardly goes there himself." And a dozen times or more Carr replied with comforting noises, none of which he himself quite believed.

There's a security desk in the lobby, and cameras, but nothing more heavy-handed in the procedures than a glance at their passports, consultation of the visitors list, and a call upstairs. Carr fights the impulse to turn away from the cameras. Someone at Isla Privada approves them, and they're pointed toward a small elevator for a slow ride to the fifth floor. Bessemer is shifting from one foot to the other.

"You have to pee, Howie?" Carr asks.

"Among other things."

A woman, fit, brisk, and fiftyish, meets them at the elevator. She wears tan trousers and a sleeveless white blouse, and has a thick blond ponytail that barely moves as she leads them down corridors, around corners, and through a maze of low cubicles.

Isla Privada's offices aren't empty, but they feel that way—like a Saturday morning, rather than almost noon on a Wednesday—and the decor is decidedly low-key. The furnishings are as muted and generic as the building itself—slate and putty and taupe. The office artwork is visual pabulum: placating and instantly forgotten, surplus from a shopping mall or an airport lounge. Even the ringtone of the telephone system is muffled to a low burr that sounds to Carr like an electronic snore. The air is cool and smells like a new car.

This is not the back office—the centralized operation that processes the transactions of all the bank and trust companies in Isla Privada's portfolio and that enables Curtis Prager to wash and move so much money so efficiently and incon-spicuously. Those offices, Carr knows, are two miles away, in an even blander building, wrapped in much more serious security. But looking over the cubicles as he passes, Carr sees no clue of the business being done here. Insurance? Consulting? Selling time-shares? It could be anything.

The woman leads them to a glass-walled conference room. She stands by the door and ushers them in with a sweep of her muscular arm. There's an oval conference table in the center of the room, and beneath the shaded windows a low credenza with trays on top. Coffee service, ice bucket, glass tumblers, and small bottles of soda.

"Sorry for the wait, fellas," the woman says. "Please have a seat." Her voice is husky, aggressively upbeat, and has a trace of Texas in it. Her skin is tanned and grainy. "We'll get started in just a minute, but in the meantime we have refreshments." She crosses the room and carries the trays from the credenza to the conference table. Bessemer reaches for a glass and a bottle of ginger ale.

"And for you Mr. Frye?" She spreads her hands toward the trays, like a trade-show model presenting a dishwasher. "Please, help yourself," she says, and leaves, closing the door behind her.

Bessemer fills a glass with ice and ginger ale and empties it in one long swallow. He picks up a cocktail napkin and wipes his mouth and his forehead. Then he goes to the window and raises the shades. Carr sees the low rooftops of George Town, bright under the hammering sun, and the busy blue harbor. Bessemer turns and begins to speak, and Carr shakes his head minutely.

"Lots of boats," Carr says.

Bessemer nods. "Curt must be running late," he says, and begins to pace.

Carr stares until he catches Bessemer's eye. "Another drink, Howie?" he asks, and slides a bottle of ginger ale across the table. Then he reaches for a glass of his own.

Twenty minutes later, Carr his finished two club sodas, and the hairs have risen on the back of his neck, though he doesn't know why. Bessemer is pacing again, but the little knot tightening in Carr's stomach isn't fallout from that. He swirls the ice in his glass and looks around the conference room, which has suddenly come to resemble a fishbowl.

"Does Prager usually keep you waiting long?" he asks.

Bessemer flinches, startled by Carr's voice. "He never keeps me waiting, and he never parks me in a conference room either. I feel like a salesman, for chrissakes."

"I know what you mean," Carr says, and he looks through the glass walls at the people in their cubicles doing god knows what. "Have you caught a glimpse of him, walking around?"

"Walking around out there?" Bessemer says, flinching again. "No, I haven't seen anything." And the knot tightens more.

And then the blond woman is at the conference room door again, still smiling, though this time apologetically.

"Fellas, I feel *terrible* about this. I just now got off the phone with Curtis, and he's not going to be able to make it in today. He's on his way to the airport—got a little emergency, and he's got to jump over to Nassau real quick. But he wants you to know he's *real* sorry for this, and he'd like to reschedule for Saturday—lunch at his place."

Carr looks at Bessemer, who is sputtering. "This is unbelievable," Bessemer says. "We came down to see Curt, not for a vacation. I'd have come in February if that's what I was after."

The blonde nods and her smile slides smoothly into a sympathetic frown. "And Curtis is *so* sorry. In fact, he'd like you to send over your hotel bill, so he can take care of it."

Bessemer begins to speak and Carr puts a hand on his arm. "That's all right," Carr says, smiling. "Things come up—

I know how it is. And Saturday should be fine, don't you think, Howie? Give us time for some golf."

Bessemer looks at Carr and nods vaguely. "Golf, sure."

The blonde's smile returns. "Great—so I'll tell Curtis Saturday."

"Saturday," Bessemer says.

The blonde makes more noises of cheerful apology and leads them out of the conference room and through the office again. The knot in Carr's stomach moves into his chest. They pass the men's room, and Carr makes an abrupt right turn.

"I've got to make a pit stop," he says, leaning on the bathroom door. "I'll catch up at the elevators." Carr pushes through, and as he does he sees the blonde's face tighten with a look of annoyance.

The bathroom is small and gray and smells of disinfectant. Carr runs water on his hands and dries them and listens to the blonde's voice dwindle down the hallway. When it's gone he throws away his paper towel, steps into the corridor, and turns left. He walks down the hall, turns a corner, and stops when he sees the conference room, and the man at the conference table, who is sporting a crew cut, a polo shirt, and vinyl gloves, carefully placing Carr's drinking glass in a plastic evidence bag.

AT THE elevators, Bessemer is sweating, and the blonde is checking her watch. Carr smiles as he approaches. "Sorry to hold things up," he says, chuckling. "Too much club soda."

The blonde returns his smile and presses the elevator call button. "So we'll see you Saturday, Mr. Frye? Mr. Bessemer?"

Carr nods and puts out his hand. "You'll be there too, Ms....?"

"Oh, I'm sorry—I never did make a proper introduction to you fellas. I'm Kathy Rink."

"A pleasure," Carr says. "Are you Curtis's assistant?"

Kathy Rink smiles wider and laughs as she squeezes Carr's hand. "Oh, no, Mr. Frye, I'm his head of security."

30

"**SHE'S EX-DEA,**" Tina tells Carr, stirring the ice in her drink, but drinking nothing. "She left eighteen months back, after fifteen years there. Spent most of her time in the New Orleans district, in Shreveport and Baton Rouge, and her last three years down south, in Honduras. She came on about four weeks back, with a recommendation from one of Prager's clients. Word is she's still got plenty of friends in the agency."

"Shit," Carr says. His voice is low and cold.

They're alone on the terrace of a bar perched over a cove, at a table by the wooden railing. The tide is rolling in, slapping at the rocks below and casting up a briny mist. Carr has nothing in front of him but the strips of a shredded cocktail napkin that are being carried away, one by one, on the wind.

"That's all I've got so far," Tina says, "but I'm expecting another call."

"And is this call going to explain just what the *fuck* happened to your intel?"

"I don't like surprises any more than—"

"It's not your ass on the line."

Tina's face is without expression and as white and still as carved bone. Her eyes are invisible behind her dark glasses, and her voice is without affect. "You want me to say it's a fuckup? Fine—it's a fuckup. You feel better now?"

"No," Carr says. He presses his fingers to his temples. "If Rink's still got federal wiring, then Greg Frye won't last. He's not built for that. He's good for a quick look-see— a criminal records check, or somebody trying to confirm that he and Bessemer were at Otisville together—but for somebody with fingerprints and access to AFIS..."

Tina nods. "She'll run right through Frye to you."

Carr looks down at the foam-covered rocks. "They took my prints when I applied, at every one of my interviews, on my first day at Langley, and a half dozen times afterward. Dennis is good, but he's not good enough to scrub all that away."

Tina leans back and chews on her straw. "Your minders still around?"

"We wouldn't be meeting here if they were. They were with us to Prager's office this morning, but not afterward, and they're not at the hotel."

"You left Bessemer there?" Carr nods. "How's he holding up?"

"He was nervous before we met Rink; he's bat-shit now. Bobby's probably scraping him off the ceiling, if he hasn't actually killed him yet."

"How's Bobby doing?"

"Pissed off, scared, ready to pack his bag."

And Bobby wasn't the only one. After parking Bessemer in the suite and phoning Tina, Carr had arranged a conference call with Valerie, Bobby, Mike, and Dennis. His story of what happened at Prager's office was met first with silence, and then angry, colliding voices. Bobby's was the loudest and most poetic.

"What the *fuck*? We pay Boyce for intel, and this is what we get—a steaming pile of dog shit? This is fucked, brother—up, down, and sideways—and I'm heading for the fucking airport."

Dennis had been slightly less noisy but no less upset, and Mike had done his yelling in Spanish. Only Valerie had been quiet, and Carr swore he could hear the gears turning in her head.

"Everybody else feel the same as Bobby?" Tina asks.

"What do you expect? The boss doesn't bring on a new security chief because he wants to keep things the same. So what we knew about Prager's personal security, and what we could infer because of Silva, is all subject to change now. The same with Isla Privada's network security, and even Amy Chun's protection—all out the window. And I didn't even tell them about the prints. Once they find out about that they won't even bother to pack."

"So don't tell them," Tina says. She looks out at the ocean, and Carr watches the breaking waves in her black lenses. She tosses her straw into an ashtray. "Four weeks isn't a lot of time in a new job," she says. "It's barely enough to figure out what changes you want to make, much less to make them."

Carr squints at her. "You think Rink hasn't changed anything yet?"

"She hasn't even been there a month."

"That's a fucking big *maybe*—and let me point out that we saw some changes today."

"We'd have to take a second look at things, of course—verify that nothing important has—"

"And you think we'll get it right on the second look? Or maybe the third? Come on, Tina."

She takes off her sunglasses. Her gray eyes catch the light and glitter like broken glass. "So your bag's packed too, is that it? I just want to make sure I get it right for when Boyce asks me."

"I don't know that there are any other options here."

"Bags packed—yes or no, Carr? 'Cause if it's yes, I've got to get the accountants working on what you owe us. And by the way, I'm going to want those diamonds back, as a down payment."

"I'm not pulling out on a whim, Tina, or because I decided it was all just too much work. This is about the wheels falling off because of an intel fuckup. *Your* fuckup."

"No one's arguing that, and trust me there's a certain lazy bastard who has a date with the inside of an oil drum, but when Boyce asks me if I think this whole thing is irretrievably screwed, I'm going to tell him *no*."

Carr's laugh is bitter. "Everybody in the stands gets an opinion. They just shouldn't confuse watching with being on the field."

"Is that really how you want to approach this?" Tina says quietly. Her smile is thin and chilly and doesn't reach her eyes. After a moment Carr looks away.

There's a gull hanging in the breeze above the terrace, eyeing the paper scraps on the table and, Carr thinks, eyeing him. He waves a hand at it, but the bird is unimpressed. He looks back to Tina. "Even if Rink hasn't made many changes to Prager's security—and even if we could verify that—there's still the issue of my prints. A day or so from now, she's going to know I'm not Greg Frye. How do you make that go away?"

"*I* don't," Tina says, and then she picks up her phone and walks to the far corner of the terrace.

She's on for a long while, walking a tiny square while she talks. The wind carries her voice in pieces. Carr can't make out the words above the beating of the surf, but her tone is tense and urgent. Her face, when he can see it, is blank, and her shoulders are rigid. The longer she speaks, the tighter his chest becomes.

Tina closes her phone, leans against the terrace rail, and

looks out at the waves. For a moment Carr thinks she might throw the phone into the sea, but she slips it into her pocket instead and walks back to the table.

"Boyce?" he asks. Tina nods. "And?"

"We have to wait and see."

31

FROM HALF a mile out, from beneath the canopy of an open fishing boat rocking gently on flat water, the Prager compound is impressive even to the naked eye. The sweep of sand is like a quarter-mile curve of new snow. The bordering palms are lush, lithe, and synchronized in the breeze. The stone stairs, terraces, and retaining walls are meticulous gray lines. The boathouse, at the end of a spidery pier, is a trim, white chapel. The three-hole golf course is like a velvet swag across the east end of the property, and the corner of a house, visible between palm trees at the west end, is like a slice of pink cake.

"Let me have the binoculars," Carr says, and Bobby passes them over. Carr adjusts the dial and details emerge in the bobbing frame. Shadowed foliage becomes careful landscaping, dense green with generous dollops of color—hibiscus, bougainvillea, ixora, and red ginger. A swimming pool casts a shimmering web on a striped awning. A gust of wind swirls tennis court clay into a thin red cloud that settles at the edge of a croquet lawn. The slice of cake turns out to be the corner of a guesthouse—a pink stucco confection with a satellite dish. Of the main house, only a section is visible—an acre or so of terra-cotta barrel tile, a length of colonnaded portico, and a line of French windows that catch light off the ocean.

"We got them curious," Bobby says. "On the beach, at the bottom of the stairs."

Carr scans the binoculars from west to east and sees them, two security grunts: crew cuts, polo shirts, dark glasses, and earpieces—first cousins to the minders at his hotel. "Didn't take long," he says. He drops his sunglasses back on his nose, pulls his ball cap down low, and hands the binoculars back to Bobby.

"I make it six minutes."

Carr nods. "Me too. Get a head count."

Bobby peers through the binoculars and Carr steps around the center console, keeping his back to the shore. He fiddles with the fishing rods and the lines that run off the stern.

"I got five," Bobby says. "The guys on the beach, one more by the guesthouse, and two at the pier, who look like they're coming to say hello."

Carr glances up and sees two men donning float vests and pulling at the lines of a red-hulled Zodiac moored near the boathouse. "Plus the two we saw on the gate," he says, reeling in the lines.

"And who knows how many inside," Bobby says. "That's seven-plus on a weekday afternoon, with nothing much happening. With a party going on, it could be twice that."

Carr stows the fishing rods and returns to the console. He flips a switch and the twin outboards start. There's a puff of pale exhaust at the stern, an upwelling of foam, and a throaty rumble that echoes across the inlet. He lifts the binoculars and sees thick faces turn, can feel their sharpened interest. The men are climbing into the Zodiac now, and Carr hears their outboard whine.

"I don't need any more," Bobby says. "How about you?"

"We've seen what we came to see," Carr says, and he pushes the throttle, turns the wheel, and carves a long white crescent in the ocean.

What they've seen is bad to worse, and it's been the same everywhere they've looked the past two days—since Carr agreed with Tina to make a hurried reconnaissance of Isla Privada's security arrangements. In George Town, at Isla Privada's back office, the new guards are practically tripping over the old ones. From Boca Raton, Valerie called to report that Amy Chun's lethargic driver is due to be replaced in the coming week by an armed one, and that her house will be swept even more frequently for unwelcome electronics. Curtis Prager's personal protection has gone from one paunchy ex-cop to three muscular crew cuts. And here at his compound on Rum Point Drive, the household detail has grown from four to something north of seven. Only Dennis has yet to report in, on the all-important state of Isla Privada's network security. If that has changed, Carr told Tina, it's game over.

Carr has the boat planing now, and just coming even with the jagged peninsula that marks the western edge of Prager's property. He looks back along their wake. The protected inlet is dwindling behind them, and so is the red Zodiac, which has barely made it to the reef, two hundred meters from shore. Carr begins a wide curve around the rocks. He sees the Zodiac slow and then turn back. He looks ahead, and in the misty distance he can make out Rum Point.

Bobby calls to him over the engine and the rush of wind and water. "You want a beer?" Carr shakes his head. Bobby reaches into an ice chest beneath his seat and pulls out a bottle of the local brew. He takes a long swallow and sighs. "This stuff sucks."

"It's what they had at the store."

"No wonder," Bobby says, and takes another drink. "This Rink chick has been busy."

Carr nods. "Seems that way."

"She's got people nervous."

"I know, Bobby."

A third swallow and he pats his mouth with the back of his hand. "I fucking hate surprises."

It's pretty much all Bobby has said for two days—how much he hates surprises, how fucked up Boyce's intel was, and that they should be thinking about packing it in. And Carr has explained, over and over, that if they can't get a handle on what changes Rink has made, or if she's changed anything material to their plans, then they would indeed call it a day. The message has a half-life of about five minutes in Bobby's brain. Dennis is even more anxious but, mercifully, more inhibited about saying so, and Carr is glad he took Tina's advice and made no mention of Rink taking his fingerprints.

As wearing as Bobby's and Dennis's worry is, Valerie's and Latin Mike's seeming lack of nerves is somehow even more so. After his initial outburst, Mike has uttered no other word of complaint or concern, but simply set about reconnoitering—an uncharacteristically cooperative soldier. Valerie has yet to say anything.

They are approaching Rum Point, and there are other fishing boats ahead, pushing north out of the sound, and swimmers closer to the beach. Carr eases up on the throttle and turns the wheel a couple of points northwest.

Bobby pulls off his T-shirt, wipes his brow with it, and leans back in his seat. His body is thick and white, a fish from a different sea. "Could be twice the security when he has a party, could be three times—we really don't know," he says. "We're just guessing at what Rink might've changed. We don't know shit."

Carr sighs. "There was a lot we didn't know when Silva was in charge."

"We knew he was a lazy drunk, and that was..." Bobby puts up his hands, searching for a word.

"Comforting?"

"There you go," Bobby says, raising his beer bottle. "We're just feeling around in the dark now, and I like it better with the lights on."

"Like I said, Bobby—if she's changed anything important to our plans, then we don't go. If all she's done is add muscle—"

"You sound like Mike now."

"Yeah? I haven't heard Mike say much lately."

"Well he's saying the same shit as you—how it's all manageable, how we should keep on keepin' on. Personally, I think his perspective's fucked."

"Which means that mine is too?"

Bobby shrugs. "You can't like a job so much you lose sight of the basics. You can't get locked in. You gotta be willing to cut your losses if it's the smart thing."

"And you think I'm not willing?"

"Hey—I want to finish this as much as anybody. I got the same time in—the same sunk costs. But there'll be other jobs."

"Not too many others this size, Bobby."

"See what I mean—locked in," Bobby says. "That's the kind of attitude that gets you killed, brother." He drains the rest of the beer, pulls a fresh one from the locker, and holds the bottle against the side of his face. He closes his eyes.

Carr swings the boat farther north. They pass day-sailers and catamarans coming out of the sound, and divers massed along the reefs of Stingray City. When the sea around them is empty of other boats, Carr cuts the engines and lets them drift.

Bobby sits up and looks around. "What—we fishing for real?"

Carr shakes his head. "You know, I had a talk like this with Declan, just before the Mendoza job—"

"Oh for chrissakes!"

"About getting hung up on a job, and losing sight of the fundamentals."

"Motherfuckin' Carr—"

"You think that kind of attitude got him killed, Bobby, or was it something more specific?"

"I thought for sure we were done with this crap."

"We're done when I say so, and I'm not there yet. But here's where I am, Bobby: I'm down to the short strokes on the last job I ever want to work; I've had a nasty surprise with bad intel; and whenever I've asked a question in the last four months about what happened in Argentina I get answers that are at least fifty percent bullshit. So I'm nervous. And I don't want to be nervous anymore. I'm fucking tired of it. I'm tired of wondering who's got my back and who's going to stick something in it. If I'm going to finish this job, I need to know what's what, Bobby, and you're going to tell me."

Bobby shakes his head slowly. "Mike said—"

"Mike isn't here, Bobby. You're going to tell me."

Bobby chuckles and opens his beer. He takes a long swallow. Then he looks over his shoulder at the empty ocean. "Or what—you're gonna make me swim back?"

"We're pretty far out, so let's not have it come to that."

Another drink. "What the fuck do you want me to say, Carr?"

"I want to know what happened that night."

"Jesus, I've told you—"

"Talk to me about the barn. Talk to me about the money in the barn."

Bobby looks up. He shakes his head and laughs softly. "Mike thought you knew. In fact, the fucking guy thought I told you."

Carr sighs and looks at the sketchy clouds. He nods and smiles minutely. "Well, now he's right."

"Aw fuck!" Bobby barks. He pushes his sunglasses into his hair. His eyes are bleary and buried deep in a nest of lines and folds. "You fucking prick. That was bullshit, Carr—total fucking bullshit. What are you, practicing to be a cop?"

"Yeah, really sorry, Bobby. I feel just awful about betraying your trust. Now talk about the barn."

"Fuck you."

"So you're going to try the swimming?"

"Fuck you," Bobby says again, but there's less to it now. He lets his sunglasses fall to his nose, and he takes a deep breath. "Everything I told you about our run up to Bertolli's place, and everything I said about our running out again— all that was true. The only bullshit part was about the barn. They didn't hit us before we went in; they hit us after—after we came out."

"Who's *we*, Bobby? Who went in?"

"All four of us—me, Mike, Ray-Ray, and Deke. It was pitch-fucking-black, like I said, and cold—cold enough to see your breath if it wasn't so dark. We came up real quiet— coasting in at the end. There was a chain on the sliding door, and we clipped it. Then we popped the door lock and went inside.

"The goddamn place reeked of dirt and horse shit—it came out like a big cloud—but there were no horses. No, it was just like Deke said it would be—a long row of empty stalls, and one at the end that was outfitted as a strong room. Steel wall panels, a big reinforced door, this giant fucking lock that was about as useful as skates on a pig, and some really stupid wiring. We snipped the wires, jacked the door frame right off the wall, and opened her up like that." And Bobby snaps his fingers.

Carr starts at the sound, and it breaks a spell he didn't realize Bobby had woven. The darkness, the oiled weight of weapons and tools, the rich, humid scent of earth and horses, the metal tang of adrenaline on the tongue—Carr could taste it and smell it and feel it all. He could practically see Declan, hulking but somehow graceful as he moved through the shadows. Bobby is watching him, looking worried.

Carr tugs at the bill of his cap. "And inside?"

Bobby drags a hand across the back of his neck. He's staring at his feet, at the beer bottle, empty now, at anyplace but Carr. "Inside was money—bricks of euros, banded and shrink-wrapped, very neat. It was like Deke said, just not quite as much of it."

"How much?"

"We took out about two."

"Two million?"

"About. In two duffels. Ray-Ray had one, Mike took the other."

Carr nods slowly. "Split evenly—a million in each?"

"Pretty much."

"And then what?"

"And then we came out to the vans, and it was like I told you—they came around that hangar and lit us up."

"As you came out of the barn?"

"As we were getting back in the vans."

"And Mike still had the duffel?"

"He had one; Ray-Ray had the other."

Carr nods again and watches a cruise ship churn across the horizon to the north. "Then what happened?"

"Then it was lights, camera, action: yelling, shooting, hauling ass out of there—exactly like I said."

"Except you left out the part about hauling ass with a bag full of money."

"Yeah, well, the driving was the same, and so was the shooting."

"And the safe house, and the call from Declan—were those same too?"

Bobby blots his face with his balled-up T-shirt and looks at Carr. "I swear to Christ, that was straight up—all of it."

"But you and Mike decided not to mention the money. Why?"

"It was Mike's idea," Bobby says, slouching in his seat. "After Mendoza, we didn't know what the fuck was going on—if the Prager job was still on, who was gonna run things, hell, we didn't know if there was gonna be anything to run. And Mike said it was us who almost got our asses shot off—not you or Val or Dennis. We'd earned the money, and why the hell should we pay into the kitty for a job that might not happen."

"Except, as it turns out, the job is happening—and it's been happening for a while now. But I guess you two never revisited your original reasoning."

Bobby sits up and sticks out his chin. "It was us—"

"Who almost got your asses shot off—I heard you the first time. So, you lied about the money. Anything else you want to clear up?"

"Fuck you. Nothing else."

"No? You didn't kill Declan then? You didn't sell him to Bertolli?"

Bobby's face and fists clench tight. "You keep talking like that, ocean or no, you're gonna catch a beating."

Carr shakes his head. "So what was the take?" he asks.

"I told you—we got about half."

Carr pulls off his sunglasses. "Don't give me this *about* crap, Bobby. How much exactly?"

Bobby reaches into the ice chest and pulls out a fistful of crushed ice. He sits down and runs it over his neck and shoulders. "One point two even."

"And what happened to it?"

"In a bank—banks—finally, and what a pain in the ass that turned out to be. That much cash—it's a fucking albatross.

Took forever to get it moved, converted to dollars, give it an acceptable past, and get it deposited. I see why we pay Boyce to handle all that crap. Mike needed help to get it done."

Carr is standing now, out from under the canopy. "Help from who, Bobby?"

Bobby smiles and reaches into the ice chest for another beer. He pulls the cap off and takes a long drink. "That's a funny story," Bobby says. "Nando fixed it for us—set us up with a couple of friendly bankers in Miami. Remember Nando? It was a real blast from the past when Mike told me he was in touch. He knows all about this shit now. Guess he's come up in the world."

32

THE DREAM leaves him sweating and breathless, grasping for the story line even as it fades in the predawn light. Something with his father. Something with his mother. The courtyard in Caracas, the bedrooms in Mexico City. The beds empty. A booming, piratical laugh. Carr wakes holding nothing more than sheets.

He runs water on his face and walks into the living room. The walls are bathed in shifting blues and yellows from the television, playing silently to Latin Mike, who is stretched out on the sofa. A shopping channel from the States—makeup and jewelry that is not quite gold.

"You buying, Mike?" Carr says quietly.

Mike yawns widely. "Maybe the eyeliner."

Carr nods at Bessemer's bedroom. "Howie sleep tight?" he asks.

"Went in there with a bottle about midnight," Mike says. "Hasn't come out since."

Carr opens the bedroom door and looks inside. Bessemer is a snoring mound in a landslide of pillows and blankets. A bottle of Bombay Sapphire lies on its side, on the end table. Carr closes the door. "The guy puts it away," he says.

"More every day," Mike says, and he stretches and scratches and wanders to the terrace doors. He looks out at the glowing pool and the gray ocean. "You want to watch that. He's got to be upright for Prager."

"He will be." Carr walks to the bar and fishes in the little refrigerator for a Coke. "You're good to stay the morning?"

Mike nods. "You think Dennis got anywhere last night?"

"We'll find out."

A new salesman appears on the screen, with a pitch about a moisturizer.

Mike points and laughs. "Should buy some of this shit for Bobby. Guy looked like Larry the Lobster when you brought him back."

Carr nods. "I told him to use sunscreen."

Which is a lie. Carr had watched as Bobby drank beer and grew ever more pink, but he had said nothing about getting burned. What he had done was make Bobby repeat his story several times more, and answer questions about Nando and Valerie.

About Nando, Bobby had said little, besides that Mike had kept in touch with him over the years, and that the fee Nando had charged for helping them launder money "wasn't robbery." About Valerie he'd said less.

"She's never asked about the money, and I've never told her. If she knows something, she heard it from Mike."

"Mike tell her a lot of secrets?" Carr had asked, and he'd gripped the canopy rail tight enough that his fingers ached.

"Fuck should I know?" Bobby had said, but he'd looked away.

A silence followed, during which Bobby drank another beer and Carr replayed his afternoon in Miami against the new backdrop Bobby had painted. It was Bobby who'd broken the silence, with a decorous belch and an observation.

"Mike won't put that money in the pot."

"I'll save him the trouble—I'll just deduct it from his cut. From yours too."

"He won't like it."

"And how about you, Bobby?"

Bobby had shrugged. "I'm not crazy about it, but I wasn't crazy about the sneaking around, either. I figure if we're gonna do this job, then let's get it done. I want this fucker over with. But that's me—Mike's another story."

"I'm not going to lose a lot of sleep over it."

"So, am I supposed to tell him about this, or what?"

"Do what you want, Bobby."

It doesn't seem to Carr that Bobby has yet told Latin Mike anything, though with Mike it wouldn't necessarily be obvious. Maybe Bobby has been too busy tending his sunburn.

BESSEMER IS still asleep when Carr leaves the suite, and Mike is still on the sofa. Carr is careful on his way through the lobby, and watchful, but there is no reappearance of Kathy Rink's men. The sky is painted pearl gray as he crosses the visitors' parking lot, and already the day's heat is building beneath it. There's a rumble of thunder off to the east as he climbs into Mike's SUV and drives away.

The workhouse is at the end of a quiet lane, on a canal that feeds into North Sound. It's a stucco box in faded blue, with a tiled roof and plaster embellishments around the windows. From the street, Carr can see into the sandy backyard. There's a metal dock there and the fishing boat is tied up alongside it. Dennis opens the door. A week on Grand Cayman and he's paler and thinner than ever—a red-eyed, unshaved reed. He puts a finger to his lips.

"Bobby's still crashed," he says softly. Carr follows him in. The main room is white and raftered, and the big front window has a view of unkempt hedges, milky sky, and planes angling toward the airport. The furnishings are a hodge-podge of hotel castoffs: fraying slipper chairs, sagging leather and chrome armchairs, water-stained end tables, and the ashtrays of a dozen defunct lounges. Dennis has three laptops open side by side on a chipped glass dining table, behind a stack of high-speed modems, coils of cable, and a platoon of empty soda cans.

"You want coffee?" he asks Carr. Carr nods and Dennis disappears into the kitchen, reappearing with a steaming mug.

Carr takes a drink. It's bad. "When's the last time you slept?" he asks.

Dennis's smile is skewed and slightly goofy. "A while ago."

"Hope you were doing more than just surfing porn sites."

A blush spreads up Dennis's neck. "Not just porn."

Carr puts his coffee aside. "So what's new in the virtual world of Isla Privada Holdings?"

"That's a nontrivial question," Dennis says, rubbing his chin and taking a seat before one of the laptops. Carr girds himself: Dennis gets pedantic when he's tired, and he's tired now. "Security on their VPN wasn't totally stupid to begin with. I mean, aside from the happy gap we want to exploit, the multifactor authorization is pretty cute. And the rest of the stuff—it may be textbook, predictable, maybe even lazy, but it's not *totally* stupid. It's good enough, for instance, that if you look at it too hard—look *actively*, I mean, poke around too much—they're going to know you're there. And they're going to poke back." He looks up at Carr, his eyes shadowed but earnest. "We don't want that."

"We don't," Carr affirms.

Dennis opens four packs of sugar over his coffee mug, stirs with a pencil, sips at it, and smiles. "So, a nontrivial question—how do you look inside the box without taking the lid off? Not so easy, unless..." Dennis taps a forefinger lightly on his temple.

"Unless you're you—I get it. So what's changed?"

Dennis drinks more coffee. His fingers beat a droning drumroll on the tabletop. "A few things. They've upgraded their routers; they've implemented better filtering on inbound and outbound packets; and they're scanning their servers better. Still textbook, but at least a more recent edition. In fact, if I was going to mount a denial-of-service attack on them, I might actually have to spend more than ten minutes planning it."

"I didn't think we cared about that stuff."

"We don't."

Carr counts to ten and struggles to keep the impatience out of his voice. "What's changed that we care about, Dennis?"

"For the moment, nothing—at least from what I see. The network access protocols and authorization layers are the same. The out-of-band component, to the user's cell phone, is still in place. Last night, I walked through video of Chun as she was logging in yesterday, and I synchronized it with the sniffer logs. Everything looks the same."

"And our gap?"

"From what I see, it's still there. Once you pass through the authorization layers—the password generator, the thumbprint scan, the call back to the cell phone with a second password—and you get onto the network, access to Isla Privada's processing system is by password alone. And there's still no cross-check between the network access and processing system. So if I've got Curtis Prager's processing system password, then that system thinks I'm Curtis Prager, and it lets me do everything Curtis Prager can do, even if I've gotten onto their network using Amy Chun's ID."

Carr sighs. Something loosens in his chest, but it tightens again when he looks at Dennis. "There are a lot of qualifiers in what you said, Dennis—'for the moment,' and 'from what I see.' They're not particularly reassuring."

Dennis's fingers drum faster on the table. "They shouldn't be. I can't see too far into their network without hitting trip wires, but I've seen enough to know that their environment is changing. They haven't fixed the hole that we want to climb through yet, but I'd say it's just a matter of time."

Carr sighs again, but there's no relief in it. "How much time?"

Dennis shrugs. "Ask Kathy Rink."

TINA'S HOTEL room overlooks a garden, with lavish beds of jacaranda, frangipani, and hibiscus massed around a weathered stone fountain. The garden is empty and the flowers are limp and restless in the humid breeze. Carr turns from the window.

"You should be smiling," Tina says from the sofa. "It's all good."

"You call it good; I call it fucked up, though maybe not completely fucked up. *Maybe* not. There's a difference."

"Semantics."

"Call it that when it's *your* ass hanging out."

Tina chuckles and unfolds herself from the sofa. She wears a simple gray skirt and a short black T-shirt, and her white-blond hair is pulled into a short ponytail. She pads barefoot across the room to refill a glass of ice water from a pitcher.

"Come on, Carr—the system stuff hasn't changed, security's tighter but still manageable, and your prints came back to Kathy Rink with Greg Frye's record attached—and only his record: that's good news." Carr looks at her and raises an eyebrow. "What?" Tina says.

"I'm just wondering how you managed it—the finger-prints, I mean."

"*I* didn't."

"Boyce, then."

"I don't ask, and he doesn't tell." She smiles at Carr but he doesn't return it.

"This is more than just ordering off-menu—more than calling in a favor here and there. This is pulling some serious weight, and I have a hard time believing you don't know shit about it."

Tina returns to the sofa, folds her white legs beneath her, and smooths her skirt. "I know about gift horses, and where not to look."

"I'm serious, Tina."

"So am I. I'm not talking about this anymore, and if you've got half a brain you won't either." Her eyes are flat and icy and unwavering, and finally Carr turns back to the view of the garden. "How's Bessemer holding up?" Tina asks.

"He's pickling himself in gin."

"He going to keep his shit together for Prager?"

"Mike was worried about the same thing. He will."

"And Mike, and the rest of your crew—how're they doing?"

Carr takes a deep breath and turns around. Tina's eyes have lost some of their chill, and that makes it easier. "I found out what happened to Bertolli's money," he says, and he tells her about Bobby's confession, and about the afternoon he spent in Miami, walking up and down Brickell Avenue. Tina is perfectly still; her face is without expression while Carr speaks and in the squirming silence that follows. Finally, she clasps her white hands together and puts them in her lap. Her voice is soft.

"Well, they're busy beavers, aren't they? Maybe you're not giving them enough to do. Too much time on their hands."

"I'm sure that was the issue."

Tina frowns. "There's plenty here for me to be pissed at—like the fact that I'm only just now hearing about this— but I'm doing my best to rise above it, and so should you." Carr nods and Tina continues. "Assuming Bobby's not full of shit, this explains where some of the money went—though not all of it."

"Bobby said Declan had the rest. If he did, then it went up with his van."

"Maybe. You buy that Bobby and Mike had only half the cash?"

"Why lie about that? He's no more of a shithead for walking off with the whole take than he is for walking off with half of it."

"Maybe," she says again. "And what about tipping off Bertolli? You don't think those two had anything to do with that?"

"I think Bobby was telling the truth about that."

"And you've proven to be such a good judge."

Carr bites back his first response and rubs his chin. "They sell Declan to Bertolli, they sell themselves in the bargain. They were all getting shot at together."

"If you buy Bobby's version of events."

"What about your witness—Bertolli's runaway gunman— did he have orders to shoot at only two out of four guys?"

Tina shakes her head. "Maybe Bobby and Mike were willing to roll the dice—warn Bertolli and take a chance that in the ensuing shit storm Declan would get iced and they could split with the cash."

"That's a hell of a chance, Tina. Takes large brass balls to make that bet, or a tiny little brain."

Tina shrugs skeptically. "Mike and Bobby don't fit that profile? Well, you'd know better than I.

"But what about Fernando—what the fuck is he doing with these guys? Last I heard he was slapping up condos in Cabo or something. Guess the real estate market's driven him back to a life of crime." She shakes her head. "And Valerie in on it too—who'd have guessed she couldn't be trusted?" Tina looks at Carr and smiles thinly.

"I don't know what she's in on, or since when."

"Ask her—I'm sure she'll give you a straight answer."

Carr looks at the garden again. The wind has picked up and the flowers are shaking their heads at the darkening sky. "You don't think she would?"

Tina's laugh is like a blade. "It's what you think that matters. Do you trust her—do you trust any of them—to do their jobs? This late in the game, that's what it comes down to: honor among thieves."

"Fuck trust—I'll have their money. They need me if they want to get paid."

"Now *that's* a working relationship," Tina says, nodding. She shifts on the sofa, stretching out her legs. "And speaking of which—what about our little project down south?"

"What about it?"

"The unanswered questions—who tipped Bertolli, and what happened to the rest of the cash—you want to spend more money on them? Should I keep asking around?"

There's a rumble of thunder outside, and fat drops of rain against the glass. The garden is dark, the flower beds a uniform gray.

"Keep asking," Carr says.

THE WIND is gone and the rain falls straight and heavy; the short sprint from parking lot to lobby leaves Carr soaked.

He shivers as he steps into the elevator and presses the fourth-floor button. He's alone in the car and the door is nearly shut when a hand slides in and bumps it open again. And then Valerie is there, wet from the rain. She presses the button for three, waits for the door to close, and presses her mouth against his.

33

HOWARD BESSEMER is a vision in seersucker: clear-eyed, pink-cheeked, hair slicked and shining—an altogether healthier vision than his recent diet should allow. He sits erect and alert in the passenger seat, scanning the approaching coast, the whitecaps, the immaculate sky, as Carr bears left off Frank Sound Road onto North Side Road. Bessemer's window is down and his face is turned into the salt breeze, and he reminds Carr of a dog out for a ride.

"Day like today, you see why people move here," Carr says.

Bessemer smiles. "Wait till you see Curt's place. It's not quite San Simeon, but it's a hell of a spread."

Carr nods. "Prager live there all by himself?"

"Him and the staff. Every now and then he sets up a girl in the guesthouse."

"Girl as in girlfriend?"

"As in hooker," Bessemer says, smirking. Carr lifts an eyebrow. "Always pricey, though. Very high-class."

"No doubt," Carr says.

They ride on in silence, Bessemer watching the sea, and Carr, despite their destination and the mounting tension, failing to keep his mind from the night before. Lack of sleep casts a dreamlike scrim over his memories of the evening— burnishing the images and shuffling their order.

Even from across the room, Valerie's voice was close in his ear. "You want this job done, and so do I. I did what I had to do."

Her hands were cold under his shirt. Her hair was wet and smelled like lilac and an airplane cabin.

"All I know about what happened down there is what Bobby and Mike told us. The first Mike said anything to me about euros was the day before we went to Miami."

Her mouth tasted of airline wine, and it seemed to be everywhere at once.

"Bobby and Mike talked about Nando sometimes, and so did Deke, but I never met him until that day in Miami."

Her dress was wet, and it peeled away like a shedding skin. She left it in a pile beside the minibar.

"Amy's gone for two days, up in New York. I'm booked on the first flight back to Boca tomorrow morning."

Her legs were smooth and slick, and the hollows of her neck were full of rain.

"Mike was going to pull out of the job if I didn't help him wash his money—and he was going to take Bobby with him."

Her room was on the third floor, overlooking treetops and a loading dock. She kept the lights off and opened the drapes.

"Bobby told Mike that you knew, and Mike told me, and then I got on a plane down here. I didn't want to talk to you about this on the phone."

Her lips were searing.

"The e-mail from that coffee bar? That was to Nando. He said no cell phones—messaging only. He was superparanoid."

In the dim light, her skin was like matte gold.

"That afternoon, with Mike, that was the only time. You want this job done, and so do I. I do what I have to, and I'm not going to apologize for it."

The rain grew heavier, and it made a tearing sound as it fell through the leaves.

"Have you thought any more about afterward—where you want to go, what you want to do? 'Cause if you haven't, I've got ideas."

North Sound Road becomes Rum Point Drive, and Bessemer clears his throat. "We're coming to it," he says, and a surge of adrenaline drags Carr from his reverie.

Prager's property announces itself to their right, with a wrought-iron fence and high, dense shrubs that obscure the ocean view. A while longer and they reach the gate.

It's tall and steel and topped with cameras, and adjoined by a green pastel bungalow. There are two men inside and Carr recognizes one of them from the airport tail. The man comes out wearing a trained smile and a Glock on his hip. He's carrying an iPad and Carr sees two pictures on the screen: his own and Bessemer's. The guard glances at the photos and at them and rests a hand on the car roof.

"Mr. Frye, Mr. Bessemer, welcome. Mr. Prager will meet you at the main house. Just stay on this drive—you can't miss it." As he speaks, the gate opens and he steps aside and waves them in.

The drive is crushed shell and it's bordered by close-cut lawns and ironwood trees sculpted by the constant winds. It curves gently west and rises up a hillside that he knows, from the broader topography, must be man-made. Another curve and they're at the top, where the drive empties into a wide circle of pavers, set in a herringbone pattern. There's a fountain in the center, marble, pale pink, like the inside of a baby's ear. A marble fish stands on its tail within, and the braid of water falling from its mouth makes a prosperous sound. Across the circle is the house.

Its architectural pedigree is indeterminate—an uneasy hybrid of Italianate, Spanish Colonial, and Georgian—with *big* the only unifying principle. Beneath the tiled roof, its stone walls are yellow—goldenrod in the main parts, going to a butter color for the arched colonnades and the ornament work around the windows and doors. There is a portico in front, and two glossy black doors. They stand open, and Curtis Prager is in the threshold, in sandals, linen trousers, and a pale pink polo shirt. Kathy Rink is at his side, in a green golf skirt and with a smile fastened on her face.

Carr glances at Bessemer, who is smiling oddly and humming softly, tunelessly. Carr wonders if he's taken something. "Shit," Carr whispers, but when he pulls up to the portico, Bessemer sharpens.

Bessemer is out of the Toyota before Carr has switched off the engine, a big smile and a big hand extended. There's a clumsy hug and biceps squeezing, and then Prager holds Bessemer at arm's length. He's taller than Carr expected, with more ropy muscle on him. He seems to dwarf Bessemer.

"Jesus, Bess, you look like shit. What the hell have you been doing to yourself?"

Bessemer grins and ducks his head almost shyly. "Just the usual misdemeanors. But what about you—you keep a special portrait in the attic, or something? Drinking pints of virgin's blood? You look twenty years younger."

"*Virgin's blood.*" Prager laughs. "That's the pot calling the kettle. I just do a day's work once in a while, and then I get on a tennis court or in a boat. Get some oxygen in my blood, instead of pure ethanol."

Prager claps Bessemer on the shoulder once more, and Bessemer ducks his head again, and it occurs to Carr that he's witnessing a sort of theater: an imitation of camaraderie, an acting out of Bessemer's subordination. He's not sure who the intended audience is. Maybe himself. Maybe they do it for each other.

There's a final lockjaw laugh, and Prager turns to Carr.

His eyes, in his lined, brown face, are the color of sleet. His hand is cool and wiry. "And you must be Mr. Frye—at long last. Sorry for the scheduling screwup, but this week has been one fire drill after the other."

"There are worse places to kill time," Carr says. "And call me Greg."

Prager nods. "I'm Curt. Now, I hope you'll bear with me a bit longer, Greg, before we sit down." He looks at Kathy Rink, who looks inside the house and beckons.

Two men appear, both stocky with crew cuts, one holding something that looks like an old-fashioned walkie-talkie. He smiles politely and approaches Bessemer, while his partner waits, eight feet off.

"Mr. Bessemer, if you could spread your feet apart and hold your arms straight out from your sides, I'll sweep you down real quick. Mr. Frye, you'll be next."

THERE ARE platters of shrimp, crab legs, and scallops on crushed ice, a tureen of ceviche, bowls of gazpacho, frosted pitchers of iced tea, and plates of sliced fruit, all on a linen-covered table, under a wide awning. Beyond the awning, there are trees with songbirds in them, and a hillside descending in terraces to the beach and the swaying sea.

"Kathy insists on a frisk," Prager says, smiling across the table at Carr and Bessemer. "Personally, I think she likes it."

Rink smiles just as brightly. "It's what you pay me for, Curt, and I'm sure Mr. Frye—Greg—understands."

Carr nods and raises a glass of iced tea. "I'm all for hobbies."

Howard Bessemer squeezes a lemon wedge over his plate. "That other fellow you had—what was his name—he never saw the need to have me felt up."

Carr watches over his glass as Rink seeks out Prager's eye,

and Prager nods to her minutely. "See what you were missing?" Prager says, and he dips a shrimp in red sauce and eats it.

"When it comes to security, Howie, it's smart to change things up now and then," Carr says. "Otherwise your boys get stale." He looks out at the ocean, the sand, two patrolling guards; then he looks at Prager. "Your private island?"

Prager smiles. "Not an island, but private."

"It's nice, but don't you miss home?" he asks Prager. "The States, I mean."

Prager eats another shrimp. "This is home to me. It's the only place I miss."

"But there's no issue with you going back stateside?"

"I go back when I need to," Prager says. "And what about you, Greg? And you are Greg today, right—not Glenn Freed, or Gary Frain, or Craig Farley? Is Boston still your base, Greg, or are you resettling in Palm Beach?"

Carr knows he's supposed to be impressed that Prager knows Greg Frye's aliases, and intimidated, and he lets his face tighten. "I do business in a lot of places. People come to me if they need to, and they don't seem to care much where I am or what I call myself, as long as I meet my obligations. Palm Beach is okay, though. The real estate market's still plenty soft."

Kathy Rink pats her mouth with a linen napkin. "That what you're doin' there, Greg, bottom-feeding?"

"That's real estate, right? Making money off somebody else's stupidity. Or their shit luck."

"Too true," Prager says approvingly. "But property's just a sideline for you, isn't it? I mean, you didn't come to talk to me about mortgage financing?"

"I need a banker. And maybe it's possible a banker could need me."

Prager's smile is indulgent. "They always need customers, otherwise they'd have no business. But strictly speaking, I'm not a banker, Greg—I run a holding company. And I don't have customers, per se, I have investors—typically, quite large ones. That said, Isla Privada does own several financial institutions in Florida. If you need an account set up, I'm sure we can help you out."

Carr spears a fat scallop on his fork. He dips it in a dill sauce and pops it whole into his mouth. "I really like your paranoia, Curt," he says, chuckling. "But it's a fucking conversation killer. Would it help if she pats me down some more? Maybe a cavity search?"

Kathy Rink's laugh is throaty and loud. "Can it wait till after lunch?"

Carr winks at her and looks at Prager. "I think you have some idea what I do, and what I'm looking for. I came here to do business, not to hang out by the pool or tiptoe around."

Prager shrugs. "As I told Bess, I'm happy to listen. But doing business is something different, Greg. The truth is, I don't know you from Adam."

"Howie's not a good reference?"

"You're here only because of his introduction. But with all due respect to Bess—and he knows I love him—an introduction is not quite the same as a reference. Bess doesn't actually do business with you, whatever that business is—he can't vouch for you that way. So you don't come with the same kind of pedigree most of my new clients come with."

"The fingerprints didn't tell you enough?"

Prager glances at Rink. "They tell names and dates and places, Greg," Rink says. "Which could add up to somebody interesting, or could be somebody who's a little vulnerable."

"Vulnerable to what?" Carr asks.

"To being squeezed."

"Squeezed? By who?"

Rink chuckles. "It's a long fucking list of acronyms. We'll run out of daylight before I get through 'em all."

Carr smiles and works some incredulity into his voice. "You think I'm a cop?"

Prager smiles back. "I don't know enough about you to think anything at all, Greg. That's why, for now, it's better that I just sit and listen. If what you have to say is interesting, I may decide to spend the time and money to find out more about you—pretty much all there is to know. If not, we will have had a pleasant lunch and we'll say good-bye."

Howard Bessemer partly stifles a belch. He looks at Carr and shrugs. "I think that's your cue, Greg."

34

THEY LEAVE Bessemer with the remains of lunch, and they walk as Carr talks—he and Prager in the lead, Kathy Rink trailing. It's a slow saunter around the grounds, and they stop occasionally to admire the horticulture or the view, but throughout, Prager and Rink maintain a careful silence. No questions, no comments, not even a sigh. Carr has waited a long time to make this pitch, and he knows Frye's business as well as Frye himself might, if he weren't fictional.

"It's a simple operation: I'm basically a middleman, a wholesaler. I buy stones in quantity—sometimes large quantities, sometimes smaller lots—and I resell them to other middlemen, or to retailers. The nature of my suppliers is such that I pay significantly discounted prices, so I can offer merchandise to my buyers at a price point way below other wholesalers, and still maintain a very fat margin. As you'd expect, it's a cash business, end to end: my suppliers want only cash, and I take only cash from my buyers.

"I started out regional—the Boston area, and New England—but, my trip to Otisville aside, I'm good at what I do and I've been successful. I can handle quantity in a hurry in either direction—buying or selling—and I can ship it, so now I've got suppliers and buyers all over the United States and abroad. Like I said before, they come to me, and I can do business anywhere. I keep my overheads low, in part by contracting whatever services I need—security, transpo, storage, whatever—so, no employees. I spend a few months here, a few months there, but I'm based pretty much nowhere, and that's how I like it.

"I figure my banking needs are nothing new to you. I've got cash to move, and to put on deposit somewhere—with somebody who's not going to file a whole lot of paper. I want to invest what I deposit—build a diversified portfolio, nothing too aggressive, but with some international exposure. China definitely, maybe India—we can talk about it. And I need someone who can help me repatriate my assets—give them a boring history, something I can pay taxes on, though not too much. But something that'll stand up to an audit. And of course I want access—cash on demand, wherever I happen to be, in the States or abroad.

"In terms of quantity, I've got ten bucks I'd want to place up front, and I'd be looking to place maybe two bucks a month afterward. Maybe more sometimes."

Carr pauses as they approach Prager's pink guesthouse, waiting for some reaction but getting none. The guesthouse has a wall of French windows on the ocean side that open onto a patio. There are two tables there, with umbrellas and chairs, and Prager sits in one and watches the surf unfurl. Rink sits next to him and looks at Carr, who continues.

"What's different about my setup—where maybe there's an opportunity to work with somebody like you—are my buyers overseas. I have a lot of them—in Europe, Latin America, Asia, all over—a whole network of gray market independents. And all they do, all day long, is buy and sell stones—for local currency, for euros, for dollars, for pretty much whatever you want. Cash goes out, diamonds come in; cash comes in, diamonds go out—all day long, and no questions asked. And they all know how to ship."

Carr pauses again, waiting for a response. And he gets one, after a fashion: Prager looks at him for a long while and raises an eyebrow before he stands and strolls away. Carr follows, and Kathy Rink follows him. They pass a greenhouse and a low cinder-block building painted the same pink as the guesthouse. It's the size of a two-car garage, and it has a tin roof and roll-down metal door. The door is open, and two young black men are inside, talking, laughing, and doing something with the gardening equipment ranged around the walls. They fall silent as Prager passes. The path curves toward the beach again, and when they hit the sand, Carr continues.

"Stones are a lot easier to move than bulk cash," Carr continues, "and a whole lot harder to trace. They're easier to store and secure, and easy to convert to cash when you need to—especially with a network like mine at your disposal. How much simpler does your operation become if you don't have to worry about moving cash—if you can move diamonds instead? Or better yet—if somebody is moving the diamonds for you? How much does that improve your margins? And how much more can you charge your clients for access to this kind of network?"

Carr finishes as they climb the stairs that lead from the beach to a vast blue swimming pool. They cross flagstones, headed toward more glass doors. Carr sees Bessemer, still at the table under the awning. Bessemer raises a hand in salute, and Carr waves back and looks for cameras, remembering where they're mounted, figuring the blind spots. The three remain silent as they go into the house, down a paneled hallway, past what looks like a wine cellar, and up a flight of stairs.

At the top of the stairs, past a study, a game room, a music room, through an atrium, and down another paneled corridor, is Prager's office. It's white and glass, minimally furnished in an aggressively modern style—a monk's cell with Barcelona chairs, a pair of Rothkos on the wall, and a view of palm trees and a Caribbean garden. Prager takes a seat behind a brushed aluminum desk that looks like a knife blade and that is bare but for a laptop, a large, wafer-thin monitor, and a phone. Rink takes one of the guest chairs. Carr takes the other and tries not to look at the laptop or at the thumb-print scanner plugged into it. Prager clasps his hands behind his head, leans back in his chair, and sighs.

"You're a guy off the street, Greg. Yes, you know Bess, and you have a little story to tell, but basically you're a guy off the street." Prager says it quietly, with a faint smile that is almost regretful. Carr says nothing.

"You could be a big deal, or a big waste of time," Kathy Rink says. "Or you could be something worse than a waste of time. How're we supposed to know?"

Carr shakes his head. "I'm confused. Are you saying no, or that you want to know more?"

It's Rink who answers. "Maybe he's saying you haven't sold him yet."

Carr shrugs and looks at Prager. "I'm not a salesman. It seems to me you're either interested or you're not."

"I don't know if I'm interested," Prager says. "I don't know if you're anything besides talk."

Carr lets a silence descend, and then he nods his head. "How about I get something from the car?"

Prager nods to Kathy Rink, who picks up a phone. In a moment a crew cut appears. "Take Mr. Frye to his car, and then bring him back," Rink says. "Anything he brings with him gets scanned."

The crew cut leads Carr out. When they return, Carr is carrying a slim metal attaché case.

"You checked it?" Rink asks, and the crew cut nods and leaves. Carr places the case on the desk and turns it so that the latches face Prager.

"I take it I'm supposed to open this," Prager says, and Carr nods. Kathy Rink comes around the desk to stand beside her boss. Prager looks at her and she lifts the lid.

Prager is silent for a moment, and then smiles thinly. "Very dramatic, Greg. They for real?"

"You expect me to say they're not? But I'm going to leave them with you, so you can check them out yourself."

"How much is here?"

"In carats or in dollars?"

"Dollars."

"Loose like that—three bucks, plus or minus. A lot more when you turn them into earrings and bracelets. But I figure you'll check that too."

"This a big lot for you?"

"Nope."

Prager leans back and sighs again. "So you're a guy off the street with a story and props—albeit, expensive props."

"Which makes me more worried, not less," Rink says. "Not many folks can afford this kind of window dressing. Assuming they're even for real."

Carr reaches across the desk and closes the attaché case. "I guess this is where I say thanks for lunch."

Prager puts a hand on the lid. "If you were in my shoes, would you do it differently?"

"It would depend on how much I wanted your business," Carr says.

"The dollar amounts you're talking about are rounding error," Prager says, shaking his head. "Not even that."

"Then I guess it would depend on how interested I was in access to this network—what kind of problems it could solve for me, what kind of new revenue streams it could bring."

"And if you were interested?"

"I'd ask you to open your kimono—at least a little."

Kathy Rink clears her throat and frowns. Prager ignores her and nods slowly. "And if I ask?"

Carr rubs his chin and looks at Prager. "Open the briefcase. Look in the lid pocket."

Prager lifts the lid and lowers it again. He holds a black flash drive between thumb and forefinger. "What's this supposed to be?"

"My kimono," Carr says.

35

CARR WALKS into the suite, and Latin Mike and Bobby look at him like children at a Christmas tree. Bobby's face is red and peeling. "Did he take it?"

Carr closes the door behind Bessemer and nods. "He took everything. When I left, the jump drive was sitting on his desk, right next to his computer."

Latin Mike sighs. Bobby smiles and puts out a fist. Mike taps it lightly. "So now we wait," Bobby says.

"We'll know as soon as it's plugged into anything with an Internet connection," Carr says.

"When what gets plugged in?" Bessemer asks from behind the bar.

"Gotta be the next day or two," Mike says, ignoring him. "He's got that party next weekend, and afterward he's on his road trip."

"Prager invited us to the party," Carr says. "I want to be far away by then."

"What's supposed to get plugged in?" Bessemer asks again.

"I gave Prager some information on a jump drive—information about my business, and some of my colleagues abroad. It should give him a better idea of what I've got to offer." Which only seems to make Bessemer more nervous. Bobby and Mike exchange looks, and Carr smiles thinly.

"Why don't you sit in the sun a while, Howie," he says. Bessemer shrugs and carries his gin and tonic to the terrace.

Bobby shakes his head. "Seriously—how long will that shit hold up?"

"Not long," Carr says. "The names are real, and they're really diamond dealers, all over the world, all active in the gray market. But only one of them—a guy in Singapore—knows the name Greg Frye, and that's because he's been paid to know it. I told Prager that the Singapore guy's the only one with approval to talk about my business. I told him if he likes what he hears, I'll okay the others to talk too."

"And this Singapore guy—what's he gonna say?"

"Something plausible. Given what Boyce is charging us, it better be. With a little luck, though, Howie will have done his thing and we'll be gone before it's an issue."

Latin Mike looks out at Bessemer, and then looks at Carr. "How did he do today?"

"He was fine," Carr says. "Kept it together, didn't speak unless he was spoken to, focused mainly on the food."

"And you think he'll keep on keepin' on?"

Carr nods. "He has only one more thing to do, once Dennis tells us the drive's been plugged in."

"So I guess it doesn't matter that he's asking a lot of questions," Mike says, nodding. " 'Cause pretty soon it won't matter how much he knows."

"He's my problem, and I'll take care of him."

"He's everybody's problem if you don't, *jefe*."

"I said I'd take care of him."

Mike looks at him, and doesn't look away when Bobby clears his throat. Bobby puts a hand on Mike's shoulder. "Once that thing's plugged in, we zip up and get out, *amigo*, so we better start packing."

Bobby and Mike depart, and Carr collapses into an armchair. The two of them seemed to take up more than their usual share of space and oxygen, and Carr is relieved to be alone. His breath leaves him in a long sigh, and the tensions of the day—Prager's relentless skepticism, Rink's barely veiled hostility, the constant fear of a wrong word from Bessemer, the constant feel of cameras on him, like a finger tapping incessantly on his skull, and all the pumping adrenaline—hit at once. His shoulders cramp, his legs tighten, and the sweat that stayed away, even through the day's heat, rises suddenly through his shirt. A bitter taste washes through his mouth. His stomach twists, and for an instant he feels his lunch coming up. And then his cell burrs.

"You're answering the phone," Tina says. "That's a good sign."

"I've got all my fingers and toes too, at least so far."

"Prager was interested?"

"We'll see just how much."

"No word from Dennis yet?"

"Not yet."

"What's taking so long?"

"Prager's a busy guy. I assume he's got some other things to do before he gets around to researching me."

"You'll call when you hear?"

"I'll call."

To stay in the chair is to sleep, Carr knows, so he hoists himself up and goes to the bar. He fills a glass with crushed ice, club soda, and limes, and looks at Bessemer on the terrace. He's numb in a lounge chair, his head to one side, a leg dangling— a puppet without strings. His round face is empty, and Carr thinks again of Bessemer's son, Simon—his watchful eyes, his suspicion. Bessemer's glass is balanced precariously on his belly, in the grip of limp fingers. Carr opens the terrace door and retrieves it. Bessemer mutters something he can't make out.

. . .

CARR SHOWERS and changes his clothes, and when he steps into the living room again, he finds the daylight fading and Bessemer sprawled on the sofa. His shoes are off, and his shirt is untucked, but he's out just as cold. Carr shakes his head and picks up the room service menu.

He's just about made his choices when his phone rings again. Carr crosses the room at a run.

"You don't call?" Valerie says. "I've got to depend on Mike to let me know? What's the matter, you tired of me?"

He sighs. "I figured you'd call me."

"I guess you figured right. It went well?"

"So far so good, but he hasn't done anything with the drive yet, and that's what matters. Chun is back from New York?"

"Yeah, and she has no trips planned for a couple of weeks."

"And her security?"

"Nothing new since last time," Valerie says. "You going to let me know when you hear something, or am I going to have to keep chasing you?"

"I'll let you know."

There's a long pause, filled by the soft hiss of the ether, and then Valerie sighs. "It's just around the corner now. You come to any decisions about what you're going to do with yourself afterward?"

"I'll let you know."

Carr looks at Bessemer and can't imagine him going anyplace, and decides against room service. He has a light dinner in one of the hotel restaurants, and afterward he kicks off his shoes and rolls his pant legs and walks along the shore. The beach is empty but for a few couples, strolling arm in arm, and Carr gives them a wide berth. The sea breeze has turned cold, but a tropical lassitude still trails him across the sand.

Too long on the roller coaster, Declan called it. "Yer jacked up so long, you get used to it—used to the fright and paranoia, and then you get stupid. You know you're supposed to stay scared, to stay alert, but you can't seem to care enough to make it happen. Too tired and bored to save yer own goddamn life. And it always comes at the worst feckin' time—right at the end, when you need to be on top of the game."

Right at the end—it's where Carr is at last: Dennis says the word, Howie makes his call, and then it's Valerie's turn, a matter of little more than typing. And then...what? A flight north, to watch his father disintegrate? A flight south, to watch Tina's men sift ashes? A flight into the sunset with Valerie? One too many options to settle by the toss of a coin, and Carr wonders if it really matters which he picks. *Too tired and bored to save yer own goddamn life.* Too tired, certainly. He thinks about Bessemer, in a heap on the sofa, and of Latin Mike's admonition: *He's everybody's problem if you don't.* . . . His throat tightens and a clammy sweat breaks out across his forehead.

The incoming tide is lapping around his ankles when his phone goes off, and he answers without looking at the number.

"Dennis?"

"Who's Dennis?" Arthur Carr asks, and Carr can tell right away that his father's been drinking.

"Someone I work with. Is everything okay?"

"I'll call some other time, if you're working."

"It's fine. Are you all right?"

"All right?" Arthur Carr snorts. "You know she's leaving, don't you?"

"Who's leaving?"

"Eleanor Calvin—who else would I be talking about?"

"She told you she was moving away?"

"The question is, Why didn't you tell me? She said you've

known for weeks. Is this privileged information? Maybe you think I'm a security risk."

"I didn't want to say anything until I'd made new arrangements."

"*New arrangements*—what the hell do I need *those* for? I didn't like the old arrangements you made, and now that she's walking out, I don't need any goddamn new ones. The hell with that disloyal bitch."

"Is she there?"

"What if she is?"

"Put her on the phone."

His father's laugh is jagged. "Well, she's not here. She walked out on me. Said I could fix my own dinner if I didn't like her cooking, and that if I was going to curse—"

"What did you say to her?"

"I had no idea her sensibilities were so—"

"What did you say?"

"Nothing much, and I can't imagine she hasn't heard the word *whore* before."

"For chrissakes!" Carr says, and he realizes he's shouting, and that the few people on the beach are staring.

Arthur Carr laughs again. "In fact, I'm sure she's heard worse."

Carr sighs and walks toward the jetty that marks the edge of the hotel property. "You can't talk to her that way, Dad," Carr says softly. "You can't expect her to put up with it."

"Do you have any idea what *I've* put up with?"

"You can't talk to people that way."

"*People?* She's not people—she's my goddamn wife, and I'll talk to her any goddamn way I please."

The breath catches in Carr's throat, and there's a rushing noise in his ears. When he speaks, his voice is soft and even. "We're talking about Mrs. Calvin, Dad."

There's angry silence on the other end, and then an

embarrassed cough. "What the hell are you saying? I know who we're talking about."

A wave catches Carr as he reaches the jetty, lifting him and banging his knees on a rock. The sound of surf against stone drowns out the sound of his father's hasty good-bye.

"Fuck," Carr says aloud.

When his phone rings again, he thinks it's his father calling back, but it's not.

"Jesus, Dennis, I've heard from everybody *but* you today," Carr says, leaning against a rock. "Please give me some good news."

"I would if I could."

"The fucking thing's still not plugged in?"

When he answers, Dennis's voice is thin and tired. "I got the message ten minutes ago. It's plugged in all right, just not into Prager's computer."

36

BOBBY HAS exhausted his many variations on *fuck this*. He hunches forward on the sofa in the sunny front room of the workhouse and runs his hands though his hair. When he looks up at Carr, he looks as though he's come through a hurricane.

"It's the worst fucking Plan B I've ever heard," Bobby says.

"No argument," Carr says. "It sucks. So give me an alternative." He looks at Latin Mike, who stares longingly at a jet dwindling in the sky.

"It's for shit," Mike says, "but I got nothing better."

"You can get the hardware?" Carr asks Bobby.

"That's not the problem. I've got the boat; a couple of WaveRunners won't be an issue. The problem is all the fucking variables."

"And the putty?"

Bobby shakes his head. "I know where I can get it, the det cord too—equipment's not the problem. The problem is too many variables—too many places where the fucking wheels can fall off."

"Let me worry about those."

"That's not a lot of comfort," Bobby says. "No offense."

"Then give me an alternative," Carr repeats.

Bobby shakes his head and puts his hands through his hair again. Carr looks at Dennis, who is thinner than ever—a ghost-eyed wheat stalk. "And you're sure it'll load, even if the screen's locked?"

"Screen locked, power-saving mode, waiting for a password, whatever—I'm working down below the operating system. If the computer's switched on, it'll load. Fifteen seconds, max. The LED will blink green."

"What if the computer's not switched on?"

"Then switch it on—it'll load. It'll just take a little longer—a minute, maybe."

Latin Mike gives up on the airplane, lights a cigarette, and blows smoke at the ceiling. "What about Bessemer—can he handle it?"

"It's a party—mostly he has to handle eating and drinking. He's good at that."

"He'll have to say his piece to Prager in person. You think he can do it?"

Carr nods. "A case of nerves will make him more plausible."

"Long as he doesn't crap his pants, *jefe*."

Carr stands and stretches. He hasn't slept and his eyes feel like an ashtray. "I'll let you guys start putting it together."

Still bent forward, Bobby laughs bitterly. "You don't know what they're going to do with a party going on. How do you know they won't call the locals? I don't want to find myself playing hide and seek with a coast guard cutter."

"Rink won't do that," Carr says. "She's still new. She wants to prove herself."

"You don't know," Bobby says, shaking his head. "You don't know shit."

Carr shrugs and walks to the door. "No argument there, Bobby."

THERE'S A tin-roofed shack, painted bright blue, on the side of the road to the airport, where the fat counterman serves fresh fish-and-chips and cold beer, and where Carr meets Tina. It is well past lunchtime, and they're the only ones sitting at the open-air counter. Carr drinks an iced tea and eats fries from Tina's plate, which is otherwise untouched.

Tina watches heat rise from the asphalt. Her voice is low and tight. "Isn't that your job, to plan for these things?" she says. "To have a fallback when shit goes wrong?"

Carr laughs. "I did plan for it. Of course, my plan assumed that Eddie Silva was still running security, and I didn't find out he wasn't until I was standing in Prager's offices. Remind me again who's responsible for that triumph of intel."

"Fuck you," Tina says, without much conviction. "You think this will fly?"

Carr shrugs. "The bigger question is whether Greg Frye will last until the party."

"It's not much longer."

"Yeah, but Dennis tells me Rink's been busy. She's poring over what was on the flash drive, Googling like mad."

"Doing it herself?"

"Apparently."

"I'll call Singapore—make sure our guy remembers his lines."

Carr nods. "If he does, and if Rink stays focused on the info on the flash drive, Frye might last. If she starts digging deeper into his criminal record—trying to talk to arresting officers or prosecutors—we're hosed."

Tina's jaw clenches. "Just a few days more," she says, and she jabs her fish with a fork.

CARR HAS a laptop open and aerial photos of Prager's property spread out on the coffee table. He's looking at a floor plan of Prager's house when Howard Bessemer walks in. Bessemer is fresh from the hotel spa, wrapped in spa terry cloth, shod in spa slippers, and admiring his new spa manicure. He stops when he sees Carr and stares at the coffee table.

"That doesn't look like packing, Greg," Bessemer says.

"Don't worry, Howie, we're going home—right after the party."

Bessemer's spa glow vanishes, replaced by a nervous pallor. "You said we were leaving before then."

"Change of plans."

Bessemer looks down at his terry-cloth slippers, and then at the tabletop again. "That can't be good."

"It'll be fine, Howie," Carr says, and he returns to his work.

"What do we—"

"It'll be fine," Carr says again. "Just think about what you're going to do afterward. It'll be fine." Bessemer looks at him skeptically and Carr ignores him until he goes away.

Carr isn't lying to Bessemer. An uncharacteristic calm settled over him the night before, as Dennis delivered the news, and it hasn't abandoned him yet. The adrenaline started pumping as he began laying flesh on his skeletal fallback plan, and it's built with every detail he's added, but it hasn't jangled him. In fact, there's something oddly comforting about it.

He studies the photos and drawings, memorizing points of entry and egress, camera fields and blind spots, alternate routes and dead ends, and it reminds him of his training days at the Farm. His heart rate is up, his fingers are drumming on the table, and there's a hum in his gut that he recognizes as eagerness. Carr can almost hear the rough brogue and smiles to himself. *Roller coasters*—after all this time, here, on his last job, he's finally developed a taste for them. Declan would be proud.

THE CALL comes in the empty night, when it seems even the ocean is still. The voice on the other end is held together with tissue paper and trembling breath, and Carr almost doesn't recognize it as Eleanor Calvin's. When he does, he's certain she's calling to report a death, but he's wrong.

"He is...I don't know...I can't find him anywhere. I came over this afternoon and...the ambassador was gone."

37

CARR IGNORES the phone twitching in his pocket for the third time in ten minutes, for the hundredth time since dawn, and focuses on the Stockbridge cop shifting nervously on the porch steps. He's young and earnest, and every time he speaks his Adam's apple jumps behind the collar of his uniform shirt. He reminds Carr of Dennis.

"There's nothing new since the Lenox PD called this morning, to say they found his Volvo in the town lot. They haven't found anyone who saw the ambassador park it yet."

Carr bites back the reflexive correction and nods. "My mother is buried in Lenox. He may—"

"Mrs. Calvin told us. Lenox has a man doing drive-bys in case he shows up there, but they haven't seen him yet."

"Did they check the local inns?"

"Lenox checked the inns in town, the Staties checked the motels along Route Seven. Nobody's seen him."

"How about the car? Did it look like he'd slept in it? Did it look broken into?"

"Broken into?"

Carr sighs. "Is it possible it was stolen from someplace else and dumped in Lenox?"

The cop reddens. "I...Lenox didn't say anything special about it, but I can ask them."

"I'll ask myself, when I go up there. What about the temperature last night?"

"The temperature?"

"How cold did it get up there?"

The cop squints, and then it dawns on him. "No, no—he would've been okay. It was in the low sixties last night."

Carr nods. "You'll tell the Lenox PD I'm coming up?"

"Sure, Mr. Carr," he says. "Did you have any luck finding his cell phone, sir? Because if it's turned on—"

"It was in his sock drawer. The battery is dead."

The cop's Adam's apple leaps, and he shakes his head regretfully. "We'll be in touch then," he says, and he walks down the path to his cruiser.

Carr rubs his palms over his face, which feels thick and numb. His eyes are sticky and he smells like airports and rental cars.

Eleanor Calvin is inside, red-eyed, sniffling, smaller. "Tim Binney," she says. "He's a nice boy. I just wish he had more to tell us."

"Uh-huh," Carr says. Even with the shades up and all the windows open, the house is gloomy, and it reeks of food and heat and mildew. Carr swallows hard, tries not to breathe too deeply or to look too closely at anything.

He fishes his phone from his pocket and scans through a long list of missed calls. Mike, Bobby, Bobby, Mike, Valerie, Valerie, Valerie. He turns the ringer on, and as soon as he does the phone burrs. Valerie again. He turns the ringer off.

"Your phone is always ringing."

"Work," Carr says. He looks up at Eleanor Calvin. She's crying again. "Mrs. Calvin, it's not your fault."

"Yes, it is. I knew he was upset. I knew he was confused. I just never thought he would...I lost patience with him."

"He has that effect on people."

She shakes her head. "No. I was stupid. He was upset and confused and frustrated, and I shouldn't have argued with him. I didn't know that Volvo still ran. I didn't think he had the key."

"I took it away last year, but he must've had a spare. He was upset even before he found out that you were moving?"

She nods. "He's been agitated for weeks, on and off."

"About anything in particular?"

"He's been talking about your mother."

"Why?"

An embarrassed look crosses her face, and she looks away from Carr. "Her birthday is coming up, dear—next Tuesday. She's always on his mind, this time of year."

"What does he say?"

Eleanor Calvin's cheeks redden. "He curses sometimes, the way he cursed at me—but I don't think he means anything by it. Other times, I can tell he misses her. Just a few days ago he was talking about...I don't know, I suppose it might've been a vacation the three of you took. And there was something about a fairy tale—King Midas, I think, and a maze. Honestly, I couldn't follow most of it. Does it mean anything to you?"

Carr looks at her and shakes his head.

THE LENOX Police Department is headquartered in a reassuring brick building with columns and dressed stone trim that dominates the south end of Main Street. But when Carr steps through the heavy doors, into the heat and glare of the afternoon, he is not reassured. The Lenox force is no larger than its Stockbridge counterpart, and its strengths run similarly to directing traffic and protecting weekend homes.

Manpower is stretched thin in this high season of outdoor concerts, dance recitals, and outlet shopping, and though the stocky, gray sergeant promised they were doing all they could, Carr knows it's not much.

There's a bench outside headquarters, in the shade of a wide oak and with a view of cars streaming toward a concert at Tanglewood. Carr takes a seat and sighs. His bones are leaden.

The sergeant had led him out back, to where the Volvo had been towed, and let him look over the car. There wasn't much to see. The doors had been unlocked when the Lenox cops found it, but there were no signs of a break-in. It was as mud-spattered and pollen-caked as it had been when Carr had seen it last, decomposing in his father's driveway. Inside, it was bare and sour. No motel keys or gas receipts or maps with circled destinations. The sergeant had told him his patrols would keep an eye on the lot where the Volvo had been found, in the event Arthur Carr returned for it. Carr had nodded and thanked him.

What had he expected them to do about a man who'd simply gotten in his car and driven away? Did he think they would organize a posse? Call out the bloodhounds? Dredge the Stockbridge Bowl? And really, what had he expected to accomplish up here himself? What the hell was he doing?

Latin Mike had asked a similar question, in a call Carr had made the mistake of answering in the Miami airport, while he waited for a flight to Boston. "Forty-eight hours to game time, and you *fucking* disappear on us? The fuck's the matter with you, *cabrón*? This job's not hard enough as is—you got to walk off in the middle of the night?"

"I told Bobby that I'd be back in time."

"I don't give a shit what you told him—I want to hear it for myself, *pendejo*. I want to hear about this *personal business*—or maybe you just lost whatever balls you pretended to have."

"I'll be back before the party, Mike."

"That's all you got to say? I got money sunk in this thing, asshole—I got *plans*—and if you fuck them up—"

Carr had hung up then, and had answered only one call since, from Valerie. He was about to board the Boston flight, and her voice was soft and worried. He could barely make it out over the announcements.

"Bobby said you had an emergency. Are you okay, baby? Can I do anything?"

"Just keep people calm," Carr had said. "I'll be back soon." If Valerie had said anything in reply, he hadn't heard, and he couldn't bring himself to talk anymore. Bobby, undaunted, had turned to texting. His last message summed it up nicely: "4 q s hole."

A bus rolls by, leaving behind a cloud of diesel and an impression of wrinkled faces and wispy white hair at the windows. Carr hoists himself from the bench, rubs his eyes, and drives to his mother's grave.

THE CEMETERY is two miles outside of town, off a pitted road and behind a leaning wrought-iron fence. There's a chapel by the gate, with black shutters, peeling white clapboards, and a steeple with no bell. Carr doesn't come here often, and when he does, his heart pounds. It's pounding now, as he follows the path that climbs the hillside, and his face is warm, though not from exertion.

Her grave is near the top, by a stand of maples and a white stone bench, and with a view of distant woods and a nameless blue pond. It is not a family plot—no relatives lie to rest nearby—it is simply a place his mother picked out when she learned that she was dying. He wasn't sure what about the site appealed to her. Maybe it was the pond, or maybe it was the company of strangers.

Her stone is granite—Dark Barre, from Vermont, Carr recalls

from a corner of his exhausted brain. The chiseled inscription is simple: *Andrea de Soto Carr*. No dates; no epitaph; no embellishments of any kind. Carr rests a hand on the curved top. He doesn't fight the hammering in his chest or the burning in his eyes, doesn't resist the vertigo. It's a much diluted version of the feeling he'd had, at age fourteen, when his father told him she was gone. The rushing in his ears, the ground opening beneath him, the free fall, the sense that there was no bottom. There's something consoling in the memory of that initial terror. He'd survived it once; he could do it again.

The time between her diagnosis and her death was short—a matter of months—and Carr spent it sleepwalking. His vision, it seemed, worked only on things very close— his hands, his feet, a book—or very far away, but not in the middle distances, no place other people might occupy. Other people were an abstraction—like shadow puppets. Most of what they said seemed irrelevant or garbled, and he himself said very little in response.

What he remembers best of his mother from that time are her hands, white and narrow, strong until the end. She took up knitting again, something she said she'd done when she was younger. He remembers the white hands working, the skeins of dark wool, the click of the needles, the pieces she made that were neither scarves nor hats, but simply long, dark panels. He remembers too the streaks of gray that appeared, overnight, in her jet-black hair, and how her collarbones became so pronounced—the bones of a ship, laid bare by a storm. *Denial* was not a word he knew in this context, but later someone explained.

He can't look for too long at the stone, and so he focuses on the flowers placed beneath it—a wilting bouquet of gladiolas in yellow, pink, and white. Her favorite flowers, in her favorite colors—the same as the bunch he's holding now. He guesses that the older ones have been here for a day.

38

IT'S THE white stone bench that does it. He sits on it, in the shade, for some time, looking at the flowers on her grave—the ones he brought and the ones his father left there. He runs his hand over the smooth stone, lets the coolness seep into his fingers. He studies the veins and seams—like threads—in the marble. He remembers her knitting, the coiled wool. He lets his eyes close and listens to the patrolling bees. He lets Eleanor Calvin's voice echo. Something about a vacation, about a fairy tale—King Midas and a maze. And then his eyes are open again, and he's up from the bench, trotting down the hill toward his rental car.

There are still lawn tickets available for the Boston Symphony Orchestra concert, and Carr buys one, but declines a program. The music will not start for hours, but the manicured lawns of Tanglewood are already busy with concertgoers spreading blankets on the grass, laying out picnics, pursuing their wandering toddlers. Carr sticks to the gravel paths and makes his way south and west, toward the formal gardens. It's been nearly thirty years since he was last here, but somehow he remembers the way.

The gardens are bordered by boxwood hedges, as high and thick and dark as they are in Carr's memory: looming green walls; gnarled, intricate roots; and, cut at intervals in the hedge, portals so narrow that even children must stoop to pass. Carr turns sideways and ducks low, but branches catch at his shirt.

It is quiet on the other side of the hedge, and the air is still. The boxwoods are shorter inside the garden, but high enough that the aisles between them seem narrow and clutching. Certainly Carr remembers them that way, remembers running headlong down those corridors in the fading light, remembers the thrill and fear, the sensation of walls closing in, the blind curves, sharp turns, dead ends. Remembers it as a maze—a labyrinth, his father called it.

Mrs. Calvin heard it wrong: not *Midas*, but *Minos*—King Minos, of Crete. Not a fairy tale, but a myth. He remembers his father's voice, chasing behind him, calling, in a bad imitation of Boris Karloff: "Beware the labyrinth. Beware the Minotaur." Carr was six. His father had been thinking about leaving the Foreign Service and was interviewing with the Economics Departments of several colleges in New England. They'd made a family trip of it. He'd never seen his parents so relaxed before, or ever again.

He's moving at a run when he comes to the white marble bench. It's at the far side of the garden, where two boxwood lanes empty into a clearing. It's broad and smooth, with a high curved back and a worn inscription, and it's cracked and stained by weather and much use. His father sits at one end, one leg crossed over the other, arms folded in his lap. He's studying the lawn, and he's so still and pale he might be made of marble himself.

Arthur Carr looks at his son without surprise, and with a faint, wry smile. "Minotaur chasing you again?"

"What the hell do you think you're doing?" Carr says, catching his breath. "Where the hell have you been?"

His father scratches his head and narrows his gray eyes. "Have you eaten lunch? I could use a sandwich."

· · ·

AT THE diner, his father orders a roast beef on rye. He tries to order a scotch with it, and has some trouble with the waitress's explanation that beer is the best she can do. In the end he has a Heineken. Carr orders tuna fish, and goes outside to make phone calls.

He watches his father through the window while he talks to the local police and to Mrs. Calvin, and makes arrangements for the Volvo to be towed to a garage. Carr glances at his missed calls list, and sees more messages from Valerie and Mike, and one—an hour earlier—from Tina. He goes back inside.

Arthur Carr's reading glasses are perched on the end of his nose, and he's scanning the ads and the children's games printed on the paper place mat. "Calling the office?" he asks, as his son slides into the booth. "I expect you'll be getting back soon."

"It wasn't work. It was about you."

"Not a particularly compelling subject," his father says, chuckling. "Who's interested in that?"

"Mrs. Calvin, for one. She was worried sick."

"Damned dramatic. Doesn't she have anything better to do? Shouldn't she be packing?"

"For chrissakes, you can't just take off like that."

"Nonsense—people do it all the time. They're here, and then—poof—they're gone, just like that." There's a connect-the-dots picture on the place mat, and his father moves his finger from number to number. "Christ, some people can vanish while they're standing right in front of you. They're in the very same room, but it's like they're not there at all. She had that trick down cold."

"Mrs. Calvin?"

His father looks up and scowls. "Don't be thick—you know

who I'm talking about. You're just like her, for chrissakes—playing dumb when you want to, but taking it all in. She was a hell of a poker player, you know."

"I didn't know that."

His father squints at him behind his glasses. "So, maybe not taking it *all* in," he says, and a sly smile—as at a private joke—crosses his face. "It's her birthday coming up. Did you remember?"

"On Tuesday."

"It was always hard to shop for her. Who knew what she wanted? Nothing I had to offer." The smirk again, angrier this time. "For example, I never knew her taste in cigarette lighters. And I was never much of a tennis player, either. Always hated doubles."

Carr takes a deep breath. His father mentions Hector Farías only rarely, and when he does the reference is always oblique. And always he baits his son to respond—to ask about his mother and Farías, to offer some comment—but Carr never does. He's relieved when the waitress brings their food.

Arthur Carr is hungry, and in short order half his sandwich is gone, and so is half his beer. He pats his mouth with a napkin and sighs. "Her cooking isn't so remarkable," he says. "I'll take a few meals here every week and be just fine, and the hell with her."

"Don't start again," Carr says. "She won't be around for much longer, but for the time being, you've got to make this work. You've got to be civil, at least."

"Silence is the best I can manage," Arthur Carr says, and drains his beer. He turns his attention to the connect-the-dots picture again.

Carr shakes his head. "She does a lot for you."

His father looks up. His eyes are unfocused and confused for a moment, and then they sharpen. He crumples the place mat into a small white ball. "What exactly did she do for me, besides end my career and turn me into a cuckold and a laughingstock? Am I supposed to be grateful for that?"

Carr's jaw tightens. "I was talking about Mrs. Calvin," he says softly.

"I told you not to do that—pretend to be stupid. You know damn well who I'm talking about."

Carr looks around the diner. It's nearly empty, and he takes a deep, unsteady breath. His voice is a raspy whisper. "You want to have a conversation about her? Fine—let's have at it. You want to know what she did for you? For one thing, she put up with your crap for all those years. She put up with your absences and your anger and moving house every other year, and she still managed not to kill you. I'd say that was a fair amount. So she had a lapse in judgment—can you really blame her? She tried to find some happiness, and didn't think it through. She's not the first one."

Arthur Carr lifts his half-glasses off and pinches his nose between his thumb and forefinger. "*Some happiness*—is that what you tell yourself? Is that what you really believe?" His words are slow and his voice is quiet, and his expression is like a flickering candle, shifting from surprise to triumph to regret. "All that watching, and you never saw anything."

"I saw you red in the face, and heard the endless griping about your career—as if your failings were somehow her fault. You and your goddamn career."

"My career…Jesus." His father shakes his head. "You *are* an idiot."

"So much for conversation," Carr says, and he picks up his tuna sandwich.

"All that watching…," Arthur Carr says, and he lowers his voice. "Don't you understand? If it wasn't for *my* career, she wouldn't have had one."

"Had one what? What are you talking about?"

"I'm talking about her career."

"Her career? She didn't have a career—she never even had a job."

Arthur Carr's laugh is bitter. "She *always* had a job," he says. "My job enabled her job, for chrissakes. It was her *cover*. *I* was her cover. *You* were her cover. *Her cover*—do you understand it now?"

There's a rushing in Carr's ears, a step he missed. "What? What are you talking about?"

"You insist on being dense. She was Agency, your mother—in the Directorate of Operations. You understand what I'm saying?"

There's vertigo, a feeling of the ground opening beneath him, and it's hard to get the breath out of his lungs. His fingers are splayed on the table. "What the hell...? What are you saying?"

His father looks suddenly tired. His voice is a dry whisper. "Your mother was with the Agency, for chrissakes. She was a CIA officer."

Carr doesn't remember getting the check, or paying it, or leaving the diner, but somehow they're in the parking lot and he's grabbing his father's arm. It's thin and light—a bird's bone. Carr hears his own voice, but it's far away and attenuated—a radio in a distant room. "I don't know who you think you're talking about, but it's not. . . . You're confused, Dad—you're seriously confused."

Carr stares into his father's face, into those gray eyes, but try as he might, he can't find confusion there—can't find anything but exhaustion and regret. He tells himself his father can't keep a thought straight any longer—can't find the thread, much less hold on to it. He doesn't know the difference between Mrs. Calvin and his own wife half the time. He tells himself these things, but his voice is tinny and remote and in his heart he knows it's full of shit.

A woman's voice cuts across it all. "There a problem, mister? You need a hand?" It's the waitress, calling from the diner door. She's holding a telephone, scowling at Carr, and staring at his hand on his father's arm.

Arthur Carr waves with his other hand and smiles. "We're fine, thanks. My son's just driving me home."

On the way, Carr's head is wrapped in cotton wool, and he can't tear it loose. He pulls over just before Lee, when he realizes he's not seeing the road. His father is unsurprised, and looks out the window at a crow picking at a flattened squirrel. The light is lengthening, tinted at the edges with orange, and a hum of insects rises from the woods. Carr draws a deep breath and his father turns toward him.

"Hector Farías," Carr says softly.

His father nods. "He was one of her sources, one of the agents she ran. He was her prize."

"She...she knew he was Cuban intelligence?"

"Of course—that's what made him so valuable. He was one of their senior guys; he was connected everywhere in the region. He was a star, and she had turned him and was playing him back to Havana. In theory, at least."

"And in reality?"

"He was playing her."

"The whole time?"

"The whole time."

"It was years that she knew him...all those places we lived. She never suspected?"

Arthur Carr sighs and turns to the window again. The crow draws a strand of gut from the dusty carcass. His beak is glossy, and so black it's nearly blue. It's an eternity before Arthur Carr speaks, and when he does, his voice is like dry leaves. "That's what the record says."

Carr turns in his seat. "What does that mean?"

Carr's father runs a forefinger down his long nose, to his

mouth, and to his chin, which has begun to quiver. "She wasn't stupid. Your mother had her flaws, but that wasn't one of them."

The rushing grows louder in Carr's ears. "You're saying she *knew* she was being played? The whole time?"

"She sussed it out early on."

"She *knew*? She told you that?"

Arthur Carr studies the crow, hopping around the squirrel. After a while, he nods.

Carr can't seem to fill his lungs, and he throws open the door of the rental car and stumbles out into the road. The driver of a passing truck leans on his horn and yells, and leaves a cloud of dust in his wake. The crow flies off. Carr walks slowly to the edge of the woods, and slowly back, the whole way watching the ground. When he returns, his father has the passenger door open and is sideways in his seat.

Carr looks at him. "She *knew*, but she let it happen—she participated in it. She . . . she was a traitor." The word sounds strange in his ears—something foreign or archaic.

Arthur Carr makes a tiny, rueful smile. "Well, yes," he says. "Why?"

"Why do you think?" his father says. "She loved that son of a bitch, and she thought that he loved her. Who knows, maybe he did."

Carr gazes at the treetops, the orange clouds, the coming twilight. "But that's not in the record, you said. That's not the official story."

"No."

"Why not? Why didn't the Agency come after her? Why didn't they prosecute? Put her in jail? Jesus Christ—why did they ever let *me* in the door?"

"The counterespionage people wanted to come after her. They were embarrassed and angry, and they wanted a full investigation and someone they could burn at the stake."

"What stopped them?"

Arthur Carr stretches his legs in front of him. He massages his right knee. "I did," he says softly. "I vouched for her. I pulled what strings I had left at State. Finally I threatened to go public if they didn't let her be. It wound up costing me every chit I'd ever collected over twenty-plus years, and my pension too, but eventually they decided to call it incompetence rather than treason. So that's how the record reads." He flexes his knee and looks up at his son. "The only thing the Agency hates worse than being embarrassed by the opposition is being embarrassed by them in public. You'd think they'd be used to it by now."

Carr watches him rub his bony thighs and flex his aching fingers. He looks thin and brittle—like a leaf the wind might carry off. Another truck passes, another dust cloud settles. The crow returns and curses at them.

IT IS six a.m., and Carr is in Terminal A at Logan, waiting for his Miami flight, still waiting for the spinning to stop. He's at the gate, watching but not following the highlights of a baseball game on the wall-mounted TV, when someone steps into his view. She's wearing a black dress and dark glasses, and her bare arms are paper white. Her lips barely move when she speaks, and her voice is flat.

"He wants to talk to you," Tina says. "He wants to know if there's some reason you don't answer your phone." She takes off her glasses and makes a tiny flick of her eyes. Carr looks over her shoulder, down the long row of gates. Even at a distance, Mr. Boyce looms like a cliff.

39

THEY'VE GONE over it once. They've gone over it twice. Now, as darkness settles on the workhouse and wind sweeps through the palms in the front yard and bumps the boats against the metal dock out back, they go over it a sixth time. Carr makes Bobby walk it through: the sequence, the timing, the signals, the routes in and out, the alternate routes, the rendezvous, the alternate rendezvous, and the contingency plans—meager though they are.

"And the minimum window is?" Carr asks when Bobby pauses.

"Five minutes. Five fucking minutes. How many times do I have to repeat it?"

"No less than five between the opening and the finale. Longer if you've got a receptive audience, but no less than five."

Latin Mike snorts from the sofa. "You don't know how many guys they're gonna have in the house, for chrissakes. You don't know if this is gonna distract them."

Carr answers without looking at him. "Loud noises get attention." Mike snorts again, and Carr ignores him. He turns to Dennis. "What's the weather forecast?" he asks.

Dennis is pale and skittish behind his laptop. He glances

at the screen. "Mostly sunny and breezy tomorrow, with heavy surf from the storm. Weather service says it should hold off until after ten tomorrow night, and even then we should only get the edge of it."

"They downgraded it?" Carr asks.

Dennis nods. "Tropical storm Cara now."

"Is it gonna fuck things up at the airport?" Bobby asks.

"We get out before ten we should be okay," Dennis says.

"So let's get out before ten," Mike says, lighting a cigarette.

"That's the plan," Carr says. Mike snorts again. Carr looks at Bobby. "The surf's going to be rough. You okay with that?"

"We're good."

"Good," Carr says. "Let's go over it again."

IT'S ELEVEN when they stop. Dennis buries his head in a computer. Mike grabs a whiskey bottle, plugs a cigarette into his mouth, and goes outside.

Bobby stretches and yawns. "Howie still sober?" he asks Carr.

"He was when I left him this afternoon. You were good with him."

Bobby shrugs. "Babysitting gave me something to do. He was jumpy without you."

Carr rubs his grit-filled eyes. "Nice to feel wanted."

Bobby looks at him, laughs ruefully, and shakes his head. "Fuckin' Carr," he mutters.

Mike is sitting on the front steps, drinking from the bottle, blowing smoke, looking at the sky. Carr walks around him.

"Guess you've given up tryin' to be like Deke," Mike says. "No pregame party tonight, right? So I got to make my own."

"Make it a small one. It's an early day tomorrow."

"I'll try to fit you in—unless something else comes up. Maybe I got to get my teeth cleaned or something."

"Give it a rest, Mike. I was gone for, what, a few hours?"

"It was more than a day."

"And now I'm back, so spare me."

Mike is fast—up and at Carr almost before the whiskey bottle hits the dirt. One hand goes to Carr's neck, his thumb in the hollow of Carr's throat. The other hand holds a knife. "If I didn't need you whole, *pendejo*, you wouldn't be," he says. "*¿Está claro?*"

"Very clear," Carr says quietly. "You feel better now that you got that off your chest?"

Bobby calls from the steps. "It's nice you boys are so glad to see each other."

"Piss off, *cabrón*," Mike says, but there's not much to it. He doesn't resist when Bobby hooks his arm and hauls him away.

"You know the world is fucked when I'm the voice of reason," Bobby says, turning Mike toward the house, "but maybe we should all just keep our minds on the job and save the rest of the bullshit for later."

It was, Carr thinks, driving back to his hotel, the same advice Mr. Boyce had given him in Boston.

Tina had stayed at the gate while Carr followed Boyce into the first-class lounge. It was empty, the attendants conveniently on a break. Carr was too tired to speculate on the coincidence. Even off the golf course Boyce was dressed in black, and he seemed much larger.

"Family," Boyce said, as he settled into an armchair. "What are you going to do with them?" Carr had no answer, and Mr. Boyce shook his head. "But that's no excuse. Pros don't make excuses. You have problems, I have problems—everyone has problems. But so what? You do your job, and *then* you deal with your problems. Get it the other way around, and you're no good to anyone. You want to look after your father, you'll keep your goddamn head in the game."

Boyce's words and rumbling voice had filled the room, and Carr had nodded in the right places. He kept nodding later, back at the gate, where Tina had reported in a low voice that Kathy Rink had called her man in Singapore.

"She was on the line for nearly an hour, listening to him talk about Greg Frye. Our guy thinks she went away satisfied."

Carr nodded. Tina had looked at him and hadn't liked what she'd seen. Before she left, she'd gripped him hard by the arm. "You better get a coffee or a searchlight or something, and get your head out of whatever fog bank it's in. You go sleepwalking into Prager's place, you won't walk out again."

Even now he can feel her fingers on his wrist.

Carr pulls through the gates of his hotel, and into a parking space. He shuts off the engine and sits in the dark and silence.

You want to look after your father? Look after him—it turned out he didn't even know him, didn't know either of them, and never had. *All that watching and you never saw anything.* What was it he had seen for all those years? What he'd wanted to see? What he'd needed to see?

Carr had driven back to Stockbridge on autopilot, and Arthur Carr had dozed the whole way. Carr helped him up the porch steps; he weighed no more than a handful of straw. His father stretched his legs on the sofa as soon as they got inside and closed his eyes, and Carr had walked around the room. Though maybe *walked* wasn't quite right. *Wandered* might be closer; *staggered* closer still.

The vertigo that had come on in the diner, along with the news about his mother, was back again, and as he moved about the living room he had to reach for things—a doorknob, a windowsill, the dusty furniture—to keep from falling or floating away. Eventually he fetched up beside the piano.

The photographs were still there, in their tarnished frames, and Carr stared at them while his head swam and his father snored gently. His father at the lake; his father in cap and gown; his mother in a garden, or at a party, or at a dance. He'd spent his life looking at these pictures, and now it was as if he'd never seen them before. The people behind the dirty glass were strangers to him, and what he thought he'd known about them was less than smoke.

Carr switched on a lamp and gazed at the photo of his father at the lake, and suddenly the small, pale face seemed to wear not a smirk, but a shy grin. And in the commencement picture, Arthur Carr's smile didn't look bitter—it looked nervous, but excited and even hopeful. Carr shook his head and picked up the photo of his mother.

The dark hair, blurred by movement, the luminous skin, the graceful neck and white teeth, the finger of smoke between lips that were just beginning to smile, or to speak to someone out of frame—he knew the pieces, but he couldn't make them whole. Carr closed his eyes and tried in vain to retrieve another image of her, to hear the sound of her voice again, and the words she'd whispered as they peered from the windows, to feel her hand around his again. He breathed in deeply, straining to catch a trace of gardenias and tobacco, but found only the musty smells of his father's house and of the humid night. An ache burrowed deep in his chest—deeper than bone—a wound where something had been excised badly, and with a dull blade. It was like losing her again. It was worse. His throat closed up and his eyes burned.

He looked up to see his father, watching him from the sofa.

"What are you doing?" Arthur Carr asked.

"Looking at pictures," Carr whispered.

"What pictures?" Carr held up the photo in its frame. His father squinted at it. "I didn't know that was up there."

Carr rubbed his eyes. "Where's it from?"

His father shrugged. "That picture? Someone's wedding, I think. I don't remember whose. It was before you were born."

Carr cleared his throat. "You saved her. You said that you saved her from...from a full-blown investigation."

"That's what I said."

"But you didn't say why—why you did it. After everything she did—all those years—why did you protect her?"

Arthur Carr shook his head. "Why did I. . . . She was my *wife*, for chrissakes—your *mother*. What was I supposed to do? I wasn't going to let them..." He shook his head some more, and then he sighed and closed his eyes. "I told you— don't be thick."

SITTING IN the hotel parking lot, Carr reaches for his wallet. The photographs are inside, creased and antique-looking alongside Gregory Frye's fabricated identifications. His father by the lake and at commencement, his mother at some forgotten wedding. They are part of a narrative—the story of his parents, his father the embittered bully, his mother the brave, long-suffering victim—that is undone now: unraveled and debunked, like Santa or the Tooth Fairy, but even more ridiculous. Carr lays the pictures on the dashboard, smooths them out, and looks at them for a while. Then he folds them up again and tucks them away with the rest of his false papers.

40

DESPITE THE sun and the honeyed breeze, Carr's fingers are cold and white. His elbows are stiff and his legs heavy, and when he moves them they feel clumsy. His chest is too small for his lungs, and too brittle for his hammering heart. It's fear, he knows, and adrenaline. He takes a slow breath in and lets it slowly out again, then shifts the champagne flute to his other hand. He flexes his fingers until the blood comes back, and he watches Curtis Prager grab a waiter by the arm.

Prager points at the carpaccio on the silver platter. "That's wagyu beef," Prager tells a banker from Panama City, "and what those bastards in Miami charge for it makes me think we're in the wrong business. Clearly, the real margins are in cows." The Panama City banker laughs as if it's funny, and so does everyone else within earshot, and Prager moves on through his guests. Carr hangs back, pretends to sip his champagne, and looks at the crowd.

It's an off-season party—not as large, Carr knows, as some of Isla Privada's charity events, but still a good-size turnout of local dignitaries, favor-seekers, would-be business associates, and other sycophants. It's a handsome crowd too, expensively dressed in regatta casual: the men in variations of Prager's outfit—white ducks, linen blazer, and deck shoes—the women in gossamer, bare arms, and sandals with intricate straps. Like birds, Carr thinks, all plumage and bright chirping. All appetite too. They flock around the white-jacketed waiters as they emerge from the caterer's base camp in the guesthouse, swooping on trays of sushi, sashimi, oysters, and high-margin carpaccio.

Except for its lawns and patios and first-floor bathrooms, the main house isn't open to unescorted guests, so the crowd has flowed mostly to the beach. Carr is at the east end of the beach, near the boathouse pier, leaning against the red Zodiac that has been pulled up on the sand. He watches as his host makes his way slowly, convivially, westward. Handshake, peck, nod, chuckle. Shoulder squeeze, smile, nod, move on. There's a quartet set up on the guesthouse patio. They're laboring over a samba, and it seems to Carr that Prager has matched his movements to their rhythms. Peck, nod, chuckle.

Kathy Rink prowls in Prager's wake, like a pilot fish in an orange muumuu. Her eyes scan restlessly over guests and staff, her head pivots left and right, and her cell phone is constantly at her ear. Carr can understand Kathy Rink's nerves: this is the first of Prager's periodic soirees to take place on her watch. She wants it to be a smooth afternoon, as seamless and unblemished as the breezy blue sky. Carr allows himself a tiny smile and hopes it will be the worst day of her life.

He takes another pretend sip and scans the crowd for Howard Bessemer. He spots him at a bar set up in the shade of a palm. His jacket is hung over his arm, and he's laughing at something a heavyset redhead has said. Given the sweating and fretting of the morning, Carr thinks he looks improbably relaxed.

"I don't feel like going to a party," Bessemer had whined from beneath his blankets. "I feel clammy. I think I'm coming down with something."

"That's a hangover, Howie," Carr called to him. "Have some coffee, and it'll go away."

"I don't see why I have to go anyway. What do you expect me to do there?"

"I expect you to eat and drink, and when I tell you, to ask Prager to do that favor."

"But I don't feel—"

"You do it, Howie, and we're headed home tonight."

Bessemer leans against the bar and laughs some more. Carr shakes his head and checks his watch. He checks the empty ocean north, and the jagged peninsula to the west. He can't see them, but he knows Bobby and Mike are out there now, beyond the rocks. They'll call when they're ready, and then they'll wait for his say-so. He checks his watch again. Time to lift the latch.

Champagne flute in hand, Carr crosses the beach and climbs one of the stone stairways. He cuts across the croquet lawn toward a fieldstone patio and the main house. His heart pounds harder as he walks, and his legs are reluctant. He passes two women headed for the beach. They smile at him and giggle as they teeter by. The taller one reminds him of Valerie, though she's not as arresting, and for a moment he wonders where Valerie is and what she's doing and if he'll see her tonight. He touches his ear, but there's no earpiece there, no whispering voice, no breath that he can almost feel. Then his mind comes back as he approaches a pair of glass doors. Laughter, music, the chatter of the crowd, all fade behind him. He takes a deep breath and doesn't look at the camera mounted above. He pulls at a handle and hears Declan's brogue in his head. *Nothin' like a house in the dark, lad.* Nothing like one in broad daylight, either, and filled with security guards.

The hall is quiet and the air-conditioning sends a shiver down Carr's arms. His footsteps echo on the polished stone floor. He has spent hours squinting at the floor plans of this house, and on them he's found three places he might enter when the time comes. Today, after walking the grounds, counting and recounting the guards, watching the flow of guests and staff, and visiting several bathrooms, he has narrowed his list to one.

Down the hall, on the right, is a powder room. It's small and windowless, and Carr has already been there once today. Just past the powder room, around a corner to the left, is a stairwell, with stairs climbing up. Past the stairs, across the hall, and three paces down is Carr's way in.

It's a rectangle labeled LAUNDRY-2 on the floor plans, but it's not the room's function that interests Carr, it's the small window set in its wall. It's in a casement-style frame, and because of its size and ground-floor location, and the dense hibiscus growing just outside, it has no view to speak of. What it does have, by Carr's careful calculation, is a position outside the view of any of Prager's security cameras.

As on Carr's prior visit, one of Rink's security crew cuts appears at the end of the corridor, to make sure he doesn't wander too far afield. Carr raises his champagne glass.

"Toilet?" he asks the guard.

"Of course, sir," the guard says. "Right here." He points toward the powder room. Carr steps in and locks the door. He lifts the toilet lid and pours his champagne down in a thin, noisy stream. Then he sets his glass on the edge of the sink and starts unrolling toilet paper.

"A little help," Carr calls, as he steps out of the bathroom.

The security guard comes down the stairs and around the corner, and almost slips on water that's begun to flow across the powder room's threshold. "Oh Christ," the guard says.

Carr smiles sheepishly. "I think it's clogged," and he points his glass at the toilet and the water and bits of toilet paper flowing from the top of the bowl.

"You think?" the guard says impatiently, a look of disgust on his face.

"I tried jiggling it," Carr says, and raises his hands helplessly. He looks down at the spreading water and moves out of the way, careful to keep his shoes dry. The guard steps gingerly into the bathroom, and Carr backs away.

The guard shakes his head. "Christ," he mutters.

When the guard emerges from the powder room, his knuckles are skinned from wrestling with the jammed water valve under the toilet tank, and his trouser knees are soaked. The hallway is empty, and the patio door is just swinging shut.

Outside, crossing the lawn, Carr feels the sun's warmth for what seems the first time. He takes a deep breath and at last there seems to be some oxygen in it. The music returns, coming to him on the warm, gusting breeze. His shirt, he realizes, is stuck to his back. He's suddenly thirsty, and he heads for the bar set up at the edge of a terrace looking over the beach. He orders an ice water and checks his watch and his phone vibrates.

"We're all right," Bobby says. His words are indistinct against the background noise of water and wind. "We're getting bounced around in the chop pretty good, but we're ready to rock. And you?"

"So far, so good. It should be soon."

"Soon would be aces."

Carr pockets his phone and looks out at the ocean. The sea is boiling around the reefs offshore, and platoons of whitecaps stagger drunkenly this way and that across the bay, to fling themselves on the sand. To the east, the sky is painted with a milky wash. Carr shakes his head and wonders how long the weather will hold.

He walks along the terrace and scans the beach, looking for Prager and Rink. He spots Prager, surrounded by a knot of petitioners and making his way east from the guesthouse. He doesn't see Kathy Rink immediately, but knows she can't be far behind. Suddenly, Howard Bessemer is at his elbow.

"Are we almost done?" Bessemer asks. He's pink from heat and from drink, and there are damp circles under the arms of his blue button-down shirt. His blazer hangs over his shoulder like a drowned thing.

"Soon, Howie."

"We're going to get some of that storm, you know. Sometime tonight they said on television, maybe sooner."

Carr nods and looks again for Kathy Rink. "Thanks for the update. You should head back to the beach and get something to eat. And switch to soda water."

Bessemer grimaces, unfastens another button on his shirt, and wanders off.

Carr picks out Prager again—smiling, nodding, drink in hand—walking up a shaded path. He sees no sign of Rink and checks his watch once more. It would be better, he thinks, if they were down by the water, but the thrashing surf and the sky and the tightening in his stomach tell him there's no point in waiting. He pulls out his phone.

"I'm headed in," he tells Bobby. "Put three minutes on the clock and go."

"Three it is," Bobby says over the wind. "Clock is running."

Carr finishes his ice water, places his glass on the bar as he passes, and heads back toward the main house. He rounds a corner and there's an orange blur to his right. Kathy Rink drops a thick, manicured hand on his arm.

She squints up at Carr. "Been lookin' for you, Frye. What the hell have you been up to?"

Carr looks at her, at the security man at her side, and at Curtis Prager, approaching from the beach. Carr smiles and shrugs. "Enjoying the view, enjoying the hospitality, and wondering if that's all I'm here for, or if somebody wants to do business."

Rink's squint turns into a scowl. "Jury's still out when it comes to business, but we want to talk more. And now's the time."

"Great," Carr says, smiling. The knot in his stomach tightens, and there's a ticking sound in his head.

41

CURTIS PRAGER grips Carr's arm and steers him back toward the terrace bar. Rink and her security man fall in behind them. Prager's face is flushed and shining and fixed in a wide smile. Rink's scowl deepens.

Prager sweeps his arm in the direction of the beach. "Not bad, eh? Raising how much today, Kathy?"

"About two hundred thousand," Rink says.

"For who?" Prager says.

"Hospital," Rink answers. "Kids' wing."

"Kids' wing." Prager chuckles. "I'm a hero. *They* ought to pay *me* to grip and grin with this crowd for so long. Be a relief to get on the plane tomorrow."

Carr nods appreciatively. Prager leans on the bar and orders a ginger ale from the barman, who pours it into a tall glass and disappears at some unseen signal from Rink.

"Kathy spoke to your man in Singapore," Prager says.

Carr smiles and manages not to look at his watch. "How'd it go?"

"It went fine," Rink says. "He says you're tough, and reliable, and discreet, and smart, and that you generally walk on water. Which I'm guessing doesn't surprise you. It would've been pretty stupid to point us at someone who wasn't gonna say good things."

Carr shrugs. "So besides learning I'm not stupid, it was a waste?"

Rink starts to speak, but Prager shakes his head. "Not a complete waste," he says, "but we don't know this guy. We don't know any of the names you've given us so far. The bottom line is, Greg, we need to talk to someone we know. Someone we know, who also knows you. You understand—we need a reference."

Carr hears an engine drone, and for a moment he thinks it's Bobby and Mike, but it's too fast and too far off—an airplane. Carr nods. "I get what you're saying—I just don't know what to do about it. I don't know about you, but most of the people I deal with don't want their names traded back and forth."

"So maybe there's nothing else to talk about," Rink says, and she drums her fingers impatiently on the bar. Carr appreciates the sentiment.

Prager shakes his head. "Or maybe Greg can think about some of the people he buys stones from. Maybe we can talk to some of them."

Carr nods, as if he's actually considering it, as if he's thinking of anything besides getting to the house. And then he hears another engine drone.

It's two engines, this time—close, throaty, rough running, like dirt bikes—coming from the water. His three minutes are up. Prager glances toward the beach and knits his brows.

Carr clears his throat. "I'll think on it," he says, nodding, and the engine sounds grow louder. And now the ambient chatter of the beach crowd changes. A collective chuckle rises, and then a gasp.

Prager shakes his head and peers down at his bay, and his party guests, gathered on the sand. Carr leans left and catches a glimpse of two WaveRunners chasing each other through the whitecaps, rooster tails flying, engines stuttering and echoing across the bay. Bobby is on the red one, Mike the gray. Both of them wear flowered trunks, muscle tees, and aviators. They weave in close to shore—fifty yards or less—and Carr can hear their whooping and hollering and see the bottle of beer that Bobby is waving around. It's a nice touch, but Prager doesn't appreciate it.

He turns to Rink, and his face has darkened. "What's going on, Kathy? Who are those assholes in my backyard?"

Rink is blushing, and already on the move. She waves to the security man at her side, pointing him to the shore, and she puts her cell phone to her ear, but it's all too slow for Prager, who strides angrily toward a stairway that leads to the beach. Kathy Rink hurries behind, saying something into her phone. All Carr catches is "boat in the water," and then she's gone. He checks his watch and heads toward the main house.

He tells himself not to run, but it's hard to listen. On his way across the lawn, he sees a pair of security guys who have no such inhibitions: they're in full sprint toward the beach, with their radios squawking. Carr sees the fieldstone patio ahead, and before he comes within range of the camera, he veers right.

He is quick across the patch of lawn at the corner of the house, and quick into the stretch of heavy plantings. He keeps low as he moves between the greenery and the house, and stifles a yell when two red birds dart screaming from the bushes. He fights to keep his breathing under control, and when he reaches the dense hibiscus and kneels by the window whose latch he has broken from inside, he has to struggle to hear the buzzing of the WaveRunners over his own gasps. But there they are, along with exclamations from the crowd. Carr looks at his watch and figures that Mike and Bobby have begun their game of chicken.

Carr peers into the laundry room, takes a last look around

the grounds, and sees no one. He dries his hands on his sleeves, works his fingers around the frame, and swings the window open. He checks the flash drives in his pocket again and climbs quietly in.

Carr closes the window and stands between the washing machine and the utility sink, listening. He hears the cycling of the air conditioner, the gurgle of water in pipes, the pounding of his heart, and nothing else. He looks at his watch again. Bobby and Mike have promised him a minimum of five minutes, of which two are gone. He crosses the room, drops to the floor, and looks through the gap beneath the door. There's no one in the hall, and he stands and opens the door a crack. A blade of air slips in, and cools his face. Behind it come voices.

They drift down the stairwell—men speaking and, through a screen of radio static, the voice of Kathy Rink. Carr can't make out her words, but her anger is unmistakable. The men find it funny.

One voice is Southern and deep: "Pine and Colley don't get that fucking Zodiac going, the old broad's gonna swim out there herself—turn those drunks into chum."

The other has a Midwestern twang: "Sounds like she's gonna make chum out of Pine and Colley. For chrissakes, how hard is it to flip a fuckin' starter switch?" Carr smiles to himself. They can flip all they want, he thinks, it won't do much good with the battery unhooked.

The laughing voices recede, and Carr opens the door wider. He touches the flash drive in his pocket again, like a charm, takes a deep breath, and climbs the stairs.

He is in a wide, windowed hall with white paneled walls and a view onto a courtyard garden. Too much glass—not a place to pause. To the left is the game room, and Carr can see green felt—the corner of a pool table. To the right is the music room, and the gleaming lid of a grand piano.

Carr goes right, the floor plans unfurling in his head—music room, hallway, office. His ears are straining; the muscles in his legs are quivering.

The music room is an exercise in monochrome—black piano, white rugs, black leather chairs, white leather sofas—but still too much glass for Carr's comfort. His footsteps are silent on the rugs, and he crosses quickly to the opposite door. And freezes.

A maid comes from behind the curving staircase, and it is only the basket she carries, and its high pile of linens, that saves Carr. He drops beside a white leather settee, crams his heart back into his chest, and listens as she climbs the stairs. Sweat runs down his face and along his ribs, and when he stands again it's like lifting a boulder. Somehow he manages to place one foot before the other.

He cuts across a sunny atrium and makes it to the final hallway. He pauses, listens, and hears voices in the library. It's at the end of this same hall, across from Prager's office. Which means it's on the ocean side of the house, and has an ocean view. The voices are low, and Carr is trying to decide whether they belong to the security staff when a radio squawks and answers the question.

Carr checks his watch: his five minutes are gone—he's in overtime now. So, wait or go? The radio chatter cuts in again—an angry, urgent blast: something's happening on the water. Something worth watching, Carr hopes. And then, behind him, there are footsteps approaching. So much for waiting.

Six paces down the hall. Six paces through quicksand. Through wet cement. Six paces without air or sound, and with his vision a narrow tunnel, the office door at the distant end. And then he's in. He doesn't bother to check if anyone else is there, but no one is. His shuddering sigh is almost sexual, and for an instant he's giddy and light-headed. The windows are big and bright and full of palm trees and sky. The Rothkos rise above him like twin suns. He's transfixed by them, and imagines lifting them from the wall, prying them from their frames, rolling the canvases. He takes a deep breath, laughs, and shakes his head.

Carr reaches into his pocket for the flash drive and steps to the aluminum desk and stops. He stares at the desk, and at the flash drive in his palm. He squints and his eyes run over the desk, from end to end. He walks around it, and looks beneath it. He looks around the starkly furnished room for a drawer to search, or a cabinet, but there are none. He returns to the desk, thinking he must somehow have missed it. His gaze returns to the nearly bare surface. *Phone, monitor, cable.*

"Fuck," Carr whispers.

Prager's laptop is not there.

"Fuck," he says again. Only the voices in the library keep him from shouting it.

He puts the flash drive in his pocket and rubs a hand across the back of his neck. Where would Prager take the thing? Not to the Isla Privada offices—he doesn't go there. So where else? He probably takes it on trips. Trips like the one he's making tomorrow, to Asia, by way of Europe. Leaving tomorrow, so packing today. So he's packed the laptop and left it...where? Where's his fucking luggage?

Two places jump off the floor plan: a cloakroom, just off the main entry hall, and Prager's bedroom. Going to the cloakroom means crossing the entire main floor of the house; going to the bedroom—the master suite—means going upstairs. So, the bedroom first.

Carr doesn't remember the trip down the hall and back across the atrium to the curving staircase, but somehow he's climbing the stairs. There are footsteps below, and voices, and radio chatter. Carr hurries to the top.

Upstairs, the polished stone floors and raised white

paneling give way to glossy wood and silk wallpaper. Carr passes a line of bedrooms, each one done in a different ocean color: sea foam, turquoise, aquamarine, and each with an ocean view. The maid is in the last one, a silhouette on a balcony, watching the action on the bay. Carr doesn't realize she's there until he's already passed.

"Shit," he says to himself.

The master is at the end of the hall, behind a pair of teak doors with gleaming brass hardware. The doors aren't locked, and the mechanism is almost silent. Chest heaving, Carr closes them behind him.

He's in a sitting room, with a fireplace, a big ocean view, and none of the austere minimalism of Prager's office. The sofa and chairs are fat and silk-covered, in blue and gray stripes, the rugs are Persian, the low tables are teak, and the pictures on the wall are tinted engravings of sailing ships. Outside, through glass doors and beneath a green awning, there is a large balcony that wraps around all three of the suite's exposures. And in the corner, near the fireplace, there is luggage: two large leather suitcases and a leather duffel, open and half-packed on folding stands. Pressed shirts, balled socks, but no laptop.

"Shit," Carr whispers. He looks at his watch. Nearly nine minutes since the show began. He walks into the bedroom.

It's like the sitting room, but with a king-size bed instead of a sofa and chairs, and a small teak desk near another set of balcony doors. Carr sighs deeply and smiles. Like the sitting room, only infinitely better: Prager's laptop is open on the desk.

He nearly laughs aloud when he touches the space bar and the screen lights with a message asking for a password. He pulls out the flash drive, feels for a USB port, and plugs it in. And then Carr hears the almost silent mechanism of the teak doors, and his heart lodges in his throat.

He drops low, peers into the sitting room, and sees a door swing open and the maid walk in. She's dark and serious-looking behind the basket of folded laundry. She crosses to Prager's bags, picks through the basket, and places a stack of underwear on a table beside the luggage.

Carr looks behind him, at the open doors of Prager's walk-in closet. He looks at the flash drive. Fifteen seconds to load, Dennis said, and the LED would blink. How long has it been in? Did the light blink? *Fuck!* The maid stacks undershirts on the table and lifts the basket, and in two quiet steps Carr is in Prager's bathroom.

It's like an old-fashioned bank—chrome and marble from floor to ceiling—and Carr stands behind the door, trying not to breathe. He watches through the crack as the maid stows clothing and glances out the window at the bay. She glances out often, as if something new is happening, and now she goes to the balcony doors. When she opens them, Carr can hear the buzzing of the WaveRunners along with a new sound— the angry sputter of an outboard. The Zodiac is running.

The maid stands in the open doorway, watching, shaking her head, and from down the hall Carr hears a voice.

"Yo, Sylvie!" a man calls.

"In here," the maid answers.

"Shit," Carr says to himself. He looks around the bathroom. It's huge, with a soaking tub, a steam shower, double sinks, and views of the garden. And straight back, its own pair of glass doors to the other side of the wraparound balcony. He looks through the crack again, and sees two crew cuts headed down the hall. One waits at the doorway to the master suite, the other—the one whose khakis have damp knees—comes in smiling.

"You watching the circus out there, girl?" he says. "My boss'll have a stroke if we don't chase those boys away." He steps onto the balcony and runs his hand over her back.

She giggles and knocks his hand away. "And so will my boss, she finds you up here wasting my time." The crew cut laughs and slides his hand lower, but Carr is watching his partner, who still stands in the doorway.

The maid giggles again and points at the water. "Your boss got her wish. They've run away behind the rocks. Show's over, I guess—no more circus."

Carr's whole body tenses and the crew cut on the balcony says something, but his words are lost in the flash and the *whump* and the rattling of windows. Carr feels the shock wave in his chest, and the maid is screaming now, and both crew cuts are on the balcony yelling *what the fuck*, and Carr steps into the bedroom. He stays low and pockets the flash drive, and then he's back in the bathroom, through the glass doors, onto the balcony, and over the rail.

42

OFFSHORE EXPLOSIONS have a muting effect on parties, and Prager's party is not immune. The jetty screens his guests from seeing the blast itself, but they hear it and feel it and see the smoke. There are cries of surprise, then silence, then a milling confusion. And then the rush to be as uninvolved as possible.

Amid the hunt for valet tickets and the hasty good-byes, no one notices Carr's sweat-soaked shirt, or the scratches on his face and hands from the pindo palm that broke his fall. No one notices him listening intently to a voice on his cell phone. No one notices his smile as he puts the phone away.

Carr glides weightless through the crowd, with Dennis's words still echoing: *It's loaded, boss, nice and clean.* He touches the flash drive in his pocket, and tells himself to slow down, to focus. Now it's Declan's voice he hears: *Don't fall in love with yer own genius, lad—there's no greater arse than the one gets shot while he's staring in the mirror. Yer not home till yer home, and maybe not even then.* Carr runs a hand down his face and wipes the grin off.

He finds Howard Bessemer by the guesthouse, holding a glass and staring at the jetty. He's pale and sweating and shaking his head. "Now's the time, Howie," Carr says.

Bessemer swallows hard. "Jesus Christ," he whispers. "Did you see what happened? Did you hear that noise? Did you see who it was on those things?"

"I know, Howie, everything's fine. It's time now—just like we went over. And then we go home."

Carr has worried this part to death. Would Howie balk? Would he freeze up? Would he fold altogether? For an instant, Bessemer tilts sideways, threatens to buckle, but the prospect of *home* has a bracing effect on him. He steadies himself on Carr's shoulder, nods curtly, and reaches into his glass for a chip of ice.

"Where is he?" he says, chewing.

Prager is outside the main house, smoldering. He's accepting quick, embarrassed farewells—one after the other—from his guests, and Kathy Rink is standing several paces off. She is paler even than Bessemer, and maybe more jumpy. Her shoes and the hem of her floral dress are wet, as if she's been in the water. When she speaks it's to bark at her men. When Prager speaks, she twitches.

Bessemer hangs back while Carr says his good-bye. Prager's eyes catch for an instant on a scratch on Carr's face, but he's got other things on his mind. They shake hands quickly.

"The police are on their way," Prager tells him, irritation swelling in his voice. "So you'll want to be on yours. Unfortunate we didn't get to talk more, but as you can see," his eyes flick to Kathy Rink and then to the cloudy sky, "this day has gone to hell." Carr nods. "Give her your number," Prager says. "We'll arrange a secure call while I'm on the road, and after you've had a chance to think some more." Carr nods again and moves off. When the line of departing guests ebbs, Bessemer steps up.

His shirt is dotted with sweat, his jacket is a limp balloon, and his tie has surrendered. He pushes a hand through his thin hair and puts it on Prager's arm. His head bends close.

Carr can't hear what he says, though he and Bessemer have been over it enough that Carr knows it by heart. But he has no trouble hearing Prager's reply.

Prager shakes Bessemer's hand off, and his face is an aggravated red. "For chrissakes, Bess—this can't wait until business hours? What the hell do you think I am, a fucking teller?"

Rink, the guards, the parking attendants, and the few guests who remain turn their heads. Prager doesn't seem to care, and neither does Bessemer. He's a determined petitioner, and his hand goes to Prager's shoulder. This time Carr catches some fragments of his speech—*serious guy* and *wants it yesterday* and *not kidding*.

Prager shakes his head, but his expression slowly cools from anger to a resigned acceptance of what seems to be his fate today. "All right, already," Carr hears him say wearily.

When he gets into the passenger seat, Bessemer's hands are shaking. Carr looks at him, and Bessemer answers before the question is asked. "He said he'd do it soon. He said he'd call when it was done."

Carr pats his knee and drives through the gate.

They rendezvous off Rum Point Drive, beside a snack shack damaged by some long-ago storm and never repaired. The parking lot is weedy and cracked. The nearby cove is empty but for the open fishing boat, rocking at anchor. Bobby and Latin Mike stand on the narrow, shingle beach. They're in blue shorts, polo shirts, and ball caps, watching the clouds and drinking beer.

Bobby turns when the car pulls in. "Man of the hour," he says, smiling. He lifts his beer bottle in a toast. "From the motherfucking jaws of defeat."

Mike smiles too. His teeth are very white. "You like the show, *jefe*? You like the time we gave you?"

Carr sheds his jacket and shoes and socks. Something

loosens in his shoulders. "I liked it fine, Mike," he says, smiling back. "You guys were fucking amazing." He's surprised by how much he means it.

"And Howie?" Bobby asks. "How'd he do?"

Bessemer laughs nervously. "I was fucking amazing too."

"Fuckin' a," Bobby says, and there's laughter all around. Bobby passes out more beers and they toast. Mike takes a long pull and wipes his mouth. "What's *soon* to Prager?"

Carr shrugs. "Howie told him it had to be today, and he's flying to London tomorrow morning, so..."

"Phone charged up, Howie?" Bobby asks.

"A hundred percent," Bessemer says, and Bobby nods approvingly.

They watch a boat go by, east to west, a mile or so out. Carr can see flags, many antennae, and a big radar array. He turns to Bobby. "The WaveRunners?" he asks.

"Wiped clean, in pieces, on the bottom," Bobby says.

Carr nods, and the boat passes from view. He takes a long swallow and exhales and all the air seems to leave him. He can already feel the beer. He closes his eyes and listens to the wind in the ironwood trees, the waves against the shingle, and Bobby, Mike, and Bessemer laughing at something. The water washes over his feet, and he's not sure if he can move again.

Carr stands this way for he doesn't know how long, and when Bessemer asks for another beer, he opens his eyes. Bobby hands the beer over and Bessemer's phone rings.

Bessemer freezes, and Carr takes the bottle from his hand. "You should see who that is," he says quietly.

Bessemer reaches into his pocket. He stares into the phone's display. "It's him."

Bobby shakes his head. "Soon was soon," he says.

Carr nods. "Nice and easy now, Howie."

Bessemer swallows hard and thumbs a button. " 'Lo, Curt," he says. His voice is brittle and high. Head bowed, he listens intently. Carr sees his fingers whiten around the phone. Finally, Bessemer nods. "I can't thank you enough, Curt—you're a lifesaver. Have a great trip, and I'll call when—"

Bessemer takes the phone from his ear and looks at it. "The bastard hung up on me."

"Fuck that," Mike says. "Did he do it?"

Bessemer nods. "Thirty-seven thousand transferred from Isla Privada to my Palm Beach bank."

Bobby and Mike exchange high fives just as Carr's phone burrs. He steps away and answers. Dennis's voice is a shaking whisper. "We got it," he says. "Prager's password. We got all the parts now."

"Nice work," Carr says quietly. "You finish cleaning up; those two will be back to give you a hand." He closes the phone and turns around. Bobby, Mike, and Bessemer stare at him—eager and frightened. Carr nods and smiles.

They don't sigh in unison, but there is something in their collective silence that feels that way—relief, release, deflation. They look at one another and smile and shake their heads in disbelief. And then they are in motion. Mike wades out to the boat. Bessemer heads back to the Toyota, and Carr takes Bobby's elbow.

"Nice and clean at the house, Bobby, and nice and easy at the airport."

Bobby laughs. "I know—we're not done yet."

"Almost, but not quite. So let's not—"

Bobby laughs harder. "I know, for chrissakes—*yer not home till yer home.*"

Carr smiles at him. "So let's get there in one piece."

Mike starts the engine and calls to Bobby. "Come on, *cabrón*, this weather's not holding, and I want to make the earlier flight."

Bobby looks at Carr, and behind him, at Bessemer. "What about your housekeeping?"

Carr's stomach knots and a prickle of sweat breaks on his forehead. "It's covered, Bobby."

"We could take care of it here and now."

"I said it's covered."

Bobby shrugs. Mike brings the boat in close, and Bobby climbs in, and they roar off toward Rum Point. Carr stares at the clouds stacking in the east.

Bessemer is behind the wheel on the way back to the hotel, driving carefully, and Carr is in the passenger seat making calls. His first one is to Tina.

The tension is plain in her voice, and so is the relief when Carr tells her. "Christ," she says chuckling, "you couldn't have called sooner?"

"I waited until I knew for sure."

"The way you were at Logan, I figured hearing from you today was at best a sixty-forty thing."

"Happy I could disappoint you."

"Your guys are buttoning up?"

"And flying out, assuming this storm doesn't shut things down."

"They should be okay."

"Watching the Weather Channel, are you?"

"What else am I supposed to do while I'm waiting for you to call?"

Tina asks about flight times and arrivals and when he expects to be in Boca, at Amy Chun's place. Carr answers, but his mind is already on his next call.

Valerie's voice is a taut whisper. "You fucking asshole. You know how long you left me hanging? What the fuck happened?"

"It's done."

There's silence on the other end, and then a long breath. "Don't bullshit me."

"I'm not. We've got it."

Another silence, longer this time. "So that's it then," she says finally.

Carr glances at Bessemer, whose gaze is fixed on the roadway. "Almost. I'll call you when I get in. How are things there?"

"I'm at her place now. She should be home in a couple of hours."

"We'll see you there tomorrow."

"And then what?"

"What do you mean? And then we're done."

"I'm talking about afterward. You made any decisions about that? 'Cause I know where I'm going; I just want to know if I'm going there alone."

"I haven't had much time to think about it lately."

"How much time does it take? You either want to or you don't."

Carr glances at Bessemer again. "Can we talk about this later?"

"Not too much later—Amy will be back. Or were you asking for more time than that?" Carr is still searching for an answer when Valerie hangs up.

BESSEMER PACKS quickly, humming to himself while he does it. Afterward, he goes behind the bar and mixes a gin and tonic. "For the road, Greg?" Carr shakes his head, and Bessemer raises his glass to the room. "I'll miss the old place," he says. "Such fond memories."

Carr smiles and shakes his head. "Best to have none at all of these past few weeks, Howie. Best to get on with whatever it is you're going to do."

Bessemer looks at him for a long moment, and then he finishes his drink. "Do I have time for a shower before we leave?" Carr nods and Bessemer disappears into his bedroom.

Carr reaches into a duffel and pulls out the Glock. He drops the clip out, checks the load, and works the slide. Then he snaps the clip back in. He can hear the shower running in Bessemer's bathroom, and Bessemer singing badly. He thinks about Bobby and Mike—*He's everybody's problem if you don't*—and he thinks about Bessemer's son—*I don't really know him*—and he slides the clip out again.

"Fuck it," he says aloud. He opens the balcony door, drops the clip into a stand of dense foliage below, and feels as if a piano has been lifted from his chest.

Carr looks up at the shrouded sky. He thinks about flight delays, and the connections from Miami to Palm Beach. He thinks about his mother and father, and the house in Stockbridge, and about Valerie. He goes inside and picks up his phone.

He tries her three times but gets no answer, and wonders if Amy Chun has come home already, or if Valerie is simply ignoring him.

Bessemer emerges with wet hair and fresh clothes. He drinks a final gin and tonic and watches with amusement as Carr wipes down the rooms. Top to bottom, back to front. Carr makes Bessemer close the door. On their way to the elevator, Carr wipes off the empty Glock and drops it behind the ice machine.

They pause beneath the portico when they come out of the lobby. Rain is falling, in fat, erratic drops, but the sky promises more. It's dark now, and the trees are swaying. The lights in the parking lot are on and shaking on their poles. Bessemer curses softly, and they trot across the asphalt.

Their car is at the far end of the lot, in a space beside a light pole. As they approach, Carr notices that it's the only light not lit. There's a sedan parked in the next space that wasn't there before. It's dark—black or blue—and it's familiar to Carr, though he's not sure from where. A few steps closer and he sees that it's a Nissan, and Carr stops in his tracks. Bessemer jogs ahead and Carr calls out, and there are footsteps behind him.

Carr drops his bag and whirls, and headlights come on, and catch him full in the face. A hand clamps on his wrist and tries to fold it into a come-along hold. Carr pivots and throws his elbow up and something crunches. A voice yells *motherfucker* and the hand falls away, and Carr pivots again, out of the light, as another voice yells *stand clear*. Carr hears a pop, feels a sting on his back, hears a hissing sound. And then the sky lights up, and so do his arms, and legs, and skin, and bones. And then it all goes dark.

43

THERE'S BLOOD in his mouth when he comes to. He tries to feel it with his hand, but can't because of the restraints. They're the stiff plastic kind, and they're tight behind his back. And then there's the matter of the hood. Someone yanks it away and Carr is blinking into a hard white glare.

There are shapes behind the lights—charcoal figures pacing, pointing—and when the rush subsides in Carr's ears, he can make out voices. Men's voices, and a woman's.

"What's your name?" Kathy Rink says. "We know it isn't Greg Frye."

"I don't give a shit about his name," Prager says. "I want my fucking money back."

Carr's having trouble with the words—their meanings don't keep up with the sounds. And he hasn't taken any money—not yet. He tries to look at his watch, but again the restraints stop him. He hasn't taken any money. The air is damp and smells of newly turned earth.

There's a noise to Carr's right, something between a groan and a sob. He turns and sees the hood torn from Bessemer. His head lolls to one side. His face is white and wet with tears, and there's a triangle of blood spreading from his nose down across his mouth and chin.

"And you, you fat lying fuck!" Prager shouts. "I trusted you."

There are shuffling feet and urgent whispers behind the lights, and Carr tries to look around. He sees a concrete floor beneath him, and open space above. To his left, half in shadow, there is a workbench covered with empty terra-cotta flowerpots, coils of garden hose, and sacks of potting soil. To his right, in a sodden heap in the corner, he sees what's left of his and Bessemer's luggage. Everywhere there is the clatter of rain on a tin roof. Bessemer groans again.

"Not me," he mutters.

"Anything broken, Howie?" Carr says softly.

Prager steps from behind the wall of light. He's in shirt-sleeves, and his hair is wet and wiry. Cords pop in his neck, and veins pulse. Carr is fascinated by them. Prager grabs him by the collar, and Carr can smell his sweat and his fear. "What the fuck did you say? Come on, say it again."

"Curt, please," Kathy Rink says sharply. "Let me do my job." She emerges from the glare and puts a hand on Prager's arm.

He flicks her away like a bug. "I keep waiting for you to start," he says disgustedly. "Find my money. Find out what the hell he did to my system."

Carr blinks his eyes, trying to clear them. Maybe it's the lingering effects of the Taser, or his collision with the pavement afterward, but his mind is split into several pieces. One piece is trying to establish a basic fact set, and to make it sit still. Someone has hit Isla Privada, ahead of schedule. Prager has found out about the theft. Prager has found out about him. Prager is going to kill him.

Another piece is a storm of questions. How did Prager find out? Was there a camera he hadn't seen, a switch he'd tripped? Was he spotted in the house? He doesn't think so, but anything's possible. The biggest question—who has stolen Prager's money—Carr scarcely needs to ask, even in his fractured state. It's someone in his crew. Maybe everyone in his crew.

Yet another part of him tries to figure the timing. How many hours passed between Dennis reporting that his spyware had scooped up Prager's passwords, and Carr being tasered in the hotel lot? Enough time, certainly, for Dennis to call Valerie. Enough time for Valerie to sit down behind Amy Chun's desk. Enough time to do any number of things, if the people doing them had discipline and a plan. Carr tries to look at his watch again and strains against his plastic cuffs.

The last scrap of his mind is the busiest—a panting, scrambling thing, searching every inch of this arena of light, probing the shadows at its boundaries, looking for a way out. Flowerpots, garden hoses, potting soil, an upside-down wheelbarrow, what might be a spade, what might be a rake, a garden tractor that is missing a wheel—he's struggling to turn any of it into a key. Kathy Rink isn't letting him think.

She's sitting on a stool now, her face close to Carr's. "I said, 'What do I call you?' " Her skin is grainy, and there are deep lines around her mouth. Her breath smells of old coffee.

"My name's Greg Frye, but call me what you want."

"But that's not your name, is it?" Carr tries a smile, but the cut in his mouth hurts. "Though your diamonds are for real, and your prints came back as Greg Frye, which—I gotta admit—gives me a scare. You some flavor of cop, Greg?"

Carr shakes his head. "You seem to have your mind made up about things."

"Your prints come back as Greg Frye, and there's a file for Greg Frye with the Bureau of Prisons, but after that…" Rink shrugs. "How'd you manage that?"

"If you think I'm a cop, shouldn't you be a little more careful with the merchandise?"

Rink holds his Greg Frye passport up. "Not so much, Greg. You and Bessemer checked out of your hotel, and the last anyone heard you were headed for the airport. I want to, I can have a couple of guys with your names on a plane to the ass end of nowhere, just as soon as the airport opens up again. Your handler'll think you two ran off together.

"Now, how 'bout you tell me where your buddies are—the ones who put on the little show this afternoon?"

Carr smiles again. "It seems like something's happened here, and you think I'm involved."

"*Something's happened here?*" Prager calls from the shadows. "My whole system is locked up. I might as well be fucking *blind*." Kathy Rink looks sharply at him, and then turns back to Carr.

"I know a lot of people," Carr continues. "Let me make some calls. Maybe between the two of us we can figure out what's going on."

Kathy Rink produces Carr's cell phone from somewhere. "Who do you want to call, Greg? Give me your password, and I'll ring 'em up for you. And speaking of phone calls—who do you think would call Curt, out of the blue, with a heads-up about wire transfers? What reason would they have, and why would they throw your name around?"

"There are people up in Boston who don't like me much."

"They're not alone," Rink says, smiling, and she pats the side of his face.

There's a noise behind Rink—a metallic complaint, like a rusty garage door—and the sound of rain grows louder and a breeze blows in. There's movement beyond the lights, and a man steps into the arena. It's one of Rink's crew cuts, carrying several rolls of duct tape. His nose is packed and bandaged, and there's dried blood on his polo shirt. He glares at Carr through blackened eyes.

There are two other men with him, and they don't have crew cuts. One is a suntanned fireplug, with a peroxide pony-tail, a camo wife-beater, and tattoos from his collarbones to wrists. He's got towels over his shoulder and a slant bench under his arm, and he smiles at Rink with crooked teeth. His colleague is small and slim and shaved egg-bald. His skin is the color of oatmeal, and he's wearing dark glasses and pressed fatigues. He's got a plastic water jug in each hand—the five-gallon kind that go on water coolers—and he sets them down in front of Carr.

"I tol' him we didn't need so much," the fireplug says to Rink. His accent is deeply Southern. "When does it take even a gallon? But he don't listen."

"I like to be prepared," the egg says. His voice is soft, his accent from nowhere.

Kathy Rink tosses Carr's phone and passport into the corner, onto the remains of his luggage. "We won't waste a lot of time going round with threats, or any of that *we can do this hard or we can do this easy* crap, okay? We both know you're not gonna say shit unless you have to—and even if you did, I wouldn't believe it. Besides, after what you did to me today, there's no way I'm gonna miss this opportunity."

The fireplug laughs and puts the slant bench down. He kneels and begins to adjust the angle. Howard Bessemer moans. "Jesus Christ," he says, his voice a choked whisper. "This wasn't me. None of this was me."

Rink turns to him and frowns. "My problem with you, Howie, is I'm not sure what you're good for. I mean, I don't need to put you on the board here—I could just smack you in the head and you'll tell me whatever it is you think I want to hear. So what exactly do I need you for?"

Bessemer cranes his neck, trying to see beyond the glare. "Curt! Come on, Curt!"

And then the lights go out.

Prager's is the first voice Carr hears. "Son of a bitch!" he shouts. "Son of a *fucking* bitch!"

"Flashlights!" Kathy Rink calls. "Somebody get some lights here."

There's scraping, stumbling, cursing, and then two thin, shaky beams cut the black. A pool of light spreads at Kathy Rink's feet, and another at Prager's, and then there are radio voices in the air. Someone calls from the darkness: "Power's out at the main house too." To which Prager responds: "You're *fucking* kidding me."

Two more flashlight beams emerge from the dark. Two crew cuts, wet with rain, emerge behind them. "It's a blackout, sir," one reports. "The whole north end of the island's dark."

Prager's voice quivers with anger. "Which is why I have emergency generators and two big tanks of diesel. So where the hell are my lights?"

"They're trying, sir. There's a problem—with a fuel line, they think. They're working on it, but it's slow going in the dark." Prager curses fluently, and Carr stifles a laugh.

There's throat clearing, and then the fireplug's voice. "This isn't the kind of thing you want to do by flashlight, Kath. I'm up for it if you are, but truth is, we might drown the fucker without meaning it."

Rink curses under her breath. "How long till we get the lights back?" she yells.

There's whispering and radio static, and then an answer. "An hour, maybe two."

"Fuck!" Prager shouts in the dark.

For a moment there is just the rain, hammering at the roof, sweeping through the foliage, and then Rink speaks. "I'm thinking we should take a break, Curt—wait till we have light to work by." There's no response from the darkness, and she tries again. "Curt?"

There's an embarrassed cough, and one of the crew cuts answers nervously. "He left, ma'am. I think he went up to the house."

"Shit," Rink whispers, and then, in a louder voice: "Let's button it up for an hour, boys." She points at two of her crew cuts. "Colley, Marco—you two are outside." And she looks at the fireplug. "C'mon, Vic, I'll buy you and Amory a beer."

The fireplug nods, and the egg smooths his fatigue pants. "I want Pepsi," he says.

44

THERE ARE footsteps, and the beams of light tremble and diminish, and the garage door scrapes down. The sound of rain is muted, the breeze vanishes, and the darkness is complete.

Bessemer sobs. "Is this part of it? Leaving us in the dark."

"It's a blackout, and let's hope it lasts."

"I don't even know where we are."

"There's a shed next to the greenhouse, with garden equipment in it. I'm pretty sure this is it."

Bessemer sobs again. "What the hell did you get me into?"

"Now's not the time, Howie. Now we get the hell out of Dodge. Can you walk?"

"Walk? I don't know if I can stand. My face hurts like a son of a bitch; I think they broke my nose. Besides, where am I supposed to walk?"

"I'm leaving, and you'd better come along."

"Are you kidding? I'm not going anywhere—you think I want to get in deeper?"

"It doesn't get deeper than this," Carr says, and he stands and shuffles slowly forward, navigating from memory. Around the slant bench, the water jugs, the light stands, toward the tractor. His shin smacks into something smooth and metal.

"What are you doing?" Bessemer says.

Carr turns around and stretches his arms back. "I hope I'm turning on a light," he says. He runs nearly numb fingers across a landscape of plastic textures—pebbled, cross-hatched, tacky, and smooth—until he finds the ridges of the tractor's little steering wheel. Then he reaches down and scrabbles over knobs and switches until he touches a key. Carr turns it, and the tractor's headlights come on—sickly beams that barely cross the room. To Carr, they are flares in a mineshaft.

Bessemer's voice is a frightened hiss. "They'll see!"

"The only windows are in back, Howie—those narrow slits near the ceiling. No one will see."

Carr follows the light to a workbench on the wall. He peers at the tabletop, then turns around and strains his arms back until his fingers catch the garden shears. "Stand up," he tells Bessemer.

"Why?"

"Because that way there's less chance I'll slash your wrists."

"What?"

"And for chrissakes stand still."

It takes two tries, back-to-back with the shears, and though Carr doesn't slash Bessemer's wrists, he does slice through his trousers and a chunk of his belt.

"Now cut mine," Carr says.

Bessemer cuts the plastic in one clean pass, and Carr massages his wrists and cold hands. "Now what?" Bessemer says.

"Now sit down again, and put your hands behind your back." Carr carries his own chair to the back of the room and places it beneath one of the narrow windows. He goes to the workbench, retrieves a pry bar from a hook on the wall, and stands on his chair.

"What are you doing?" Bessemer says. "We can't get out that way."

"No?"

"Maybe you can fit through, but I can't. Are you going to leave me here?"

Carr reaches up and slips the pry bar between the cinder-block wall and the window's aluminum frame. He grunts with effort and then there's a sound of rending metal and breaking glass, and he looks down at Bessemer. "Better sound the alarm, Howie."

And Bessemer does. Loudly. Loud enough to be heard over the lashing rain.

The metal door rolls up and two flashlight beams catch Bessemer in mid-yell. "The *bastard*, the *son of a bitch*—he left me here. That fucking prick went out the window and left me here!"

The lights dart and circle and find Carr's chair, and the broken glass and mangled window frame on the floor. Rain is blowing through the rectangular gap.

"Shit," the taller crew cut says. He draws his Glock and crosses to the window. His partner draws his gun too, but stays in the doorway, and Carr takes him first—the pry bar to the crotch, to the kidney, to the back of the head. There's an explosive bellow and the taller crew cut turns, is frozen for an instant, and brings his gun up.

And Carr is on him at a run. He clamps both hands on the Glock, forces it down, and drives his shoulder into the crew cut's chest. The crew cut goes back against the wall and the gun goes off and Carr snaps his head down hard on the bridge of the crew cut's nose. There's a crack and the crew cut's grip loosens. Carr tears the Glock free as the crew cut hits him with the flashlight. It catches him on the shoulder and bounces hard against his ear, and Carr hammers the crew cut again and again on the side of his head until he goes over.

Carr is breathing hard as he strips the guards of flash-lights, guns, radios, cash. He goes to the corner and runs a light over their wrecked bags. He picks through the pile and retrieves their wallets and passports.

Bessemer is still sitting, gripping the seat of his chair. "Jesus Christ," he whispers. "Are . . . are they dead?"

Carr rubs the side of his head and stands in the open doorway. "Not yet," he says, "though Rink might change that. We better get a move on; someone probably heard that shot."

Outside they are drenched in an instant, and their flashlight beams are swallowed whole.

"Christ!" Bessemer says, struggling to keep up. "Is this even a path?"

"It'll take us to the boathouse," Carr says, "assuming we can stay on it."

"What do we do there?"

"Get in a boat."

"In this? Are you crazy?"

"I don't like it, but I don't like cutting across the property either, much less making it over the fence. I don't know how many men Rink has here, but it won't be long before they're all out looking for us. They're not going to look for us out there."

The wind gusts and twists, shoving them sideways, shoving them forward, shoving them back. Palm fronds snap past them and sand scours their faces. The ocean is a flailing, howling thing, much too close in the dark.

"The money," Bessemer shouts, though he is right at Carr's back. "I thought nothing was going to happen until we were in Florida."

"That's what I thought too," Carr says, and he pulls his mind away from a thousand questions about who did what, and when they did it, and where they are right now. There's a squawk on the radio, and Carr stops and holds it to his ear.

"Dammit," he says. "Someone's calling the guys at the toolshed."

"What do we do?"

"Go faster."

But they're not fast enough. They're not halfway to the boathouse when a ribbon of light appears behind them. "They've got power in the guesthouse," Carr says, and he looks up through the whipping trees. "And in the main house too."

"And there," Bessemer says, pointing. There are lights at the boathouse, and more lights moving down the path.

Carr looks back. "They're coming from the greenhouse too," he says. He grabs Bessemer's collar and hauls him off the path, through bushes and branches, onto wet sand. The surf is white and frenzied before them, streaming across the beach and past the line of palm trees. The bay is boiling ink.

Carr drops the guns and radio to the sand. "Take off your shoes," he shouts.

Somehow Bessemer's face finds new terror. "What?"

"You a strong swimmer?"

"*What?*"

"It's a simple choice: stay here and die, or take our chances out there."

"There is no chance out there."

"We'll head west, around the jetty. There should be some protection in the bay, but we need to stay clear of the rocks."

"We...we could hide."

"They're going to search every inch of this property until they find us, Howie, and when they do, they're going to torture us and kill us. So now's the time."

Carr wades in and the cold is like a fist clenched around his lungs. He loses his breath and nearly loses his footing, and in two steps he's up to his neck. "Now, Howie."

Bessemer looks around wildly and sees lights approaching. His chest heaves as he kicks off his shoes, and he's fighting for breath when he calls to Carr. "Wait up!"

45

CARR IS badly wrong about the bay: there is no protection—not from wind or wave or hungry currents, or from the constellation of debris that swirls and collides just below the angry surface. The lights from shore dim with the first swell, and disappear altogether with the second, and suddenly he's fifty meters out. Or is it a hundred and fifty?

The sea heaves in every direction, and the wind makes shrapnel of the whitecaps. Carr's feet tangle in what feels like plastic netting, and something hard—a fence post swept from somewhere—glances off his thigh and leaves his leg numb and useless. A sheet of drywall—peeling, dissolving—shatters across his back. There's a roll of carpet, a shipping pallet, chicken wire, and a drowned chicken. It's like swimming through a landfill, or in Dorothy's twister, though actual swimming is all but impossible. Carr flails and twists and tumbles, coughing, spitting, wrestling for breath, and the only thing louder than the wind and rushing sea is his hammering heart.

Bessemer vanishes immediately, carried off without a cry, and Carr doesn't see him for what seems a choking eternity—until he spots a white arm rushing past, struggling vainly against the riptide that he himself has just escaped.

Carr sees him spin away—the white arm, the benign, round face, the sad, thin hair like sea grass—and then he calls Bessemer's name, fills his lungs, and kicks out after him.

The rip takes hold of Carr again—shoving, pulling, twisting him around—and he loses Bessemer behind a wall of water. He manages a sloppy breaststroke, but can't keep the ocean out of his mouth. He calls out, but the wind tears the words from his throat. He sees a shape that may be an arm, or a leg, or a tumbling body, and he lunges forward, through a breaking wave.

His fingers hook on something and he takes hold of an ankle. Bessemer is floating facedown. He finds his belt and flips him over. Carr slides an arm under Bessemer's arm and across his chest, and Bessemer's head rolls back against Carr's shoulder. Even in the dark, through the spray, Carr can see the ashen face, the blood flowing down his cheek, and the deep, depressed gash at Bessemer's left temple. He puts his ear to Bessemer's mouth and hears faint, uneven breathing.

"Howard," he yells, again and again over the wind, and Bessemer mutters weakly. The rip is pulling them out and under, and pulling Bessemer from him. Carr strikes out perpendicular to the current—to what he thinks is the east.

The current is twisting them, and he fights to keep Bessemer's face out of the water. His legs and shoulders are cramping, and his fingers, wound in Bessemer's shirt, are numb. He closes his eyes and concentrates on his breathing, on coordinating it with his kicks and his sculling arm, on ignoring the lead in his thighs and the weight clutched against his chest. And finally he finds it—the metronome he's been straining to hear, the rhythmic four count that silences the wind and the flailing sea: his heart, his lungs, in, out.

Carr loses himself in the cadence and loses track of time, and then, suddenly, the outbound surge is gone. They're free of the rip. Carr keeps kicking and realizes that another current, a lateral one, is pulling them slowly eastward. He lets it carry them, lifting his head to look for lights or land or anything at all, but he sees only darkness. They're well out of the bay now, he's sure—well beyond the reefs—and the waves are larger here and even more chaotic. One lifts them up high, and for an instant Carr sees a light, or thinks he does, and then another wave breaks across them, nearly tearing Bessemer from his grasp. Carr catches his arm, pulls him close again, and gets a better grip across his chest, and it is only then he realizes that Howard Bessemer has died.

46

FROM THIS height there's no trace of the storm—just pale sky, turquoise sea, and the edge of Cuba—brown and green and wrinkled as a fallen leaf. No trace, but he can still feel it moving in his arms and legs, and in his gut: a surge, a lift, a queasy drop. He can still hear the roar. Or is that the jet's engines? Carr signals the flight attendant and asks for another coffee and a blanket. Half a day since he came out of the water, and still he can't get warm.

He doesn't know how long he was in. Hours, certainly. Long enough for the lateral current to carry him miles to the east. Too long for him to hang on to Howard Bessemer's drowned and battered body. A wave finally tore it from his grasp, and some time afterward—he didn't know how long—Carr's foot found a sandbar, and eventually the shore.

It was a spur of rock off Old Robin Road, and there was a house under construction nearby, and a trailer to shelter in, once Carr had kicked in the door. He collapsed on a sofa, slept, and dreamed of nothing. In the drizzly morning, he'd hitched a ride with some housepainters to George Town.

A barefoot man in damp, salt-stained clothes hadn't raised as many eyebrows as Carr had expected. Maybe the locals wrote it off to the exigencies of the storm, or the eccentricities of tourists. Maybe it was Carr's still-wet cash that preempted their questions. In any event, it got him a ride to the strip mall, where he bought clothes and a toothbrush and a prepaid cell in a discount store. He washed up and changed in the store's bathroom, then sat on a curb and made phone calls.

The first one was to his father, and the relief he felt when he heard Arthur Carr's voice—*Why the devil are you calling? You never call*—took him by surprise. The next ones were to Valerie, and Bobby, and Dennis, and Mike, and Tina, and they all went unanswered.

Two tries, three tries, and then he'd taken a taxi to a cruise ship pier. He'd invested in sunglasses and a ball cap there, with a smiling pirate turtle stitched above the bill, and joined a large group of tourists riding a shuttle bus to the airport. He'd spotted two of Rink's men in the terminal, but he stayed with the crowd and kept his ball cap low, and he didn't think they'd seen him. At the gate he'd made more phone calls, but with no more success.

The operational puzzles—clothing, transpo, evasion— had kept Carr's mind focused, anchored to the present and to the next step. When they were solved, and his pace slowed, other questions had crowded in. Questions about timing, about passwords, about access to Amy Chun's laptop. About where the fuck the money was. Carr had no answers to them, but he didn't mind that they filled his head. They gave him something to do and left no room for his anger, or for the images that seemed to rise up whenever he closed his eyes—of Howard Bessemer, white and drowned and dropping through black water.

Carr wakes with a start, and for an instant Bessemer's soft round face floats before him. He squeezes his eyes shut and opens them again and looks out the window. In the distance he sees the towers of Miami.

. . .

IT'S BLUE dusk when he arrives in Boca Raton. The rendezvous is on a quiet street of breeze-block homes in earshot of 95, and just two exits from the airport. Like every other house in the neighborhood, it's a neat, one-story rectangle, with a shallow pitched roof, a carport, and a brown lawn. It's painted some pastel shade, maybe pink, maybe yellow, though in this light everything is gray to Carr. He drives past the house and turns the corner three blocks down.

The whole ride up from Miami, he's thought more about the timing—how tight it was, how rapid the sequence of events. Dennis gets Prager's password. Prager's money is stolen. Prager gets a call, telling him he's been robbed by Greg Frye. Prager grabs them from the hotel lot. All in the space of not quite three hours. By then, Dennis, Bobby, and Mike would've been in the air, en route to Miami—according to the plan, at least. But no one seemed to care much about the plan these days—not about Carr's plan, anyway.

He's thought about Dennis too. Young Dennis, skinny Dennis, pimply Dennis, tentative Dennis, genius Dennis. It's hard for Carr to believe that he's involved, but impossible to figure a way that he's not. Dennis and Valerie both. Dennis had Prager's password, Valerie had access to Amy Chun's hardware. They couldn't do it on their own, but they could do it together, and Valerie could be very persuasive.

He drives past the house a second time. The carport is empty; the shades are drawn; no lights—the house has a buttoned-up look. The streets are quiet. Few cars and no pedestrians. He turns the corner, parks two blocks down, and sits behind the wheel for forty-five minutes, until night has finished falling.

There's a tension in his stomach as he walks down the empty sidewalk, and it winds tighter as he vaults the alley fence into the darkest corner of the house's backyard. No lights back here either, and no open windows. Buttoned up. He's soft and quiet moving up on it, but that's more habit than anything else. He has the feeling he could launch fireworks and no one would care. The house has that look.

He stands against the back wall, by the screen door, and listens. A chorus of night bugs, a television playing in Spanish, half a block down, and the ceaseless whisper of 95. Nothing from inside. He takes out his cell and punches Dennis's number once more and holds the phone away from his ear. He rests his head against the door, and hears—very faintly—a ringing from inside.

"Fuck," he says aloud, and he cuts off the call and punches Bobby's number. Again, faintly, a ringing inside. "Fuck," he says again. He snaps on plastic gloves, takes a flashlight and a screwdriver from his pocket, and wishes he had something more substantial.

He slides the screwdriver into the frame and the back door opens with a whisper, and the smell hits him right away. It's one that's familiar, but still, his stomach nearly empties. He rubs his eyes and pulls his shirt up to his nose and steps inside.

It's a small house, and the smell has filled it to bursting, and so have the heat and the flies. It takes no searching to find them: they're in the living room, Bobby sideways on the sofa, Dennis genuflecting by a card table. Carr can't tell how long they've been dead.

He stands over Bobby's body and runs the flashlight up and down. There's a beer bottle on the cushion next to him, and the remains of a cigarette that scorched his pants and the flesh underneath. The flies buzz and hover and Carr shoos them away from Bobby's head. He can see the entry wounds then—one to the back of the neck, one to the back of the head. He can't tell if there are powder burns.

Dennis also has two wounds, also to the head and neck. His laptops are missing, but his clothes are there, still packed in a duffel, as are Bobby's. Mike's are not. Carr stands stock-still as a van drives slowly past, and then he leaves. He waits until he's in the alley, two blocks away, before he throws up.

47

THERE'S ONLY one place left for Carr to go, but it isn't late enough yet, and he needs a shower. He takes a room at a Fairfield Inn near the airport and stands under the spray for a long time. He uses all the little bars of soap and all of the shampoo, but still it's not enough. Wrapped in a towel, lying on the bed, he tries to work the puzzles—the efficient double taps in both bodies, the lack of struggle, the missing laptops, no Mike—but nothing will sit still. He sees Dennis, dumped like lost luggage beside the table. He sees Bobby's wry, irritated, tired face. *Fuckin' Carr*, he hears him say. He can hear the flies and feel them lighting on his hair and arms.

AMY CHUN'S gated community has decent security, but the golf course abutting it does not. The cart path that runs along the sixth fairway is bordered on one side by palms and lush plantings, and on the other side by an eight-foot wrought-iron fence. Amy Chun's house lies just beyond, across an empty street. Crouched on the golf course side, Carr watches. Just past midnight, just after the security cruiser makes its half-hourly run, he climbs over.

The house is modern and glass, all planes and angles, and

the landscaping is all about privacy—tall bamboo, fanning palmettos, and long ornamental grasses. Path lights pick out a white gravel walk that disappears into the foliage.

All the windows that Carr can see are dark. He crosses the street quickly, finds heavy shadows, and waits. Nothing moves, nothing but bugs make a sound. Carr is quiet approaching the front door. It is massive and metal clad, and there's a discreet sign nearby, warning of alarms and armed response. Carr would be more concerned if he couldn't see the control pad through the door sidelight, and the status indicator glowing green, for disarmed.

He follows a path around the back to a long deck. It looks out on a man-made pond and a garden of rocks and combed gravel. In the dark it looks to Carr like the surface of the moon. Glass doors run the length of the deck, but the glass is dark, and Carr can see nothing inside. He takes out his phone and tries Valerie's number, and then Mike's. He gets no answer, and hears nothing from inside. He's not sure if he's relieved. Then he punches Amy Chun's number.

The phone is loud through the glass. It rings five times, and then the voice mail kicks in. Amy Chun's voice is crisp and businesslike, and her message is brief. Carr closes his phone and pulls on his plastic gloves. He turns on the flashlight, takes out the screwdriver, and takes a deep breath.

Amy Chun's air-conditioning is efficient, but the cool temperature doesn't mask the odor. It hits Carr harder this time, and he has to hold the door frame until his head stops spinning. He turns on the flashlight, shrouds the beam with his hand, and follows the smell.

Through the living room, down a short hall, to a frosted-glass door, half-opened and marred by a jagged crack. Amy Chun's office. Despite the overturned chairs, the crooked pictures on the wall, and the books and papers on the floor, Carr recognizes it from Dennis's spycam video.

The desk is askew, but Chun's Isla Privada laptop is there, along with the other hardware—the password generator, the fingerprint scanner, and Chun's cell phone. And there is blood too.

It's on the edge of the desk, and the arms of the chair, but most of it is on the floor, in the corner, around Amy Chun's body. Her back is against the wall, and one bare leg is bent beneath her. The other is straight out in front. Her arms are at her sides, and her hands lie palms up on the floor—a supplicant's hands, Carr thinks. Her head hangs down, and her long black hair hides her torso. Carr is grateful he can't see her face.

The smell is stronger here, and Carr's head is spinning again. He can't look away from her hands, her pleading fingers, and he feels embarrassed—as if he's come upon her in the midst of something deeply private. The flashlight seems a terrible invasion, and Carr turns it off, but even in the dark he can see her hands.

He remembers her walking with Valerie beneath the arcade, their heads bent close, their fingers brushing. He remembers the bar in Houston, the green paper lanterns hanging, the smell of beer and cigarettes, Bobby and Dennis watching Valerie. He sees Howard Bessemer's pale hands, and his pale, round face drifting away. And suddenly, desperately, he needs air. Carr turns and the beam hits him full in the face.

It's a hard blue light, and he can't see who is behind it, but the glint of the chromed gun barrel is unmistakable, and so is the bass rumble of the voice. Like thunder, but not at all distant.

"Where are you rushing to?" Mr. Boyce says. "And where the fuck is my money?"

48

INHALE, EXHALE, *not too fast,* Carr tells himself, and he shifts carefully in the long grass.

November is early summer down here, but to Carr the pre-dawn sky looks like winter, and the ocean—dead calm—looks frozen. The beach below is like a field of ice, and the sun—still a waxy splinter on the horizon—looks coated with frost. Carr knows the forecast calls for another warm day, but there's nothing warm about the ground he's lying on, and nothing soft about the grass. It feels like winter ground to him.

Carr moves the binoculars slowly along the coastline, but there is little to see. Some fishing boats to the north; to the south something larger, and farther out at sea. A tanker maybe, or a cargo ship. The beach is empty but for a stray dog worrying a carcass—a gull's perhaps—a quarter mile away. He can hear a jet far off, but can't see the lights. The only other noise is the wind. Of the ten armed men ranged along the hilltop with him, he sees and hears nothing. Even the man beside him is practically invisible, which is a considerable achievement given his size.

"Watch the flare off the lenses," Mr. Boyce whispers. Carr nods and scans the binoculars down, to the house at the bottom of the hill, at the edge of the sand.

It's a modest house by local standards, a cottage really, without the cantilevered decks, sweeping windows, or vast infinity pools common to its newer neighbors. But still, a nice house. Thick, whitewashed walls, red tile roof, fences and patios of rough local stone, a vegetable garden in back. Carr studied the site survey at the records hall, in town, and knows it sits on nearly a dozen acres—from beachfront to the top of this hill. Nice, and not cheap.

A yellow light appears in a window—a kitchen window, Carr knows. Boyce sees it too. "He a morning person?" Boyce asks.

"I don't know what he is," Carr says.

Nearly three months of tracking him—tracking both of them—following money and rumors and bodies across half the world, and Carr still doesn't know. He knows they were damn smart, though—that he knows without a doubt. The web of wire transfers that emanated from the initial one—the one that relieved Curtis Prager of one hundred million dollars—was intricate and broad, similar in concept to what Carr had planned, but more complicated.

Prager's money was quickly split into fifty separate transfers of two million each, and sent to fifty different banks around the world, into accounts owned by fifty shell corporations. Within hours of the theft, while Prager was still struggling to get Isla Privada's systems working again and to notify his correspondent banks that something was amiss, those accounts had themselves been emptied by still other transfers. The layering and structuring of electronic payments continued for days, until the money came to temporary rest in banks in Luxembourg and Switzerland, in accounts owned by yet another set of shell companies.

Then came the cash withdrawals. There were nearly forty of those, over the course of five days, in Zurich, Basel, and Luxembourg—in amounts ranging from one million to three million euro. They made for heavy briefcases, but nothing a healthy courier couldn't handle. Once in cash, the money became nearly impossible to trace. Carr suspects it didn't travel far—to banks down the street from the banks it came out of, most likely, and into another set of accounts.

It was elaborate, and it must've taken at least a year, and a fair amount of money, just to set up the shell companies and open the bank accounts. A lot of planning, and more discipline than Carr would've expected from him, but maybe that was her influence. There's motion on the beach, and Carr shifts the binoculars. The dog is in the water now, snapping at sea foam, his jaws closing on nothing. Carr knows how he feels.

Three months of staring at account numbers, wire transfer logs, bank statements, flight manifests, and security camera footage have left him feeling alternately like an accountant and a cop, and both of them empty-handed. But dead ends, bleary eyes, overcaffeination, and exhaustion notwithstanding, he hasn't minded the work, or even Boyce's microscopic scrutiny of him while he does it. In fact, he's welcomed it—welcomed anything that occupied his brain, and left room for nothing else. Not for thoughts of how blind he was, how foolish, or how wrong. Not for guilt or hungry rage.

Mostly, the job has fit that bill, but even amid the columns of numbers, the megabytes of data, and the stacks of paper, there's been downtime. The flights are the worst, and commercial or private makes no difference. Something about the long sleepless stretches, or the darkened cabins, or the dead, cold air, or the unceasing grind of the engines, or maybe all of those things together—something summons them. Memories of Bobby and Dennis in the workhouse, in Boca—the flies and the smell—of Ray-Ray in the morgue, in Mendoza, his blackened bones and clawing fingers; of Howard Bessemer, white and bloated and spinning through the waves; of Amy Chun's hands—

"Kitchen window," Mr. Boyce whispers.

Carr shifts his binoculars and sees a silhouette moving in the yellow square. "Can you tell who?" he asks.

"No," Boyce says. He touches the mic on his neck and whispers something. They watch in silence, and after a while the shadow disappears from the window. After another while, Boyce sighs and lowers his binoculars.

"You called your father last night?" he asks Carr.

"You know I did."

Boyce nods imperceptibly. "How is he doing?"

"He's okay. I'm sure you know that too."

"I don't eavesdrop."

"Your distinctions are too subtle for me."

Boyce smiles. "How's he getting along with Margie?"

"As well as he does with anyone. Which is not well."

"She was an army nurse for twenty years—I think she can handle it. Margie can stay on with him, you know. She likes it up there."

Carr shakes his head. "After this, I go back. That was the deal—that, and the money. Nothing's changed."

"I just want you to know you have options."

Carr points down the hill. A door has opened near the kitchen window, and a rectangle of yellow light falls on the patio stones. A shadow—the elongated shape of a man—fills the rectangle. The shadow is still, and Carr finds that he's holding his breath. The door closes again and Carr sighs.

Boyce chuckles softly. "He's like a dog, sniffing the air. His hackles are up, but he doesn't know why."

Carr looks at his watch and looks at the sky. Three months, and the end is a hillside away. He feels his heart rate rise, and a tightness spread through his shoulders and down his arms. "He'll know soon enough."

Boyce turns to look at him. "You're sure about going in alone?"

"I'm sure. You'll be cleaning up with sponges otherwise."

"And you don't want to bring anything?"

"The wire is enough," Carr says. "There'll be more than enough guns in there." Three months.

Mr. Boyce reads his thoughts. "It's been a long time," he says in a quiet rumble. "A long time chasing. A lot of time to think. To brood. I know a little something about disloyalty, but now's not the moment to get impatient or sloppy or... emotional."

Carr's laugh is quiet and rueful. "I thought I was just tired."

"You are. Anger is tiring."

Carr rubs a hand across the stubble on his jaw. "The light's coming up," he says.

Boyce checks his watch and whispers something into his mic. He waits for an answer, and then looks at Carr. "It's time then."

Inhale, exhale, not too fast.

49

CARR IS quiet down the hillside and across the patio, but when he opens the door he knows he hasn't been quiet enough.

Declan is looking up from a newspaper spread on a long table. He's holding a pair of reading glasses in one big hand, and a Taurus nine-millimeter casually—almost carelessly—in the other. Neither one of them moves or speaks, and blood rushes madly in Carr's ears.

Then Declan smiles. It's huge and crooked, and it engages every crag and freckle on his ruddy face. His eyes gleam, and Carr would swear the light gets brighter. "You got grass stains on your knees, lad, and you look like pickled death. You better have yourself a coffee." The brogue is stronger than ever.

Carr nods slowly. "Coffee would be good."

"I just put the pot on. There's breakfast too, if you like. Fry up some eggs?"

"Just coffee, I think."

"Coffee then," Declan says. He slips the gun into the waistband of his pajamas and pads barefoot across the tile floor. He takes two mugs from a cabinet. "And would you close the door, lad—unless your friends are comin' too."

Carr shuts the door. "Not yet."

Declan smiles. "Not yet," he repeats.

"You lost some weight," Carr says. "And I like the beard—even with all the gray. You look good." Actually, he looks older to Carr—leathery, smaller, and somehow desiccated, like an old boot.

"Death agrees with me."

Carr smiles. "You don't seem too surprised."

"Had a feeling the past few days. Not even a feeling—more like an itch I couldn't reach, or a yen for something, but I didn't know what. So, not entirely surprised."

"Surprised it's me?"

Declan shakes his head. "When I heard you'd gotten yourself away from Prager, I figured if it was anyone, there was a better than even chance it'd be you." He points a thumb across the open living room, at what Carr knows is a bedroom door. "I told her that. And I told her yesterday that something was up. But she wasn't havin' any. She said I was paranoid—*an old woman* was how she put it. She can be... unkind."

Carr nods. "Yes, so I've seen."

The coffee is ready, and Declan pours it out and carries the mugs to the table. He fetches a can of condensed milk from the pantry, shakes it, and punches the top with a can opener. "I remember you like this stuff," he says. Carr pours some milk in, stirs, and takes a sip. Declan smiles. "I can see you're feeling more spry already."

Carr nods, but actually he's more exhausted than ever. He studies Declan across the table and tries to find some other feelings. Rage? Hatred? Disgust? He's harbored them all over the long months—nurtured them, savored them sometimes—but now they've abandoned him. He tries to conjure them up, recalling images of Bobby and Dennis, of Howard Bessemer's white face and Amy Chun's pleading hands—images that he's run from for three months—but it's like turning out empty pockets. There's nothing there.

Or almost nothing. He looks at Declan's shoulders, slumped in striped pajamas, his gray-streaked beard and graying hair, the little gold hoop—that's new too, and even more ridiculous than the beard—his reading glasses and bloodshot eyes, and finds a speck of something. A grain of... pity? It confuses Carr, and he's relieved to have questions to fall back on.

"So, how was it supposed to work?" he asks.

Declan drinks some coffee and smiles ruefully. "Not to put too fine a point on it, lad, but you weren't supposed to walk away from Prager's."

"It was hardly a walk."

"I can only imagine. But if you'd stayed put, it would've looked like your crew had fucked you, and then fucked one another: three down and the other two in the wind, and no one to say different. Boyce could beat the bushes for them as long as he wanted, but in the end who would he find?"

"And of course no one would be out looking for you."

Declan smiles. "Death benefits."

"Which, I gather, was the point of the theatrics in Mendoza."

"I needed room to move, yes, and also some extra operating capital. Setting up that pipeline wasn't cheap."

"It was goddamn expensive for Ray-Ray."

Declan's face darkens for a moment. "Don't think I was happy about it—I wasn't. I'd planned for him to drive with Bobby and Mike on the way out, but things were a little crazy."

"No crazier than you wanted, though. I mean, it was you who gave Bertolli and his men the heads-up about the raid, right?"

Again the smile. "They were more eager than I expected."

"They didn't shoot you off that road, though. That was you again, right?" Declan nods modestly. "And you had a ride waiting out of there?"

"A four-by-four. I drove off-road after that, back to Mendoza, and it was hell on my kidneys."

"And the body alongside Ray-Ray's?"

"The fellow that brought me my four-by-four."

Carr shakes his head. "What did you do in Mendoza?"

"I laid up for a couple of weeks, then made my way to Mexico. Short hops, nice and easy."

"Home free, while we were weeping at your grave."

"From what I heard, you two weren't doing much weeping—you and Val."

Carr's throat tightens. "You didn't worry we'd scrap the job?"

Declan laughs. "Walk away from that payday? I knew you a lot better than that." He points his thumb at the bedroom door again. "She was worried about it, though—worried about you running things, frankly—but I told her you were the man for the job. Told her to help you out too—lend a sympathetic ear, and so forth."

"Thanks for the vote of confidence," Carr says softly. He drinks some coffee and struggles to get it down. "Bobby and Mike didn't share your faith. They didn't like my management style. Half the time they were ready to walk. So was I, for that matter. The rest of the time I was thinking that they'd sold you to Bertolli. That's why I made a deal with Boyce—told him I'd stay on only if he'd look into what happened down there. But I guess you know all about that."

"I was touched when I heard, lad—really."

"But not worried."

Another rueful smile. "Well, no—there was never much chance you'd find anything I didn't want found. And you know my thoughts about idle hands—I figured the more you had on your mind, the less opportunity there was of you getting into anything too troublesome. Bobby and Mike and their money-laundering shenanigans were a surprise, it's true—those feckin' pirates—but it helped to keep you busy.

"And in the end, you pulled it off! It was a knotty piece of work, with all sorts of unexpected shite falling on your head, but you made it happen. A true classic!"

Carr shakes his head. "Then I went and fucked things up by not letting Prager kill me."

"You left us scrambling, yes, but I was still a dead man, and we had faith in the pipeline we'd laid down, and that we'd left no trail to this little hidey-hole. And so I must ask you, lad—what brought you to our doorstep? It wasn't following the cash, was it?"

"No, you covered those tracks too well. We did find Mike's body, out in the 'Glades, and we found that guy you dropped in Lake Worth—the Russian kid. He was what—your computer guy?"

"He was no Dennis, but he was good enough to steal Prager's password off the server Dennis's spyware sent it to. Of course, we did tell him where to look, didn't we? But he was good enough to bring Prager's systems down for close to a week. That was a help—a nice head start."

"We found one of your couriers too, in a landfill outside Frankfurt."

Declan snorts. "And he deserved every screaming second of it, the suited prick—running off with my luggage like that. I'd kill the bastard again if I could."

Carr nods. "I'm sure. Anyway, he's about as far as we followed the cash."

"Then how did you manage it?"

"It was the real estate."

"What—this place?"

"You used to talk about this neck of the woods, once upon

a time, when you played retirement geography—you and Bobby and Mike and Dennis and Ray-Ray. You used to talk about Punta and José Ignacio and La Paloma—this whole stretch of coast. How wide the beaches were, the blond sand, the fishing. And then, about two years back, you stopped talking about it. You just dropped it—never mentioned it again. You talked about plenty of other places afterward—in Vietnam, in Thailand—but not here."

"Fuck me. I didn't think anyone was paying attention."

"I was. It was your favorite place, and then it wasn't. Was that when it started, the planning for all this—two years ago?"

"Who keeps track?" Declan says, smiling. "A pretty slim reed, though, wasn't it—some game we used to play?"

Carr nods. "It was grasping at straws, for sure—but what else was there to do? The money trail was cold. So I looked for purchases of private homes—beachfront property only—made by foreign individuals or companies where payment was in cash. Anytime in the past two years. Anywhere from Punta, north to Costa Azul. It was a shot in the dark, but this stretch of coastline isn't all that long. Hell, the whole country isn't that big. Turned out there weren't so many purchases to sort through. And, of course, Boyce has the resources."

Declan's face darkens and he shakes his head. "Doesn't he though, lad—a whole feckin' empire at his feet. And have you finally sussed out who it is you're working for?"

"It didn't take much figuring. All that access, all that data, the intel reports…"

"Your old dad will be pleased to know you're serving your country again."

"I'm a consultant," Carr says, frowning. "A subcontractor."

Declan's laugh is bitter. "That's what you tell yerself. That's how it starts. The bastard doesn't want Prager's money, you know—he never did. He wants Prager himself—

his very own bent banker as a pet, and all that intel on Prager's clients, current and future. He was going to squeeze Prager—threaten to rat to his clients that a hundred million of their money had walked out the door—if Prager didn't roll over."

Carr nods. "Which is what he did. Boyce squeezed, and Prager rolled over."

"So things worked out fer him after all—that's grand."

"Don't kid yourself—Boyce is out of pocket one hundred million plus some hefty expenses. He wants his money back. And I want mine."

Declan's laugh is full of irony. "Ah, young Carr, is that what all this is about to you—nothing more than money?"

Carr pushes his mug across the table. His face is hot. "I could ask you the same. Was this just about money to you? Was it worth the fucking body count?"

"Don't moralize, lad. I'm a thief—same as them. Same as you."

"I didn't slaughter the men I worked with."

Declan stands quickly and runs a hand through his hair. "You think that's what I set out to do?"

"I think you have an amazing ability to rationalize just about anything. That firefight at Bertolli's place, being out there in the dark, blasting away, making it up as you go—I think you love shit like that. It's right up your alley. I think the only thing you love more than money and yourself is risk—and fuck the collateral damage. If there are bodies in the street, it's their own damn fault for getting in the way."

"They knew the downside of this work, same as you. They knew what could happen."

"Bessemer didn't know it. Amy Chun didn't know it."

"Bessemer was never going to make it, and Chun was questionable."

Carr's jaw aches from clenching. "And what about our

own guys? Did they know that their biggest risk was the man they were working for? For chrissakes, they trusted you!"

"Trust? You naive ass—you think they wouldn't have sold you out? You thought they'd ratted me to Bertolli. You thought they were going to do the same to you—and they might've, lad, given half a chance. Look what they did in Mendoza: ran off when the shooting started—with a chunk of my money, mind—and then lied to you about it. They're professional liars! You're telling me you trust men like that?"

Carr shakes his head in disbelief. "You don't seriously believe that, do you?"

"You should thank me for opening your eyes. They were thieves and killers, not my feckin' kids. You were on borrowed time with them, same as me—only I had borrowed more."

"So that makes it okay, then? We were going to fuck you eventually, unless you fucked us first?"

Declan waves a hand, as if he's shooing a fly. "This is a young man's game, and I was too long at it. It was just a matter of time, and that bastard Boyce wasn't going to let me retire. He won't let you go either, you'll see."

Carr pushes away from the table and looks out the window. Light is swelling in the sky now, and the ocean is yellow and scored with whitecaps. He looks at Declan—a grizzled old man in rumpled pajamas, with a gun in his hand. He reaches once more for those feelings, but it's just empty pockets.

"I can't even follow your bullshit anymore, Deke. It's too convoluted, or I'm too tired. It's all just noise."

Declan squints at him and at the Taurus, and slides the gun onto the table. His smile is thin and tired. "Maybe the simple answer's the best, then. Maybe I did it for her."

Carr laughs coldly. "You did it for *love*?"

"You sound shocked."

"I expect cynicism from you, not delusion."

Declan's smile is tired. "Not a believer, lad?"

"In a love that has you killing your own? I don't call that love."

"You think it's all paper hearts and stolen kisses? You're not *that* young, Carr. You've read a book or two."

Carr sighs. "I hope she's worth it."

Declan laughs bitterly. "Too soon to tell, lad," he whispers.

Then the bedroom door opens, and Tina walks through. She's wearing fatigue pants, a black T-shirt, a black plastic holster under her left arm, and another on her right hip. Her platinum hair—longer now—is tied in a tight braid. She slams a clip into a Glock as she crosses the living room, and slides the gun into her shoulder holster.

She shakes her head in disgust. "If I have to listen to much more of this, I won't wait for Boyce to shoot me. I'll do it myself."

50

THERE IS heat in Carr's face again, and a rushing sound in his ears, and the feelings that eluded him with Declan come surging back now. He looks at the Taurus on the table, and has to make a fist to stop himself from reaching for it.

"Long time, Tina," he says.

She purses her lips. "Not long enough, if you know what I mean," she says, and looks at Declan. "You pat him down?"

"Jaysus, girl, he's not come here to throw down. If that's what he wanted, he'd have done it already."

"That's your view. Pat him down."

Declan rolls his eyes and puts up his hands in mock despair. "Indulge her, lad," he says. Carr stares at Tina for a moment, and then he stands and puts his palms on the table and spreads his legs. Declan is quick and thorough, and there's only the slightest hesitation when his fingers find the mic taped between Carr's shoulders. He smiles at Carr and looks at Tina. "Like a baby," he says.

Tina goes to the kitchen window and looks up the hill. Then she turns to Carr. "Great. Now if you two are through catching up, we can—"

"Not quite through," Carr says softly.

"What, more questions? Let me guess—Valerie?"

"I want to know what happened to her."

Declan coughs nervously. "Come on, lad, you—"

Tina cuts him off. "He knows what happened to her. He knows."

Carr nods slowly, as his chest tightens. "It was at Chun's place?"

"She never saw it coming, if that makes you feel better. And it was clean. And fast."

The floor is shifting beneath him and Tina's voice is faint. Carr sits down again, carefully. Declan is staring at the floor, and Tina is back at the window. "I shouldn't have let Chun see it happen, though," she continues. "That was a mistake. The woman went fucking ape-shit—put up a hell of a fight."

"Where?" Carr says. His voice is small and choked. "Where is she?"

"Valerie? Burial at sea, due east of the Boca Beach Club, four miles out or so. I don't know the GPS coordinates or anything."

The room seems to darken, and Carr's knees shake. "Christ," he whispers, and he closes his eyes and there is Valerie in Napa, the candlelight on her arms and neck, her hair coming loose from its braid, her smile. And there she is in Portland, the dying orange light on her face, her hands cold under his shirt. *Maybe that's what we'll do afterward, you and me. We'll conduct a little research to find some happy couples. We'll be like archaeologists.* And there is her amber voice, close in his ear, intimate. *Afterward.* And there is the weight of her, above him, the heat of her body washing over him. Carr's chest aches, and his bones are lead.

"Regret's a bitch," Tina says from somewhere far off. "You spent all that time wondering about her, but she wasn't lying to you. You ask me, I think she liked you. She put up with your whining, which was more than I—"

"Stop talking," Carr says. He is surprised to find himself

on his feet, his chair overturned. He wants the Taurus, but Declan has a hand over it and is shaking his head.

Tina looks at Carr. "At last, something we agree on: enough fucking talk. How many men out there?"

"Too many," Carr says.

"I count seven," Tina says. "Am I right?"

Declan chuckles. "You planning on a war, love?"

"I'm not planning to go anyplace with Boyce."

"Darlin', I think they've got us fair and square."

Tina crosses her white arms on her chest. "The hell they do. We've got Carr. If they want him back in one piece, they'll let us walk."

Carr's laugh is jagged and loud. "You think anyone on earth cares if I'm in one piece?"

"You better hope Boyce does," Tina says. "Otherwise this is going to be a mess, and you'll be the first stain." And she slips the Glock from her shoulder holster and points it at Carr.

Declan laughs. "We have a better negotiating position than that, girl. Boyce wants his money, for chrissakes, and recovery's easier with us than without. In fact, it's impossible without us."

Tina's mouth puckers in disgust. "You think I'm going to deal away my money?"

"It's not just *your* money."

"Whatever."

Declan smiles and walks around the table. He puts a hand on Tina's shoulder. "I like to mix it up as much as the next fellow, but it's nice when there's at least the ghost of a chance. You know Boyce as well as I do, love. He leaves no daylight."

Tina shakes off his hand. "You *are* a fucking old woman. After all that work, the time we put in, all the goddamn bridges we burned—you're ready to deal it away? Well, I'm not." She turns the Glock on Carr again. "How many men out there?"

"I forget."

Declan's smile is unwavering. "Who says we have to deal it all away? That's what negotiation is about. I'm sure Boyce will agree, recovering some money is better than recovering none at all." He puts his hand out again.

She steps back and keeps her gun on Carr. There are pink spots on her cheeks, the first time Carr has ever seen color there. His mouth is dry and he looks again for the Taurus, but he can't see it on the table.

Tina shakes her head at Declan. "You're mister diplomat now? Sure, Boyce might negotiate—and then he'll hose us once he has the cash. And then where will we be? I'm getting tired of asking, Carr—how many fucking men?"

"Two. Four. A hundred. Go out and count them yourself."

Declan drapes a big arm on her shoulder. "We'll still be alive, love. Even a shit deal is better than dead."

Tina ducks from beneath his arm and draws the second Glock from her hip. "The hell it is. If you think I'm—"

Declan hits her with the Taurus on the side of the head, and Tina crumples to the floor. He kicks her guns away, kneels beside her, and checks her breathing and her pulse. Then he slides all three guns across the tiles to Carr. "Better than dead," he says, and he picks Tina up and carries her to the sofa.

BOYCE AND five of his men are on the patio when Carr opens the door. The men go inside. Carr hands Boyce the guns. "You hear it?" Carr asks.

"I heard. I'm sorry about Valerie."

"So am I," Carr says, swallowing hard. "It wasn't a surprise, but…"

"Knowing it is different."

Carr leans heavily against a whitewashed wall, dizzy for a moment in the morning air. "You'll deal with the money?"

Boyce nods. "Why don't you sit down?"

Carr waves him off. "I'm fine."

Boyce looks at him for a moment and then puts out a massive hand. They shake and Boyce goes inside, and Carr walks through a gate in the stone fence and down to the beach.

He keeps walking until the sand is firm beneath his feet, and then he stops and watches the ocean, and the waves unfurling. The stray he'd seen at dawn is back, rolling and splashing in a tidal pool. His coat is heavy with water, glistening like a seal's, and he's holding a piece of driftwood in his mouth. A boy comes down the beach now, with a leash and a yellow tennis ball. The boy whistles; the dog attends. Not a stray then. Carr looks north and sees a lighthouse in the distance. He thinks about walking there, but finds that he's kneeling in the sand and that he cannot move.

EPILOGUE

IT IS February, and Stockbridge lies under a blanket of new snow. The storm that spread it moved on before dawn, and the morning sky is blue and painfully bright. Carr wears sunglasses to shovel and salt the drive, the front steps, and the stone walk out to the mended gate, and he keeps them on while he drinks a cup of coffee on the porch and watches a town plow throw pillars of snow into the air. When his coffee is gone, he stacks bales of newspaper into his pickup—yet another load for the recycling center. The bed is nearly full when a black Mercedes pulls into the drive. Carr pushes his sunglasses into his hair and takes off his gloves.

A liveried driver walks carefully around the car and opens the rear door. Mr. Boyce emerges, too large to have ever fit inside. He squints in the glare, turns up the collar of his black overcoat, and smiles.

"I thought I might be too early," Boyce says. His deep voice is somehow muffled in the snow.

"I'm up with the chickens," Carr says. "But I wasn't expecting visitors."

"I thought I'd tell you in person that the money's finally settled."

"About time."

"Declan doesn't make anything easy."

Carr nods and crosses his arms on his chest. "Tell me the final numbers."

"After expenses, et cetera, the recovery netted seventy-eight five, of which a third stays with me, and two-thirds—that's fifty-two million and change—goes to you. Per your instructions, ten of that goes to Bessemer's kid—"

"Simon."

"To Simon Bessemer, of Boothbay Harbor, Maine; another five to Maureen Shepherd, of Eugene, Oregon—Dennis's mother; and five more to Elaine Geller, of Bethpage, Long Island—Bobby's sister."

"What about Mike?"

"There might be an aunt in San Diego. We're still looking."

"And Valerie?"

Boyce shakes his head. "Daniel Finch and Dawn Schaffer—the mother went back to her maiden name—both deceased, no siblings."

Carr lets out a breath that hangs in the air like a ghost. "Finch," he says quietly, "that was her name? Valerie Finch?"

"*Anne* Finch," Boyce says. "That was her real name. Anne Elizabeth Finch."

Carr swallows hard and stares for a while at a snow-covered fir. "Her parents...do you know where they're buried?"

"In Texas, at a place near Austin."

"Both of them, in the same place?"

"Same place. Why?"

"I want to get something—a stone or something—near her parents. Could you—"

Boyce nods. "What do you want on it?"

"Just her name," Carr says.

The plow passes again, going in the other direction, and the chains sound to Carr like sleigh bells. He and Boyce watch as it recedes down the road, and then Boyce takes an envelope from his coat.

"It's a statement," he says. "It lays out the recovery, the expenses, the split—everything."

"What about the tax situation?"

"That too. You're square there—with the feds and the Commonwealth of Massachusetts—all documented and paid up, as far as they're concerned."

"Thanks," Carr says, and tucks the envelope in his back pocket. "And thanks for the courier service."

"I figured I'd see for myself how you're doing."

Carr shrugs. "I'm still racking up the frequent-flyer miles at the dump and the recycling center, and they throw rose petals at my feet at the hardware store."

"How's your dad?"

"Some days he reads to me from the *FT*, other days I read to him, and then there are the days he craps his pants. It's up and down, but the general trend is down. He's dying."

Boyce nods gravely. "And the help situation?"

"A new one started Monday. She's a few years out of nursing school, worked in a dementia unit, over in Springfield. Nice kid, very eager. I figure she'll last two weeks."

"Say the word, and I'll have Margie back tomorrow. She did fine with him before, and it would give you a break for a while. A little time to do something else."

"Something else?"

"I've always got something else that needs doing."

"I have my hands full here," Carr says.

"Any thoughts about what you might do ... afterward?"

Carr tenses at the word. "Not a one."

"A man's got to do something."

"Maybe not. I've got a lot of money now."

"I don't see you as the idle type."

"I just need some practice."

Boyce smiles and shakes his head. "You sure about Margie—about taking a break? This sort of thing…it can be long, and none of it is easy."

Carr shrugs again. "He's my father."

Mr. Boyce nods and grips Carr's hand. He walks to his car, and the driver comes around to get the door. Boyce pauses and turns back to Carr. "You never ask about them—about Declan and Tina. Not once."

"There's nothing I want to know," Carr says, and Mr. Boyce folds himself into his Mercedes and is driven away.

Carr brings his coffee mug inside. The front hall is warm and smells of soap and floor wax and fresh paint, and the living room smells of apple wood from the fire he built the night before. He raises the shades and white winter light pours in and pools on every polished surface—the floorboards, the andirons, the silver bowl on the mantel, the silver frames atop the gleaming black piano.

The frames are empty still—the photographs of Carr's parents lost in Prager's toolshed, or in the storm, or maybe to the sea—and the glass panes are like black windows. Arthur Carr has assured him that there are other photos of them— *just as damned blurry*—in a box somewhere in the attic, but Carr has yet to look. It's freezing up there now, and there are dozens of boxes to search, and Carr knows that in these matters his father is not reliable.

Carr straightens the frames on the piano, carries his coffee mug to the kitchen, and raises every window shade along the way.

NEW POCKET BLACK LIZARD EDITIONS

WHITE SHOTGUN

BY APRIL SMITH

While on indefinite leave from the FBI, Special Agent Ana Grey learns about a half-sister, Cecilia, living in Italy. She's even more surprised when the FBI calls with a high-stakes assignment: travel to Siena, Italy, and go deep undercover to gather intelligence on presumed international drug kingpin and mafioso Nicoli Nicosa—Cecilia's husband. As Ana gets to know the sister she never knew she had while trying to maintain her cover, the city of Siena is gearing up for the legendary Palio, the oldest horse race in the world and the annual venting of ancient rivalries.

Thriller

BLACKJACK

BY ANDREW VACHSS

A savage murderer is leaving a trail of eviscerated bodies all over the world. Despite knowing the Cross team as ultimate mercenaries, a shadowy team of government operatives hires them to track and capture—but not kill—this elusive hunter. When a pattern is finally deduced in the seemingly random strikes, the Cross crew devises an elaborate plan that will put their leader directly into the creature's path. Andrew Vachss's first Cross novel mixes a murder-for-hire story with a horror novel in this mind bending, spine-tingling new thriller.

Thriller

CRIME & GUILT

BY FERDINAND VON SCHIRACH

By turns witty and sorrowful, unflinchingly brutal and heartbreaking, the deeply affecting, quietly unnerving cases presented in *Crime and Guilt* are remarkable examples of minimal prose that is as mesmerizing as it is affecting. In "Fähner," a small-town physician and avid gardener betrays little emotion when he takes an ax to his wife's head, an act that shocks the locals but provides a long-awaited reprieve for the good doctor. In the startling story "Love," a young man's infatuation with his girlfriend takes a grisly turn when he comes to grips with his unconventional—and uncontrollable—impulses to truly know a woman. Attempting to hurdle through a midlife crisis, a housewife staves off depression with the rush she derives from the act of stealing in "Desire." And in "Snow," an old man whose home is used as a way station for a heroin ring agrees to protect the identity of the lead drug runner, who nonetheless receives his comeuppance.

Short Stories

ALSO AVAILABLE
Blind Man's Alley by Justin Peacock
Dead Line by Stella Rimington
The Garden of Betrayal by Lee Vance
Layover in Dubai by Dan Fesperman

POCKET BLACK LIZARD
Available wherever books are sold.
www.randomhouse.com